overeXposed

USA TODAY BESTSELLING AUTHORS

TATE JAMES
HEATHER LONG

overexposed

Tate James

Heather Long

Tate James

Heather Long

Overexposed
Copyright © Tate James, Heather Long 2024
All rights reserved
First published in 2025
James, Tate
Long, Heather
Overexposed

Cover design: Steph at Vicious Desires Design
Editing: Gretchen Stelter

content warning

Your mental health is important to us! If you need any specific information about what might be included, please contact one of us at
contact@heatherlong.net or contact@tatejamesauthor.com

Triggers include:

- Family illness
- Medical debt
- Physical assault (not of a sexual nature)
- Assault by an ex/Domestic Violence
- Mentions of self harm
- Car accident

Dear Readers,

In a world where the idea of celebrities and stars is ever changing, where the red carpet is rolled out, and every appearance is a potential photo op, it's easy to forget that behind all of the flashing cameras, blind items, and gossip channels, these are all *real* people.

Let's be honest, the drama, the spice, the scandal, and all the larger-than-life moments and personas are what keep us tuning back in for more. Whether it's a rock star hooking up with an athlete, a reality television queen who flirts with an actor on the red carpet, or a power couple who make all the public appearances together but go their separate ways in private... This is what it means to be a part of our celebrity culture.

Overexposed invites you to join us in diving headfirst into the glamor and chaos of this existence. From the first page to the last, you'll be transported to a world where nothing is really ever what it seems and that's exactly how we like it.

Prepare to straddle the line between the polished perfection of their silver screen lives and the untamed reality of what behind the scenes really is. Remember, the paps, for all they may irritate, are as much a part of that ecosystem as the celebrities themselves.

The gossip, the whispered rumors, the social media frenzy—these are all the ingredients of this intoxicating cocktail of fame, fortune, and *formidable* men and one exceptionally determined woman.

So buckle up, grab your popcorn, and get ready for a ride

filled with laughter, tears, and a few juicy tidbits you won't soon forget. Because when it comes to fame, the story's never just about what happens—it's about how we choose to tell it.

It's going to be a wild, hilarious, and unforgettable journey. Pinky promise.

xoxo
    Heather & Tate

To all our favorites, we're not procrastinating. This is a side quest.

prologue

No one plans to become a celebrity stalker—a car-chasing, privacy-smashing, garbage-diving predator ready to feast on red-carpet prey. No one plans to climb unscalable trees, make friends with every catering service waiter, dog walkers, and morgue attendants.

Everyone comes to Hollywood seeking the dream. No one comes here planning to rip open those dreams and expose the seedy underbelly, not even those of us who grew up on a steady diet of it and understood that, in the ecosystem of notoriety, the predators and the prey were symbiotic.

We needed the celebrities' scandals to create headlines and they needed us to maintain their front-page status. It was a straightforward—albeit ugly at times—business and my father raised me to be a practical woman.

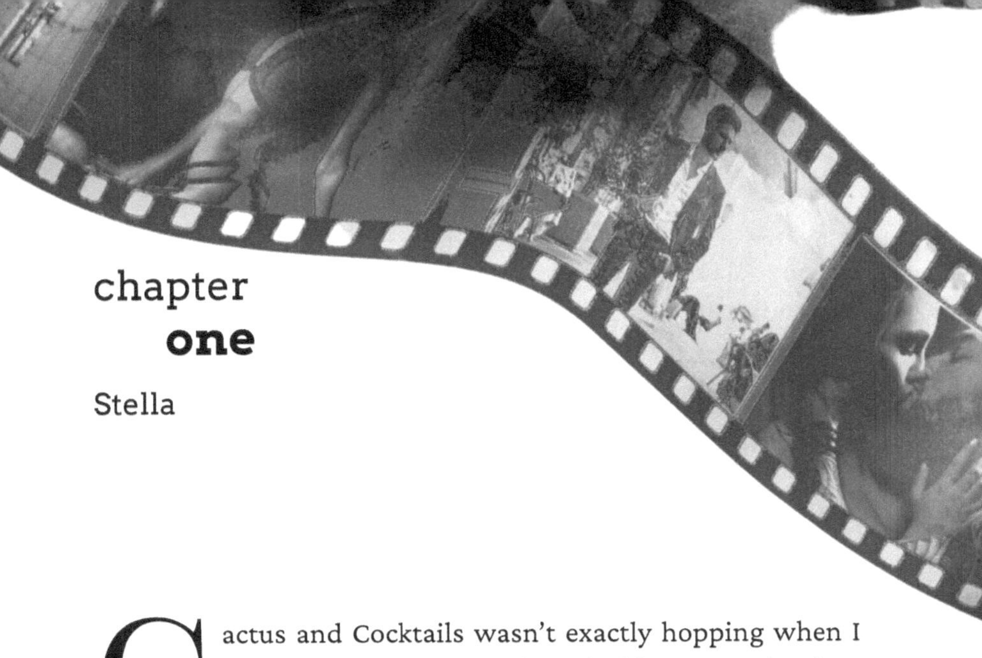

chapter
one

Stella

Cactus and Cocktails wasn't exactly hopping when I parked in the broken and cracked lot next to it. Then again, the sun was only beginning its descent. Besides, the place wasn't one of the trendier bars. It had fallen off the radar for the hip and the hot two years earlier.

Maybe three.

I didn't really track the ones that went away so much as the best ones for stargazing, the clubs the celebs went to in order to be seen, and the staged opportunities were good for a few hundred here and there.

Photographers made money, the celebs got free press—it was a win-win. Most of the time. It was also usually jam-packed with fans and wannabe paps who were looking to make their mark.

Some of those little shits would elbow you in the face for a slightly better angle. I flipped the visor down and knocked open the mirror to give myself a critical eye.

I'd just spent the afternoon haunting the *other* party venues currently in favor. With award-season prep already in full swing and the film festival at Balboa Pier starting this weekend, the stars were flying in from their homes in

Montana, Wyoming, Nevada, Northern California, and New York.

Oscar season was always in style. Balboa Pier happened to be one of the premiere festivals for launching potential contenders for the gold statues. That meant if you wanted a shot at the early buzz, you wanted applause and maybe a prize at the festival.

It also meant the celebs who wanted to party for real headed to the hangouts known for more discretion and security. Getting in and out of those took experience, skill, and lately a friendly smile. While I'd been around and I knew the business, I wasn't a *known* face, so they hadn't banned me yet.

After I touched up my lip gloss and let my hair down from the clip so it fell around my face, I checked my phone where it was connected to the camera. I'd uploaded the five very nice shots I'd gotten of the past year's award favorite with his wife, and their very close friend, lounging at the Mercantile.

Considering all three had been making out with each other, the pictures were of the extra-spicy variety. They may not net me much right now, but they were good to have on standby. I loaded them to the cloud, then sent one off to tease my contact at the gossip channel.

They liked to verify before they would buy. I didn't have a problem with the women making out or the director alternating between his wife and their friend. If they were happy and it was consensual, well, party on. They were in public and they were popular faces, especially the ingenue who was rumored to have a breakout role.

If she went viral, these pics were gonna be gold. Worth the past eight hours of floating in and out of the local spas, wine bars, and clubs. Now, it was time for a break. I checked my watch, then secured the camera back in its bag.

The Cactus and Cocktails was known for its heavy pours

rather than watering the crap out of its house liquor. I checked the phone for messages, then grabbed my purse and slid out of the car. A cool breeze carried the sweet scents of fried foods and bad decisions. Both specialties of the place in front of me.

The exterior was a kind of burnt-sienna color. They were going for a southwest aesthetic, with the cacti painted on the stone walls. The effort ended out here though. I locked the car and headed for the entrance.

Someone pushed open one of the heavy doors, letting out a fragrant cloud of melted cheese, meat, beans, and spices. Hell yes, the nachos here were just this side of perfection.

They were also the second reason why the C and C went to the top of my list. The margarita pitchers were only five bucks on Wednesday nights. A fact my wallet and I had appreciated for a few years. While I wasn't a broke student anymore, I did have to watch the dollars.

I headed right to the bar. I didn't need a booth or a table. I wanted the corner seat...but my steps slowed at the sight of someone already sitting in my favorite spot.

Any hope that he might just be sitting there to get a drink died with the fresh plate of nachos delivered to him as he tilted up his bottle of beer to drink. His gaze was fixed on a hockey game playing on one of the big TVs mounted behind the bar.

As tempting as it was to stomp my foot, I swallowed the sulk and jerked my big girl boots back on. I came for margaritas, food, and...I stared at the game on the television for a minute.

Yeah, I didn't care about the hockey but I'd watch 'cause it was that or doomscroll on my phone. Ignoring the long length of bar that stretched down the room, I went past *my* corner spot and slid onto a stool two seats over. Not close enough to invade his space but definitely close enough to score the seat when he abandoned it.

Plans were good.

The bartender gave me a friendly smile and raised his brows. "Be right with you," he said with a lift of his chin as he popped out a few more bottles and removed their caps to set on the tray for the single waitress who was working tonight.

That was fine. There were menus somewhere, laminated and kind of sticky, but they hadn't changed what they served in all the years since they opened, so I didn't need one anyway.

The team in dark blue scored and the team in the lighter blue looked pissed. Two of the players shoved at each other, but they broke it up the minute the ref was on them. It might be fun to watch after all.

"What can I get you?" The bartender wasn't model perfect, but he definitely had a good face and better hair. Five bucks and a pitcher of margaritas said he was an aspiring actor.

"Pitcher of the classic margaritas with a plate of nachos." I kind of wanted a cheeseburger, but I'd pace myself. If I got a second pitcher, I'd get a second meal.

"Sure thing," the bartender said, giving me a friendly little wink.

I kept my grin at friendly and let my gaze travel right past the flirt to the television. The guy to my right snorted when the bartender headed away and I glanced at him.

The black baseball cap shaded his eyes but didn't do a damn thing to hide the strong jawline and chiseled cheekbones. I didn't stare because (a) I didn't care that he was sitting there except he was in my seat and (b) I was done for the day.

If he wanted to sit there pretending to be nobody, who was I to argue?

The smell of his nachos was making my stomach grumble, but Mr. Happy Wavy Hair with his expensive smile was back with the pitcher of margaritas, a glass, and a card with his name and number on it.

"Thanks," I said, keeping the smile polite but distant and then glanced past him to the game. Oh, it was a commercial. Fine, whatever. The bartender lingered for a moment, wiping things down while I poured my drink.

"Another beer," the seat usurper ordered in that bedroom baritone that melted women's panties. I didn't mind it, but I was a little more flame retardant.

"Sure," the bartender took the distraction and went for his beer.

Blowing out a breath, I lifted my fresh glass of margarita in a half toast to the man on the right. "Thanks."

"Don't mention it," he said, shifting a little on the stool. He was keeping his gaze fixed on the television. A little too fixed, like he wanted to make sure I didn't think he was flirting with me.

Again, totally fine with me.

"I'm not who you think I am," he informed me before the bartender returned with his beer. Thankfully the waitress needed him and a couple of fresh patrons took seats at the other end of the bar.

"You know," I said idly, "I wasn't going to comment, but yes, you are who I think you are." The thousand-dollar smile was the thing heartthrobs were made of. It didn't hurt that he had the body to back it up.

I'd clocked him as soon as I saw the jawline. The jeans, beaten-up boots, and plaid button-down over a cream-colored Henley were hardly a disguise. If he thought the baseball cap was working, he needed to get better advice.

"No," he said, cutting me a look. "Trust me, I'm not."

"Don't know you well enough to trust you," I retorted. "You know what I do know?"

He sighed. It was so long-suffering and put-upon, I was tempted to leave him be. "No," he said, finally cutting those piercing blue eyes toward me. Damn, rough really did suit him. "What do you know?"

I touched my tongue to my teeth before I licked some of the salt right off the rim of my glass. Another mouthful of margarita washed it down perfectly. I held his gaze the whole time.

"What do I get if I'm right?"

His eyebrows shot upward. "What do you *get?*"

"Yes, what do I get? You think I'm wrong. I know I'm not. So what's my prize if I get it right?"

He frowned, head cocked as he studied me for a long moment. "What do you want?"

Now that was a loaded question, but then my nachos arrived and the moment burst. Good, 'cause that first glass had already gone to my head and I was having a hard time not just throwing back this second one.

The bartender slid the plate in front of me and the combination of cheese, spices, and meat made my mouth water. Not to mention the warmth of the chips.

"Can I—"

"You can go away," my new friend told him.

The bartender blinked but retreated immediately.

"Blunt," I said. "But effective."

"He's annoying and you're not interested. It'll be easier for him to take the rejection from me." He motioned to me with the bottle of beer. "You didn't answer my question."

I lifted a loaded chip and shoved the whole thing in my mouth. Hot, spicy, and crunchy—the perfect combination. I washed it all down with another mouthful of icy cold margarita.

Oh, there was a thought.

"Another pitcher of margaritas. Maybe a cheeseburger."

He blinked. "Maybe a cheeseburger?"

"I haven't finished my nachos, so maybe a cheeseburger. It sounds good, but I could be full. Another pitcher of margaritas though, that sounds even better." I was also going to be halfway through this one in no time at all.

"Fine," he answered. "Another pitcher of margaritas and maybe a cheeseburger."

Excellent. I loved winning bets.

"You're Gem Harrison," I said, before refilling my glass. His expression was priceless. Even stunned, he looked hot. It was hard not to laugh at him because he genuinely seemed stumped.

"How?" He frowned. "Nobody ever guesses me first?"

"(A) I wasn't guessing," I reminded him. The buzz from the first two margaritas hit my system and I scooped up another nacho. "And (b) that info will cost you."

I had no idea what, but I was really enjoying his surprise. He didn't respond immediately and I dug into my nachos again. The crunch was everything, and I was so damn hungry, I could probably eat the plate itself.

"Fuck it," he muttered. "What will it cost?" The curiosity was absolutely flashing in those stunning eyes.

"You're in my seat."

Literally the first thing that came to mind and it popped right out. So I took another bite of nachos while he turned that information over in his head.

"You want this seat?"

"Yes," I said around the mouthful, covering my mouth with my hand. "I do. I love that seat. It's got great angles on the room."

He eyed me for a moment, then slid out of the seat, moved

his drink and nachos over before swapping them with my plate and pitcher.

"Hell yes." I hopped down and danced the two steps over to claim my prize. The seat was warm, and there was just something deeply satisfying about winning my seat.

I was on a roll.

Taking the stool right next to me, Gem studied me. "Payment made. Tell me… how did you know?"

I could have told him anything. I could have said it was the way he was seated, kind of hunched and not wanting to be noticed. I could have said it was the calluses on his hands or how they were rougher looking. He didn't get manicures anymore.

Lots of things I could just make up on the spot, but this was fun, so I went for the truth.

"You have a scar," I told him, reaching over to brush my thumb against that jawline, then down to his chin. "Just here. It's small, almost minute, but in the right light you can see it. Your brother doesn't have it." Then because all of that probably sounded suss as fuck, I added, "Don't worry, I'm not a stalker. I don't give a fuck who your brother is or your prior career or even who either of you are banging. I just like to notice details."

His identical twin and current legitimate Hollywood movie star. There were so few these days. Gem could still be one too; he'd started out on television like his brother. But when Seven made the leap to the big screen, Gem chose another path.

I was still tracing my thumb against that scar and enjoying the way his pupils seemed to widen, then contract. The faint scrape of stubble on his jaw rasped against my skin. He really did have a nice jaw.

A loud burst of laughter came from the doorway and then a collective groan from the other end of the bar. The sudden noises jolted me out of the warm haze, and I pulled my hand back.

Nachos and margaritas, I reminded myself.

"You play pool?" He gestured toward the green felt–topped tables on the far side of the bar.

"Maybe," I said, grinning in spite of myself. "Did you want to play?"

"Only if I can set the terms for the wager."

Oh, now I was intrigued.

"I'm listening…"

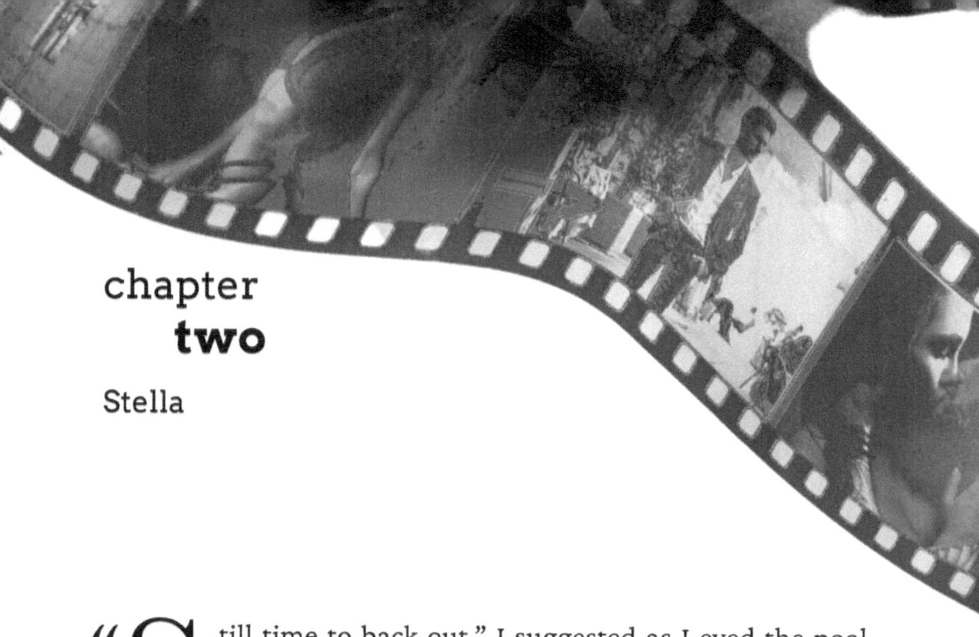

chapter
two

Stella

"**S**till time to back out," I suggested as I eyed the pool table. We'd carried my pitcher, glass, and the nachos over. He'd finished most of his but he hadn't touched mine. He did, however, order a fresh pitcher for me along with another beer for him.

"I think not," he told me with a faint smile as I chalked the tip of my cue. He'd racked the balls we acquired after he dropped the pair of twenties on our friendly bartender...whose name was Flip.

I hoped he'd made that up because it seemed unnecessarily cruel to do to your child. "I'm just offering you options," I said, setting the chalk aside and reclaiming my glass for a long drink.

"I'm good." Amusement sanded over the words despite his controlled expression. He really didn't want to be noticed and that thousand-watt smile probably brought all the lookie-loos to the yard. I didn't have the heart to tell him that the ball cap was doing nothing to hide his famous face.

"Well, then keep your eyes on me and get your best flirt ready." I winked before I leaned over to do the first break.

"My eyes are right where you want them." Since he was

behind me when he said it, I didn't doubt he was looking at my ass. I gave it a little shake for him before I refocused my attention. The jeans I wore were relaxed and comfortable. They looked good but they were far from skin tight.

I sent the cue ball flying across the table in a perfect crack to break. The balls scattered and the solid red dropped into the corner pocket. That was one.

"Nice," Gem said, the compliment seemingly genuine. "Still sticking with your bet?"

"I'm no welcher," I said as I took another long swallow of my margarita. They were perfect and the buzz was polishing away the roughness of the day. "You said you wanted me to shock you—again."

Which in and of itself was kind of funny. Apparently *everyone* thought he was his twin and the fact I didn't had truly stunned him. Funny and sad really. Glass down, I circled the table, looking for my shot.

He sighed, and I had to bite back another smile. "You just want to get out of what I win."

"Oh, you're not winning it," he said with a ridiculous amount of confidence.

"Four in the right pocket." I made the shot and it went right in like a good little ball. "Aww, you're going to hurt my feelings."

With a dry look, Gem snorted. "I told you the guy already thinks I'm Seven. Hitting on him is a hard no." The bartender kept glancing at us. I didn't think the guy was gay in the slightest, but the hero worship when he looked at Gem was funny.

"Yet you took the wager." At my reminder, he smirked.

"Accepting a wager doesn't mean I've already lost, Slick." The exaggerated drawl on the last word made me grin.

"Fair enough. Six in the side." I took the shot and sank it.

Gem tracked my progress as I lined up each shot. After the fourth one dropped in the called pocket, I drifted back to my nachos and ate a loaded one.

The vibrant-blue eyes seemed to burn as we locked gazes. Instead of commenting, he just shook his head and took a long drink of his beer.

Touching my tongue to my lips, I held his gaze for another beat before turning back to the table. The weight of his gaze was back on my ass. I called the next ball and sank it, but it was a narrow thing, brushing the eight ball, which drifted far too close to a pocket for my taste.

The flood of adrenaline added a little weight to the thumping of my heart. It also added the slightest tremor to my hands. I mean, it could have been the margaritas, but I was almost certain it was the adrenaline.

My next ball didn't drop into its pocket. I clicked my tongue against my teeth as I glanced over my shoulder. "Guess it's your turn."

"Guess it is." He put his hands on my hips and nudged me away from the table. Unlike me, he didn't pace the table nor did he give it any kind of study. He just lined up his shot. "Striped red in the corner."

The snap of the ball was followed by the crack as he struck his target and then it dropped. He barely waited for it to have vanished before he followed the cue to line up his next shot.

"Blue in the side..."

He pulled off a sexy bank shot from the side bumper and in the ball went. Prowling around the table like a man on a mission, he lined up his shots and knocked every single one in, and he didn't go near the damn eight ball, perched in its precarious spot next to the pocket.

I knocked back the last of the margarita in my glass when he straightened up. Every ball of his was gone and all that was left was the eight ball. He met my gaze, smirk in place, then he winked before he said, "Eight in the corner."

In the ball went like a good little bitch. I saluted him with my empty glass before setting it aside. "I guess you were serious."

He circled the table to stand in front of me, pool cue in his hand. "So...time to pay up."

Right. I licked the salt from my lips and gave him a once-over. "Like I said. I'm not a welcher. You won fair and square."

"It was down and dirty, but I'll take your word for it."

I polished off the last of my first pitcher. I still had most of the second. Right... "Okay, stud. Grab the pitcher. I'll grab my nachos and you follow me."

He frowned. "Follow you where?"

"Hotel across the street. You're getting us a room, and then we're gonna see if we can get you balls deep in my pocket." It was a horrible come-on, but I said it with a straight face because I was definitely riding a really good buzz and he was hot as fuck.

Yes, he won, but he was a dick about winning cause he didn't want to pay the forfeit if he lost. Fair enough. I grabbed my plate of nachos and headed for the door. When Flip started to hold up his hand, I waved him off. "I'll bring the plate back."

It wasn't like I was announcing to the whole bar we were going across the street. Neither one of us had raised our voices. At the door to the bar, I glanced back to see Gem staring at me, mouth slightly open like he wasn't entirely sure I was serious.

"Come on," I called, then shoved the door open with my hip and stepped out into the fresh air. It hit my flushed skin like a balm. I scooped up one of the nachos, they weren't as crunchy now, but they definitely hit the spot. Hotel rooms usually had cups or glasses and if not, I wasn't opposed to drinking from the pitcher.

I could mostly walk in a straight line and I started for the hotel that was located across the little side street from the bar. If I got there and he didn't show up, well, he hadn't said he would.

Might be disappointed...

Eh, no, I'd definitely be disappointed.

Right, I was just passing my car when I slid to a stop. I set the plate of nachos on the hood and dug out my keys. I'd just opened the driver's side door when Gem appeared in my periphery.

"Cutting out?" The hesitation in his voice gave my ego a little boost.

I flipped open the glove compartment, then dug out a couple of condoms and withdrew them. I never relied on the guys to provide protection. Nope, they gloved or there would be no love. Also, I preferred to make sure I knew the condoms were good quality and not as likely to rip.

When I fanned the pair at him, his mouth formed another little O, and I had to chuckle. Sliding back out, I straightened and met his gaze. "Are you *that* shocked that I would want to use a condom?"

The silence stretched out between us as I shut the door. Then he set my margarita pitcher down on the hood next to the nachos. "Slick, you've been blowing my mind all evening."

"Well, then maybe you should buckle up, cowboy," I said, closing the door with a slam and sauntering to him. He really did look sinfully good. Whether he'd ever played a cowboy or not. "It's still early."

He slid an arm around my middle and hauled me to him. Six foot two was damn impressive when I was only five foot six and not in heels. But he didn't make me stretch before he dipped his head.

Honestly, I had no idea what I'd been expecting when he

kissed me. I planted my hands against the hard muscled wall of his chest just as his mouth locked on mine. A dozen thoughts ignited, then scattered half-formed under his slow, sensual assault.

Firm lips held mine captive and despite his hesitation inside, he teased with his tongue until I opened to him. I was not a hard sell. The man kissed like he wanted to lick up every drop of my margarita. The tongue wrestling was just a perk.

The very rigid evidence of his attraction thickened in his jeans and a shudder raced up my spine. He bumped me back against my baby blue car and then his hands were on my hips and he picked me up. My butt landed on the hood and our heads were even.

Oh, this was much easier and not a strain on the neck. I scraped my nails down his chest and he slid his hand under my shirt. Not once did he let me up for air. My heart raced as my thighs bracketed his hips. Even as he tugged me forward, there was just not enough friction.

Wrenching my face from his, I stared up at him. It was definitely a thrill to find him panting as hard as I was. "Hotel?" 'Cause we weren't fucking on the hood of my car and I wasn't doing it in the back seat either.

He closed his eyes, head back as his throat bobbed with a hard swallow. Was it that much of a struggle for him?

Before I could ask, he pulled me up against him until his erection was firmly pressed against the apex of my thighs. If not for two layers of denim, we could be getting seriously intimate right now.

"Hotel," he said. "Let's go." Then he picked me up like he was going to carry me over there.

"Nachos," I argued, and he paused. He shot a sidelong glance at the hood of my car. "Margaritas too. We have a long night ahead of us, and we should definitely carb up."

"Fuck me." He exhaled the two words like a prayer, and I enjoyed sliding down him.

"That is my plan," I promised. He let me go long enough to grab the pitcher and I got the nachos, and then we were heading to the hotel with his arm around my waist. We probably made a sight as he kept pausing to kiss me.

I could get used to that. Once at the hotel, he handed me the pitcher and said to wait, then he disappeared into the building. Thankfully, he was back out not even five minutes later, key in hand.

Laughing like a pair of idiot teenagers fucking around after curfew, we hustled down the row of doors to one away from the street. The hotel was barely a three star, but it was clean and the walls weren't paper thin—I might have stayed here once or twice in the past after a night of drinking at the C and C.

Once in the room, I set my nachos on the table and he put the pitcher of margaritas next to it. His wallet and keys hit the table next. I tugged the purse strap up and over my head and dropped it in the chair. I tossed the condoms on the bed, then reached up to pull that damn baseball cap off his head.

"Better," I said as I tossed it onto the other chair.

"Not yet," he said in a voice that held a lot of promise. "But we're getting there."

Maybe it was the huskiness or the way his eyes swept over me in the half light of the hotel room. I went from being buzzed and light to overheated and needy.

"One question," I said as I jerked off my boots, then stripped off my shirt and bra.

"I'm clean," he said, like I'd asked if he'd had an STD check. The minute my shirt hit the floor, I went for the buttons of my jeans and paused to stare at him.

He wasn't moving, but his mouth was open, his gaze glued to me.

"Shit," he swore, then shrugged out of the plaid before he yanked the Henley off in a smooth one-hand over-his-shoulder move to tug the fabric up and over.

Damn. Those muscles I'd felt earlier were right there, ripped and cut in all the best ways. *Strip first, look after*, I ordered myself.

My jeans and panties hit the floor. The air-conditioning in the room chose that moment to kick on with a clank. The rush of cold air blew right across my breasts and my already-taut nipples tightened further.

"You're fucking gorgeous, Slick," Gem said as he stood from dropping his jeans and boxer briefs. His cock was red tipped and already angling up. Oh, that was going to do real nicely. It was long and it was thick and it had some lovely veins already popping on it.

"Thank you," I said. "You're not so bad yourself." But when he reached for me, I put a hand on his chest and he went still. "Question," I reminded him.

"I thought I answered already."

"You told me you were clean," I said. "Thank you, that's good to know, but that wasn't my question."

"Then ask," he practically growled. "But it's going to cost you."

The cost was being hauled to him and his mouth slamming down on mine. His hands were hot and callused, and he stroked them down my back to my ass. The fact that he picked me clean up until his dick was resting against my cunt but he didn't start humping away just made him all that more attractive.

I had to fist his hair and tug to get him to lift his head. I didn't wait for his permission.

"Do you prefer to be on top or on bottom?"

His eyebrows shot up. A ripple of dark, humor-laced pleasure went through me. "Goddamn, Slick, I could get addicted to you."

"Not an answer."

He turned and tossed me onto the bed. "You have two condoms. Let's find out which I prefer…"

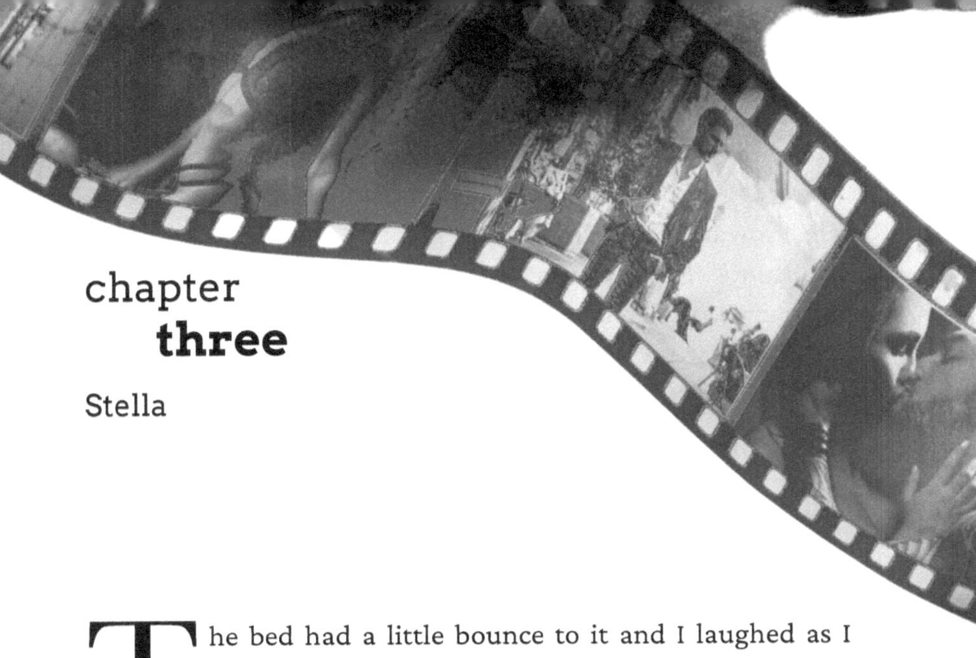

Stella

The bed had a little bounce to it and I laughed as I pushed up onto my elbows. This angle did him a lot of favors, or maybe he was the one doing all the favors. I slid my foot back toward me, but he caught my ankle and pulled me back.

"Where do you think you're going?" There was a possessive edge to the words as he flexed his hand on my ankle. Before I could answer though, he dropped down over me. Catching his weight on his hands, he boxed me in a blanket of masculine warmth and his very erect cock bumped my stomach.

"Well, I was on my way to get you," I teased, wrapping my arms around his neck. The heat pouring off of him was glorious. The room's air-conditioning might have been chilly, but my nipples weren't taut peaks just from the cold. I slid my legs apart, inviting him to cradle himself against my hips. "But then you came and got me."

It probably wasn't anywhere near as funny a thought as it struck me. Laughter bubbled out of me when he dipped his head and went for my throat. The half-mouthed kisses interspersed with bites threatened a riot in my system.

"Slick," he murmured, giving a gentle thrust that teased his cock along the slit of my cunt. He wasn't trying to sink in, but the slow grind with so little friction had me shifting beneath him. "You are something else."

"Hmm." I hummed a sound as he kept mouthing kisses along my collarbone. The scrape of his stubble added little pricks of sharpness to each soft kiss. It was a slap and tickle in the best way. Especially when he kissed a path to my breast. "You like being shocked."

I dug my nails into his shoulders as he sucked a nipple against his teeth so tight, a cry burst out of me. The sting and pull was so much—too much—and the harder he teased, the tighter I gripped him.

It was like his whole body pulsed against me and then he released the nipple with a noisy pop. The cold air across the damp flesh added another layer of sensation—more. It was like all the blood rushed into the tortured peak and it went cold, then hot, and then he blew a breath over the pebbled skin.

Hips bucking, I went for his hair to keep him from doing that again. It was too damn much, but he had both of my wrists in his clasp. Once he pinned them over my head, he studied me with the piercing brilliance of his blue eyes.

"I thought you wanted to know if I liked being on top or bottom?"

Fighting my panting breaths, I stared up at him. "I didn't think that involved nipple torture."

"Oh, Slick." He damn near groaned that nickname he'd stuck me with. Not that I was complaining. No, definitely not complaining despite my defiance. "I think it's going to involve everything with you."

Then he was kissing me again. The slow grind of his body against mine just kept reminding me of how fat and heavy his cock was—and that it wasn't inside me. Most guys were good with the *roll on the condom and fuck you stupid*. A good ten minutes if you were lucky, and I could almost get the orgasm out of it, if I gave them a hand.

Gem, it seemed, wasn't giving me any hands as he returned to teasing my nipples. He went back and forth between them, alternating between long, slow licks, then sharp bites. Occasionally, he rubbed his cheek against the too-sensitive flesh and I'd be writhing all over again.

"You're so wet," he whispered against my ear. "I can smell you."

"That's kind of gross," I admitted, but then, I couldn't smell anything of myself. All I could feel or taste or smell was *him*. There was a headiness to his scent—sunshine, sand, and maybe more than a little salt and tequila.

I licked a line right up his throat when he lifted his head. It was a strain because he wouldn't let go of my wrists, but I wasn't really struggling. There was something sexy as fuck about being pinned in place while he made me squirm.

Suddenly he sat up, releasing my hands as he brought his thighs to rest on either side of my chest. The softness of the hair on his legs teased me, and he wasn't keeping his weight on me, but I couldn't move away.

It also gave me a lovely eye-to-cock view with his *flushed so red it was actually tipping out purple* dick. With my hands back, I wrapped my fingers around the stiff erection and gave him a couple of slow pumps.

"Hmmm...want to do that with your mouth?" The dark interest in his question sent another thrill through me.

Tilting my head, I met his gaze. He had a condom in hand. Oh, that sent another frisson through me, a zing of electricity from breasts to cunt and back again. Running my tongue over my lower lip, I switched my attention to his cock.

"Give me a little room?" At my prompting, he lifted his

weight some and I pulled up onto the pillows. It gave me some options. I didn't look away as I wet my lips again, then licked my palm before I stroked his cock from base to tip and back again. The springy hairs at the base there were softer than I expected. Maybe he'd waxed once upon a time.

That definitely softened the pubic hairs when they grew back in. Uncomfortable but worth it for the smooth skin. I preferred laser these days when I could afford it, but I was back to waxing right now.

With his gaze fixed on me, I parted my lips and then teased his tip over them like I was putting on gloss. The dribble of precum was warm and salty. I'd barely gotten a taste when he surged forward.

My eyes watered at the weight of him pressing deep, but I kept swallowing around him until he pulled back.

"Fuck me," he whispered. "I want to fuck that mouth of yours..." He didn't give me a chance to respond as he put action to his words. Every snap of his hips sent him deeper. He bumped against my throat, then down.

Every stroke filled my mouth with a fresh bit of salt and sweet flesh, his low grunts egging me on. He twisted one of my nipples as he fucked my mouth and I moved my head in a slow motion, to add to his thrusting.

The tears splashed against my cheeks as he slammed a hand to the wall and gripped the headboard. I relaxed my jaw as he kept pumping. When it was too much and I needed to breathe, I slapped his thigh once.

He pulled out immediately, his breath coming in harsh, ragged pants.

I went looking for the condom he'd dropped while he stared at me. As soon as I tore the foil from the corner, he shifted to slide his fingers to my cunt.

Thumb on my clit and drawing circles, he dipped two fingers into me. I arched my hips in invitation. I was definitely soaking wet and more than ready for him. After the way he felt in my mouth, I had faith he was going to feel even better inside my cunt.

Smoothing the condom on, I savored the way his pupils looked fatter and blown as he stared down at me. Keeping my legs spread as he worked his fingers in and out, I surged up to meet his teasing thrusts. When he curled his fingers and stroked that spot inside even as he increased the pressure of his thumb, I fought to hold on to the pleasure he drowned me in.

It was a strain. I was almost there and so ready to come, and then he pulled his hand away.

"Fucker," I swore, as I wrenched my eyes open to meet his laughing gaze.

"Don't worry, Slick," he promised, licking his fingers off before he gripped my hips and pulled me down until my thighs were against his chest and his cock lined up with my cunt. "I've got you."

Those were the last three words I heard as he filled me with a thrust of his hips on the last syllable.

"Fuck…" The word exploded out of me as he pulled back and then pushed himself in again. The angle gave him all the control and he kept my legs locked to him as he stared down at me.

Every bump of his hips seemed to impale me harder on him. Whether I was just intimately aware of every inch or just that turned on, I had no idea. But I was here for this. My breasts bobbed as he picked up the pace.

Then the man added a goddamn twist to his hips and he was hitting that spot over and over again. The earlier strain redoubled and a litany of "fucks" fell from my lips as he pursued my orgasm with a kind of relentless fervor that gave no chance for breath.

The bed slammed against the wall and the thump of the headboard to the drywall added a distinctive tempo to his strokes. Writhing, I scrabbled at the covers. I wanted to reach for him or touch him, but he had me on my shoulders, half-pinned, as he rocked me.

The orgasm that ripped through me was so loaded, it left me dizzy. And, holy fuck, he was still going. My mouth was open as he added a few more thrusts until he stiffened and came with a hard grunt.

He let my legs go slowly, as he dropped down and then he was draped over me—all hot, sweaty, and panting. Just like me. I swore he still felt hard inside me. I had no idea how long we lay there before he started kissing my shoulder.

Eventually, he sat up and, with care, pulled the rest of the way out. I lay there, uncaring of my sprawled position as he rose on shaky legs.

Smugness floated up inside of me. I'd done that to him. Well, I helped. He'd kind of done most of it. I was far more into participation than I'd gotten that time around. He disappeared into the bathroom. A flush of the toilet and water running in the sink later, he reemerged.

He had a washcloth in his hand. Like the genuine fucking gift he was turning out to be, he paused at my pitcher of margaritas.

"More?"

I sat up. "Oh, yes please."

More sex? More margaritas?

Yes, the answer was still yes.

He filled the glass and carried it over. Before he handed it to me, he stole another kiss. I downed half the glass before I offered him a drink. He used the cloth to wipe me down.

I made use of the bathroom, half wondering if this was where the fun evening ended. To be fair, I'd definitely gotten more out of it than I'd planned. Returning, I found him sprawled on the bed, stroking himself lazily.

His cock was already semi-hard. Well, that was nice. Definitely a feature.

"Round two?" I teased.

"Yep," he said, curling his fingers toward me. "Now you get to be on top."

That had my cunt clenching all over again. "Too bad we only have one more condom."

"You only have one more," he said. "I have three in my wallet."

Eyes closed, I tilted my head back in triumph before I got myself another drink. "That, my good sir, will definitely get you another blow job."

Who needed sleep?

chapter **four**

Seven

The incessant, never-ending buzz of my phone on the glass-topped nightstand was what finally dragged me out of my deep sleep. I fucking *hated* being woken up by my phone, but whoever was calling seemed fucking desperate.

"What *the fuck* do you want?" I barked into the phone without even opening my eyes to see who was calling. Either it was someone I knew, and therefore they knew better, or it was a journalist...and quite frankly they could go fuck themselves.

"Open your goddamn emails, Seven!" my manager, Jerry, snapped back. "Or your socials. Or the fucking internet. It's fucking *everywhere*! Why *the fuck* would you do something so stupid, *now* of all fucking times?"

The fury shaking his words made me sit up, sleep haze evaporating in a flash of dread. "What are you talking about, Jerry? I was dead asleep until you blew up my phone."

"Me? Just me?" He scoffed. "Bullshit. I bet every reporter with your number has tried to get through to you this morning. Fuck knows they've been harassing the shit outta me."

Scrubbing a hand over my face, I put Jerry's call on speaker and checked notifications. Sure enough, I had *dozens* of missed calls and voicemails. I had notifications for social media turned off, but when I opened the app, I wondered if maybe it was broken.

Then I saw the images.

"Whoa. *Whoa.* Jerry, what the hell? What is this?" I exclaimed, sweat breaking out all over my skin as I frantically checked my missed calls again. Sure enough, there were a handful from my longtime girlfriend, Clara Belle, and I groaned.

Jerry inhaled deeply. Smoking. Jesus Christ, I'd driven him to smoking again. "You tell me, Seven," he coughed on the exhale. "This scandal will *not* go down well with Carriage Pictures."

"Fuck!" I roared, resisting the urge to throw my phone across the room. Instead, I sprang up out of bed and stalked out of my room, slamming the door open as I went. "I'll call you back, Jerry."

My manager started to protest, but I ended the call right as I reached Gem's bedroom door. My fist pounded against it, then I shoved my way in without waiting for a response. He was my identical twin; there was no privacy between us.

"Gemini!" I bellowed, searching his empty room with a glance. "Where the fuck are you?" I all but kicked his bathroom door open, then growled my frustration to find it also empty. His bed was perfectly made and his bathroom spotless. The fucker wasn't even home, and by the look of things, he hadn't been all night. Our cleaners didn't make the beds this early.

My next stop was downstairs to hammer on Ollie's bedroom door. He, thankfully, had actually come home last night. We'd all been out at an exclusive club in the penthouse of the Covington, and Gem had left early, grumbling some shit about hitting the gym in the morning. Ollie and I had stayed way too late, playing Texas Hold'em and drinking forty-five-year-old Port Ellen whiskey. Hence my irritating behind-the-eyes headache right now. Or shit, maybe that was from the photos splashed all over the tabloids of my *fucking idiot* twin brother hooking up with some random chick in a parking lot.

Problem was, the tabloids all claimed it was me.

And I, among other things, had a very committed, very *public* relationship with Hollywood's sweetheart Clara Belle Lafleur.

Or I used to anyway.

"What's going on?" Ollie asked, scowling at me with sleepy eyes. "Why all the shouting? What's Gem done?"

I shoved my phone in his face, too irate to explain. A picture was worth a thousand words anyway, and there were a half dozen pictures to choose from. Hell, there were even sensationalist headlines to accompany.

Superstar Seven Harrison Caught Cheating!

Slimy Seven Shows His True Colors!

Seven Harrison Sets His Career on Fire With Mystery Woman!

"Oh shit," Ollie spluttered, jaw dropping as he scrolled through. "Bro...when the fuck did this happen and why didn't you tell me?"

My head might have just exploded. Fucking half-asleep dickwad. I smacked him in the side of the head in an attempt to wake him the hell up. "I *didn't!*" I roared.

"Ow," Ollie protested, rubbing his head, then, "Oh. Ohhhhh. Gem. What a moron."

I grabbed my phone back. "Exactly! And the little dick isn't even home right now to fucking explain himself. Where is he? He said he was hitting the gym early but his bed wasn't slept in."

Ollie yawned, running a hand over his messy inky-black hair as he exited his bedroom. "I reckon I know where he spent the night based on those pictures." He chuckled, and it irritated the fuck out of me. It wasn't *his* relationship or career on the line.

"Those pictures weren't from last night," I muttered. "They were taken in the parking lot of Cactus, and I know he was drinking there on Saturday night. So where the hell is he now?"

Right on cue, the huge front door of our house swung open and my mirror image came strolling through in his signature baseball cap and sponsored athleticwear.

"You two are up early," he muttered, brushing past both Ollie and me as he headed through to the kitchen. "Figured you'd both be nursing hangovers with how hard you were hitting the scotch last night."

"I would be if Seven hadn't woken me up just now," Ollie admitted, grabbing a couple of vitamin juices out of the fridge and offering one to me. "You're in *big* trouble, Gemini Harrison. *Huge* trouble. But first...who was she? Fangirl, right? You fucked her, I hope."

My twin quirked a puzzled brow at our best friend. "The fuck are you talking about? I went hiking through Runyon Canyon before dawn because I couldn't sleep. No fans, certainly no fucking."

"He is talking about the pictures of *me* hooking up with some hot brunette all over the tabloids this morning," I snapped, losing my cool all over again. "Don't act like you don't know about it, Gemini. I sure as fuck wasn't the one picking up chicks at the Cactus, regardless of what fucking TMZ thinks."

Gem choked on the Gatorade he'd just taken a gulp of, then coughed and spluttered for a moment before staring at me in shock. "Excuse the fuck out of you?"

My eyes narrowed and my fist tightened so hard that I was

at risk of shattering the glass juice bottle I held. "You. Heard. Me."

Ollie yawned again. Loud. "Where's your phone, Gem? Haven't you seen the blow up?"

My brother shook his head, still looking like he'd seen a ghost. "I left it behind."

Fucking typical. He never took his phone with him when he went for hikes, claimed it was too easy for people to find him and he wanted to be *alone* with nature. To help clue him in, I tossed him my phone and it unlocked for him thanks to our identical faces.

"Oh. Fuck," he whispered, his eyes wider than a dinner plate as he scrolled. "What the hell? Sev, this is bullshit. She knew *perfectly well* that it was me and not you. I can't believe she fucking—" He broke off, running a hand over his face with a groan. "Sev, bro, I'm so sorry. She seemed so *normal.*"

I frowned, confused. "What makes you think the chick had anything to do with the photos? You just got papped, dude. It happens to us all the freaking time. You *know* that. Remember when Ollie got papped coming out of the family-planning clinic a few years back?"

"Yo, dude," Ollie interjected, "they share the same building as my dermatologist. I was getting my skin checked for melanomas!"

"Paps don't fucking care. They sell whatever story makes them more money. And apparently *Seven Harrison Cheats On Clara Belle* sells more magazines than *Gemini Harrison Breaks His Dry Spell.*" I threw my hands in the air, silently cursing the fact that my own fame was preventing my brother from just living his life. But at the same time... "*Fuck,* Gem. You know better!"

Gemini was staring at my phone, his brow furrowed as he zoomed in on the images. "Foxy bitch," he muttered under his breath, but there was a weird, little smile on his lips like he was remembering a hell of a good night.

Come to think of it, he'd been in a *crazy* good mood that next day. I guess he really had broken his dry spell in spectacular fashion, and honestly, good for him. But if he could hook up without destroying my life, I'd be a lot happier.

"It was her car," he said in a quiet, thoughtful voice. "The pics...they're all taken from *her car* and since there were no slimy paps hiding out in the back seat, I'd bet my shorts they're stills from a dashcam."

"Whoa," Ollie commented, peering at the pictures again. "So she knew who you were...but still sold these to the dirt media as it being Seven? Rough."

"Not necessarily," Gem said, defending the mysterious woman. "Maybe she sold them as *me* and the breaking publication decided to slap Seven's name on it. Wouldn't be the first time."

My phone rang again, and Gem held it out to show me Jerry's name flashing on the screen. I shook my head and he rejected the call. Barely a moment later, it started again and this time when he held it out, Clara Belle's name flashed.

"Shit," I breathed. "Gem, I swear to fuck—"

"Dude, what do you want from me? I don't have a time machine." He was irritated now and understandably so. Tossing me a middle finger, he answered the call for me and put it on speakerphone. "Clara Belle, honey, it's Gemini."

"Fuck you, Gem. Put Seven on." My girlfriend had a vicious tongue on her, despite her carefully crafted image as Hollywood's darling.

"He's right here," Gem replied, raising a brow at me, "but I wanted to get ahead of things and tell you those photos are of me, not him. I met a woman the other night and was a little bit indiscreet, and—"

"Do you think I'm an idiot, Gemini?" Clara Belle snapped. "Obviously it's you. Anyone with half a fucking brain knows it's you. Seven isn't that goddamn stupid, especially now with the Carriage Pictures deal on the table."

A huge sigh of relief gusted out of me to hear her say that, and I sagged to sitting on a barstool as Gem handed the phone across the island to me. "Thank fuck," I groaned. "Clara, baby, you have no idea how worried I was that you were calling to break up with me."

There was a pause on her end. Then she gave a small laugh. "Oh, Sev...I *am* breaking up with you. Honey, you know I love you, but this scandal is going to be *huge* for me. Awful for you, don't get me wrong, and I really do feel bad about all of that, but I'd be an idiot not to take this opportunity."

Shock rendered me speechless for a moment and I just stared at my phone like maybe I'd heard her wrong. We'd been together for four years, and I'd been planning on proposing to her once the Carriage Pictures deal went public. It was all planned out between our publicists. I'd spent millions on her ring and everything.

"What the fuck?" I exclaimed eventually. "Clara, I didn't cheat on you. Those pics are of Gem!"

"I know," she replied, her voice dripping with false sympathy, "and, Sev, this hurts me just as much as it hurts you. But the media thinks you're a lying, cheating scumbag. There's no coming back from that, and you have to see how fantastic this will be for me! I'm the heartbroken, jilted woman here. My agent is already getting calls for new roles I never would have been considered for previously. This could win me an Oscar, Sev! Really, if you loved me, then you should be happy for me."

Fucking *speechless* all over again.

Ollie and Gem looked just as shell-shocked as I was feeling, their jaws basically on the floor as they enjoyed a front-row seat to the systematic destruction of my whole damn life.

"Clara, what the *fuck*?" I asked again. My brain was too numb to form much more thought than that. "You're breaking up with me because you want public sympathy to win roles? How about you just become a better actress and stop pretending to be such an airhead, then directors will take you more seriously?"

For all her many faults, Clara Belle wasn't an idiot. She was sharp and business savvy, but she was a mediocre actress who'd never cracked it past straight to streaming rom-coms and the occasional art house women's fiction flicks. Still...that was a low blow.

Her outraged gasp told me she thought so as well. "There's no need to get nasty, Seven. It's nothing personal, and you'd do the same in my shoes. I'd say we can stay friends, but you know how it goes. The story is juicier if we hate each other. Bye, boys, good luck with Carriage now." Her nasty, little chuckle before she hung up told me she *also* believed my career was in the toilet from this.

"Fuck!" I exploded, leaping out of my chair and clenching my fists. I wanted to hit something so badly, but I couldn't risk messing up my hand when I still had a few days of shooting left on *Death Mission* before it was done.

"Wow," Ollie murmured in a sigh. "She is a piece of fucking work. Bullet dodged, bro. Seriously. I'm kinda glad she's gone."

I spun around to glare at him, incredulous. "Ollie! I was supposed to fucking marry that woman and she's...she just... What the *fuck?!*"

Gem was oddly quiet, and I swung my gaze to him. My emotions were all kinds of conflicted because he didn't do this deliberately. He didn't ask for any of this and had expressed his discomfort with fame in a multitude of ways over the years.

We'd started out acting together as children, swapping out in the same roles to share the workload while we were still young, but the older we got, the less enthusiastic he'd been to take new parts.

Several years back, he'd quit acting entirely and slipped into the shadows as a stuntman and body double. As far as the media was concerned, though, Gemini Harrison was no longer an actor and he liked it like that. Except, of course, I was going from strength to strength on the silver screen and we, unfortunately, shared a face.

"I'm sorry, Sev," he said quietly. "I should have thought it through."

Mentally, I forced myself to calm the fuck down. He looked so crestfallen, and I knew beyond a shadow of a doubt that he felt entirely responsible for what had just happened with Clara Belle.

"It's not your fault, Gem," I gritted out, scrubbing my hands over my face. "It's not on you. This is the paparazzi fucking with our futures *again*. Filthy, soulless bottom-feeders."

Ollie grunted his agreement, no stranger to the paparazzi treatment himself. "Why *didn't* you think it through? You're normally so careful."

My twin's face flushed pink, and he ran a hand through his hair that matched mine so perfectly. Our arrangement with him working as my stunt double was invaluable. No one could match what we had, which was why Carriage Pictures had even taken an interest in me for their new action-hero franchise. I couldn't do it without him, and I wouldn't want to. He was my other half, and it just fucking sucked that he couldn't be his own person.

"Uh, well...I'd had a few drinks," he mumbled, seeming sheepish. "And this woman...Jesus she was something else.

Knew immediately that I wasn't Seven, then nearly kicked my ass at pool…" He trailed off with that weird, little smile on his lips again.

Ollie grinned, clapping his hands together. "Shit, dude, you're fucking smitten! What's her name? Are you seeing her again?"

Gem screwed up his face, looking regretful. "Uh…"

I rolled my eyes. "She sold pictures of him to the tabloids, Ollie. Of course he isn't seeing her again. Right, Gem?"

He shrugged. "Couldn't even if I wanted to. I never got her number and she was gone before I woke up." Then he cleared his throat and ducked eye contact as he added, "And I didn't get her name either."

My jaw dropped, but Ollie cracked the fuck up.

Before I could give Gem grief for his irresponsible decisions, the doorbell rang, then rang again and again. I rolled my eyes, knowing full well who I'd find even before I sauntered over to open it.

"Morning, Jerry," I drawled, letting our manager in with the weight of dread across my shoulders, "welcome to the shit show. Clara Belle broke up with me, and Gem didn't even get that chick's name."

Our manager stared for a moment, so hard I worried his eyes might pop out of their sockets. Then he glared at Gemini. "So I take it you didn't have her sign the NDA? That explains a lot. So much. What the *fuck* did I do in a past life to deserve this?" His slightly sobbing question was sent heavenward, and I bit back a smile. Jerry was a drama queen.

He'd fix this all for us, I was sure of it. He was the best in the business, so if Jerry Thompson couldn't untangle this mess, no one could and we were all fucked.

chapter
five

Stella

Nothing made me happier than seeing my bank account sitting in the black for the first time in too damn long. Even after paying off all the crucial bills, such as power and water, and chipping away at Dad's in-home care bills, I still had money left. Not a lot, mind you, but enough that I could treat myself to a drive-thru Starbucks on my way through downtown LA.

My phone rang as the barista handed over my venti brown sugar oat milk shaken espresso with vanilla sweet cream on top. It was 100 percent a splurge drink, and I felt expensive as hell for even ordering it.

"Hey, Dad, everything okay?" I asked after accepting the call on speakerphone in my lap. There was no Bluetooth in my '57 Chevy Bel Air but she was divine to drive and had ample space for camera equipment, so I wouldn't trade her in for the world.

"I saw the pictures, Shutterbug." His voice slurred slightly, which was a result of his head injury. The injury may have ended his career as a paparazzi, but it had saved his life. Without those brain scans, they never would have found the tumor until it was too late to operate. Now he was bed-ridden and required in-home nurse care, but he was alive. That was the important part.

I wet my lips, a small amount of guilt curling through my chest. "Mmhmm, not the best quality but what can you expect from dashcam stills, right?"

He sighed, and it sounded distinctly disappointed. "Stella. I don't like you doing this work. What happened to that job you were working over at the Grove? That was a good job, wasn't it?"

I rolled my eyes skyward as I came to a stop at a traffic light. He was talking about the waitressing job I had at a swanky pizza restaurant. "I got fired, Dad. Some guy grabbed my ass and I broke his nose. Besides, even you have to admit, I'm kinda good at this celebrity-stalking shit. Maybe even better than you."

His laugh was more of a cough, but I'd take it. "You wish, Bug. You wish. I just want you to stay safe out there. Those men can be—"

"I know, Dad. Trust me. I'm a tough cookie. I can handle myself."

He huffed. "Well, do we need to have a talk about the content of those photos, young lady?"

My jaw dropped and I gave a horrified screech. "Ew, Dad! God, I'm twenty-five, not twelve! We are absolutely not discussing the *content* of those photos. Ever. Gross."

Dad's hacking laugh came down the phone line and I shook my head. He'd smoked for way too many damn years, but after walking in his shoes for the past six months, I kinda understood. The job took a toll on your morals, and every now and then I wasn't averse to taking the edge off. Though I went more for weed than nicotine because I respected my arteries a fraction more than that.

"Dad, I'm almost at Rodeo Drive. I gotta go," I said, despite the fact I was still a solid fifteen minutes away. "Get some rest, okay? Don't watch any more episodes without me, though."

"Can't promise anything, Shutterbug. You stay safe out there, and for god's sake, steer clear of Dillon if you see him."

I wet my lips, nodding to myself. "I will, Dad. I promise. Love you."

"Love you more," he replied, gruff as ever.

I ended the call with a sick feeling of dread curling through me. Dillon Paget was the reason my Dad wore a massive scar down the side of his head but also sort of the reason he was still here…I guessed. He was a smooth talker, a professional paparazzi photographer, and a real mean drunk.

We used to date. Sort of. Until he turned that mean my way, and my Dad intervened.

One punch. That was all it took for my whole world to fall apart.

Somehow, thinking about Dillon made me think about Gemini. Again. I'd done a whole lot of thinking about Gemini since Saturday night and had gone back and forth with my own conscience for way too long over whether to sell those photos. Ultimately, though, I accepted the fact that I'd never see him again, so what did it matter?

Did I feel bad for blowing up his brother's life? Fuck no. Seven Harrison had been in the business long enough to accept the risks. So had Gemini for that matter. At the end of the day, the paycheck was more important than any weakness toward Gem's theoretical feelings on the images.

Everyone knew that Seven was deliberately cleaning up his act to not violate the morality clause with Carriage Pictures. It meant that juicy gossip and photos of him were few and far between, and most were somehow smoothed over by his shark of a manager, Jerry Thompson.

Not these ones, though. By selling them as Seven, not

Gemini, I'd tossed a grenade into his perfectly crafted squeaky-clean image and paid off a shitload of bills in the process. It didn't matter what damage control Jerry did; I'd already collected my fee.

By the time I pulled into a parking spot just off Rodeo Drive, I'd finished my indulgent Starbucks and was in a much better mood. My friend Tessa had tipped me off that the high-end clothing store she worked at was expecting a celebrity visitor, and I wanted to poke the bear with a stick a little.

Camera slung over my neck, I walked the rest of the way and casually leaned against a lamppost in front of the clothing boutique where a simple belt cost more than a month's worth of insurance payments. My camera was far from inconspicuous but my leather jacket disguised it a little bit. Enough that the shiny blonde actress stepping out of the store with a small army of assistants carrying bags didn't see me until it was too late.

Snap, snap, snap!

"Clara Belle! You don't look particularly upset today," I called out, grinning as my camera captured the horrified expression on the beautiful woman's face. "Did you know that Seven was cheating on you? Who was the woman?"

Okay, now I was just having fun.

"Probably some filthy, obsessed fan," Clara Belle sneered, before clapping a hand over her own mouth with a dramatic gasp. "Oh my goodness, excuse me. I never should have said that." Her face screwed up like she was about to cry, but no tears escaped. "I'm just so utterly heartbroken that he would betray me like this!" This time she whined like she was actually crying...yet no moisture leaked out.

"Are you...trying to fake cry?" I asked, bemused even as my finger worked my shutter button, making sure to capture every single angle and expression from the starlet. "Oh, wow. I heard you couldn't cry on cue, but I figured you'd be a little more broken up to lose *Seven Harrison*. Didn't he basically make your career?"

To my disappointment, Clara Belle's friend came barreling out of the store toward me, hands waving. "That's enough!" she shouted as if I gave a flying fuck about her. "No pictures! Have a little respect, you filthy animal."

I barked a laugh, popping a few more frames of Clara Belle's smirking face while her friend insulted me. It was nothing I wasn't used to, even if I'd only been in the business six months.

"I said, *no pictures!*" the older woman yelled in my face, reaching out to grab my camera or push it away or *something*. Not a damn chance. I whipped the expensive equipment out of her reach, and she stumbled, her momentum carrying her forward to fall in the gutter between two cars.

Clara Belle gasped, pressing her manicured fingers to her mouth. "Oh my god, Marjorie, *get up*! What are you doing?"

More photos. This was perfect. I was the only pap capturing this too. Maybe I could actually put a dent in the hospital bills this time.

Red-faced, Marjorie reached out a hand to Clara Belle, who tried to help her back up to her feet, but it was an awkward sort of positioning. The assistants holding her shopping bags just stood there watching too, none of them really giving two fucks to help out.

Unable to help myself, I pretended to brush past the actress as if to leave, only to bump into her and send her sprawling on top of her friend in the gutter. Then, of course, took more pictures.

"You *little bitch!*" Clara Belle screeched, her sweetheart mask slipping away to reveal the shrew beneath. "I'll sue you for this!"

I scoffed, clicking the shutter button at dizzying pace as I backed away. "Good fucking luck with that. Hey and sorry about Seven cheating. That woman in the photos looked like she would have been fantastic in bed. It's no wonder he didn't fight for you."

Low blow, even for me. Antagonizing the celebrities wasn't *technically* a job requirement but sometimes a girl just needed to go the extra mile to get the shot. Besides, this fucking bitch was begging for it.

Clara Belle let out a feral shriek and I genuinely thought she was about to swing at me as I continued taking pictures, but her friend quickly intervened. A few harshly whispered words in Clara Belle's ear and suddenly that sweet-as-peach-pie mask was back in place, and she dusted herself off as though she were running for Miss Hollywood.

After that, nothing else came even close to getting a rise out of her, so I called it quits and went back to my car. I took the time to carefully pack away my equipment into the padded cases in my trunk, then climbed into the low driver's seat with a satisfied sigh.

It wasn't glamorous work, hell it wasn't even very moral, but it was work. And it was a heck of a lot more exciting than waiting tables at a pizza restaurant...not to mention better paid.

A scroll through my phone showed me the news was still blowing right the hell up about my hookup pics with Gemini. Or rather...Seven cheating on Clara Belle. I snorted a laugh at how stupid the media was to just lap that up without questioning which twin it was. Technically, Gem gave me the idea himself when he said that people *always* guessed Seven first.

"Shit," I muttered, rubbing at my sternum.

I needed to stop feeling guilty. Gem was hardly innocent to

the ways of paparazzi and media, and he hadn't exactly made me sign an NDA or anything. I wasn't breaking any rules. But I still sort of regretted leaving the hotel room like I did, sneaking out while he slept soundly. It'd been *so tempting* to stay, but ultimately it never would have worked out. When he sobered up, he'd have regretted everything.

At least this way I got something out of it—more than the incredible sex, of course.

With a sigh, I sent off a message to my favorite photo buyer with the subject line "Clara Belle on the verge of a mental breakdown?"

It was enough, I knew, to pique her interest. I'd send the photos themselves later, once I'd sorted through, edited, cropped, and all the other finishing touches. People seemed to forget, sometimes, that paparazzi were photographers and some of us actually gave a fuck about quality and composition, rather than just a breaking scandal.

If you snapped all three, you were absolutely the winner.

chapter
six

Stella

One of the advantages to being not only new to the paparazzi circuit but also a young, pretty woman was that I could gain access to places that the greasy, overweight old-timers parked outside couldn't get into. In just a few months, I'd built up quite the closet of various uniforms after discovering no one blinks twice when you show up at the back door and claim to be with the caterers.

Sure, I couldn't really wander around a private party taking pictures, but it did allow me access to vantage points that others couldn't get to. So while the morning after a lavish party there were fifty-seven different versions of the same celebs standing in front of the same doorway, wearing the same thing and looking equally irritated by the flash cameras, I was submitting my totally unique perspectives looking into the garden or up at a balcony or, my favorite, couples sneaking out the service entrance to "avoid being photographed."

My hot target for the evening was supposed to be Seven and Clara Belle, but in the fallout from the cheating scandal, neither of them attended the party. Instead, I found myself snapping a few not-for-sale pictures of Olivier Griffiths smoking a cigarette in the garden. It wasn't newsworthy; he was just a beautiful man to look at through the lens. Tall, broad, raven-black hair and eyes to match, he made the perfect action-movie villain. The kind of character women secretly hoped would turn out to be endgame for the heroine.

His smile was utterly to die for as he spoke with an older gentleman, and I zoomed in to keep him the main subject of my frame. Simply stunning.

Part of me sort of hoped that Gemini might be at this party too. He and Olivier were best friends, and it wasn't uncommon for them to attend industry events together, so I'd have been lying if I'd said I wasn't quietly hoping I could catch a glimpse.

No such luck, though.

After some hours, I wandered back around to the staff entrance and sat on the tail of a refrigerator truck while waiting for drunk celebs to wander into my frame. Mostly they were just stars sick of smiling, but every now and then I'd catch a pairing that hadn't yet gone public.

"Bingo," I whispered, clicking a few sneaky shots of a silver-haired gentleman leaving with a woman who was very definitely *not* his wife. The hand planted firmly on her ass said they weren't just sharing an Uber home too.

Pleased with the results of my work, I hopped down off my spot and silently applauded my decision to wear chunky-soled boots rather than heels. Most of the guys out the front were probably long gone, having grabbed their shots as celebs arrived, but I was patient.

"I thought that was your car," a familiar voice came from the shadows as I crossed the street.

My footsteps faltered, and I drew a quick breath before continuing on. Never show fear to a predator—they'll rip you to shreds. Not wanting to engage in a verbal sparring match, I ignored my violent ex-boyfriend and popped the trunk to store my camera equipment safely.

"Ignoring me, are we? Come on now, Stella, don't be like that. You know you miss me."

I just barely closed the trunk before he grabbed my hip, shoving me forward against the car and boxing me in. Fear rolled through me, but I clenched my jaw and refused to shrink away.

"Get your filthy hands off me, Dillon," I snapped, spinning around and giving him a hard shove. He stumbled back a couple of steps, just enough to show that he wasn't totally sober. *Fuck.* I'd have happily gone ten rounds with sober Dillon, but drunk Dillon was another matter entirely.

His eyes narrowed and his lips twisted in a sneer. "You think you're too good for me now, Stella? Now that you've whored yourself out to the big-time action star? Huh? Yeah, I recognized you in those photos, you slut."

"You're drunk." It was better to not confirm or deny. Keep the focus on him. One thing he liked was his ego being stroked, and he hated to look like a fool. Why the fuck he was drinking when he was supposed to be working was none of my business.

Instead of fumbling for a defense though, he closed the distance between us and gripped my throat. Fuck. One minute I was on my feet, the next, I was slamming into the trunk of my baby.

The angle made kicking him impossible. The pressure from his hand against my throat cut off my oxygen. I dug my nails into his forearms, but it was easy to forget that he worked out enough to build up muscle. He also had a solid seventy pounds on me, none of which was flab.

Mouth breathing the liquor fumes into my face, he glared at me. "Bet Daddy is real proud of his little whore spreading her legs to snap the story."

The flat look in his eyes made them seem almost devoid of

humanity. The twisted look on his face robbed it of all its attractiveness. Of all people, you'd think I would recognize that, in this town, beauty really was just skin deep and not fallen for the tousle-haired bad boy with the striking eyes, chiseled jawline, and rugged appeal.

"Yeah, bet your daddy doesn't know what a freak in the sheets you are." He flexed his fingers on my throat as I tried to get a foot up and between us. "Maybe I should tell him?" He punctuated the last five words by banging my head against the trunk.

Each blow sent pain lancing into my skull. Even worse, my vision was going spotty. I had to breathe. The more he squeezed, the more difficult it became. Nothing I did had an effect on him. Nothing...

Suddenly, he yanked me upward and just as abruptly let me go. I sucked in a desperately needed breath and damn near choked on it. Coughing, I staggered toward the sidewalk. A series of grunts penetrated my oxygen-deprived brain and I half fell as I twisted to see two figures locked in a struggle a few feet away.

One was definitely Dillon, but I couldn't make out the other. I sat abruptly, trying to focus. It was like I had a dirty lens and everything was smudgy. A series of hard blows rained down on Dillon.

Both men had dark hair. Dillon wasn't in a full suit. The other guy was. I wanted to cheer when my knight in whatever the hell designer suit he was wearing landed an uppercut that clacked Dillon's teeth together.

I was still trying to get enough air back into me. Between the blurry eyesight and the fight to breathe, it was hard to get a fix on what was happening. But then the guy in the suit literally leapt and slammed both of his feet into Dillon's chest.

Holy shit.

I gaped as Dillon went down. He tried to get up, but the suit was already on his feet. With a pivot, he slammed his foot into the side of Dillon's head and that was all she wrote for the slimy piece of shit I used to date.

Just a head wound, I thought almost bitterly. Maybe they'd find some screw loose in him. I blinked and the suit went from standing over Dillon to squatting right in front of me.

Oh, those were some pretty damn eyes. The light was hitting them and made the blue in them practically shimmer. No wonder he was getting more roles as a sexy romantic lead. Olivier Griffiths was a hell of a lot better looking up close.

Even the indistinct, hazy version of him. Kind of reminded me of when they would put Vaseline on a camera lens to give women a more ethereal look.

"Hey there," the sexy bastard said in that sexy beast of a voice that sounded like a melodic growl. He could play all those hot-man-of-privilege roles or even the urbane, suave spy while still getting rough.

Perfect guy really.

"Hey there," he repeated. "You still with me?"

"Hi," I answered him belatedly. "You're bleeding."

The red on his shirt was not from wine. Wrong color. It was dripping from his nostril too. He swore and pulled a handkerchief out of his inner pocket and blotted at his face.

"Huh," I said, kind of bemused. "Didn't know people still carried those. Sorry that the dickwad got a couple of shots in."

"Don't worry about it. Dickwad is unconscious. Hopefully he wasn't a boyfriend or something."

I waved that off. "Ex. Very ex. I wish he were a thousand miles behind me ex." Maybe that was going a bit far. The harder I tried to squint to look at Olivier, the more my head hurt. "I should get up."

"Maybe not yet." Olivier put a hand on my arm to keep me

in place. My legs weren't really cooperating anyway. "You okay? You look a little out of it?"

"Not drunk," I told him and held up three fingers. "Scout's honor."

"Not the Scout's sign," Olivier said. "But I believe you." He glanced over his shoulder to where Dillon lay in a crumpled heap. Maybe we should drop him around the corner with the rest of the garbage. "Still, we should probably get you to a hospital."

"No hospital," I said with a snap and gripped his arm. "Absolutely not." Dad's bills were more than enough. Our insurance barely covered a dental cleaning, much less an emergency room visit. "I'll be fine. Totally had worse."

I had no idea when, and I was kind of croaking when I spoke, but fuck it. I surged to my feet and Olivier followed me up. That might have been a mistake on both of our parts. My stomach rolled as the world spun.

"I think I'm going to puke," I warned him. I wasn't able to focus on much but he could definitely get out of the way. One minute I was standing, the next he swept me up and got me over to one of the dumpsters. The smell was repugnant, but it decimated what little resistance I had left and I threw up.

Thankfully, it'd been a few hours since I ate, so it was mostly water. But it still hurt like a bitch and burned my throat. The dry heaves that followed sucked even more.

"Easy," Olivier said, he had the handkerchief up to my mouth and dabbed at it. "All good?"

"Sure, peachy." I even managed to give him a thumbs-up.

"You need a doctor," he informed me. "Your pupils are huge."

"Thank you," I told him. "I think you're sexy too." I patted his chest. "But not tonight."

The corner of his mouth quirked upward. "Right. That's it, definitely the doctor."

"No," I told him and pulled away. "I can take care of myself. No doctors. No emergency rooms. No doc in the boxes. Just...let me take care of me."

"Lady," he muttered, "I need to get the fuck out of here, but no way in hell am I letting you just stagger off with a concussion."

"You can't go home with me," I told him. "I don't take strangers home. Even if you're technically not a stranger cause I know you...but...you know I think I'm gonna be quiet."

The more I talked, the worse my throat hurt. Olivier gave me a hard look. "If you pass out, I can just take you to the hospital."

"Please don't."

"Goddammit," he swore again, then looked over at Dillon before looking back at me. "Too many damn vultures here tonight to argue about this. If you won't let me take you to the hospital or home, you're going home with me."

"Okay." Then I frowned. "Wait...why do I have to go home with you?" He was talking too fast. He whipped his jacket off and pulled it over my shoulders before he slid an arm under my knees. The ease with which he swept me up sent my head spinning.

"Don't throw up," he ordered as he strode away from Dillon and my car. "I can't fucking believe this." The last came out a mutter. "Jerry's gonna fucking kill me. Seven's gonna kill me. No fucking way am I sticking around for the bottom-feeders to get their shots."

"Oh." Right. The other paps. "None out here," I told him and patted his chest. "I was alone."

"Good to know no one was around to help you. Anyone ever tell you to not park out back of big hotels?"

"Nope," I said and then we were suddenly at a car. There was a click of locks and he pulled open the door of the low-slung Jaguar. "Pretty kitty."

Olivier settled me into the passenger seat as I transferred my petting from him to the seats. The leather was really soft. He snapped a seat belt across my chest, then popped open the glove compartment. A rustle of paper brought me back to the present and he put a bag in my hands.

"Hang on to this. If you need to puke again, throw up into the bag and not the floor."

"Good plan," I told him as he closed the door and circled the car. Cleaning this car would probably cost a fortune. The engine purred to life. Really sexy kitty. Then he was backing out and we were leaving the hotel, Dillon, and my sweet baby behind.

I'll be back, I promised my baby mentally. Dillon would surely be found and they could scrape his drunk ass up off the ground. Head against the seat, I closed my eyes. All the headlights were kaleidoscoping or streaking past me.

They hurt my brain.

"You know," I said. "I probably shouldn't be driving."

"You don't say?" The sarcasm raked against me.

"You're funny," I said. "And cute."

"I thought I was sexy?" The teasing growl made me laugh. Oh, that fucking hurt. No more laughing. I put a hand up to my head.

"Sure, I should probably say thank you too, but it's getting hard to focus."

"Close your eyes, Snow, I'll have you somewhere safe soon." I was half out of it, but I swore he also said, "And Gem better be home when I get there or I have no idea what I'm going to do."

chapter
seven

Gemini

Leaning forward against the counter, I shifted my grip on my cock. The strokes weren't quite what she'd done to me, but staring down at the blurry images, I could almost picture the sass in her green eyes. They sparkled when she smiled, and there was so much goddamn humor in her smile.

But no lie, all that gorgeous, black hair spilling over the pillows while I drilled into her? That was an image that could make me come. I'd wanked to it a few times this week. My dick stiffened and that slow, rolling burn began to ascend my spine when a chirp came from the security system.

The fuck?

The relief I chased evaporated as I pivoted to glare into the bedroom. We had intercoms in the whole damn house. It just made it easier to find each other when we were in a hurry. Another chirp...

Goddammit. Someone had left the button on downstairs again. The chirps were the security system disarming downstairs. The thump of a door closing and then Ollie said, "That's it Snow, one foot in front of the other."

"Hmm." Whatever she said in response was muffled, but

the fact *Ollie* was bringing home a girl had me stuffing my dick back into my pants and zipping up. It would take too long to get back to the edge.

I snagged my phone off the bathroom counter before I headed out of the bedroom and diverted toward the stairs. I hadn't been sleeping that well this week anyway. When I wasn't haunting the Cactus, I'd gone to the gym. The tabloids were having a fucking field day at Seven's expense, and it didn't matter that we knew it wasn't him in the photos.

The only thing I really hated was the fact my girl couldn't miss the damn picture or the circus they generated. The chances of her giving me a call were slim to none. Course, I hadn't exactly given her my phone number and she had been gone when I woke up.

Best fucking night's sleep I'd had in a year.

"Okay, that's it," Ollie said.

"Hey!" The husky, feminine voice promised all kinds of dirty things and my dick stiffened immediately. Right, so it got off to my girl and apparently Ollie's bedroom piece. "I can walk."

"Just stay there," Ollie said, and I followed his voice to the sunken living room. Weird place to take a date. We rarely brought women home. Clara? Yeah, because Seven had dated her for years, but random hookups?

The last thing I expected was to find *my girl* with Ollie when I walked into the room. He shot a look at me, relief written all over his face.

"What the actual fuck?" I demanded. Ollie had a hand on her leg and was on one knee in front of her like he was about to go down on her. The black-haired siren of my wet dreams groaned.

"Shit," she muttered as our gazes locked.

"The name is Gem, Slick. You knew that, remember?" I

reminded her, and I shook my head. What were the chances I'd be jerking off to the thought of her and she showed up here?

Wait—what *were* the chances? Dismissing that for the moment, I focused on where Ollie's hand was.

"You two know each other?" Ollie swung his relieved gaze from me to Slick, then back again.

"You could say that, and you want to get your hands off my girl?" It wasn't really a suggestion but the sudden urge to pop the guy who was practically a second brother and was definitely a best friend burned through me. I had to consciously force my hand to uncurl.

"I'm trying to keep her from getting back up," Ollie protested. "She took a hell of a hit. Some jackass attacked her behind the hotel."

The words had me really focusing on her. The lights were all on dim here, so I hit the switch on the wall to turn them up to full brightness. Slick jerked her face to the side, grimacing. A ring of red marks encircled her throat.

"I brought her back here because she refused a hospital," Ollie was saying. "I beat the shit out of the guy and got him off her, but there were paps everywhere tonight, and the last thing I needed was my photo taken standing over the dude."

Crossing the room, I nudged Ollie out of the way as I cupped Slick's chin and tilted her head.

"I'm fine," she argued with me even though she was still squinting badly. The husky voice must be a byproduct of the attack. She had a far smoother voice, like whiskey going down slow and sweet.

"Easy, Slick," I said, shuttling aside the dozens of questions springing to mind. Yeah, the red marks were definitely going to bruise and there were four—no five half-moon marks, probably from nails digging into her skin. "You kicked the shit out of this asshole?"

"Oh yeah," Ollie said as he rose, then raked a hand through his hair. "He was banging her head off the car. And she is really woozy, threw up already."

"I am not," Slick argued, and she made a pathetic attempt to shove me back and stand. Yeah, she definitely was woozy.

Cupping her face, I lifted her gaze to mine. The lights were definitely hurting her. "Cooperate please," I said. "Let me identify the issues and we can take care of it, and then we'll turn the lights down again."

Her grimace needed no interpretation, nor did her wince as I began to work my fingers over her scalp. I tried to keep it gentle and ignore the silken feeling of her hair on my skin. A little tougher considering I didn't have to imagine the spill of it now.

"Ow, fuck." The sharpness in the first word and the echo of pain in the second assured me that I'd found the tender spot. There was some swelling, but I wasn't feeling the bone move.

That was a relief.

"Easy," I said as I rose and leaned over her to part her hair and get a good look. There was no blood on my fingers, so I didn't think it had broken the skin. That said, she needed care.

"Can we turn down the lights now?" If she didn't sound so damn miserable, I might have left them on just to get even with her for her ditching me to wake up alone. But that was being a dick and I didn't want to be a dick right now.

Maybe later, when she was feeling better.

"Hey, Ollie, turn them back down and get me a couple of ice packs and some water."

"Sure," Ollie said. "Right away, Mr. Gemini, I'll get that for you."

I ignored the sarcasm. "Get the med kit for your hand too. You tore up your knuckles."

"Fuck," Ollie swore as he strode out of the room after

dimming the lights. I leaned back on my knees and stared up at her. The little sigh of relief as it went darker wasn't manufactured.

This was the same woman who kicked my ass with her sharp tongue and playful gambling. She'd also rocked my fucking world, and I'd gotten it up more than a few times that night. It had been a long time since that had happened.

"Hang in there, Slick," I said. "We'll get you fixed up. You have any allergies I should know about?"

"You have a medical degree that I should know about?" The snappy response pulled a reluctant smile to my face.

"Certified paramedic," I told her. "Helps with the work and when we get into scrapes."

Her mouth formed a silent O.

"If you want a doctor, I can totally take you to one." Ollie probably should have forced the issue with her. The longer I studied her eyes, the more I worried. They were definitely dilated and she wasn't focusing well. I had no doubt there was a concussion, but now I had to worry about a subdural hematoma.

"No," she argued. "I'll be fine."

"Still singing that tired verse?" Ollie asked as he returned with a bucket of ice that also held water bottles and ice packs in one hand and the first aid kit in the other.

"Look," she said, twisting to try and find him but she wavered a little. Not a good sign. "You saved my ass, I appreciate it. But you don't need me to be here and I'd rather be somewhere else."

"Damn, Slick," I said before Ollie could jump into the conversation. "Way to wound a guy. I know you got off... I even remember you screaming my name more than a couple of times." My dick gave a pulse at the reminder.

"I guess you two really do know each other," Ollie

muttered as I cracked open one of the water bottles and pressed it into Slick's hand along with a couple of painkillers.

"You could say that," I told him. "Drink that slowly. Your throat sounds bad. Gonna wrap an ice pack on it and put another on your head."

I was glad she wasn't bleeding—at least visibly. She couldn't quite hide the pained expression as she took a drink.

Her eyes were half-closed and it gave me time to just study her while I wrapped one of the ice packs around her throat. The Velcro would keep it in place. We had all kinds of ice packs in the freezer. Our injuries varied, so we needed to be flexible.

The night I met her, she had been dressed in jeans and chunky motorcycle boots. They'd been cute on her and had done fantastic things for her legs, but this was a whole different style. She wore the same boots but instead of a T-shirt, she had a nice blouse and black skirt. Nothing high-end but definitely attractive. Maybe a waitress uniform? Was she a cater waiter maybe? Ollie's suit coat didn't go with the rest of the outfit, but maybe that was my jealousy talking.

Frankly, her outfit screamed "comfortable" and not "please hit on me." Hell, it didn't even say "let's party." The barest trace of makeup seemed present, but it was hard to tell in the dark. Then I checked her fingers to reassure myself.

No rings.

Good.

She didn't need the accessories to look good... Also it was reassuring to see she wasn't married because that had definitely crossed my mind when she disappeared without a trace.

"That feels good," she admitted when I had her lean back against the ice pack. "The ice, I mean."

"It's okay to say you like my hands on you," I said and she let out a snort.

"You wish."

"I know," I said, then traced a finger down her cheek. The red marks on her throat were definitely going to bruise, but her face was unblemished. It didn't look like the guy punched her. I wanted to know more about the jackass that attacked her.

Her eyes slitted open, and I could practically feel the impact of her trying to focus on me. What I didn't like was how large her pupils still were. I needed to check for reactivity. I hadn't managed it when the lights had been on earlier.

"Are you two done? Or do I need to leave you alone?" Ollie's dry tone hit the right note and reminded me that we had company *and* that Slick and I had a lot to discuss before we hit the sheets again.

But that was definitely going to be a *when* and not an *if*.

"Fuck off," I told him cheerfully as I stood. "Let me see the hand."

"Asshole," Ollie responded, then thrust his hand at me. The knuckles were definitely scraped up. The bleeding had all but stopped. His gaze went past me to Slick. "Didn't know she was *that* girl."

"Wouldn't expect you to," I told him. "You can't really see her face in the pictures."

"Can see her body," he countered, and I smirked. He did not have to remind me about that. "But all I saw when I came out was some guy trying to strangle her as he beat her head against a car."

The image *that* painted just pissed me off.

"Pulled a *you* on him," Ollie continued as I cleaned his knuckles, then applied some antibiotic ointment. They'd heal up in a couple of days. Fortunately, he'd just finished filming a picture and had a few weeks before another one started.

"A me?" I asked as I glanced up. His attention was still on Slick.

"Yeah, you from *The Dead Keep Walking*." Ollie grinned. It was one of the first action flicks we'd done as adults. It was also the picture that cemented my desire to get out of being an actor and to focus solely on stunt work. I'd done all of my own stunts on the picture.

Carlisle "Candy" McShane had been the head of the stunt group. He was old Hollywood and he'd taken me under his wing. I missed the old coot. Shaking off that reminder, I repacked the first aid.

"I did a lot of shit in that movie. What scene are you talking about?"

"You remember where you jumped and hit the guy with both feet right in the chest. Then rolled up and roundhouse kicked him?"

"Yeah," I said slowly. It was a stupid move. The double kick was effective, but it also dropped you on your own ass. You had to be fast.

"Did it like a champion." Ollie dusted off his shoulder and grinned like an idiot, then he sobered. "What are we going to do with her?"

That was a damn good question.

chapter
eight

Stella

id I fall asleep on the mega-celebrities' couch while they chitchatted about some old movie? Yes. Undoubtedly yes. I was tired, for one thing, and my head hurt enough that I firmly believed sleep was the only cure.

Strong, warm arms scooped me up, rousing me from my rest slightly and I groaned as the daggers through my brain lit up once more.

"Where're you takin' me?" I mumbled, not really putting up much of a fight because...brain daggers.

"Bed," Gem responded, his deep voice like a soothing balm as he carried me. "But you can't go to sleep, okay? You've definitely got a concussion so you need to stay awake."

I scoffed lightly, not bothering to open my eyes. "Now I know for sure you don't have a medical degree. That's total bullshit, and it's been proven that sleep is actually the best thing for the brain to heal."

His soft laughter was like a warm blanket wrapping around my cold body. "Well, you're not slurring your words so that has to be progress."

My reply was just a huff as I snuggled my face into his

chest. Fuck he was sexy. Why did I sneak out in the dead of the night again?

Gemini carried me up a flight of stairs, then gently laid me down in a huge bed that smelled strongly of cedarwood, clove, and patchouli. It smelled of Gem.

"Am I in your bed, Gemini Harrison?" I mumbled, trying to get comfy and regretting the waitress uniform I wore for the party.

He hummed a sound of confirmation as his hand stroked down the bare length of my leg. Just as I started to think he was instigating sex, he began unlacing my boot. Oh yeah. Shoes in bed wasn't the best idea.

"You are in my bed, Slick. Is that a problem?"

No. But I was curious and wanted to tease him a bit. "Don't you have guest rooms in this fancy mansion?"

Another of those low, soft chuckles that made my insides tighten. "We do, actually. Several guest rooms."

"Mmhmm," I murmured as he tugged my boot off, then moved to the other one. "Then why am I in *your* bed, Gem?"

He didn't answer as he unlaced my second boot, then tugged it free. His long fingers wrapped around my foot and his thumb rubbed my arch in the most delicious way. "Because I want you to be, Slick."

"Oh," I replied, a little at a loss for what to say back to that. I wasn't used to men being so...*secure.*

Gem rubbed my feet a moment, then got up with a sigh. "I'm going to grab you a T-shirt, all right? You can't sleep in that."

I snuggled my face deeper into his pillow, inhaling his scent. "I thought I wasn't allowed to sleep?"

He laughed again. "I thought I wasn't a doctor? Stay awake a little longer, though. I want to make sure you're comfortable."

I didn't do as I was told, drifting back to sleep and needing Gem to wake me up in order to change out of my blouse and skirt and into the soft, oversized hockey jersey he'd picked out.

"Am I allowed to sleep now?" I grumbled once he'd tucked me in. "I feel like I got the crap beaten out of me tonight."

He exhaled heavily, his lips brushing my wrist in the ghost of a kiss. "Yeah, you can sleep. I think once those painkillers kick in, you should be feeling a lot better."

He started to stand up, but I grabbed his wrist to stop him from leaving just yet. "Thanks, Gem," I whispered, my eyes just barely open to see him. "I owe you one. And probably owe Olivier at least two for saving my life."

His brow furrowed a moment, then he kissed the inside of my wrist this time. The warmth of his lips left a brand behind. "No thanks necessary...though I would take your name if you're willing to offer it."

A startled laugh burst out of me, and I instantly groaned at how it hurt my head. But still... "You don't remember my name? I'm so fucking insulted." And yet I was struggling to contain my laughter.

"You never told me," he responded with a touch of outrage.

I grinned, letting my eyes shut fully. "Oh well. G'night, Gemini."

His frustrated sigh amused me to no end. "Sweet dreams, Slick."

Despite the heaviness of my eyes, I didn't expect to drop right into sleep. Yet the next time my eyes opened, time had definitely passed. My bladder protested, demanding attention.

Lifting my head, I found Gem sprawled next to me, sound asleep. While he was close enough for his heat to warm me, he wasn't touching me. Hushed twilight draped the space. The blinds were closed, along with the curtains. A soft light shone from within the bathroom. The dim glow but a glow nonetheless.

The soft light was enough to let me make out the shapes in the room. Easing out of the bed, I made a beeline for the bathroom. The ache in my head had improved. I tested the knot on the back of my skull and grimaced. That still sucked and it hurt when I messed with it.

Right, don't touch it, idiot. The mental castigation made me smile. After I peed, I washed my hands and then got a drink. My throat ached but it wasn't too bad. At least my larynx wasn't crushed. On quiet feet, I drifted back into Gem's bedroom.

I debated searching for my clothes, then slipping out before he woke. I hadn't wanted to leave with Olivier in the first place. I knew they were friends but I hadn't expected them to be sharing a house.

Gem being here had been a blessing and a curse. Then he'd also been so damn gentle. His probe for my name and reaction to me teasing him had also been funny. Instead of getting dressed and leaving, I was staring down at Gem's sleeping form and imagining all the ways I could wake him up.

Running my tongue over my lower lip, I closed my eyes. *You should leave. Get your shit and go. Nothing good can come from waking him up.*

I almost snorted at myself.

Okay, yes, I can definitely come and he'd make sure too. The man had a gift. *Still a bad idea.*

Despite already being on the losing side of that debate, I ticked off a few more reasons to *not* wake him up. None of them competed with the one pressing reason coiling tighter and tighter inside of me.

I wanted to wake him up.

I wanted *him.*

That night at the club had had nothing to do with work and everything to do with him. Did I sell those pictures? Yes. Did I plan them? No. Right now, I didn't have a single camera on me. I wasn't even sure where my phone was…

Gripping the hem of the hockey jersey he'd dressed me in, I whipped it off. I shed the bra and panties right behind it before I slid back beneath the covers.

The sheets were silky soft, and it was warmer closer to him not that I'd noticed the chill. As I eased over to him, he let out a little sound in his sleep and shifted. I went still as he turned toward me and wrapped an arm around me.

I waited to see if the skin-on-skin contact would wake him, but his low, slow breaths didn't shift. He was well and truly out. As much as I wished it were brighter in here so I could study him more, I savored the intimacy of being wrapped up close under the blankets and surrounded by our own bubble of darkness.

Just us. No one else. Not the fans, the tabloids, or even just the public to come between us. I traced my fingers over his pec. If I recalled, there was a tattoo just beneath his fourth or fifth rib, with a line of dialogue or a quote scrawled there in text.

I hadn't gotten a chance to read it. Frankly, I'd been too busy feeling him to be looking at him. With a series of gentle kisses, I worked my way down his chest to his abdomen. The waistband of soft shorts. They'd dragged lower on his hips and left me his adonis belt to explore with my fingers.

The peak of his erection was right there as I nudged the waistband lower. It wasn't quite fully hard yet, but the semi stiffened as I wrapped my fingers around him. One stroke from root to tip and back again.

He was every bit as thick and heavily veined as I recalled. A low sound vibrated in his throat as he stretched under my light touch. The heat of his leg against my breasts was a light tease but not like the way his scent filled my nostrils.

There was a muskiness but also a clean, almost woodsy scent to him. Maybe it was the room or the sheets or like when he brought me in here and the combination reminded me of *him*—it was just Gem.

The languidness in his muscles only lasted until I wrapped my mouth around the tip of his cock. The slow dip and shallow thrusting motion stiffened him gradually. The weight of him on my tongue accompanied by the low sounds he released fueled my motions.

With a stroke of my hands over his thighs, I nudged them wider and slid over so I was more firmly between them. The angle worked better. The chiseled strength of his muscles were a delight to explore even as he pressed deeper into my throat.

I checked the motion with care, not wanting to gag or hurt my throat. Thankfully, swallowing around him was more of a delight than a pain. Oral sex wasn't for everyone, but I enjoyed it—with the right partner.

Gem was very much that partner. He'd gone down on me more than once. It was nice to savor the corded muscle in his body as tension began to radiate through him. A harsh inhale almost made me smile.

"Slick?" The sleepy voice vibrated with a kind of husky need. It had me rubbing my own thighs together. The man had a voice that was sex on a stick, and right now, I very much wanted to ride that stick.

That said, I wanted to do this too. At the question in his words, I rolled my tongue around the tip before stroking it along the underside of his cock and taking him deeper.

"Holy fuck," he groaned. "Slick...if this is a dream, don't wake me up."

A laugh shook me at the demand and plea rolled into one.

His breathing came in sharper, little puffs. I could almost imagine the surprise on his face. He did like it when I shocked him, right?

Delight curved through me when he threaded his fingers into my hair. He fisted it but not to pull or jerk. Instead he just held on and let me set the pace. I caressed his hips and when he thrust upward, I stroked my thumbs in circles.

"Fuck," he swore, but I pressed my face all the way to his abdomen, settling my nose to his skin and then pulling all the way back. Relaxing my mouth, I held just there with his tip on my tongue.

Light teasing strokes of my nails raised goose bumps along his skin. His hand flexed in my hair and then he gave a tug toward him as he thrust, and I took him all the way to the throat again.

His next words came out a garbled groan. Pleasure flushed through me as I focused on rolling my tongue around his head, then stroking the hot, velvety skin at the base with my fingers.

Each teasing lick or firm caress earned me more groans until it became an entire litany of them. His muscles tensed and his feet were flat against the bed even as he seemed in a fight to keep his thighs open. Despite his hand in my hair, he didn't hurry me along, only tugged me back whenever I lingered overlong on the tip of his cock.

Was I doing that to tease him mercilessly?

Maybe a little.

I indulged myself again and again. There was just something so decadent about exploring his every reaction and a man who wasn't remotely opposed to revealing them. I slid my hand under to his balls as he began to shake, massaging them lightly. The harsh, little explosions of breath and the trembling in his thighs and abdomen told me everything I hadn't realized I needed to know.

Ceasing playtime, I went in avid pursuit of his pleasure by increasing the pace and the pressure while still stroking his balls. His strangled "Slick" was the only warning received as he released the first spurt of cum. I swallowed around him again and took him deep as more spurts joined the first.

The bitter and salty taste was heavy on my tongue, and the rich scent of him filled my nostrils. His hand flexed in my hair as he gave an involuntary jerk with his hips. I stuck with him, breathing through my nostrils as I swallowed every drop, then added more teasing strokes as I licked him clean.

Smugness filled me as I released him with a little pop. There was something altogether heady about his reactions. Then he hauled me upward, abandoning any pretense of my control. His mouth fused with mine as he tumbled me onto my back.

chapter
nine

Stella

The next time I woke, the twilight of the room was illuminated by the sun peeking around the edges of the blackout curtains warned me it was time to go. I hadn't meant to go back to sleep, but a couple of orgasms had done wonders for my headache. My throat still hurt, but I would survive.

Lifting my head, I studied Gem where he sprawled. I was on my stomach, but he was on his back and his hand was quite firmly on my ass. Naked, pleasantly sore, and relaxed, I could probably close my eyes and go back to sleep.

Bad idea though.

The lightest of snores told me Gem was still out and I sighed. The night I'd spent with him before had been an escape, a good time without strings or attachment. That I got some good shots from the dashcam by accident? Just icing on the cake.

Tonight? Tonight had been a choice and one I refused to regret. That said, it was also time for this Cinderella to turn back into a pumpkin and roll out. I needed to pick up my car before it got towed.

As much as I wanted to stay right there in the bed, I forced myself to ease out from under his hand. I slipped off the side like a thief seeking to escape detection. Which I kind of was. Course, the only thing I'd "stolen" tonight was a lot of fun and some comfort.

Regret tried to settle in my stomach as I stole another look at the bed. *Nope*, I told myself almost resolutely, *don't do that*. It wasn't until I gathered my clothes to get dressed that I realized I had no idea where my panties ended up.

They could be tangled in the bed. The bra was right there hanging off the edge. I did find my phone in the clothes. Go me. Gem didn't so much as stir as I dressed. Leaving commando might be a bit chilly, but I'd cleaned up after I peed so hopefully it wouldn't be messy.

Boots in one hand, I tiptoed over to the door before I allowed myself one last look at the shadow sprawled in the bed. In a moment of whimsy, I blew the sleeping man a kiss and then opened his door.

The light in the hall was almost too bright. I hurried through and then closed the door as quietly as possible. Squinting, I glanced left and then right. The wide hallway didn't offer any clues on which way the stairs were. Gem had carried me up here so it was definitely *up*stairs.

After flipping a mental coin, I went left. It wasn't a long walk before the hall turned to arrive at a large balcony that twisted into a long staircase that descended into the foyer. From the marble tile below to the paintings on the wall decorating the path to the gorgeous crystal chandelier, the place screamed wealth and celebrity.

Of course they were stinking rich. Seven hadn't released an unsuccessful movie in years. Olivier also lived here, so if they were pooling resources, they were fucking rolling in it. At the end of the day, they had carved out their own little palace, and I very much needed to Cinderella my ass right out of here.

I descended the steps, hanging on to my shoes. I could put them on at the bottom. I checked my phone; it had about 30 percent. Enough for me to get a rideshare back to my car. Better to wait to call for it when I was down the block.

The windows alongside the wide double doors were frosted, but the light outside was definitely brightening. *Let's go, Stella*, I told myself. *Time to get the hell out of here.* I didn't want to give the competition any walk-of-shame shots.

"Excuse me."

Dammit. So close.

With a grimace, I pivoted and tried to school my features into something more neutral. Seven Harrison stood in the archway separating the foyer from a sitting room of sorts. Dressed in a button-down open at the collar with the sleeves rolled up to reveal tattooed arms, he met my gaze like he often welcomed guests at far too damn early in the morning.

"I was just leaving," I said, rather than try to stammer out some excuse. I was an adult as was Gem. So no explanations required.

"Actually, you're not," Seven said, before gesturing to the sitting room. "Join me. We need to have a conversation."

I raised my eyebrows. "No," I said. "We don't. I have places to be."

I didn't make it even two steps toward the door when Seven said, "The alarm is on and the door is locked. You won't be able to open it."

Cutting a glance back over my shoulder, I narrowed my eyes. "Then enter the code and let me out."

"Eventually," he said, almost too agreeable. The placid expression on his face was total bullshit. He might be Gem's height and have his dark-brown hair and stunning blue eyes, but there was a coldness to Seven.

That chilly, calculated layer threatened to slice at you if

you dared to get too close. I had no idea why people couldn't tell them apart, even without the scar I'd noticed on Gem's chin—a scar that was definitely absent from Seven's chiseled jaw.

"Please come in," he said, motioning to the sitting room again. It wasn't until he shifted that I noticed the crystal decanter on the side table with a tumbler that held a few drops of amber liquid. The table in front of the chairs, however, had a contract on it. "This won't take long."

Debating how serious he was about the door still being locked without the code to also disarm the security system, I studied Seven's posture. His shoulders were rigid and his manner distant. The polite neutrality in his voice didn't remotely touch his eyes.

The man glared at me like I was the devil incarnate. Interested on a faintly perverse level, because I'd hardly done anything to earn his ire, I moved toward the sitting room. As soon as I took a step, he lead the way.

"Sit there," he said, waving an almost imperious hand toward the settee in front of the coffee table. "You can review the NDA, then sign it."

Apparently, he expected me to just hop to it and do as I was told. Wow, was he about to be disappointed. "No."

"I have a copy you can take with—" He paused, then snapped his gaze to me. "What did you say?"

"No," I repeated.

"What do you mean no?"

"I mean no, n-o. No. I won't sign your NDA. I'm leaving now."

"You have to sign the NDA," he informed me and it was almost amusing how truly outraged he was, except I had no interest in being held hostage by America's asshole here.

"I have to die and pay taxes. Everything else is optional. I need to go," I said, checking my phone. The morning wasn't getting any younger.

"You don't understand." Seven followed after me and caught my arm. The tug had me spinning back to face him. Only his resemblance to his brother kept me from hitting him with my shoes. I'd had enough manhandling, thank you.

"I think the one failing to understand the word *no*, would be you. You want me to sign a contract. I do not want to sign a contract. You have nothing I need or want, ergo you have no leverage to incline me to sign."

"Except you want to leave," he snapped, though his eyes narrowed on my throat.

"Are you saying you're planning on kidnapping me, Mr. Harrison? I assure you, that won't end well for you or any deals you've got cooking with major studios." Showing my own hand? Maybe. I tugged my arm out of his grasp. "Now, am I setting off your alarm or are you opening the door?"

I was over the conversation.

"Of course I'm not planning on kidnapping you," the actor snapped. "You need to sign the NDA because we don't bring women in this house. We have reputations to protect. You've been in here. I want to keep our privacy intact."

"Well, bully for you, I guess. If you open the door, I'll leave you to your privacy."

His negative little growl of a groan almost made me smile. Frustration edged his movements as he raked a hand through his hair. "It doesn't hurt you to sign the NDA."

"It doesn't help me either." I shrugged. "Maybe you should make your girlfriend sign one and leave me out of it."

His lips compressed and a vein throbbed in his forehead. I probably shouldn't enjoy needling him so damn much. At the same time, if he just got out of the way, I'd be out of here.

I wasn't planning on advertising my night in Gem's bed or

repay Ollie and Gem's kindness by selling the story. I didn't have my camera either. But no, I wasn't signing some stupid document.

"You think I don't know who you are?" Seven demanded, real anger threading through every single word. "You think I don't know you're the one who was in those photos with my brother? Or how you managed to get him into position to take them?"

"I don't *care*," I told him, holding up one finger.

"What?" Surprise flashed in his eyes.

"Are you hard of hearing?" I asked, studying him. "That can be a problem when there are a lot of explosions on set, but you seem to be struggling in understanding me."

"My hearing is just fine," he snarled, gripping my biceps and then pulling me right over to the table despite me dragging my feet.

Yeah, I wasn't standing still. Seven might be the fancy-pants actor out of the pair, but he was hardly a slouch in the muscles department.

"Sign the damn paper," he snapped, pointing at the table. "Now."

This time when I tried to yank my arm out of his grip, it wasn't going anywhere. "I'm not a dog."

"I don't *care*," he parroted back at me. "You're going to sign the damn document."

"Or *what*?" I glared up at him even as he stared down at me.

That vein in his forehead pulsed and his lips were almost white from how hard he mashed them together. The faint hint of alcohol on his breath didn't suggest he was drunk, but if I was in for a penny...

"Maybe you should switch to coffee, Mr. Harrison. Between the booze and your hearing issues—"

"I do *not* have a hearing problem," he snarled. "But I know a bottom-feeder when I see one. You're signing the damn page if I have to hold your hand and make you do it."

"I'd like to see you try," I snapped back. Only this time, I managed to swing my boots in my free hand and smacked him square in the shoulder of the arm he was using to keep me still. His hand opened reflexively and I raised my phone like a talisman, video *on*. "It's been a pleasure, Mr. Harrison... want to say anything to your fans to add to that little rant?"

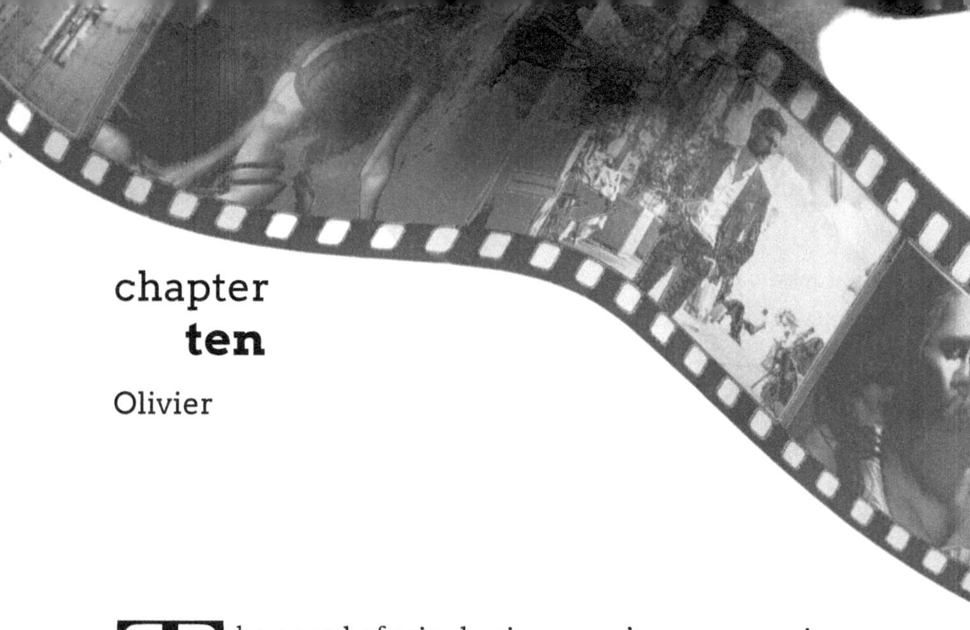

chapter
ten

Olivier

The sound of raised voices wasn't uncommon in our house. Living with two hothead identical twins came with its ups and downs...lately a lot more downs than ups as Seven struggled to accept Gemini's quiet distancing from the Hollywood scene. But the inclusion of a husky *female* voice arguing back was what roused me from slightly hungover sleep.

That wasn't Clara Belle. She was a hell of a lot more *shrill* when she was mad.

Stumbling out of bed, I scrubbed the heel of my hand over my eyes and grimaced at the sting in my knuckles. That was the reminder I needed to recall the events of the night before. I'd been decently drunk, in my defense. Really, really should *not* have driven, but I'd perfected the art of functioning under the influence before I was even legal to buy alcohol.

Hollywood taught us former child stars all kinds of shit that we had no right learning.

Still, I found it hard to regret my actions in saving that sexy waitress from the piece of shit beating her head into that car. The whole Gem thing when we got home was just a perk. I'd heard them going at it a few hours ago, and it sounded...*hot*.

Lucky bastard.

"...want to say anything to your fans to add to that little rant?" the sexy-legged vixen sneered right as I stepped into the room where she was brandishing a phone in Seven's face.

She was barefoot and disheveled but still blazing hot. Goddamn Gem, I owed him a punch in the dick for robbing me of this hottie.

Seven's jaw clenched and his eye twitched, but he was 100 percent aware that her video was recording. He'd never jeopardize his Carriage Pictures deal. Not now that it was so close to being signed.

"Okay, what's going on here?" I interrupted before things could get out of control—or *more* out of control than they already were.

The dark-haired bombshell whipped her head around in surprise at my voice, and Seven took advantage of her distraction to snatch the phone out of her hand.

"Hey! That's my private property, asshole!" she snapped, that voice just as husky as I remembered from the night before. It reminded me of her injuries, and I tried to get a better look at her throat. Was it bruised?

Seven retreated a few steps out of her reach as he deleted the video, then pocketed her phone with a smug smirk. "Okay...and? What's your point?"

"Give it back!" she demanded, advancing on him like she planned to pin him down to retrieve her phone. Seven put out his hand to keep her at bay and shot a frustrated look my way.

"A little help, Ollie? This feral trash panda is refusing to sign the NDA, and I, for one, am not letting her fuck up my career any more than she already has." He pointed to the paperwork sitting on the table. "Just sign it and you can leave with your phone. It's that simple."

"This is kidnapping!" the woman exclaimed in outrage, her

high cheekbones tinted with color, betraying how angry she was as she turned to address me. "This dickwad won't let me leave until I sign his shitty contract."

I yawned, ruffling my fingers through my hair. "Technically not kidnapping, Snow. More like...uhh...false imprisonment, maybe? Or unlawful detention? Something like that. I guess maybe it would fall under kidnapping except Sev didn't abduct you from anywhere; he's just not allowing you to leave. Hmm, I dunno, there must be a word for it."

Seven shot me the most perplexed look, shaking his head slightly. "Ollie, bro...what the fuck are you talking about?"

I shrugged. "Beats me, I'm still half-asleep. How's your head, Snow? You took some wicked knocks from that prick last night."

The sexy thing just blinked at me in confusion. "It's fine," she muttered. "I mean, it hurts but I'll live."

"What happened?" Seven asked, looking between the two of us like we'd both just grown tails and started dancing the macarena. "How do you two know each other? Didn't Gem bring this bitch home with him?"

I shook my head. "Nope, I did. You want a coffee before you go, Snow? Hah, that rhymed." Chuckling to myself, I headed for the kitchen and silently prayed she would follow.

To my relief, she was either still concussed enough or simply confused enough to do just that and leave Seven pacing around like a bear with a sore head while I fired up the Italian espresso machine that sat in pride of place on the marble countertop.

"Wait, hold up," Seven called out, following us a moment later. "What do you mean *you* brought her home? Gem—"

"How do you take your coffee, Snow?" I asked the leggy brunette as she leaned her hip against the island. I wasn't in the mood to walk Seven through all the events he'd missed, so it seemed easier to ignore him entirely.

She pursed her lush pink lips, and gave Seven a long side-eye before replying. "Black, please. No sugar."

I nodded thoughtfully, prepping the hopper with fresh beans. "Coming up. Want it in a takeout cup so you can complete your sneak out before Gem wakes up?" I shot her a teasing wink and was rewarded with a pretty blush.

"She's not going anywhere until she signs the fucking NDA!" Seven roared, slapping the contract down on the island counter. We had dozens of them and used them like fucking toilet paper. Literally everyone in our lives has been required to sign one.

I rolled my eyes, yawning again. "Obviously. Snow, sweetheart, I know Sev is being a boorish idiot, but surely you understand the need for our privacy."

Her expression blanched a little and her eyes softened. "Yeah...I do. But I'm not signing that. Sorry, Olivier, I really do appreciate your help last night—Dillon could have killed me if you didn't intervene—but signing that does nothing for me. Thanks but no thanks."

Conversation had to pause a moment while I ground fresh coffee into the group head, the burrs loudly whirring and making it impossible to be heard. Then when it finished, I gave the total babe a curious look.

"I don't get it. Why won't you sign it anyway? Unless you were planning on sharing all the intimate details of your night in our house with *People Magazine* for some ludicrous payout?" I snickered at my joke, but no one else did. In fact, the pretty girl shifted her weight from foot to foot and smoothed her hand over her hair in a clear sign that she was uncomfortable.

Seven, on the other hand, smirked like a Cheshire Cat.

"Funny you should say that, Ollie. I guess you don't know what your stray cat does for a living, then?"

She rolled her eyes, giving Seven a sneer. "Don't be so fucking dramatic, Harrison. I have no intention of selling my story to *People*."

I frowned, sure I was missing some vital piece of information. "What do you do for a living, Snow? Aren't you a waitress?" Because the skirt and blouse were identical to the cater waiters who'd been working the party last night. I had assumed...

She gritted her teeth, glaring absolute daggers at Seven. "I'm a photographer."

Sev scoffed. "She's paparazzi. And she's the one who sold those pics of Gem, knowing full fucking well that it was Gem and labeled them as me."

My jaw must have hit the floor. Then I mentally replayed the events of the night before...how I'd heard the commotion and seen the asshole assaulting her from across the street. I hadn't thought my actions through—thanks, alcohol—and acted on instinct to protect her. But if she was a pap...

"Did you set that up?" I exclaimed, horrified. "What the fuck would have happened if I didn't step in to save you? That guy wasn't faking!"

Outrage flooded her gorgeous face. "Don't be ridiculous! For one thing, I don't *set shit up*, and I sure as goddamn fuck wouldn't let my psycho abusive ex beat the crap out of me in the miniscule hope a celebrity would step in to save me."

"Wait, what the fuck?" Seven asked, scrubbing a hand over his face. "I'm missing some details."

"So that's why you won't sign?" I demanded, folding my arms over my chest. "Sev, you better check her camera roll before you give that phone back. She might have nudes of Gem that she plans to peddle as you."

The pretty, little liar threw her hands up in exasperation. "I'm not a fucking pervert! Jesus, you two are carrying on like I'm some sort of—"

The loud chime of our doorbell interrupted whatever weak defense she was about to offer up, and I glared at Seven to go answer it. He huffed a frustrated sound, then crossed to the video intercom on the wall to check who was on our doorstep.

"Jerry," he announced, pressing the button to allow him entry. "Maybe he can offer better incentive for this bottom-feeding scum to sign the fucking NDA."

Snow's lip curled in disdain. "I doubt it. And unless you wanna find yourself facing charges of extortion and imprisonment, I suggest you make your peace with the fact that I will *not* sign *shit*."

"Ollie!" our manager bellowed from the foyer, sounding fucking irate. "Ollie! Get your happy ass down here and explain what the *fuck* you were thinking!"

Seven looked to me with genuine curiosity, but I cringed. Now that I knew Snow was paparazzi and *not* just an innocent waitress...I'd bet my favorite boxer shorts her punch-happy ex was also in the sleaze-media game.

"In here, Jerry!" I called back, already cursing the moment I decided to play white knight and save Gem's damsel in distress. Damn it all to hell.

Our manager strode through with brisk steps, his suit as immaculate as always despite the steam coming out his ears when he glared at me. "You fucking idiot!" he spat, throwing a glossy magazine down on the counter, then frowning at Snow. "Who is this?"

"Gem's girl," I muttered, picking up the magazine and scanning the contents of the double-page spread Jerry had it open to. "That was fast, I guess." The images were all of the douchebag's injuries and the article content was purely allegation and speculation.

Jerry was squinting at Snow with heavy suspicion, like he recognized her but couldn't place where he'd seen her before. Of course he probably paid a lot more attention to the camera sharks than I did. I just kept my head down and pretended they didn't exist.

"Is it true?" Jerry snapped, dismissing Snow from his attention. "Did you beat the crap out of a pap because you were drunk and he insulted you?"

I scoffed, tossing the magazine down. "Absolutely the fuck not." Jerry's shoulders sagged with visible relief, and I realized he thought I meant *none* of it was true. I'd best clarify. "I was a little drunk, yes, and I did beat the crap out of him, also yes. But he didn't *insult* me, nor did I know he was a fucking pap."

Jerry's eyes bugged out and he spluttered like he couldn't quite find the words to tell me how utterly *stupid* I had been. Totally not necessary—I was already aware, and I scowled at the sexy culprit herself.

"You set me up, Snow," I accused.

She rolled her eyes again, like I was being petulant. "I already said, no, I didn't. And while we're on the topic, I specifically told you *not* to bring me home with you. I remember being quite adamant that I was just fine and did not want to go anywhere with you... It was *you* who made me come here."

With impeccable timing, Gem thumped his way down the stairs with a loud yawn. "Did I hear Jerry yelling at someone?" he called out ahead of himself. "Also has anyone seen—" He broke off as he entered the room with us and locked eyes on his duplicitous girl, a huge grin lighting his face. "Slick, you're still here! I thought you snuck out again."

Totally failing to read the room, he swept her up in his

arms, perching her butt on the counter and kissing her so intimately, it nearly got me hard just watching.

"Fucking hell," Seven muttered, and I kicked the back of Gem's leg to get his attention.

He broke away from kissing the raven-haired troublemaker with a scowl, then glanced between us all with more focus. "Uh...did I interrupt something?"

"Yes," Jerry snapped. "Ollie was about to explain why he beat up a paparazzo wanker last night, and Seven was about to explain why he has an NDA form out for this woman to sign... though I think that part is now obvious. I assume you failed, once again, to get the necessary paperwork before getting your dick wet, Gem?"

Seven cleared his throat, looking like a smug fuck. "Actually, I was about to enlighten my twin to the fact that he has been sleeping with the scavengers. Literally. Your girl is a vulture, bro."

If I was under any uncertainty whether Gem knew about Snow's profession, the shock on his face would have cleared it right up. Same for the guilt and regret all over hers. Damn, this was a clusterfuck and a half.

<h1>chapter eleven</h1>

Stella

"**I** assume you failed, once again, to get the necessary paperwork before getting your dick wet, Gem?" The snotty British accent just added to the disapproval vibrating in their agent's tone.

At least, I was pretty sure that was their agent. Maybe he was just an employee. Whatever, I didn't care who he was. He was an asshole.

I shook my head. Who the hell required an NDA in order to get laid? Clearly these three assholes—okay one and a half assholes. Gem didn't count. He never asked me for one and I was more than willing to cut him some slack in this area.

"Slick?" Gem frowned at me. "Are you..."

I lifted my shoulders. My position wasn't great. Gem also didn't deserve a lie. "Yes, I'm a photographer."

He all but deflated. "So you—"

"Dropped into the Cactus and Cocktails the other day after a long day to get a drink and some nachos." My stomach actually rumbled at the memory. "You were in my seat."

One corner of his mouth kicked up even if a frown had replaced the sleepiness in his expression. "Then I told you I wasn't who you thought I was."

"And I never thought you were dickweasel over there." I waved a hand at his twin. "A fact I made clear, especially since I wanted my seat. We ended up playing pool for another wager, and then we took the party next door, where we had an amazing time."

Some of the tension around his eyes eased, only to tighten as he studied me. "Then you sold those pictures..."

"I did that. A girl has to eat. But I *didn't* set you up nor did I plan on it. I didn't even know what I had until later. We triggered the dashcam when we landed on the hood of my car."

For a moment, his grin went smug before it faded. "But you sold it as some random hookup with Seven."

"I didn't invade *your* privacy and you said everyone mistakes you for him anyway. The images were too blurry to get much past the physical size and stature and the money covered some bills. You got laid, I got laid, and by lucky chance, I made some money. No one got hurt."

"Are you for fucking real right now?" Seven demanded. "*What about me?*"

"What about you?" I said without looking away from Gem. "You're a dick, for one, and I don't know you, for two, and I don't owe you shit, for three."

"It cost me my girlfriend."

"Buddy," I said, sliding him a look. "Trust me when I say I did you a favor. Particularly since she's milking the scandal for all the press she can get."

Behind me, Olivier snorted and earned the wrath of Seven. "What? She's not wrong."

"Thank you," I said over my shoulder.

"Don't mention it," he muttered. "Really. Just don't."

"Are you four quite finished?" Jerry asked into the sudden silence between us.

"No," Olivier and Gem answered with Seven just barely echoing at the end. Currently, I didn't like these odds. Gem was in front of me, still quite firmly between my legs, with Seven at the end of the island and Olivier right behind me.

The British manager person wasn't going to be any help. So better to just defuse their bullshit so I could leave.

"What about last night?" Gem asked.

"What about it? I told Olivier to leave me alone and just let me go home. I told him not to bring me here." I jerked a thumb back toward the other man. We'd already gone over this, but I'd say it as many times as necessary. "He *insisted.*"

"You had a concussion," Gem murmured, then raised his hand toward my head. He hesitated, waiting for me to give him permission.

"Just be careful. It was hurting when I poked at it last night. But it doesn't hurt now."

"I will be," Gem promised, and with gentle fingertips, he explored my scalp. The moment he grazed the bump, I winced. Definitely still sensitive. "The headache is gone?"

"Yep, sex is pretty much the best pain reliever ever."

"Wait," Seven said, planting his hands on the island. "What the hell did I miss?"

"A lot," Olivier said. "Are you sure you didn't set me up?" The question came from behind me, and I sighed as Gem held my gaze. The same question was right there.

"No, I didn't ask my ex to slam me into my car and try to throttle me just to play coy about you bringing me back to your house where I didn't want to go." The word *throttle* had Jerry whipping back to look at me, and Seven's frown deepened. "I told Gem thank you last night and I should have said it to you as well. Thank you, Olivier, for bailing me out of that."

"Oh, this is good," Jerry said abruptly. "Not the pap part, but you were saving her. We can spin that."

"Dude," Olivier said with a groan. "Some of us are still hungover, just relax."

"I want to believe you," Gem said even as his brother threw up his hands.

"Are you crazy?" Seven asked. "She's a hack looking to make a few bills off notoriety and painting the worst possible image she can of people."

"One, I am not a hack," I informed him because, just fuck you, Mr. Harrison. "Two, if you didn't want the attention, you wouldn't be out there courting the public and the studios." With a dismissive wave of my hand, I focused on Gem again. "I wasn't trying to use you. I still don't want to use you. I was planning to leave before you got up."

He grimaced. "Again?"

I shrugged. "To be fair, this…" I waved to our audience. "This is part of why I just wanted to go. I need to get my car. I have to go home." I wanted to check on my dad. He was used to the all-nighters; he'd done more than a few himself. But if he didn't hear from me at all, he'd worry.

"Yeah, you trying to put me on video this morning really looked innocent," Seven snarked.

"I only did that to remind you that you don't get to kidnap or coerce people. I don't care what your box office receipts are. You make shitty movies."

Oh, that comment landed. He glared at me. "Excuse me—"

A whistle cut through the room and I winced. That was just a little loud. Too loud, really, and while my headache had gotten mostly better, the agitation and anger were not helping.

"Everyone back to their corners," Olivier said, pinching the bridge of his nose as he circled the island. "I need a fistful of ibuprofen and two gallons of water before I finish making coffee."

"We need to get in front of this story," Jerry said. "We'll use her to do it."

The audacity of this dickhead was astounding. Almost as bad as Seven's. "You're not using me for anything," I informed him, but the manager wasn't paying any attention to me.

"I'm sorry," I said quietly, to Gem. "This was never my plan."

"I believe you," he said after a very long pause, and some of the air whooshed out of me.

"Are you fucking serious?" Seven was suddenly in Gem's face and shoving his brother backward. "You get some pussy and just roll over for her?"

I could take offense. I didn't. But I could. Gem shoved Seven back. "Shut up. This isn't about you."

"It is about me. She used pictures of *you* to fuck up *my* life. That contract isn't a done deal yet and Clara is gone."

"Do you really miss her?" Gem asked, and the question stopped his brother in his tracks.

Right, time to go. I slid off the counter and grabbed my boots from where they'd been dropped. After tugging one after the other on, I straightened my skirt and fixed my purse where it was slung across my chest. The only thing I needed was my phone...

It was peeking out of the back of Seven's pants pocket.

"That's not the point," Seven argued. "And you know it." He twisted the moment my fingers brushed the top of my phone and he caught my arm. "You're not going anywhere," he informed me, "until you sign that NDA."

"Sev, come on—"

An alert from the gates cut through the argument and Olivier made a face where he was downing water while Jerry spoke to him hurriedly.

"Now what?" Not waiting for an answer, Seven stalked over to the intercom. An image popped up from a camera at the gate.

"Excuse me, Sergeant McBride and Officer Bright are here to speak to Olivier Griffiths regarding an incident last evening."

Seven bowed his head, and for just a few seconds, I kind of felt a little sorry for him. It was like his whole day was going from bad to worse. Then I remembered he was the prick trying to hold me hostage and I was over it.

"Fuck," Jerry muttered. "I hoped we had more time."

"It'll be fine," Olivier said, sliding a hand through his hair to finger comb it. "I'll talk to them."

"Not without a lawyer you won't," Jerry snapped, and he had a cell phone in hand. Not that I didn't agree with the British asshole.

"Great, you boys are about to be busy. If you'll just give me my phone, I will get out of your way." I really did need the phone so I could get a ride and get the hell out of here.

"You aren't going anywhere," Seven informed me with a snap.

"Seven, c'mon." Gem shot me an apologetic look.

"No, Gem, I'm sorry. This is one time I'm pulling the older brother card. I can't afford anymore snafus. You know what, maybe we should take her upstairs until the rest of this is done."

"Can you just sign the NDA?" Gem asked. "I hate asking you to do it. It'll settle him down and we can get you out of here."

"You just want my name," I said with a quick smile and then folded my arms. "But no, I won't sign an NDA." At this point, it was the principle of the thing.

The doorbell rang, and it was like a skit on the weekend comedy show as everyone went to greet the cops. The blue uniforms offered quite a bit of comfort, especially since I was going to do them all a favor.

"Oh good," I said with an aggrieved sigh. "You're here. This man kidnapped me and is trying to hold me against my will." I motioned to Seven, and the older officer frowned as he looked from me to Seven then back again.

His eyes narrowed. Oops, he'd seen my neck. Well, it was bruised but I wasn't accusing them of attacking me.

"I did not kidnap you," Seven argued. "Don't tell them that. I'm not holding you hostage either. I just need you to sign the contract and then you can go."

The sergeant cleared his throat. "Mr. Harrison, I'm sorry but you can't force someone to sign a contract. That's coercion."

The vein in Seven's forehead began to throb again. Olivier had folded his arms and I swore he was fighting back laughter at first. But the neutral expression said maybe not. Then again, he was an actor, so what did I know? Jerry looked absolutely miserable and covered his face with his hand.

"I'm not coercing her," Seven replied. "I just stressed the importance of the contract because we all need to be clear about everything before she leaves."

"If you're trying to extort her cooperation by denying her the right to leave, then that is a crime." The sergeant seemed almost apologetic. They weren't here about me or Seven, but I wanted out of here and they were my ride.

"Told you," I said to Seven, then held out my hand. "Phone, please?"

The narrow-eyed look he shot me promised retribution. He could most certainly try. He slapped the phone into my palm, then I turned a smile on the cops.

"Would you mind terribly giving me a ride out of here? My car is downtown."

The harsh exhale from Gem registered his disappointment. It couldn't be helped. Not now, and if I was lucky, this would be a moot point.

"We need to question Mr. Griffiths," the sergeant said.

"Mr. Griffiths would be happy to meet you at your precinct, say in an hour, with his attorney," Jerry inserted almost smoothly. "We appreciate any and all discretion in the matter."

The cops glanced at each other, then to the men standing there in the hall. Olivier just spread his hands. "Sorry, gentlemen. I'd like to shower and get dressed, then I'll be right down."

He was the sexiest boy next door ever and his earnestness came off as charming without an ounce of being forced.

"An hour?" the sergeant verified.

"Absolutely. Though do you have a card to tell me which one to go to? That might be helpful."

"Of course."

"Ma'am," the second officer said as he pushed the door wider for me. I slid out with a smile and when the officer looked back inside, I pivoted to give Seven the finger.

It took them ten minutes to work out the interview time and then I was in the back of the black-and-white getting a ride back to the hotel. "Do you want to press charges, Miss…?"

"No," I told him as I rubbed at the back of my neck.

"Do you need to see a doctor about your neck?" The sergeant glanced back at me. The officer was driving.

Just the thought of *more* medical debt made me nauseated, just as it had when Olivier tried to push the issue last night. "No, thank you."

"Ma'am," the sergeant said. "I understand that they're actors and the sheen of celebrity can make people forgive even the worst of behaviors, but if they hurt you, we can definitely do something about it."

Seven Harrison fucking owed me for this after being such a prick. Olivier and Gem, however, did not deserve to be painted with the same brush. "They didn't hurt me at all. In fact..."

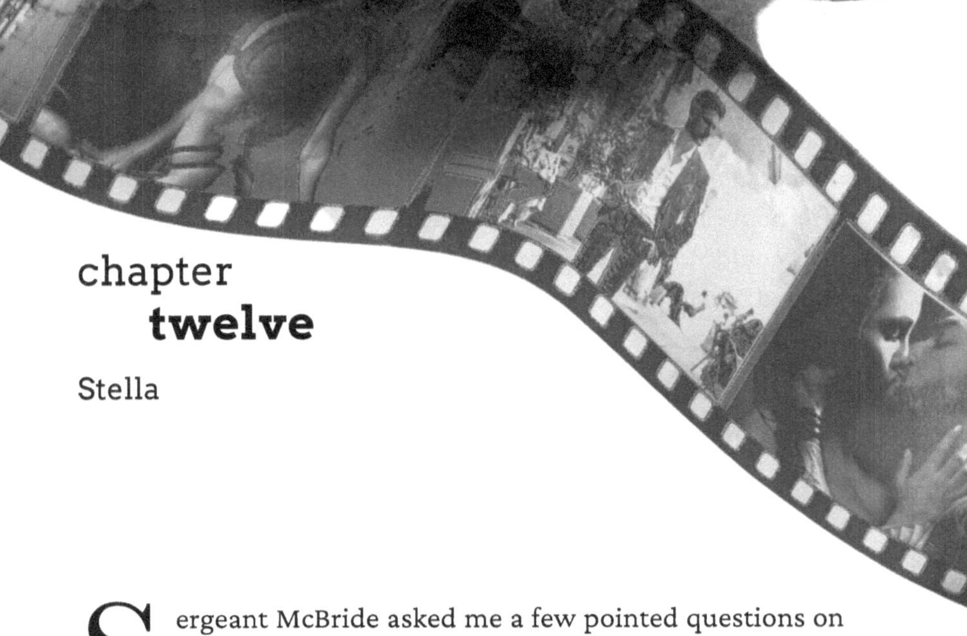

chapter
twelve

Stella

Sergeant McBride asked me a few pointed questions on the drive after I explained the assault. He wanted me to come down to the station to make a full statement. There was also the matter of pressing charges against Dillon, should I choose to.

"Mr. Griffiths was a witness?" the sergeant pressed.

"Yes, but whether or not he knows the man in question, I can't really tell you." The last thing I wanted to talk about was Dillon. He was crazier than I remembered. I could still feel his hands around my throat as he slammed my head against my car. "He saved me. That's it."

That was all I was going to say on it. Any injuries he inflicted on Dillon were in my defense. Dillon himself could get fucked. Officer Bright pulled up near my baby, and I glanced at the car. Thank fuck she was still here and not towed somewhere.

"Yours?" Bright confirmed with a hint of breathless wonder.

"Yeah," I said. "That's my baby."

"When can we expect to see you at the station to record your statement?" McBride asked.

Not groaning, I checked my phone for the time. It was almost ten. I hadn't been home since the day before. "This afternoon? I'll try to be there by four?"

I couldn't promise sooner. I needed to check on Dad. One, I needed to confirm he hadn't heard about last night and he had a check-up with the neurosurgeon this morning. No messages from him or Mom as yet, but that didn't mean they weren't coming.

"Four," McBridge confirmed. "We'll be there." Then he let me out of the back of their black-and-white.

"Thank you," I said to both of them. "For the ride."

"You're welcome." The sergeant passed me a card. "Those are my numbers. If you need to reschedule, call me. If you need a ride to the station, call me."

I frowned down at it. The more I thought about going in the more my stomach dropped. We'd tried pressing charges against Dillon before. He always seemed to slip through them or it came down to a case of he said, she said.

Dad barely remembered his attack. He couldn't conclusively say it was Dillon. Particularly after the surgery and subsequent brain-damage diagnosis.

"I'll do my best" was as close to a promise as I could get. "Thank you again." After giving a jaunty little salute I was definitely *not* feeling, I slid the card into the pocket of my skirt before I headed toward my car.

A moment later, the door shut firmly and then the car pulled away. I blew out a breath as I circled my car to the driver's side. At this point, I just wanted to—

The driver's side window was shattered inward. There was broken glass all over the seat. I swung my head around, scanning the area like I'd see the guilty party right here. Someone broke into my car. Why—oh shit. My stomach dropped and I went icy hot as I reached in to pull on the trunk release to pop it.

Even half expecting it, I couldn't suppress the shudder at the empty space where my equipment should be. My camera. The backup battery. The lenses. Everything.

It was just gone.

Bracing my hands against the trunk lid, I tried to suck in air past the constriction on my throat. There wasn't anything left in the trunk at all. Not even a scrap of material from the nylon bags.

The thief would have gotten all the memory cards too. The memory cards with the previous evening's photos. Backing up a couple of steps, I sat abruptly on the curb and bent my head between my knees.

I was hyperventilating and I had to stop it. Right now. I couldn't throw up or throw a fit. Even ordering myself to pull it together wasn't making a dent. Surging back to my feet, I slammed the trunk shut and did another sweeping scan.

Of course there were no cameras right here. It was why I'd *parked* here. A little blind spot in the hotel security. Fuck. My. Life.

Right, blind spot except I had a dash cam. I hurried around to the front of the car and pulled open the door. Even before I leaned in to check behind the rearview mirror, I already knew —the camera was gone.

Of course it was.

Goddamn vicious, backstabbing, needle-dicked weasel. Not only had he taken my equipment, he'd taken that camera, and if he did that, he probably took the drive. I opened the glove compartment, and sure enough the drive was gone.

If I'd been at all thinking clearly the night before I would never have let Olivier walk me away. I had evidence of Dillon's assault on camera. It wouldn't have been great evidence cause the camera was aimed toward the front of the car, but it would have been something.

Gone.

A few thousand dollars' worth of pictures. Maybe not a lot to some people, but it was another week of Dad's treatments. Another payment to the hospital. Part of the rent for his house. It was a drop in the bucket of all the bills, but I needed every single damn drop.

Not only had I lost all of it, but I couldn't just replace the equipment. That was thousands in equipment, memory cards, lenses...

I was lucky if I had lint to rub together in the bottom of my purse. What savings I'd had were gone. So were Dad's. Every dime we had, we'd sunk into keeping him alive. Working freelance didn't come with a great health plan. Mom worked as a nurse, and that got us some discounts, but the expenses just kept piling up.

Dad was at the doctor today.

He could need another round of treatments. More surgery. More care.

It all cost money. A lot of money.

Fucking Dillon. He attacked Dad and that put him in the hospital in the first place. The tumor wasn't his fault, but right now, I didn't care. Attacking me *was* his fault. Taking my equipment was absolutely his fault.

I should never have dated him in the first fucking place. Dad hadn't wanted me to. He'd said he didn't like Dillon's *vibes*, but that was nothing new. Dad never liked any guy I dated; it was basically in the Dad handbook to disapprove of any potential love interest. Torn between screaming and crying was not a state I liked to be in.

What I needed were solutions...

Think, Stella, I ordered myself. *Think.*

Crying wouldn't replace the equipment or pay the mortgage or even get Dad another week on chemo. I paced away from the car and then back. I also needed to get my fucking car fixed too.

Asshole.

I raised my phone and lowered it a dozen times. Who was I going to call? I already had to go down to the police station. Did I file a report on the stolen equipment? If I did that, I needed to have them come back here.

That made the most sense, though, right? File a police report? Then I'd have that to file with insurance. You know, if I hadn't let that insurance lapse to cover Dad's far costlier procedures. Protecting my equipment or saving his life?

The choice was a no-brainer.

Tears burned behind my eyes. Pinching the bridge of my nose, I forced myself to breathe. Breathe. Think it through. What options were available to me? Short-term? Long-term?

My savings were tapped. The photos I'd taken the night before would have netted me a tidy sum. So I was not only out of money in the bank, but I would be short what I could have made from last night's work.

Those were facts.

There were always events. I could go to another, get more shots, and sell those. I straightened and looked at my phone.

Yeah, even with all the improvements they'd made to smartphones, they couldn't replace a telephoto lens or the clarity of high definition. Could I make it work? Possibly.

It wouldn't be ideal and the struggle to get anything worthy of selling would be intense. So while it could fill in for the short-term, it wasn't a good fix and it had no guarantee of fiscal return.

What I needed was my equipment back or new equipment. Those were the two best-case scenarios. No doubt existed within me: Dillon had taken it. If I was lucky, he kept it in one piece and back at his place. I'd have to go to him and probably beg to get it back.

I'd sooner fuck a fire hydrant.

Worst case, he'd already destroyed the equipment. It was far more likely. Shattered it, sold it, gotten rid of it. So even if I filed charges, well, that probably would take more time I didn't have and not get me anywhere. I had no problems with filing the assault, but the robbery?

Did I have anything I could pawn to make enough to replace the equipment? My gaze landed on my car.

Oh, hell no...

Before I could follow that thought to its very negative conclusion, my phone rang. Dad's face popped up and I answered it immediately. "Hey, Dad, I thought you were at an appointment."

He coughed. "I was, but we got home an hour ago and I napped. Now I'm calling my Shutterbug."

I winced.

"Someone didn't come over this morning. Or go home last night."

"Dad," I said on a long sigh. "Are you checking up on me?"

The wheeze of his laughter pulled a reluctant smile to my lips. "I might be, but I'll never tell. You know I protect my sources."

"Yeah, you do." Even as much as the answer terrified me, I asked, "How was the appointment?" They always took so much out of him. It was why he had in-home care and only went in for very specific appointments.

"It was a lot of poking and prodding. Your mother is fussing enough for both of you. We won't know anything until the tests come back."

I sighed. Mom was a huge help, as one of Dad's paid home

helpers, but they'd divorced when I was only eight, so she couldn't be there around the clock. "Yeah, I guess I should have seen that coming."

"Think you could see your way into coming to see me and —" The hesitation was deliberate. I could almost picture him scanning the area around him in the living room where we'd set up his hospital bed. "And," he continued in a stage whisper, "bring some pizza for the inmate and maybe some of those garlicky breadsticks."

"Mom restricting your diet again?" Not that I could blame her. He had a hard time keeping down food. The richer the diet, the harder it was on him.

"You know how she is." Another cough escaped him, and then another.

The sound wracked him and it carried even if he covered the mouthpiece on our old landline phone. It was plugged in and parked right next to him. He also had a cell phone, but he liked the big phone.

"Sorry," he said, sounding winded and weary. "Needed a drink. Hate the cough, but sometimes, it's just easier to get the unpleasant stuff out of the way. Especially if it's not gonna hurt anything in the long run."

He had a point.

Dad always had a point.

"Tell you what," I said. "You had a big day today, but I'll see if I can swing around tomorrow with the pizza *if* Mom says you had a good night and your numbers are good. I don't mind tangling with her so you can cheat, but I don't want to bring you anything that'll hurt you either."

He grunted. That could be code for Mom was right there or he didn't like the offer. Or maybe both.

"Deal?" I said, staring through the broken window into my car. Sometimes, it was better to get the unpleasant stuff out of the way. Especially if it wouldn't hurt anything in the long run. Words to live by.

"Fine," he muttered. "Deal. But you're going to get a good report about me."

"I'd like that," I said, smiling. "I'll talk to you tomorrow, Dad."

"Shutterbug?"

So close.

"Yes?"

"You're okay, right? You're doing okay?"

"I'm fine, Dad," I promised him, lying with a straight face. The silence that followed my statement demanded that I fill it in. It was how Dad got me to talk when I was a teenager. The day I'd figured that out, I could have kicked myself.

I counted to sixty in my head, but before I got to fifty, he said, "Good. I worry about you."

"I know, Dad. Just worry about you tonight." Then he let me go and I exhaled a long breath.

Better to just get the unpleasant stuff out of the way. The words niggled into the back of my mind and jarred loose a fact that I'd been steadfastly ignoring since leaving the Harrison house earlier.

"It might work," I said to myself before I moved to clean the glass out of the driver's seat. It was a damn mess, but I didn't want to sit in it to drive. "It might not," I countered like I was really having this argument but I started the car anyway.

Instead of the police station or home, I headed back to the Harrison household. Seven Harrison wanted something from me.

It was a card I could play.

thirteen

Seven

It was nearly lunchtime when Jerry finally left. He planned to meet with Ollie and the lawyer before they went down to the police station. Gem fucked off to work after giving me a dirty look, like I'd been the one to make his little fuck buddy leave.

Clearly, she wanted an out and she took it. One of the cleaners stuck her head into the library.

"Sorry to bother you, Mr. Harrison," the girl said. I couldn't remember her name, but she was one of the younger cleaners. I was pretty sure she'd only started here a month ago. Not more than two months.

I shook off that meandering thought. It really didn't matter except I couldn't recall her name, if I'd ever been given it. Rather than make her feel bad, I just went for a neutral, "Yes?"

"I usually take care of the library right about now, but I don't want to interrupt you."

A couple of more caustic remarks popped into my head. *Like you're interrupting me right now and you're implying you want me to decide what you should do if you aren't cleaning in here.* Still, I swallowed the responses and shook my head.

My bad mood had nothing to do with her. She was doing

her job. A job I was currently blocking because I'd parked it in here.

"It's fine, just skip in here today. If you're done otherwise, go ahead and leave." Not that the staff reported to me. One of the best parts about having a house manager was he oversaw the staffing indoors and out. He also handled any maintenance, so we could focus on our jobs.

The blonde frowned down at the dark blue caddy in her hand. It was laden with cleaning supplies. "I don't mind waiting..." She trailed off when I glanced back up at her.

To be honest, I hadn't expected her to still be there. "No need to wait. I'm going to be in here for a few hours. I have work to do." I met and held her gaze. "You can go. Thank you."

No need to be rude to her, but also I wanted to be clear—I actually *did* have work to do. Jerry left me a stack of scripts to review. Most were probably going to be declined, but then I liked to vet the possibilities myself. Sometimes a job would appeal to me.

Carriage Pictures negotiations were ongoing. The holding pattern was irritating but a six-picture deal could set us up for a long time. It would definitely be worth it. In the meanwhile, I could afford to pick and choose from other projects.

I was skimming through a script when the intercom buzzed. It took a moment for me to process the sound. I checked the doorway first, but the girl was gone. The buzz sounded again and I rose. Script in hand, I headed for it. I needed the stretch anyway.

Pressing the button, I blinked at the woman in the pale blue car staring up at the camera. The sunglasses hid her eyes, but very little would disguise that smirk.

"You're back," I said, after connecting to the security box at the gate.

"So it would seem," she said in a lazy drawl. "Are you going to let me in?"

"That's a damn good question. What's my incentive?" Particularly since she'd been so cagey earlier. "Last time I checked, you wanted to leave so badly, you accused me of kidnapping and extortion."

She scratched her cheek with her middle finger. "Now I'm back and I want to come in."

Right. I studied her on the screen. It wasn't that high definition, and it didn't really reveal anything about her thoughts. Like *why* did she want to come in.

"Tick tock, Demon Spawn, the day is getting older." She gave an exaggerated check of her watch. And *I* was the actor here?

Demon Spawn. "That's not my name."

"No, but it was your role in last year's popcorn flick. Too bad it tanked." She blew a raspberry and gave a thumbs-down to the camera.

I scowled, unamused. "It didn't tank."

Her shrug was all indifference. "I didn't see it. I actually have good taste."

"So how do you know it tanked?"

"Because, Demon Spawn," she said, lowering the sunglasses and looking into the camera like she was locking gazes with me. It was uncomfortably intimate and direct. "I can read and it was all over the trades. Everyone knows what a flop it was, honey, even you."

I wanted to curse, but I just shook my head. The movie had the unfortunate timing of opening up between two major blockbusters. If it had opened first or opened later in the summer, it would have done fine. As it was, people just didn't watch it until it hit streaming.

Then we broke records. Yippee.

"Now, are you letting me in or am I driving away?" She revved her engine like she was considering ramming the gate. Crazy bitch probably would do it too.

Still...I couldn't make it too easy and have her think I was a pushover. "Give me one good reason to do it."

"Just one?" A dare and a challenge. Whatever game she was engaged in, I didn't want to play, and at the same time...

"Your turn, Stray, ticktock. One good reason or I'm hanging up."

She gave a dramatic sigh. "I'll let you persuade me to sign your silly little NDA."

Well, shit. That was not what I expected to hear. I leaned back from the screen like she could see me, even if I damn well knew she couldn't. It wasn't like I could argue that *wasn't* a good reason.

"Fine. Come up to the house," I told her, activating the gate to open for her. She gave a mock salute before she pushed her sunglasses back into place and then she was heading up the driveway. As if she was going anywhere *other* than the house after being granted access, but a silly part of my brain convinced me she was following my orders like a good girl.

I waited until the gate closed and no one tried to sneak in behind her. Then I made my way to the front door, more curious than anything. She'd been adamant about not signing and yet, here she was.

Opening the door, I waited as she parked in front. The car was a beauty and a hell of a classic. It looked even better in person. As much as I wanted to admire it, I made myself track her as she climbed out from the driver's side.

She was dressed exactly as she had been earlier, down to the wrinkles in her shirt. So she left with the cops and didn't even have time to change before she came back. Each new detail just added another layer to my suspicions.

"Is Gem here?" she asked as she approached. I gave it a moment, letting my gaze linger over her form. She gripped a bag that was over her shoulder, but there was no phone or camera in her hands.

"No," I told her. "If you came here looking for a story, you won't find it."

"Not why I'm here. I'm a photographer, not a journalist," she retorted. The tartness in her voice was as sharp as her smile. "Like I said, I'm here to do you a favor."

I braced a hand on the open door, not letting her in. Not yet. "You said you were here to sign the NDA."

Her smirk was downright provocative. "No, you asked me for a good reason to let me up. I responded that I would *let* you persuade me to sign the NDA."

The splitting of hairs was so fine, she should have been an attorney. Instead of backing down or changing her tune as we locked eyes, she just smiled and waited with seemingly endless amounts of patience.

What the hell did Gem see in her? Beyond the gorgeous curves, sensual mouth, and hair meant to be fisted—the list popped up so easily, I shook my head. Most of the time, Gem and I did not have the same taste in women. He thought Clara Belle was downright repulsive.

This would not be a good time to break the pattern.

"So what's it going to be, Spawn? You going to try and persuade me, or am I heading back out?" Her husky voice reminded me we were still standing there staring at each other.

A part of me wanted to call her bluff. It had to be one. She was out, free and clear, so why come back? Unless she needed or wanted something from us. The NDA was just an excuse to get in the door.

With how certain I was that she was up to no good, I

couldn't afford to let her walk without signing the NDA. It was more than just my future riding on it. That deal with Carriage Pictures could really set us all up for the long haul.

With a sigh, I backed up a step and cleared the door so she could come in.

"Thank you," she said with a too-bright smile. Already regretting the agreement, I shut the door and caught her elbow before she could head deeper into the house.

"Library," I told her, and escorted her to where I'd set up shop. Fortunately, the paperwork was right there on the sideboard, just inside the door. She didn't pull away until we were inside the room. I closed the doors behind us and leaned back against them. "Contract is right there," I told her with a nod.

She gave the room a slow perusal, spending almost no time on the stack of scripts as she turned. Then she looked at the contract before she glanced at me. "You know, I'd have thought that you could be more persuasive, what with being an actor and all."

"I'm not acting at the moment." Rather than cross the room and drag her bodily over to the contract, I folded my arms. "This is real life, Stray. My life. Gem's life. Ollie's life."

With a huff, she lowered her bag to rest on the chair nearest her. "You want to negotiate rather than persuade?"

"That would be preferable." Clearly she wanted *something*. I needed to know what that something was.

"All right, let's deal. I'll sign your NDA for a price."

There it was. She came back for a payday. I wish I could say I was shocked but I wasn't. Just kind of disappointed. "How much?"

She raised her eyebrows. "No outrage or accusations?"

I snorted. "Everyone and everything can be bought. I want your silence and to make sure you don't sell any more stories about my brother, especially after last night. You want money. Equitable exchange. How much is it going to cost me?"

She pursed her lips, then shrugged. "Twenty-five thousand."

"That's it?" Now I had some questions. She had that sum right there. Very specific.

"We can make it fifty," she countered, deadpan. The woman had no tells. "In fact, yes, great idea. Let's make it fifty."

"Fifty thousand dollars for your cooperation." It seemed a bargain at half the price, but I was more than capable of paying ten times as much.

"For me to sign your NDA," she clarified. "I have no intention of selling any pieces about Gem or photos of him. Like I said this morning, I'm a photographer—not a pervert."

As if I believed her innocent act. "You expect me to just take your word?"

"I don't expect anything. *You* want me to sign that NDA. You want it, you pay for it." She glanced at her watch, then back at me. "In sixty seconds, the price goes up."

Shaking my head, I pushed away from the doors and walked over to the contract. "Fifty thousand. Done."

"Not so fast." Those three words had me pivoting to face her. "I have a couple of conditions."

I didn't grind my teeth, but I still had them clenched and I had to push my words out past them. "Which are?"

"This is an arrangement between you and me. Period, end of story. You wire me the money, Venmo, Cash app, whatever, right now. Once I have it in my account, I sign. You have your NDA and I have the money. You don't give my name or information to anyone, including your brother."

I blinked. "What makes you think I'm going to give him your information? Or that he would even want it?"

Her expression chilled. "Nothing. Just like there's nothing that says I won't sell you out. But you have to agree to it *and* put it in that contract that *we* both sign."

"You are a fucking headache," I told her. "Trust me, I don't care what your name is and I have absolutely *no* intentions of giving it to Gem. I'd prefer he just forgot he met you."

"Well," she admitted with an exhale, "you're not alone in that."

Brutal. Was Gem shit in bed? He must be for her to be so adamant he never contact her again. I went for my phone and then eyed her. "Account info?"

She didn't play games this time; she just gave it to me, showing me her cash transfer info so I could send the money directly from my account to hers. It was my private account and not the business one, so I wouldn't have to explain it to anyone.

"Done."

She looked at her phone as it vibrated and if I hadn't been watching her, I might have missed the relief that spread through her expression. Filing that away, I picked up the pen and scrawled two sentences on the bottom of the contract and countersigned it.

When I held the pen out to her, she took it and skimmed the contract before she filled in her name, address, and phone number, then she initialed each page before she reached the final one and signed there. Stella Charles. The name suited her.

After clicking the pen closed, she straightened the papers and handed them to me. "It was lovely doing business with you, Spawn."

She snagged her bag and headed for the doors. I debated stopping her but checked through the pages first, verifying what I had seen her do. She was already at the door when I reached the hall.

"Mr. Harrison." She said it with a small smirk of mockery.

"Ms. Charles," I said it to be a dick, since her name was so precious to her.

Then she was gone and the door closed behind her. For a relatively cheap fee, I'd gotten exactly what I wanted, what we needed—a signed NDA and that woman out of our house and our lives.

So why wasn't I happy about it?

I glanced down at her hand-printed name and contact information.

Stella.

None of this felt like a win.

chapter
fourteen

Stella

Fifteen minutes after leaving the Harrison estate—or whatever they were calling it—I was still shaking. I diverted through a Starbucks drive-thru as much to get the coffee as to give myself some time to calm down.

The last thing I'd expected was Seven Harrison to be so damn cooperative. Didn't change the bout of nerves that hit when I doubled the asking price. I half expected I was going to vomit while waiting for his refusal. Then he *agreed*.

A very small, practically minuscule part of me struggled with the guilt from basically making him pay me to sign that piece of paper. I didn't need a legal document to prevent me from being some pervert cunt who sold out the guy I'd actually enjoyed a night with...Then again, I'd have happily told TMZ what an overbearing prick Seven was in real life.

Throwing Seven's ass under the bus was no skin off my nose. I gave the woman on the speaker my order, then leaned my head back against the seat. My bank account was flush. I could afford to replace all the stolen camera equipment. It wasn't going to be an overnight process, but I'd already called Paulie down at the shop to order the specific camera I wanted.

He promised it would be there in two days. Then I'd need

lenses—a whole list of things rattled through my head. I'd keep a tally. Two days of sitting idle wouldn't kill me, but I could do some other work in the meantime. Once I had my coffee and nerves in hand, I headed for my second unpleasant task of the day.

I needed to sign the report about Dillon's attack. It would help clear Olivier of any wrongdoing. While I was there, I could file a report on the break-in to my car. The broken window was a lot of evidence. But without the police report, I couldn't file with insurance.

Somehow, I doubted insurance would cover enough of the equipment to replace it. It had to be done though. The last thing I wanted to do was tell Dad that his very best camera was just gone along with my most expensive one.

Baby steps, I reminded myself. Dad didn't need to know this part. I'd killed half of the coffee by the time I got to the police station. Parking the car, I eyed the glass still on the floor. I needed to find someone to replace the window. Not an easy task for a car this old.

Again, one problem at a time. Bag strap over my shoulder and phone in my pocket, I headed into the station with my coffee. There were three people in line ahead of me. It wasn't a long wait before it was my turn.

"I'm here to sign a report from Sergeant McBride and I also need to file a report about items stolen from my car last night."

The officer behind the desk eyed me. "I'll call the sergeant, but you'll need to see a different officer about the robbery."

"That's fine."

"Driver's license?" He needed to see ID because of course he did.

I passed it over; he studied it before he ran it through a scanner to add it to his screen.

"Address still valid?"

"Yep," I answered. He acknowledged the response with a nod as he continued to type into the computer.

After he handed me my license back, he waved me to where there were three rows of hard, ugly, little plastic chairs. "Have a seat. An officer will come out to get you."

The officer wasn't in a hurry apparently. I was almost done with the coffee entirely when a man stepped out from the heavy, secured door.

"Stella Charles?"

"That's me," I said, standing. It was better to just get this over with.

"I'm Detective Doogan," he said, introducing himself, and I shook his hand. "You're here to sign a complaint and to report another crime?"

"Yes," I said, then tacked on a belated "sir" at the end. Detective Doogan was a tall, somewhat rounded man with white hair and a receding hairline that seemed to be in a full rout.

"Come on back with me. I'll take the report and we can go over the complaint."

"Should I wait for Sergeant McBride?" That was who'd taken all the information.

"He's on a call at the moment, but I have the report. We'll go over it and make sure all the facts are accurate. It will also give you a chance to correct any errors before you sign it."

"Great," I said, making sure my bag strap was secure over my shoulder. The detective went back to the door, scanned a card, and then entered a number before the lock released. "Thanks," I said as he held it open and waved me in.

I'd been in a police station before, but the last time had been about ten years earlier when I'd been joyriding with a boyfriend. Only then, I'd been stuck out front waiting for Dad to come get me. That had been a date that started out great and ended terribly.

The institutional beige wasn't that soothing to any nerves, but I just followed the detective to a little narrow, windowless room that boasted a table and four chairs. He waved me inside.

"Give me a minute." Then he headed down the hall and left me to go in and take a seat. Hopefully this visit ended better than my last one. I wasn't the one in trouble, right?

I sat down in the chairs closest to the door. He hadn't indicated there was a proper side, but I didn't like the idea of him being between me and the exit. There was a camera up in the corner, the little red dot on it a declaration that it was recording.

The detective returned with a couple of dirt-brown-colored file folders. He put one down on the corner of the table before he flipped open the second one. He removed several sheets of paper before he passed it to me.

"This is Sergeant McBride's report and complaint compiled from your statements. If you can read through that and verify that it's all true to the best of your knowledge?"

I blew out a long breath and nodded. The report was pretty straightforward. McBride had written in short, direct sentences a sequence of events that included Dillon's assault at my car, his strangulation, and the blows I'd taken to the head.

It was more than a little unsettling to see it laid out so clinically. The report also included Olivier's arrival and subsequent interference with Dillon's assault—*interference.* Such a little word for the ass-kicking he'd given Dillon.

Dirtbag.

My nose itched, but the report concluded with both myself and Olivier leaving the scene after the assault, and at that time, Dillon was fine and capable, not in need of any assistance.

I mean, that was mostly true.

He was still breathing when we left.

"This looks right," I said, glancing at the detective. He slid a card with six photographs on it over to me.

"Do you see your assailant here?" The photos were terrible and taken in terrible light. But none of them were Dillon.

"No."

"Take your time. It's always good to be certain."

"I don't have to take my time. I know who attacked me. He's not a stranger."

The detective studied me for a long moment, then he slid another card over. More photographs. There was Dillon. He was definitely younger in the picture, but the belligerent expression and cold eyes were all him.

"This one," I tapped it. "His name is Dillon Paget."

"Okay." The detective took the card back, drew a line next to the image and then passed it to me. "Initial here that this is the one you identified."

I did that. Then he nodded to the complaint.

"Sign that as well. Remember, signing it is a sworn oath in front of an officer of the law. You are swearing that what you are reporting is the truth to the best of your knowledge and recollection."

I got that.

After I signed it, he took the sheets back and collected them together in the folder.

"Why didn't you report the attack last night, Miss Charles?"

"Last night, I was a little out of it and more than a little upset." It wasn't a lie. "Olivier didn't want to let me drive so he took me back to his place."

"You and Mr. Griffiths are dating?"

"No."

"Friends?"

"Also no."

"How do you know him?"

"I don't really. Last night was the first time I'd met him."

The detective favored me with a long, skeptical stare. "You're saying the famous actor, Olivier Griffiths, came across you being allegedly assaulted by Mr. Paget. He intervened, then took you home to his mansion—and he'd never met you before?"

I shrugged. "Yes. That's what happened." The long pause as he considered me had me rethinking my own answer. The facts were facts. Olivier didn't have to help me; he could have just turned around and not involved himself.

The thing was, he *hadn't*.

"You didn't call the police and you didn't go to a hospital or see a doctor after the assault?"

I sighed "No. I didn't want to go the hospital or go see a doctor."

"You can understand how this looks, right?" There was a kind of gentleness to the question, like he was asking me to help him out here. "You say Mr. Paget was fine, but you were allegedly assaulted to the point someone else had to intervene, then you needed help afterward but didn't go to a doctor."

When you put it like that, it sounded pretty damn shady.

"Detective, I don't have any insurance. Any visit I make to a hospital or to a doctor or even a doc in the box is going to be a few hundred just to have them sit there and tell me I've got some bruises, take some pain relievers, ice it, and have a nice day."

I spread my hands as I shrugged. "I can't really afford that." Not right now. Not with Dad's medical expenses. "So, no, I didn't want to go to a hospital or see a doctor. Olivier—Mr. Griffiths tried to convince me to go but I refused. When I wanted to just leave, he refused to let me drive under my own steam because he wanted to make sure I was okay."

Fuck, now even I sounded doubtful of my own story.

"You have to admit, it's unusual for a complete stranger." The skepticism practically dripped from his voice.

"Maybe," I said. "Most people are raging assholes. Apparently, Mr. Griffiths isn't. The point is, Dillon Paget attacked me. He tried to strangle me..." To make a point, I tugged my shirt collar to the side and tilted my head. "I have the bruises to prove it. He also banged my head against the trunk of my car. If Mr. Griffiths *hadn't* done something, you might have a medical report from the ambulance that picked me up or the coroner."

Okay, that was a little dramatic. Even for me.

The detective, however, seemed to take it in stride. "All right. You said you had a robbery to report as well? Was it directly related to the incident with Mr. Paget?"

"Yes—and no." I gave him a faint smile as he raised his brows and then I explained. It took me about ten minutes to sum up everything from my equipment being locked in the trunk to what I found when I returned to my vehicle. The broken glass from the window of my car was still in the floorboard of the car.

He took notes all the way through my statement then slid me a sheet of paper and another pen. "Can you make a list of everything that was taken?"

"Yes."

"I don't suppose you have any photographs of the items or serial numbers?"

"I might have one for the camera, but I never took any photos of the camera equipment."

"Everything can help. We need to see if it shows up in any of the pawn shops, so give us as much detail as you can."

My headache had returned full force by the time I finished filling out the list. The increasing desire to pee had also invaded, but I just wanted to get this done so I could leave. The detective left me for a few minutes and typed up the report. When he came back, he had me read through it again.

The whole time the door to the room had been open, which had been nice.

"Snow," the last person I'd expected to see said from the open doorway.

Speak of the devil himself, Olivier Griffiths stood there, looking cool and suave as he glanced from me to the detective. "What are you doing here?"

A man stood right behind him, dressed in an expensive three-piece suit.

"I'm just signing my statement," I told him. "I told the detective what happened. I'm surprised you're here. I explained everything to Sergeant McBride... Why are you here?"

"I came in to answer questions as I was requested," he said, then narrowed his gaze as he glanced from me to the detective. "Why don't you have an attorney here?"

"Because I don't need one." I wasn't the suspect.

"That is not how this works, Snow," he said in a tone that made me think he was scolding a child. "You never speak to law enforcement without an attorney present. Don't you know they can lie to you? But you can't lie to them?"

"I heard that somewhere," I said, trying not to notice the fact that the detective drilled holes into the side of my head and Olivier's.

"Peter," Olivier said. "Would you mind staying with Miss..."

Olivier slid me a look and I just stared back at him. I was *not* telling him my name.

"Keep your secrets then, Snow," he murmured before he looked at his attorney again. "Stay with Snow and just make sure the cops are doing everything aboveboard?"

"I can, Mr. Griffiths, provided it's not a conflict of interest."

Olivier grinned widely. "Not going to be a conflict at all."

"Your attorney doesn't have to stay," I said. "I'm almost done." I waved the report. "I just need to sign this."

"Then it won't be a problem at all for me to review any statements that you've made before you sign them." The attorney slid around Olivier into the room. Olivier winked before he strolled away, smug as hell.

"And you still insist that you and Mr. Griffiths aren't dating?" The detective gave me a bland stare that all but shouted I was nuts.

"Mr. Griffiths doesn't even know my real name." Not that it seemed to matter a damn to Peter, the attorney, who took the statement and went over it.

So much for almost being done.

Dammit, I still really needed to pee.

<h1>chapter
fifteen</h1>

Stella

Normally the five hundred dollars to fix my broken window would have sent me into a deep pit of money despair and I'd likely have ended up driving around with a plastic trash bag taped over it until I could save the money. But thanks to my slightly shady deal with Seven, I was able to confidently accept the price and drive away with my repaired car by the end of the next day.

Paulie called to say my equipment had arrived early, and I spent a stupidly enjoyable evening at home with a bottle of wine, setting it all up. I even splurged and ordered home delivery Thai food, since Seven was paying.

If I thought about it too much, yeah it did feel a little bit dirty...essentially getting paid for sleeping with Gem. But I justified it by reminding myself that *Seven* paid me and it was for the NDA not for the sex. Sure one was needed due to the other but...semantics.

About four days after making my deal with the demon spawn, I packed myself a little picnic lunch and went to a park to take photos of strangers as test shots. There was no sense trying to familiarize myself with new equipment when I was *on* the job and potentially miss a prize shot.

An hour or so after I set up, my phone buzzed in my pocket and I set my camera down on my picnic blanket to check. Probably Dad, bored at home and wanting to know if there had been any new scandals in the celebrity sphere. You could take the man out of the paparazzi game but not the paparazzi out of the man.

To my surprise, though, it was a message from an unknown number.

Unknown Number: Are you going to be at the wrap party for War of the Mesozoic tonight? I hear there will be lots of great photo ops... Here are the details, just in case.

The next message contained an address in Malibu and a time. I blinked a couple of times, confused, then suspicious.

Stella: Who is this? I think you have the wrong number.

Unknown Number: Nah, it's the right one. Come on, Snow... take the olive branch. This party has been kept top-secret so there won't be many other paps there to steal the scoop.

I smiled, unable to help myself as I saved the number into my phone.

Stella: Olivier, did your lawyer give you my number? So much for client confidentiality.

Olivier: Wash your mouth out, Snow. My lawyer would never break confidentiality. Peter is the epitome of professionalism.

Shaking my head, I chuckled. What kind of old-fashioned gentleman uses "epitome" in a text message? Then before I could reply, my phone lit up with an incoming call from him.

"Okay, so if not Peter, then it must have been Seven," I said by way of answering.

Olivier gasped. "Seven has your number? How and why?"

Was that genuine shock or exaggerated sarcasm? It was so

hard to know, over the phone, but his voice gave me a tingly warmth regardless.

Crap on a cracker, did I have a little crush on Olivier Griffiths? Yes, undoubtedly yes. I wondered if bro code would prevent anything happening between us, since he and Gem were so close. Which then made me wonder...*how* close? Close enough to share? *Dirty Stella.*

My week was so freaking odd because the idea that I even had a chance with one celebrity—let alone two—was actually laughable. Gem was just a random stroke of luck...twice. Olivier?

"Why are you calling me? If it's about Seven's NDA—"

"I honestly don't give a flying fuck about his NDA, Snow," Olivier replied with a laugh. "I just wanted to say thank you for intervening with the police...by slipping you some inside info. The wrap parties for the *Mesozoic* franchise get crazy wild. I bet you could get some great photos if you're in the right place at the right time."

I pursed my lips, thinking it over. It sure *seemed* too good to be true...but I had saved him and his lawyer a whole lot of drama with Dillon attempting to press charges for assault. So fair was fair.

"I could possibly check it out," I murmured. "Will you be there?"

He laughed, a deep, throaty chuckle that did scandalous things to my insides. "Do you want me to be, Snow? If you asked nicely, I feel like I could squeeze it into my schedule. Just for you, though. The rest of the assholes working this movie are not the kind of people I'd willingly socialize with."

My mouth opened and closed a couple of times, and I peered at my phone to check the call was still connected, and I wasn't fucking imagining things.

"Olivier Griffiths, are you *flirting* with me?" I gasped, enjoying myself far too fucking much. Then again, he *had* saved my life, so surely it was only natural I'd developed a little infatuation.

"Call me Ollie, please," he replied with a chuckle. "Only fawning press and fans call me *Olivier*. And as to whether I'm flirting...clearly, I need to do a better job of it if you're unsure."

Oh shit. Wait, maybe I had taken more head trauma than I realized after Dillon smacked my head into my car repeatedly. Suspicious as hell, I pinched myself just to be sure. I felt it but it didn't *hurt* so I did it again...just in case.

"Ow!" I exclaimed because that one really did hurt and left fingernail marks in my forearm.

"Ow?" Olivier—or rather *Ollie*—repeated in my ear. "Did you just fall from heaven?"

I snort laughed. "That was awful. You clearly aren't allowed to improvise on set with cheesy shit like that as your go-to."

"Ah, but it made you laugh. So...will I see you there?"

I bit my lip, trying to ignore the butterflies his voice was creating. What the fuck was wrong with me? I'd literally slept with his best friend *twice*. Recently. And had a great time with him too.

"What about Gem?" I asked, unable to push that fact aside. I *liked* Gem. I just didn't want to get fucked around by some celebrity who felt like slumming it. So why, genuinely *why*, was I entertaining this call from Ollie? He was surely no different from Gemini... In fact, he was still an active movie star himself, so an even bigger red flag than Gem. Right?

Ollie gave a thoughtful hum. "You want to see Gem at the wrap party? He's not big on industry events, but I think if he knows you'll be there—"

"No, I meant... *Ugh*. I meant why are you flirting when you know I was with Gem like four days ago?" Not that I was mad about it, but at the same time...*why*? This seemed fishy.

He wasn't quick to brush off my suspicions, which was a surprise. Instead he paused a moment before replying, making me feel like he maybe wasn't 100 percent sure himself. Or maybe I was delusional.

"Well, Snow, the way I figure it, if you and Gem were going to be a *thing*, you'd have at least given him your name and number. But you didn't, which leads me to think you have no intention of walking the red carpet on his arm anytime soon." He drawled his reason with a wry tone, bordering on teasing and oozing flirtation. "I also thought we had a bit of a vibe the other night. Am I wrong?"

My heart raced. What the fuck was happening? "You aren't wrong..."

"Great. So maybe I'll see you tonight. Or maybe not. No pressure or anything, but just in case I'll text you the location of the back alleyway gate where lots of guests sneak in and out to avoid paparazzi out the front. I can almost guarantee you'll get some moneymakers there." He paused, then gave a small chuckle. "Then once I feel like our scores are settled, maybe I can take you out on a nonworking date some time."

My jaw nearly hit the grass. "We'll see," I replied, aiming for cool and collected but actually sounding like a strangled pigeon.

Another of those deep chuckles that blew my fucking mind. "I guess we will. Thanks for the chat, Snow. You really brightened up my day."

The call cut out, and I sat there for *ages* just staring blankly into space wondering whether I was, in fact, in a coma somewhere after my psychotic, abusive ex-boyfriend beat me into brain damage.

But when I didn't wake up to some nice nurse checking my

blood pressure and IV line, I figured I may as well enjoy the delusion while it lasted. So I packed up my things and headed back to my car. If I was going to work tonight, I needed to make a plan.

I also needed to stop by Dad's house and do some meal prep, so he wouldn't keep surviving on tuna and rice with siracha for *every* meal. Come to think of it, I needed to do some grocery shopping for him and now that my bank account was nice and juicy, I could actually enjoy the task.

Several hours later, I found myself somewhat regretting going crazy at the store because Dad was raking me over the coals asking what images had earned me so much cash. I could hardly tell him that I'd sold my silence to Seven Harrison for a cool fifty grand, so I took the mature approach and made a bullshit excuse to leave earlier than intended.

The fact the conversation was merely on pause rather than ended followed me back to my apartment. Dad would want me to answer, and I would work on that between now and then. Still, maybe I could distract him with something else.

I checked the cast list for the latest *Mesozoic* film: A-list, A-list, A-Minus-list. B-Plus, B, B-plus, holy shit...two A-plus plus stars. Those two were from the original film so them coming back for the final was huge, especially considering the first of the two had a nice *political* career, including six years as governor since then.

My nerves lit up like I'd been struck by lightning. When Olivier—Ollie, whatever—described their wrap parties as "getting out of hand," he was completely underselling it. The previous wrap party was rumored to have lasted almost twenty-four hours, involved a lot of drugs, alcohol, and lube as well as a pool party. The *after*-party was a lot worse.

No wonder they kept the location on lockdown. Dad had

actually nabbed a couple of the juiciest photos of his career between the previous wrap party and the after-party.

Threesomes sold like you wouldn't believe, especially if you had the money shots—and he'd gotten one of the best ever. The director, his singer wife, and their very married actor friend as well as another costar. Three men, one woman.

So Ollie wasn't kidding about the opportunities there. The money from Seven was going to do a lot of good, but the kind of photos I could get at the event could take care of the next couple of months of home nursing staff and the mortgage on the house.

If I absolutely had to give up the apartment and move back in with Dad, I would. I'd been prepared to since his diagnosis. But for both of our sakes, it would be better for him to maintain his independence, illusion or not.

In front of my closet, I stared at my options. The address Ollie sent me was for a huge house in Malibu. Phone in hand, I checked the area around the location. Getting in to private parties was challenging, even more when it was on *secured* property. Didn't mean it was impossible, but I wanted to see what I could see *first*.

The house itself was not far from Carbon Beach near Billionaires Row. Swanky. The location off the PCH made it a lot harder to get to. They'd probably have a shuttle or valets. Valet...

I snagged a red vest, then a black one, and flipped through my hangers to find a button-down white blouse. The location near the beach said fancy but also casual. A skirt it was, even if pants would be easier. I also pulled out the quintessential little black dress.

It was a practical slip of fabric. I was taking all of this with me. The nice thing about this dress, I could compress it down; then if I got inside, I could always change so I looked more like

I belonged. For now, though, I'd rather keep my distance and get my shots.

Clothes ready, I changed into something basic and then grabbed a snack and water before going over the equipment. Some of it was new, so I made sure I knew what I was doing. Not even being this prepared settled the jittery feeling bouncing around inside of me.

It was where I was going...

Not a lot of other paps, isolated location, and a real chance I could be cornered by some nutjob like Dillon. He'd hardly been put off by being in public or visible to the street when he went after me at the car.

Yeah, going there alone, without a backup or anyone knowing where I was going? Bad idea. Flirting with Ollie was fun, but better safe than sorry. I grabbed my phone and scrolled through my contacts.

Pulling up Rod Mills's number, I hit text. He was one of Dad's oldest and best friends. He had slid me a tip more than once. This was just returning the favor. It also meant someone else I trusted would be in range.

Not perfect but definitely better.

chapter
sixteen

Gemini

Seven had really quickly reminded us why we preferred him in a relationship. When he wasn't fully immersing himself in the role he was currently reading for, he was bored. And when he was bored, he was a pain in our asses. Big time. All the time he usually dedicated to Clara Belle and her expensive tastes was now shifted onto antagonizing me and Ollie and we'd both had damn gutsful of it.

So when Ollie asked if I wanted to attend the *Mesozoic* wrap party, I jumped at the chance.

We didn't bother inviting Sev... He was still desperately trying to salvage the Carriage Pictures deal and they required he basically live like Prince Charming twenty-four seven. He had to be squeaky fucking clean, and the *Mesozoic* cast parties were anything but.

Ollie had played the antagonist of the movie—his usual typecast role—and had made plenty of "friends" on set who all wanted to congratulate him on our arrival at the Malibu house where the party was held.

"No paps here?" I murmured curiously, sliding a pair of sunglasses over my eyes. It was early evening and the sunset over the ocean was bright enough to blind. "How'd they manage to keep it quiet this time?"

Ollie grinned, shrugging. "No one was given the address until a couple of hours ago. I'm sure press will catch wind of it sooner or later, but for now..." He peered back at the entryway we'd just come through like he was waiting for someone.

"Couple of hours ago? You asked me this morning." Then again, this was Ollie I was talking to. The guy had his sneaky fucking fingers *everywhere*, so him knowing the party location in advance was really no great shock.

Again, he just grinned, then headed over to the fully stocked bar on the balcony. For the most part, the cast and crew of *Mesozoic* were okay. I only had to correct a handful of people that I was not my brother and surprisingly got into an enjoyable discussion with the stunt coordinator from the franchise. He'd had to choreograph people literally riding dinosaurs and kaiju, being tossed from the jaws of hundred-foot-tall beasts and some fight scenes of epic proportions.

That was the sort of work I wanted to get into—moving the chess pieces rather than being repeatedly shoved onto the front lines as a pawn. My body was going to break for real eventually, and then where would I be?

"Seven? What are you doing here?" a slightly slurred voice interrupted us. It was like nails on a fucking chalkboard honestly.

I sighed. "Clara, it's Gem. What are you doing here? You're not in this movie." Then again, neither were dozens of other celebrities floating around the house. Once word got out, these parties tended to turn pretty wild—a literal magnet for all the loose units of Hollywood to get messy and have a good time. Or just to snag a salacious headline to revive a sinking career.

She was already way too drunk to process my words and draped her arms around my neck with a sloppy pout. "Seven, baby, you're not still mad at me for breaking up with you, are you? It wasn't personal, sugar, and I'd still totally let you fuck me upstairs if you need to blow off some steam. I saw a whole room set up with bondage stuff if you wanna do that thing—"

"Clara!" I snapped, physically removing her arms from around my neck. "Go the fuck away. Seven isn't here. But if he were, I can *guarantee* he would not take you up on that offer. Gross."

Her face twisted in an ugly sneer, the realization *finally* sinking in. "Gem, what the fuck? Ew, stop pretending to be Seven. That's so pathetic."

I rolled my eyes, not caring enough to hide my disgust for my twin's ex. Talk about a social-climbing bitch. Slick really had done Sev a huge favor by tossing a grenade on that relationship.

"You're the one throwing yourself at your ex-boyfriend's brother. If anyone is pathetic here, Clara Belle, it's you." I turned my back on her and searched the party for my best friend. It'd gotten a whole lot busier while I chatted with Dan —the stunt guy—and I winced when a vase broke somewhere nearby.

Surely by this stage the owners of these properties were decorating with Ikea. I couldn't remember the last party I'd attended that hadn't incurred heavy fees from damaged property by the end of the night. The thing about rich, famous celebrities? They had no respect for money. Or other people's belongings. It was sickening.

It took a few minutes of searching the party before I found Ollie politely fending off the advances of an up-and-coming young actress. Way too young for him, which was probably why he was carefully holding her wrists to keep her at arm's length.

"Bro, can I steal you for a sec?" I asked, tipping my head to indicate we step away.

The young actress shifted her glassy eyes my way, then gasped. "Ohmigod, *Seven Harrison*. I'm such a huge fan," she gushed, her eyes wide and her cheeks rosy. Fucking hell, she couldn't be more than eighteen...if that. She was making her big break in the newly popular "sexy thriller" genre.

I gave her a tight smile, not caring to correct her. "Thanks so much. Tina, right?"

She pressed her hand to her chest. "You know my name?" Her voice had gone all squeaky and breathless. "Ohmigod, Seven Harrison knows my name!"

Holding back my laugh, I clapped a hand on Ollie's shoulder. "You don't mind if I borrow my friend here, do you? I'll bring him right back, I promise." We didn't wait for her reply before walking away, chuckling quietly under our breath.

"Dude, she's going to be telling all her friends about how she met Seven Harrison tomorrow," Ollie snickered, shaking his head. "Poor thing looked like she was going to faint when you said her name."

I huffed a laugh. "She's so high right now, I'll be shocked if she even remembers in the morning. Clara is here, by the way, and she's wasted. I might head out...unless you wanna stay longer?" Seeing as we'd driven my car from Beverly Hills, we had to stick together.

Ollie shook his head. "Nah, I'm good. Let's get out before this turns into a fuck-fest like the last after-party for *Mesozoic*." He shuddered. "I'll never get the image of Henry Duvalle's saggy balls slapping against a sound engineer's ass out of my mind, I swear to fuck."

I gagged a little because Henry was at least seventy and not in good shape. He was a hell of a director, though. "I'm so glad I didn't attend that one." Then I paused as we approached the front entry. Distinctive flashes of cameras alerted us to the fact that at least *some* paparazzi must have been tipped off. "Should we duck out the back?"

Ollie quirked a brow at me in suspicion. "You don't wanna see if your girl is working out there?"

I glowered. "She's not my girl." His grin turned…*pleased.* Motherfucker. "Bro…you can't seriously be thinking of tracking her down for yourself. She's not interested in dating an actor. That much was *abundantly* clear with how she left our house the other day."

Ollie just shrugged. "She's not your girl, Gem." Like that was all the permission he needed to do whatever the fuck he wanted. "But yeah, we can dodge the paps if you wanna be a pussy about it. I'll get the car sent around to the side gate."

I sighed, handing him our claim check and he moved over to speak with one of the security at the door to arrange for our car to be moved around the block to the service gate.

It took another twenty minutes or so for us to *actually* escape, and even then we discovered we weren't the only ones with the same plan. Basically anyone who'd attended the wrap party but didn't want to be *known* as attending the after-party was using the service gate to avoid press.

Except, of course, some sneaky photographer had worked it out and a camera flash lit up the night in an almost strobe-light effect as Jennifer Crosse and her porn star boyfriend headed out ahead of us.

"Oh, you're sneaky!" Jennifer called out to the photographer with a laugh. "I love it. Here's one just for you."

Ollie and I slipped out of the ivy-covered gate just in time to witness Jennifer tongue-fucking her man's face while he dipped her dramatically. The camera flashed again, and I instinctively ducked my face to avoid looking directly at the lens. I hadn't thought to grab my usual baseball cap out of the car earlier and now regretted that decision.

"Give us a smile, Gemini!" the photographer called out after Jennifer and Johnny slid into their waiting SUV, and my head jerked up in the direction of the camera. "You look prettier when you smile!"

Ollie laughed, his hands in his pockets as he swaggered across the road to where the woman of my dreams sat on the trunk of a classic car with her camera in hand. She'd parked in someone's sloped driveway, giving her a fantastic viewpoint of the service gate, and I tried to pretend I wasn't thrilled to see her.

Slick... Fucking hell, my fantasies weren't doing her justice at all. She was sexier than I remembered, even as she sat there in what looked like an imitation valet uniform.

"So you took my advice after all," Ollie drawled, boosting himself up to sit beside her on the trunk. "Did you get some good shots?"

My brows rose in shock. "You knew she was here?"

My best friend just smirked. "Of course. I sent her the address this morning and even marked the service gate on a map."

"Thank you for that," Slick responded, offering Ollie a soft smile. "I hope you don't mind, I tipped off a colleague. Figured it'd incentivize people to sneak out the back if they knew the front was being smashed with paps."

"You figured correctly," I murmured. "When... Wait, how'd you send her the address?" I directed my question to Ollie with suspicion.

He just shrugged. Mysterious fucker. I rolled my eyes, knowing he wouldn't fess up when he was in that sort of mood. Besides, Slick was right here and I couldn't let a third chance slip through my fingers.

"Are you doing anything right now? Can I take you for coffee maybe?" As soon as the suggestion left my lips, I winced. It was nine at night, not exactly coffee time.

Her lips quirked like she was fighting a smile as she stared at me. The angle of her car and her position on the trunk put her nearly at eye level with me, and my hands twitched with the need to touch her. It'd be so easy to just step forward and wrap my hands around her, for her legs to slip around my waist and—

Fuck.

I was so hooked on this woman and I didn't even know her name.

"Am I doing anything right now?" she repeated, clearly amused as she raised her camera. "Yes, Gem. I'm working."

I frowned. That...yes, okay she was working. But I couldn't miss this opportunity to get her name at very least. "You're working... You just need one great photo right? One image that is exclusive and can be sold for five figures?"

Her brows rose. "Uh...yeah. But so far nothing will get me more than a couple hundred bucks."

I nodded, glancing at Ollie. "Want me to punch Ollie? I'm sure the tabloids would have a field day making up a bullshit story to accompany that image."

"Hey, whoa, time-out," Ollie protested, making a T with his hands. "Ollie does not consent to being punched."

Meanwhile, Slick looked thoughtful. She was considering it. Yes, this was good; we were getting somewhere here.

"Bro, wipe that look off your face," Ollie growled. "We've got that premiere next week and I do not need a fucking black eye to cover up."

Okay, that was a valid point. Still... "How about it, Slick? I get you a five-figure photo and you come for a burger with us?"

Her lips pursed and her dark lashes narrowed around her eyes. "A burger? I thought you were offering coffee?"

Yes. She *wanted* to say yes. We were making progress. "Slick, baby, I'll give you anything you want at this stage. Burger, coffee, my last name...you name it, it's yours. Deal?"

I put my hand out for her to shake on the deal, and she glanced at Ollie beside her. What was *that* all about? He just met her gaze with his own dark, mysterious look and the corners of his mouth kicked up. "Sounds like a good deal to me," he murmured, "so long as I don't get punched."

Slick sighed, then slapped her hand into mine. "Deal. But I don't know what sort of photo you think will fit the bill..."

I already had the perfect idea and grinned. "Wait here, I'll be right back." I walked backwards, finding it hard to pull my eyes away from her. "Get your camera ready, Slick. I'm hungry!"

Bubbling with nervous energy, I made my way back into the party and anxiously hunted out the perfect pawn to play into this scene.

"Clara, baby, there you are!" I purred, wrapping my arm around my twin's wasted ex-girlfriend. "Gem told me you were looking for me."

"Seven?" she whimpered, blinking up at me with somewhat unfocused eyes. "Baby, I knew you couldn't stay mad forever." She reached up to wrap her thin arms around my neck, and I had to turn my face to dodge her sloppy kiss.

"Come with me," I urged her, tugging her away from her friends and heading for the exit. "I wanna talk to you alone."

Her throaty chuckle said exactly what she thought I wanted to do *alone*, and my skin crawled at the mental image. How the fuck had Seven dated this irritating woman for so long? Both Ollie and I had made our feelings about her clear years ago, so Sev hardly ever brought her to the house.

As wasted as she was, it was easy to steer her out of the house and down the short path to the service gate. Then right as we were about to pass through the gate, I leaned down to whisper in her ear.

"Clara, I wouldn't put my dick in you again if you were the last woman on earth. You fucked around and chose your own fame over our four-year-long relationship and there's no going back from that. Did you know I was going to propose to you at the *Hidden Daggers* premiere? Now I'll be attending with my new girlfriend after signing the Carriage Pictures deal, and you? You're nothing but my *ex*. Washed up, has-been, *aging*—"

Oop, that did it. Her slap was harder than I'd thought she was capable of and it rocked me back a step as my ear rang. She started to shriek an insult but the flashes from Slick's camera sent her scurrying back through the gate faster than a rat into its hole.

That was…surprisingly satisfying. Seven was going to be pissed, but oh well. Some things needed to be said, and the fact she thought he was saying them? Perfection.

chapter
seventeen

Stella

I don't really know what I thought Gem planned to do when he disappeared back into the party. At the same time, it was kind of nice hanging out with Ollie for a few minutes alone.

"How's your head?" he asked as Gem ducked back through the gate. "Did you get it checked by a doctor?"

I mock gasped, pressing a hand to my chest. "You mean Gemini is *not* a real doctor? That lying bastard. I guess being a doctor and *playing doctor* aren't the same thing?"

Ollie chuckled that sexy, low sound that made my toes curl in my boots. "Okay, I get it. No doctors. I'm assuming a lack of insurance?"

I clicked my tongue. "You assume correct. Did the police drop their charges and shit for the other night? Peter seemed confident it was all straightened out."

"They did indeed," he confirmed, leaning back on his hands as he sat beside me like he wasn't one of the most famous men in Hollywood right now.

I pursed my lips, watching him from the corner of my eye as I fidgeted with my camera. "Should you be sitting out here in the open like this with me? Is this safe for you?"

He laughed again. "Are you worried we might get photographed?"

The irony was not lost on me, and I rolled my eyes with a groan. "Okay, point taken. How was the party, anyway?"

Ollie sighed, then started telling me in *far* too much detail about who was in there, what they were doing...*who they were doing* or planned to do. Apparently the rumors about the *after-party* weren't just rumors after all. When he started telling me about a particular director-actress couple who routinely invited other celebs to join them for threesomes, my jaw almost unhinged. I would never in a million years have pegged them for such titillating activities.

Before I could react to that scandal, the gate squeaked open again. I snapped back into work-mode, raising my camera and setting the focus just in time to catch Gem whispering something to a stumbling Clara Belle. Then her beautiful face morphed into shock and anger right before... *Smack!*

"Holy shit," Ollie spluttered on a laugh. "That looked painful."

It sounded painful too, but the smirk on Gem's face after Clara stormed off was downright adorable. The snap I got of that smirk and the way he slid that look at me had nothing to do with sales and everything to do with capturing the moment.

I could call it practice for the camera, but I tried not to lie to myself. Well, I tried not to lie to myself out loud. Internally? Not a problem. Gem's slow saunter to me was all playful sexuality. He really did look so damn pleased with himself. Try as I might, I couldn't help returning the grin.

"That going to work for you, Slick?" He didn't slow until he was right in front of me and his hip bumped my knee lightly.

"It's definitely not bad," I said, glancing down at my camera and then up again. Next to me, Ollie chuckled.

"She's going to make you work for a compliment, Gem," Ollie drawled. "I don't mind saying that you almost can't tell you gave up the acting gig."

For his part, Gem just snorted, but he didn't take those gorgeous blue eyes off me. The heat licking me as he stared had nothing to with being intimately aware of what he felt like rocking between my thighs. Nope, not a damn thing.

The man was far more impressive in person than on any screen. He was also so much more real.

"Just tell me it's good enough to steal you away for that coffee." Gem nudged my thighs apart so he could slide up to me. There was intimacy and then there was this sensuality. Ollie was right next to me and Gem pressing closer.

Touching my tongue to my teeth, I tilted my head as if thinking it over. That shot of Clara Belle slapping the shit out of "Seven Harrison" could easily net me a five-figure payday. Add that to what I got from the man himself, and I could call it a good week.

If only that were enough to just clear all the medical debt. If only...

Pushing away the creeping doubt and frustration, I focused on the here and the now. Each day I could bank a little more was a good day. As if by their own volition, I raised my fingers to trace the red mark on Gem's cheek. The hint of stubble there nipped my fingertips. He and Ollie both sported the unshaven look.

It was a *good* look. Then again, I couldn't imagine either of them had a bad look.

"Say yes," Ollie suggested in the least subtle sotto voce ever. "You want to say yes. You do love coffee, right, Snow? The man went and got slapped just to get your attention."

"Thanks," Gem said in a dry, droll tone, but he never took those blue eyes off of me. "I got this."

"You sure do," Ollie said, wrapping an arm around my shoulders. He smelled faintly of a whiskey, but I wasn't sure he was as drunk as he was playfully pretending to be. Nor could I quite suppress the thrill of being wrapped up in that strong arm as Gem leaned into me.

So much testosterone.

And fuck me, I was here for it.

Everything inside of me clenched when Ollie pressed his lips right up to my ear and his breath teased my earlobe. "Say yes, Snow. Let's go out together…"

Let's…

I shuddered. "Fine, yes, I owe you coffee."

Gem's smile grew and my stomach bottomed out at the delight sparking in his eyes.

"Fantastic," Ollie said, dropping a kiss behind my ear before he slid off the trunk. "Let's go."

"Who invited you?" Gem asked, raising his eyebrows.

"Me," Ollie told him without an ounce of shame. "Besides, I'm a little drunk and you drove."

A groan escaped Gem at the reminder. "I can get you an Uber or something."

"Nah," Ollie said with a smirk of his own as he held a hand out to me. "Our girl here will be much happier with the backup."

"For him or for me?" I couldn't resist asking because Gem had narrowed his gaze at his friend like he was ready to kick Ollie to the curb. I kind of hoped he didn't though—Ollie was fun and he *had* given me this tip.

Even if the tip was to "casually" arrange us meeting again. He was here and Gem was here. I had good shots and a new camera.

Ollie grinned slowly. "You're going to have to take me with you to find out. You did say yes already, right, Snow?"

The man was incorrigible. "I did."

"See? It's settled."

"Dude," Gem muttered.

"Hey, you didn't even want to come," Ollie said. "You're only seeing her cause I'm here."

The muttered comments were probably not meant for me, but they were hardly quiet about it. I nudged Gem back farther before I slid off the trunk. I tilted my head to check the gate but it was all quiet at the moment. Blowing out a breath, I popped the trunk and stored the camera in a proper safe.

If my asshat ex decided to break into the car again, he'd have a much harder time taking my shit.

"That's intense," Gem said from just over my shoulder.

"Better safe than sorry," I answered. After I had everything in its place, I closed the safe door and spun the dial. "That's my livelihood right there."

I didn't have another NDA that I could sell my signature on to fix it if the fucker robbed me again. Shuttling that thought away for another time, I closed the trunk, then faced them. The weight of all that attention being focused on me turned the night very warm, even with the breezes off the ocean.

"So where are we going?" I didn't know Malibu as well as Burbank or Hollywood.

"There's a diner in North Hollywood," Gem said, opening the driver's side door for me. "Hop in and I'll give you directions."

"Can we put the top down?" Ollie asked as he climbed into the back seat from the passenger side. "This car is definitely sexy as hell, just like her owner."

It would have been impossible to miss the look that Gem shot Ollie, but I bit back a smile as I locked the seat belt into place.

"Gem, can you hit the latch over there above the window?"

I popped the one on my side. Gem tilted his head, then released the latch. "Thank you."

Keys in the ignition, I pressed the switch to lift and roll back the top. It took it a hot minute, but there was something so satisfying about it letting it down. I pulled a scrunchie out of the glove box and then pulled my hair back and secured it.

I twisted, bracing one hand against the passenger seat as I watched behind us and backed down the drive. Awareness of both men hummed along my skin. Just before I faced front, I caught Ollie's slow grin from the corner of my eye and his wink.

Troublemaker.

Still, I was grinning when I headed away. The boys didn't choose a close-by place for coffee; instead we headed into North Hollywood and a place called the Hungry Fork, where they had all the forks to give. According to Gem, they were good people and never sold out the celebrities who came in. The slogan amused me as I pulled into the lot next to it. It wasn't the finest place I'd ever been to, but I preferred diners and coffee shops to gourmet meals.

After I put the top up, I shrugged out of the vest. I didn't need to look like a valet any longer. Freeing my hair, I shook it out and then finger combed it before hanging my purse crosswise over my chest.

As I straightened and faced the boys, I found them both watching me with the same enigmatic looks. "Problem?"

"Nope," Ollie said, then offered me an arm at the same time Gem did. It was both endearing *and* amusing. Rather than debate it, I slid my arm through Ollie's and Gem's at the same time.

"You two are cute," I said. "Don't push it."

"Pfft, where's the fun in that?" Instead of the diner, they turned toward a dodgy, twenty-four hour laundry that was right next door to it. A laundromat that was painfully bland, beige, and had lights that flickered.

An attendant was at the desk, and they barely looked up as we came inside. When I opened my mouth to ask, Gem dipped his head to murmur next to my ear. "Trust us."

With a little nod, I moved with them as Ollie patted my hand once, then pulled away to lead us all the way to the back of the place. He pulled out some tokens from his pocket, fed them into the machine, then popped it once.

The next thing I knew, the whole machine shifted to the side, opening like a door that led to a dim, velvet-bedecked hallway with a bouncer.

I shot a look behind me to where the bored attendant played on their phone and then back to the hall. The placement made it practically invisible to anyone not right here.

"Come on," Gem said in that sexy hushed tone of his. "It'll be fun."

"I thought I was the one who was full of surprises." At my quip, he grinned.

"Gotta keep up then, don't I?"

"Griffiths," Ollie was saying to the bouncer who checked something on his phone. "Reservation for three."

When had we made a reservation? More and more, this setup seemed to be getting stranger and yet I was even more intrigued. Once we were all in, the door to the laundry closed and another door at the other end of the hallway opened.

It was a speakeasy.

Shock piled onto shock. I'd heard about some of these hidden little gems, but their locations were the kind of guarded secrets that you needed national security clearance or something to find.

Ollie chuckled as a hostess stepped right up to greet us.

The interior was swanky, the music was a bluesy kind of jazz, and everything was just a little over-the-top. It took discipline to keep from gawking, but the place had a vibe that I would have loved to capture on film.

I could picture Bogey and Bacall at the bar, sharing secrets and liquor. It didn't take much to imagine Marilyn Monroe slipping in with one of her lovers to canoodle in a back corner. The fact I wanted to look at everything kept me from paying too close attention until the hostess settled us at a private, circular booth in the corner.

The boys put me in the middle as the hostess said the server would be right over. She barely left before our waitress appeared. I'd come for coffee and she was offering aperitifs.

I was painfully underdressed for this. "Just a sparkling water for now," I said to the waitress when she glanced at me. "Maybe with some lemon."

Probably better to check the prices before this got out of hand. One look at the menu though, and I was pretty much planning to stick to the water and maybe a coffee. The cheapest dish on here was almost a hundred and that was for an appetizer.

Did they serve it on solid gold plates?

"Come on, Snow," Ollie said after a beat. "You've done a lot of work. Cut loose and relax a little. Do you like wine?"

Before I could respond, Gem said, "She likes margaritas, extra salt."

"You got it," the waitress said in a sultry tone and then she drifted off.

"What do you want to eat?" Ollie asked. "That way we can get back to having fun once we take care of business."

Right. I had some protein bars in the car. "I think I'm good."

That answer didn't satisfy Ollie as he scowled at me. "Are you vegan?"

"I'm sorry?"

"No," Gem answered, knocking his knee lightly against mine. "She loves meat."

He did not just... I slid him a look and his eyes practically twinkled.

"Good. Let's go for the good stuff then..."

What did that mean?

I'd been all prepared to turn them down, particularly because I came for *coffee*. But before I could say anything, my stomach gurgled loudly.

"Right," Ollie said as the waitress returned with our drinks. How fast had they made that margarita? "We're all going to have the steaks..."

chapter
eighteen

Stella

Gem robbed me of the temptation to play vegan when the food came out. Yes, I liked meat—of both varieties, double entendre accepted. Despite not ordering the margarita, I downed a long swallow of it. Ice cold, sour, and salty—it was perfect. I managed to *not* shotgun the whole drink, but I still finished it swiftly.

The waitress snared my empty glass and replaced it with a fresh margarita. The rim of salt on the glass added an almost artistic flare. Yeah, if I was going to drink like this, I needed nachos. Still when the steaks arrived with their grilled perfection and the fat baked potatoes and buttered broccolini, I think I died a little.

My mouth watered. Every bit of it looked fantastic. Even worse, it *smelled* better. Those steak plates started around hundred and fifty. Money shots or not, I could get a week's worth of groceries for my dad for that much.

"Not hungry?" Ollie asked as he nudged the plate a little closer to me.

"I started a fast earlier today," I said, not missing a beat. The margarita helped me maintain the lie. "So, no food for me."

Frowning, Ollie glared as I picked up my drink, saluted him, and then took a sip. The warmth spread through my system, and it definitely helped to blunt the uneasy edges of being out on the town with these two devastatingly attractive men.

I knew exactly what Gem was like in bed, and he was definitely *may I have some more please*. I kind of hoped Ollie was the same. I licked some of the salt off the rim before I took another drink. Probably better to keep those thoughts to myself.

"You're kidding," Ollie said after a beat. "Right?"

"I never kid about fasting," I said, then met his gaze. "A girl has to keep her figure and the best way to do that is to alternately fast. So we're on a fasting moment. Sorry, boys…"

Eyes narrowing, Ollie leaned forward. Oh, there was even a vein throbbing in his forehead. "You didn't say anything about a fast earlier."

"You didn't say anything about this place earlier," I fired back. "We discussed coffee." I blinked. "Wait." I turned to Gem, then continued, "*We* discussed coffee."

"We did," Gem said, flicking a look from me to Ollie, then back again.

"Right, so you didn't ask me if I was hungry." Yep that logic worked. Ollie pursed his lips as he kept his gaze fixed on me. Oh, I'd really tweaked someone.

Oops.

"You need to eat," he said after several moments. "Fast or not, you were at the party for a few hours, probably had to get ready before then. The best fasts don't go longer than ten hours, so you must be nearly there. Eat." He tapped my plate almost imperiously.

"Or what?" I dared him. First, he insisted on taking me home after Dillon's assault. That worked out pretty well for me, even if I hadn't expected Gem to be there. Right, it also kind of led to the NDA.

Then he insisted on leaving his attorney to help me at the police station, no matter what I said. Peter was a good guy; he'd definitely gotten the detective to stop being an asshole. So...right, okay that also worked out.

Somehow, he got my phone number, and what did he do? He gave me a hot tip for a good place to get shots and I got them. As promised, he came through with it. I suppose it didn't hurt that he was *also* there with Gem. But there it was.

So if he wanted to *insist* I eat, I wanted to hear what was on the other side of the coin.

"Dammit, Stella, you need to eat. Especially if you're drinking like that. If you don't want the steak, I'll order you something else."

Fuck.

The world just ground to a halt. Ollie cut his gaze from me to Gem. Gem, for his part, had gone almost preternaturally still. The amused smile on his face vanished and his expression went flat.

I downed the margarita like a shot this time.

"Your name is Stella?" The quiet question carried a legion of hurt under each syllable. Knuckles whitening as he flexed his fingers, Gem didn't wait for me to answer as he focused on Ollie again. "How the fuck do you know her name?"

"Don't look at me. Seven had her name, phone number, *and* home address days ago. I just got her name."

"And my number," I tacked on. If he was going to throw me under a bus, he could get down here and let the wheels bounce over him too. "You texted me about the after-party and then called to flirt, remember? And I was all like, *what about bro code* and you were all *fuck that, Gem had his shot.* Remember?" I smiled wide, fluttering my lashes innocently as Ollie glared *shut the fuck up* daggers back at me.

Gem sat back in his seat, shaking his head. "I see."

Ollie rolled his eyes. "Oh, quit it. You literally asked if we could sneak out the back of the party because you didn't want to see the paparazzi. Remember? *She's not my girl, Ollie.*"

Well, *that* was interesting. I tilted my head and leaned forward in question. "I see," I parroted Gem in a teasing voice.

Gem glowered at his friend. "That was well after you slid into her messages, dickhead."

Ollie just shrugged, unconcerned. "Ahh, semantics. We're all here now right? Are you gonna start eating that steak, Stella? Or do I need to start ordering alternate dishes from the menu?"

Crap. My protest was at the cost of the dish already in front of me, but if he started willy-nilly ordering more plates, the cost would keep adding up regardless of whether I ate them or not. Reluctantly, I picked up my cutlery and cut a slice of the perfectly cooked wagyu sirloin.

Ollie visibly relaxed as I put it in my mouth, and then the flavors hit me and I had to hold back the moan threatening to escape my mouth. We were in the middle of a *very* exclusive restaurant-bar situation and also halfway through an argument, so moaning like Meg Ryan wasn't appropriate, no matter how good the steak tasted.

"Wait, did you fake it?" Gem asked, still scowling. Or now it was more of a pout than a scowl, but it was still sexy on him. Everything was sexy on Gem, even jealousy.

I blinked a couple of times, trying to understand the question as I cut another slice of steak and dipped it into the red wine au jus on the side. "Huh?"

Gem's pout deepened. "Your orgasms...you sure *seemed* like you were having a good time both times, but—"

I choked on my mouthful and had to cough a couple of times as I shook my head. "What the fuck?" I sputtered when I could trust myself to breathe.

Gem shrugged. "Well, it must have been really bad sex, which is sort of news to me and a pretty harsh blow to the ego, I'll admit." He sighed and swept a hand through his hair. "Are you an aspiring actress or something? If so, you're very good."

My jaw nearly hit the table, and I glanced at Ollie to see if he was also hearing this insanity. He just quirked an eyebrow at me, like he too was curious whether I'd been fucking *faking my orgasms* as some kind of...acting practice? What the shit?

"Is that... Are you serious right now? You think I didn't give you my name or number because the sex was bad?" I squinted at him, trying to process that train of thought. "I'm just going to point out that I didn't give my info to Ollie, either. He stole it from Seven, I assume. And Seven only had it because I signed his fucking NDA, and legal documents usually require those kinds of details. I specifically asked him *not* to share my details because, for one thing, I am not interested in becoming a *Snatch Squad Catch*"—the tabloid-coined name of their fangirl hookups came out of my mouth with such disdain, I shocked even myself—"and for another, I have no desire to climb the Hollywood social ladder. We had fun together, Gem. The sex was fucking amazing, and no, I didn't fake my orgasms. But that's all it was."

Both guys just stared at me for so long that I sighed and took another mouthful of steak and broccolini. The little trees had just the perfect level of crunch—not overdone and mushy but also not raw.

"I think that's valid," Ollie murmured when Gem took way too long to reply. "But I think you also underestimate how mopey and weird Gem got when he didn't know how to contact you."

Gem smacked him in the arm. "Bro, what the hell? Way to make me sound like a loser."

I bit back my smile, hiding it with more food. Now that I'd started, there was no denying how starving I was. I reached for my margarita, then paused. I had driven us all here and would need to drive the guys home again. Maybe water was the better option from here on out.

"Endearing and vulnerable, dude, it's a good thing," Ollie assured him with a firm nod.

Gem rolled his eyes, rubbing the back of his neck. "Okay I can *maybe* see where you're coming from, Stella." He said my name carefully, like he was testing it out on his tongue. "But to be clear...the sex was good?"

Fucking men. Honestly. "The sex was amazing, Gemini. Better than amazing. Best I've ever had." I delivered my praise deadpan, between bites of food, but couldn't help loving the smile that lit his face.

"Yet," Ollie murmured, smirking.

It was lucky I'd just swallowed my food when he said that, or I would have choked again.

"So if the sex was good... can I have your number?" Gem pushed. "I know this may surprise you given our reputation, but I'm actually a really cool guy to hang out with fully clothed as well as naked. Both options are freely available to you, Slick."

I smiled at his nickname for me. It sounded more natural on his lips. "Gemini Harrison...that's the worst proposition I think I've ever heard."

"Mmm, yeah, I agree," Ollie murmured, nodding. "You wanna catch Snow's eye, you need a grand gesture, Gem. Like saving her life from some psycho abusive douchewad trying to inflict brain damage."

Fucking hell. "Brain damage," I mumbled. "That would

definitely explain a lot. Are you two going to eat or just sit there letting your food go cold?"

Yes, I was fully aware I was a hypocrite.

They both took the hint to drop the subject of...whatever that fucking subject was, and Ollie smoothly shifted the conversation to telling me about the speakeasy we were dining in. Apparently there were a few of them around that catered specifically to celebrities and uber-wealthy who wanted to drink or dine like "normal" people, without worrying about scandals and press spins.

It was a good idea, but I was already plotting how I could twist that to my benefit.

After I finished my steak, Ollie ordered dessert for all of us, and I made weak protests until the sticky date pudding was placed down in front of me. Then I needed no encouragement. Yum.

It was weird and totally not how I'd expected the night to play out after Ollie's call...but I wasn't mad about it. I just needed Gem to understand that no matter how much fun we were having, I wasn't trying to date a celebrity. I was no Carriage Pictures princess, waiting for her prince to sweep her out of poverty and into the spotlight.

So long as he understood that...I guessed he could have my number.

Instead of having me drive them back to Malibu to collect their car, the guys just asked me to drop them home, which was a lot less driving. But then, of course, they spent the drive coming up with creative reasons why I needed to come inside with them.

As tempting as it was, I was enjoying the power in saying no.

"Sorry, boys," I laughed after Gem's adorable suggestion that we bake cookies because cookies taste better at midnight.

"I need to get home and sort all the images I got outside that party, then edit and go fishing for whoever is willing to pay me the big bucks for a photo of Clara Belle slapping Seven Harrison."

"Who were you thinking of pitching it to?" Ollie asked from the back seat as I turned onto their street. "Please don't say *The Nightly Mail*."

"Why not them?" I asked, confused. "They usually pay the highest fees and are a lot less fussy about image quality and brand recognition."

"They're unscrupulous bastards, that's why," Gem answered with a grimace. "The amount of lawsuits filed against them right now for slander and misinformation is insane. Let us put you in touch with a woman we know at *Bright Starz*. If it's a referral, she will pay."

My brows rose. "*Starz* usually won't pay a fraction of the other tabloids, and that's even if they'll look at the images at all. They're notoriously hard to work with."

"Because most of their images and stories come directly from the celebrities themselves," Gem confessed. "They have a handful of trusted photographers and usually only buy from them with the approval of the celebs themselves."

Huh. That made so much sense. *Starz* always had the biggest scoops and breaking news. They seemed to have the inside track on all the Hollywood proposals and on-set images. Now it made sense why they comparatively reported a lot less trash and scandal than others.

"If you can set it up, sure," I agreed. "Would Clara need to give her approval?"

Gem grinned. "Nah, they're not *that* strict. Come in, and I'll get Magnolia's business card for you."

I chuckled, shaking my head. "Smooth, Gemini, real smooth. You can text me her info, now that you've got my number." I pulled up to their front gate and gestured for Gem to lean over and put his code in the keypad.

A moment later, the gates rolled open smoothly, and I drove up the paved road to their house itself. It would have been far too childish to drop them at the gate and make them walk, even though the thought crossed my mind.

"Are you *sure* you don't want to come in?" Ollie tried one last time as I slowed to a stop in front of their impressive entryway.

I smiled, shaking my head. "No, I *want* to, but I won't. I have things to do that don't involve deluding myself into thinking this is a thing. Now, shoo."

Ollie pouted but hopped out of my car nonetheless, telling me we'd *talk soon* as he disappeared inside the house. Gem... lingered.

"Gemini," I murmured, "why are you still in my car?"

"Because I have this horrible feeling that if I let you drive away, I won't ever see you again," he admitted with a small shrug. "And I really want to see you again, Slick."

Fucking smooth talker had me all tied up in knots again, so I did the only sane thing I could think of and kissed him.

chapter
nineteen

Olivier

Still mulling over an idea of how to get Stella to join us, I dropped my keys back into my pocket even as I entered the code to turn off the alarm. Once upon a time, we didn't bother with the alarm when we were all home. But a few brave fans jumping the gate and one extremely randy chick who decided to go skinny-dipping in our pool, and that was that.

I admired the spunk it took, but if we were going to have nude women in our pool or our house, I'd just as soon be the one who picked them. Like Stella...she could definitely go skinny-dipping. I fully supported that.

Hell, I'd get naked and jump right in with her.

"Hey," Seven said as he came down the stairs. He was in shorts and a tank top. It looked like he'd come straight from the gym, except his hair was wet and he didn't look remotely sweaty. So maybe a shower *after* the gym. "You're back early."

I shrugged. "Party was a dud."

"Did you lose Gem?" Seven raked a hand over his damp hair.

"Nah, he's saying goodbye to his girl." She wasn't *his* girl totally. Not yet. Sure, she gave him her number, but only after I gave him her name. Talk about a double-edged sword. I loved Gem like a brother, and he was definitely into her.

But damn if Snow didn't get me too. It had been a while since I *wanted* to hang out with a woman even when I wasn't getting something out of it.

"His girl?" Seven's expression went through some comical contortions. "Oh, do *not* tell me it's that bottom-feeding scum pap chick."

"Dude…"

But he didn't wait to listen to me—nope, he charged out the front door to where Gem and Stella were full-on making out. Thanks to the top being down on the convertible, it was impossible to miss. *Sweet car* and *lucky bastard* were the two thoughts competing as Seven descended the steps and headed straight for the car.

"Gem," he said, snapping out his twin's name like it was some incantation. "What the hell are you doing?"

Instead of springing apart, Gem just lifted his head and said, "Fuck off, Sev. I'm kissing Slick right now."

"No shit, I'm not blind." Oh, Seven was pissed. Leaning back against the doorjamb, I folded my arms. "Speaking of which, I thought we were done with you and you weren't coming back here again."

"Hmm," Stella said, a smile flirting around the corners of her mouth. "Do you hear some annoying buzzing? I swear I've heard that sound before. It usually involves gritted teeth and nails on a chalkboard."

A snort of laughter escaped me. Unimpressed, Seven shot me a dirty look before he focused on the car. "Gem, you can do a lot better than this, particularly since she already sold us out once."

"She didn't sell us out, Sev. Seriously, take the stick out of your ass." Gem leaned back and turned to look at his brother. "I mean it."

"So do I. Since she's for sale to the highest bidder and I paid for her to fuck off, I'd appreciate getting my money's worth."

I almost wished I had popcorn for this.

Gem glared at his brother and Sev glared right back. This was going nowhere good.

Then Stella leaned back and focused on me and that had me straightening right up. Those dark eyes, sooty eyelashes, and pouty lips were everything I wanted to enjoy with or without clothes. Though, if anyone asked, my preference was definitely without.

"Ollie, is that offer of a glass of wine still on the table?"

Oh, hell yes. "Absolutely. Do you want red or white? Bubbles? I can go open it up for you right now."

"White," she answered with another smile. "Oaked chardonnay, if you have it."

Gem glanced back at her. "You'll stay?"

"Sure," she drawled. "It'll be fun. Let's just put the top up."

The temptation to laugh at Sev's utterly baffled and furious expression was right there. Thankfully, I had enough skill to keep it in check. He backed up as the top rose to close on the sexy baby blue '57 Chevy Bel Air. I really wanted to know where she found one in such pristine condition.

"Thanks, bro," I told Sev as I clapped him on the shoulder.

"For what?" he demanded, staring at me askance.

"For convincing her to stay." I grinned. "She was turning us down before." Leaving him to chew on that sour apple, I headed inside to get the wine open and let it breathe.

We'd just had food, so we didn't need snacks, but we could turn on some music. Maybe we could even move everything out to the pool.

It didn't take long for Stella and Gem to come inside or for Seven to stalk off, muttering. Then, because I was his best friend, I called after him, "You sure you don't want to have some wine with us?"

He paused midstep but didn't turn or say a word.

"Yeah, Sev, don't be a dick," Gem said, joining in. "Come have a glass of wine with Stella and us." Gem sounded a lot more gleeful about it than I was, but Sev's shoulders just stiffened and then he stalked off toward the gym.

Probably better he go and burn off some of that temper.

"Is he always like that?" Stella asked, staring after Seven with a curl to her lip that said everything about how very little she cared for him. With how he treated her, I couldn't say I was shocked.

"Yes," Gem said, right at the same time as I said no.

Rolling my eyes, I grabbed wineglasses out from behind the bar in the side of our living room. "Gem, don't be an ass. Sev is just...a little upset about the whole Clara Belle situation."

Stella wrinkled her nose. "Why? She's awful."

Gem snickered, rubbing his cheek. "You can say that again. He's not actually upset. He's just pissed off because Clara knew perfectly fucking well that was me in the photos and broke up with him anyway, because it painted her as a victim and that, in turn, gave her a boost in popularity."

"Sounds like he should be thanking me, then," she muttered, wandering closer to where I was pouring our wine. "I'm only staying for one glass, okay? I still need to drive home."

I smiled back at her. "Sure. One glass." Then I proceeded to hold eye contact as I filled hers well above the waist of the glass, pouring until it almost touched the rim.

She pursed her lips like she was trying not to laugh as she

shook her head. "Did no one ever teach you how to pour wine, Ollie? That's a pour that'd get you fired in most bars."

I shook my head. "Actually, no. We all missed out on a lot of those life skills."

She winced, clearly thinking she'd hit a nerve, since the twins and I had all started our acting careers as literal toddlers. It was all we'd ever known, and it was no secret that we'd been well into millionaire status before we were even old enough to get a "first job" like most teens.

"I'm teasing, Snow," I reassured her softly, offering her the overfull glass of wine. "I just want an excuse to keep you here."

"Flirt," she accused, then took a sip of the French chardonnay I'd chosen. "Ooh, this is good."

Gem's phone started to play a happy little tune, pulling both our attention as he fished it out to scowl at the screen. It was after midnight, so the only people calling him at this time would be a headache.

"No…" he groaned, reading the caller ID. "Goddamn it. Hello, Ricky, what's happened?"

Well, that couldn't be good. But on the other hand, at least it wasn't Jerry calling with some wild scandal hitting the morning papers. "Ricky is the stunt coordinator on *Keeper's Pursuit*," I explained to Stella as she watched Gem curiously. "They're meant to be filming a scene tonight with Seven's new stunt double."

She blinked a couple of times, with those sexy, long lashes framing her green eyes beautifully. "Gem isn't doubling for him anymore?"

Ah. I forgot that news hadn't broken to the media just yet. "Not…really. But that's in the vault, all right?" I shot her a wink and she smiled back as Gem wandered away to continue his conversation with Ricky. "Gem has been trying to separate himself from Seven's career for a while, but *Keeper's Pursuit* is the first time he's refused the job entirely. Things are not going great with his replacement, though."

"You're joking!" Gem exclaimed to whatever Ricky'd just said. "Well, shit, what do you want me to—" Pause, then deep scowl and a regretful glance Snow's way. "Come on, man, right now? I'm not even totally sober so—"

Ricky must have started talking again, and I knew Gem would give in. Everyone working the *Keeper's* franchise knew exactly how to push his buttons. As much as they butt heads, they were still identical twins and loved each other fiercely. Seven was the whole reason Gem hadn't quit show business way back when they got emancipated from their parents at age fifteen.

"Are they asking him to go to the set?" Stella asked, checking her watch and gasping. "But it's the middle of the night!"

I nodded. "Time means nothing on set. All that matters is that the lighting is right."

She seemed genuinely worried as she glanced over at Gem, who was rubbing his eyes as he listened to whatever Ricky was saying. Then he blew out a long sigh. "Fine. I'll be there in half an hour. You fucking owe me, Ricky." He ended the call and returned to us with a huge pout on his lips. "Well. This sucks."

"What happened?" I asked, sipping my own wine as I leaned on the bar top. "Someone break their back?"

Gem huffed a laugh. "I would rather that's what happened. Jean-Claude, my replacement, is apparently allergic to latex. He's broken out in a huge rash and can't wear the makeup that actually makes him passable as Seven."

I scoffed, shaking my head. "What's the stunt scene they need to film?"

Gem raked his fingers through his hair, messing it up in a way Seven would never be caught dead doing. It always confused me how people couldn't tell them apart. Physically, yes, they were identical. But they were *nothing* alike.

"Car chase, flip, and wreck."

"What?" Stella squeaked. "That sounds dangerous."

Gem's lips curled in a sly grin. "That's the job, Slick. It should be a quick one. I reckon I can get it nailed in less than five takes and be back before you finish that glass of wine, which looks like it was poured by a fucking firehose."

I snickered. "Five takes with Tai Sun Yamato as your director? Good luck, bro. You'll be lucky to escape with less than fifteen."

"Ollie, please make sure Slick gets home safe," he ordered with a serious growl underscoring his words before turning his attention to the gorgeous woman in question. "I'll text you," he murmured, then wrapped his hand around the back of her neck and dragged her into what could only be described as an Oscar-worthy kiss.

Fucking hell, it was sometimes easy to forget he could turn up the heat just as well as Seven and I onscreen. He just preferred to wield his powers in private...lucky bastard.

When he broke away, dropping a kiss on the tip of her nose, he was oozing smug satisfaction. Fucker knew exactly what he'd done, and the dizzy little stumble Stella did as he released her neck said he'd done it *well*.

"So, Snow, just you and me," I said as Gem exited the house once more. "I hear you're not bad at pool. Want to play?"

She turned to face me with cheeks flushed and lips wet, and my brain short-circuited for a moment. *Would it be sleazy of me to try and kiss her now? Yes. Okay, cut it out, Ollie.*

"Not bad?" she repeated, wrinkling her nose as she grinned. "You're kidding. That's what Gem said? I'm *not bad* at pool? What a dick. Come on, then, Olivier Griffiths. One game, and there needs to be a bet. I work better under pressure."

My dick instantly hardened at the implications of that statement. "Good to know," I coughed, attempting to subtly fix my issue before moving out from behind the bar. Now to think of a worthy bet—Gem's had ended up with the best night of his life.

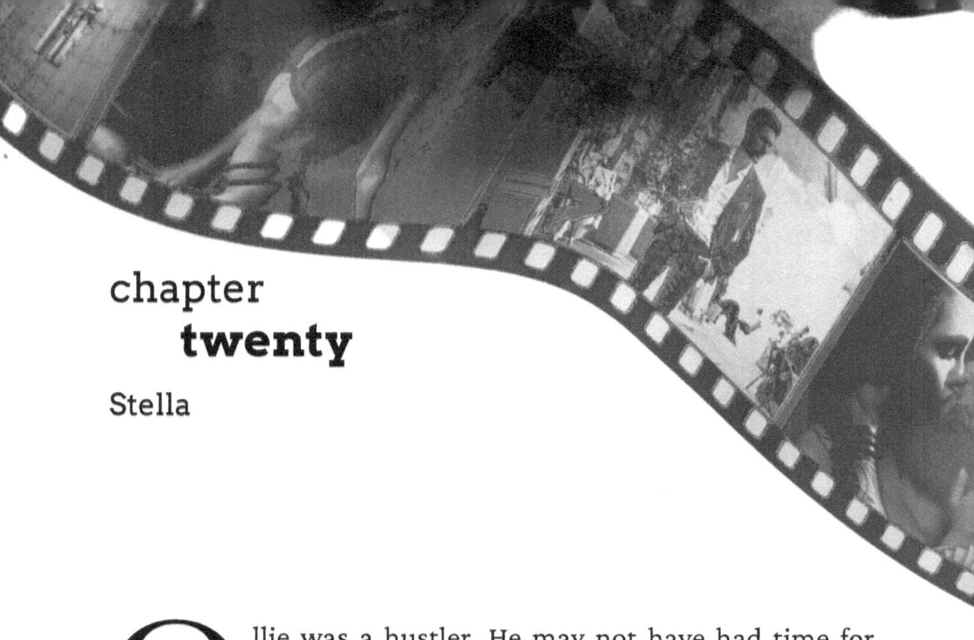

chapter
twenty

Stella

Ollie was a hustler. He may not have had time for minimum wage jobs like waiting tables or tending bar, but he certainly had time to learn pool like a pro. That and he had the audacity to act like he wasn't very good. Okay, in hindsight, I really shouldn't have been so shocked. Particularly after Gem ran the table to win our bet.

When Ollie beat me before I'd even drank half my glass, I demanded a rematch for best out of three games. It was a reasonable request since his bet was to go skinny dipping with him in their outdoor pool.

"You trying to back out on our bet, Snow?" Amusement filtered through his words as he studied me from those dark eyes.

"As if," I said with a snort while gathering the balls back together and racking them. "Considering you and Gem play with the same cutthroat technique, I'm sure you can handle it."

"Didn't say I couldn't," he said, raising his own glass and downing the rest with one swallow. "Just making sure you were still up for it."

"Absolutely." I drew a finger along the edge of the bumper

as I circled the table to reclaim my cue. "Want to make it interesting?"

"Pretty sure we already did," he murmured when I was right in front of him. "But I love the way your lips move when you're talking, so tell me what you had in mind."

The liquid smoothness in his statement sent a flutter right through me. Damn, as lines went, that was...excellent. "Flirting will get you nowhere."

"Then there's no harm in it." He punctuated the sentiment with a wink. "Are you going to tell me what you have in mind?"

Already rethinking the idea, I slanted a look at the table and kept my attention on him via my periphery. "How do you feel about strip pool?"

"Probably a safe bet to say that I'm on board, since we were betting for going skinny-dipping."

I grinned before I could suppress the reaction. "Fine, then let's do it this way...for every ball I sink, you lose an article of clothing."

"And for every ball I sink, you do," he countered, a heated look dancing with the playfulness in his eyes. Seriously, the man just oozed sex appeal and charisma. It wasn't fair 'cause it didn't even seem like he had to try.

"The winner?"

"Well, you're already down one out of three to me, so if I win round two, we head right out to the pool and you'll be ready to dive in. Don't worry, it's heated and cleaned regularly." He swirled the last bit of wine in his glass before he downed it.

"If I win, then we have to keep playing..."

"And keep losing clothes," Ollie murmured. "Not really feeling a downside here, Snow."

"Not trying for one, but I like knowing what's on the table.

Real stakes and all that." Pivoting, I faced the table. "Winner breaks."

Here was hoping he left me an opening because I'd learned that giving him or Gem one was a recipe for a loss.

"Want to add a little more spice to the game?" He shifted to stand right behind me, so close I couldn't miss the heat rising off of him or the tickle of his cologne in my nostrils. It was sandalwood and musk. It could be body wash or shampoo.

Whatever it was, it was damn attractive.

"You like to play with fire," I said, keeping both hands on my pool cue. I still had half a glass of wine left. Between the food, the earlier margaritas, the wine, and the company—not to mention some very thorough kisses from Gem—I was more than a little turned on.

With a barely there caress, Ollie ran his nose from my cheek to my ear and then to my neck, where he pressed a whisper-soft kiss. My nipples went rock-hard as a shiver cascaded through me.

"So do you," Ollie whispered. "Could be dangerous for you, Snow."

Laughing softly, I turned slightly and tilted my head to see him better. "Don't worry, Ollie. I won't melt."

"That," he said in a silky tone, "sounds like a challenge."

Playing a very dangerous game? Check.

Beyond caring if I win? Also check.

Except Gem...

That was a sobering thought. "Your break," I reminded him.

"Winner's choice," he said, his breath teasing little whirls against my skin. "So you can do the break, Snow."

Despite the air-conditioning in their very expensive home, I was definitely overheating. Licking my lips, I took a risk and bumped his hip with mine so I could change positions. His low chuckle suggested I was in no way subtle nor did I avoid rubbing against him as I circled around.

The connection had every one of my nerves lit up and on fire. Touching my tongue to my teeth, I shook my head. *Bad Stella. Stop fantasizing about what he looks like naked.*

That was almost more challenging than I cared to admit because I'd seen him shirtless in more than a few roles. The cut of his washboard abs was so sharp, it definitely threatened to slice my panties right off.

That was if the fabric survived all the heat he put off no matter how soaked they were. One delicious thought slid right into another, and I reclaimed the wineglass for a drink. Alcohol wasn't going to cool me off, but it gave me something else to think about.

Aware of his gaze on me, I took care to line up my shot. Flattening my back while my ass pushed back, I had one leg extended just slightly as I planted my foot. Focusing my attention on the cue ball, I pictured exactly what I wanted to happen.

I wanted a ball in the hole and his shirt off.

Inhale.

Exhale.

Inhale.

Exhale—shoot. I snapped the cue ball forward with a smart snap. The break was fucking perfect. Two solid-colored balls, two separate corner pockets.

Straightening, I turned to meet Ollie's smirk. "Two balls, Griffiths. Pay up."

"I never argue with a woman who is good with balls."

I rolled my eyes. "That was cheesy."

"But you still liked it," he teased. "Besides, cheese is excellent with wine." He nudged off his shoes one after the other, then took off his socks.

I snorted as he gave me an impudent look. "You want more off me, Snow, you're going to have to tap a lot of those balls."

"Challenge accepted." Wineglass in hand, I saluted him, then took a drink. Despite my early thought to slow down, I was almost finished. Facing the table again, I studied what shots were open to me. "Green in the side pocket," I informed him as I circled the table.

One sharp tap and into the hole it went. Still half folded as though I were lining up my next shot, I lifted my gaze to Ollie.

He leaned his cue stick to the side and undid his belt, slid it off, then set it to the side.

"That's just a belt," I reminded him.

"It's an article of clothing," he countered, practically daring me to argue.

"It's an accessory, but fine," I said, chuckling. "Make me work for it. Blue in the corner."

"You want me naked, Snow, just say the word." He managed to deliver that smoking line just as I made the bounce shot and sent the blue ball into its corner. "Nerves of steel. I like that about you."

This time, he didn't wait for me to look at him; he just unzipped his pants and stripped them off before folding them and laying them to the side. He sported a very nice pair of silk boxers.

At least, I thought they might be silk. They could have been cotton. The back of them was hunter green, but nothing could prepare me for when he turned around. I damn near choked on the last of my wine.

His grin was even wider.

"Why are you wearing elephant boxer shorts?" Because there was no mistaking what the elephant's trunk was supposed to be—and yes it did make me wonder if he was also erect and filling it out fully.

"I like truth in my advertising. Heard someone say once 'if you're hung like a bull elephant, you should let people know.'"

Fuck.

The moisture in my mouth dried up and I forgot how to breathe.

"You really want to know right now," he said, unabashed and open with his smirk. "Don't you?"

"With a lead up like that? Oh yeah." I gave him a once-over. He had his shirt, possibly an undershirt, and then the boxers. I flicked a look back at the table. "Three balls...I got this."

"You could," he murmured, and I made myself tune him out. Because I wasn't sure what was coming out of his mouth next, even if I was utterly enjoying the whole experience.

"Red, side pocket," I said, then made the shot and didn't look at him as I circled the table. With the cue stick, I gestured to another ball and another corner pocket, I sank it. That was two.

The rustle of fabric made me look as he stripped off the shirt and bared that very chiseled chest. Maybe not as spritzed with oil to make it sheen and ripped as he would be for a movie, but the man really had nothing to worry about. The natural beauty in his body was probably the thing sculptors like Michaelangelo sought to replicate with all that work in marble.

Fuck, it was making my fingers itch for my camera and not for pap shots. I'd bet my left nipple that I could get the most artistic shots out of him. The desire to test that theory waged a heavy battle against continuing this tug-of-war we were playing.

Because with the pool games at one to one, he would be naked and I wouldn't be skinny-dipping—*yet*.

"One more ball, Snow." It was a couple more to win the game, but I couldn't really argue. I wanted those elephant boxers off because I would never in a million years have expected something quite so *absurd* to be such a goddamn turn-on.

Dragging my gaze off him and back to the table, I pursed my lips. My shot options were limited. Still...no risk no reward. I gestured for the ball I wanted and then nodded to the pocket in the corner closest to me. It would need a hell of a bank shot.

The world bled away from me as I narrowed everything down to the shot I needed to make. I pictured where I had to strike it with the cue so it hit the bumper and rebounded perfectly.

Physics.

It was all physics.

The snap of the cue forward took all my desire with it, and the ball dropped into the pocket just like I'd pictured it. Satisfaction unfurled. Yes, I had a couple more balls to go, but frankly, I'd won as far as I was concerned.

Chuckling, Ollie reached for his shorts to strip them off, but just as he hooked his thumbs into the waistband, an alarm ripped through the house. I jerked at the sudden volume of what sounded like a cross between a klaxon on some sci-fi show and the most annoying siren on the road.

"Fuck," Ollie swore as he strode toward a wall console—boxers in place. Yes, I looked. Sue me. I followed, even as I pressed my hands over my ears. Holy shit it was loud. At the panel, Ollie punched a couple of buttons and the screens lit up with images from the exterior. My car was on one. The gate was on another. Then it flickered and there was a garage, a side garden, and—

"There," I said because something blurry was moving. It was almost too pink to stay hidden in the dark, and when Ollie tapped the screen to make it larger, I did a double take.

It was a woman.

A very *nude* woman racing across the grass from their east wall. Her breasts and her thighs had about the same amount of jiggle. I had to give her props though—she didn't slow her speed even when she crossed the white pebbled pathway in her bare feet.

The alarm cut off abruptly as Ollie pivoted to head back over to his pants. I split my attention between the woman on the screen and what he was doing.

"Sorry, Snow. I just need to call the security company. They always have someone in the area. They can come and deal with her." He had pulled his phone out of his pocket.

"Does this happen often?" I'd heard about some crazy fan encounters, but what delusion did you have to have to think that running onto someone's property naked was going to get you five minutes with the object of your...affection? Obsession? Whatever.

"That's why we have security," Ollie explained as he headed back to me, phone at his ear. "Yes, this is Griffiths," he said before reciting his address. "We've got what looks like a naked intruder streaking on the property and"—he let out such a put-upon sigh—"she's heading for our pool."

I found myself wanting to offer him some genuine sympathy because he sounded truly forlorn.

"Immediately," Ollie continued. "We'll be inside until you get here." He ended the call, his scowl deepening for a moment as the woman dove right into the water.

"It looks like a very nice pool."

"Yeah," Ollie said. "Now we'll have to clean it again."

"I'm sorry."

"It's fine," he said with another sigh. "But yeah, that's why we have security to deal with...well, that."

"Sometimes though," Seven interjected and I jumped because I hadn't even heard him come in. Granted my ears were still ringing, but Seven radiated a kind of chaotic cloud of raging disapproval. I'd notice that before I would his footsteps. "The crazies just get walked right in the front door."

Since his gaze was fixed on me, I didn't have to pretend I didn't know what he was talking about.

"My brother not enough for you, Stray? Trying to catch Ollie in your claws now?"

Since he wasn't wrong but I had zero intentions of humoring him, I faced Ollie. "Maybe I should go."

"You don't have to go anywhere," Ollie said. "Ignore Seven. It's what I do."

"I don't have a problem with ignoring him." In fact, I took no small amount of pleasure in making sure he understood I *was* ignoring him. "But there's no skinny-dipping tonight and you probably want to get dressed before security gets here."

His smirk was downright adorable. "I promise you, they've seen me worse and we didn't finish our game."

The man was dangerously tempting. "Rain check?"

Ollie dipped his head and I swore I thought he was going to kiss me, but all he did was whisper, "You better believe it," with his lips mere centimeters from mine.

Seven made a gagging noise but Ollie just winked before he pivoted and went to his clothes. Damn, I hated to see him go, but I really didn't mind watching him walk away.

I allowed myself that little pleasure at least until Seven's gagging cough grew even louder. If he weren't a grown-ass adult, I'd have sworn he just did a *slut* cough.

Finally, I cut a look at him. "Hairball?"

He glared but Ollie just laughed, and when I looked back at the screen, their nude visitor was making herself at home swimming lazy laps in their pool.

Yeah, that was definitely weird.

chapter
twenty-one

Stella

My phone vibrated as I kept one eye on the hotel's back entrance. I was set up perfectly at a table just outside a trendy bubble tea and smoothie place. I wasn't a huge fan of wheatgrass or seaweed. They had a coffee smoothie so I'd made do with that.

Despite my phone vibrating a second time, I didn't look away from the entrance. My camera was at the perfect angle, and I had it camouflaged with a couple of bags from high-end stores. With one hand under there on the shutter button, ready to take the snaps, I sipped my smoothie.

An A-list actress stepping out with her daughter's boyfriend had been all over the blinds the past few days. Dad was pretty sure when she had affairs in the past, this hotel was her favorite. It was within reasonable distance of her studio and away from the frothier places where the tourists liked to gawk.

The rear entrance was perfectly situated to let them step outside, then put on a hat or sunglasses before leaving the little courtyard. If they had a car picking them up, even better. Another buzz from the phone—it was practically bouncing with excitement.

It was probably Gem. Since I'd given him my number, we texted multiple times a day. Well, he'd texted multiple times a day and he'd called me at night more than once when I was winding down. The man wanted to know I was home safe. As much as I tried to keep a little professional distance, I had to admit, there was something really nice about the fact that he wanted to know about me.

The movement of the door pushing outward alerted me to someone exiting. Sure enough, it was a familiar woman dressed in jeans and a T-shirt with casual slides on. She had a pair of sunglasses covering her face, but that thousand-watt smile had been winning hearts and awards for over two decades.

The guy coming out with her couldn't have been a day over eighteen. Hell, I'd have been surprised if he was even that. That was, what? Nineteen-plus years age difference? I found that gross when men did it, so she didn't get an out as a woman. Particularly not a full-ass adult with a teenager.

He caught her arm and she laughed as she turned, I had my finger pressed down on the shutter, the rapid cycling of photos snapping away as she caught his face in her hands and then kissed him.

Full, open-mouthed, spit-swapping with tongues clearly visible. For someone who valued discretion in an industry that feasted on scandal, she was an idiot. At least she was being an idiot right here on the street, where I could get some good shots.

I got a few more as they faced outward. She made it to the street and waved her arm. A car glided up and she climbed in after blowing a kiss to the kid, and then she was gone.

He stared after her looking utterly forlorn. It was like all the animation drained out of him. Poor kid. Those photos were going to net a nice sum. As it was, the guys had been nudging me to keep supplying *Bright Starz*.

I'd sold them a couple so far, and the pay had been decent, the funds transferred immediately. Still not *quite* as much as I could get elsewhere. The images also didn't break immediately.

Vetting took time, I supposed. Frankly, I wasn't in this for the notoriety. My phone let out a series of buzzes in rapid succession.

"Keep your pants on, Gem," I muttered as I picked it up. Sure enough the last four messages were from him as well as the five before that. Random comments about work, the weather, and then a couple of restaurant mentions.

The phone vibrated while I was holding it and a new message popped up. This one was from Ollie, though, and I rolled my eyes when I read it.

Elephant Ollie: Good morning, Snow. How'd you sleep?

I checked the time and smiled, shaking my head.

Stella: It's almost lunchtime. Are you just waking up?

Elephant Ollie: Yep. Speaking of lunch...

We'd only been texting for a week, but I knew the game well enough to simply reply with a photo of my smoothie. He had zero faith in my ability to feed myself properly, and on more than one occasion, I'd found a full meal delivered to my apartment via DoorDash after I'd failed to answer him fast enough.

Elephant Ollie: Is that all? Just a smoothie? Snow...

Stella: I already finished my sandwich, so can't show you that but I promise it was delicious.

There was a short pause, while he no doubt debated whether I was bullshitting him. For once, I was telling the truth, though. His nagging and bullying was actually creating better eating habits for me, and my energy levels were reaping the benefits. My concealer use had drastically reduced with fewer dark circles under my eyes too.

Elephant Ollie: Good girl. That's what I like to hear.

I groaned out loud. Ollie was a fucking flirt *and* a tease, so I swapped to my messages with Gem instead. His latest one was asking if I wanted to go hiking with him tomorrow morning.

I wrinkled my nose as I typed out my reply, smiling to myself.

Stella: I'm so curious how I made you think I'm an early-morning hike kinda girl, Gem.

Gemini: Okay, fair. But I can't exactly take you out for ice cream at the Santa Monica Pier or...anything normal. Hiking is private, and you'd look so fucking hot in activewear.

He had a good point. If I wanted to spend time with him in any real capacity, it couldn't be a "normal" date in public. Not with his—and Seven's—level of fame. Still, hiking was not my thing.

Stella: We could go for a drive?

It was the closest I'd come to agreeing to a date all week, and he was quick to jump at the opportunity.

Gemini: Done. When? Now? Pin your location. I'll pick you up and we can get a picnic basket from Kitty's Katering on the way.

Stella: Geez, Gem, play it cool. You're a celeb, for fuck's sake. Act like more of an aloof twat waffle, or you'll make it too hard for me to remain unattached.

Crap. As soon as I sent that, I regretted it. I was doing exactly what I was teasing him about: acting way too fucking excited. Showing my cards way too early and risking rejection. Fucking hell. I needed to keep this complicated and messy, so I wouldn't lose myself.

I swapped back to my text thread with Ollie, like the self-sabotaging bitch I was, but before I could type anything, Gem's response message appeared on my screen.

Gemini: Good. Attached is exactly what I want. Attached to me, my name, my bed...you name it, Slick, I want you attached to it. Location?

Fuck. Me. Now I was having mental images of being handcuffed to his bed while he had his filthy way with my body...while Ollie stood there watching.

I wet my lips, trying and failing to push those *vivid* thoughts from my head.

Stella: I can't today. I'm heading over to the Covington to see if I can snap some shots of the gaming streamers staying there.

Gemini: You can't take the afternoon off?

I sighed heavily because I really wanted to take him up on his offer. Especially now that I was picturing how dirty a picnic in the hills could be with him. I wondered if Kitty's Katering sold nacho plates for old time's sake?

Stella: I wish.

Biting my lip, I considered just leaving it at that and not elaborating further, but something about Gem made me want to explain so he'd know I wasn't playing hard to get for the simple fun of it—and maybe so he'd understand *me* a little better.

Stella: My dad isn't well at the moment and his medical debt increases daily. Add to that the fact he needs in-home nurse care and can't work. This job is the only thing keeping us treading water. Rain check, though? I do want to see you...

I hated opening up. It made me feel itchy. But I liked Gem enough that I actually wanted to offer him a sliver of honesty where my workload was concerned.

Gemini: Shit, Slick. Okay, I'll stop distracting you in that

case. Knowing you* WANT *to see me is enough for now. Text me when you're home, so I know you're safe.

"Fucking hell," I groaned aloud. He was almost too perfect at this stage. A horrible little voice in my head wondered if he was preparing for a role and using me as part of method-acting prep. Maybe his character dates a poor, plain commoner? Crazier things had happened in Hollywood.

Elephant Ollie: Gem said you'll be at the Covington later. I'll arrange dinner for you in their restaurant.

The two of them were killing me in the best possible way. I wanted so fucking badly to just launch myself headfirst into this *utterly insane* ménage situation they seemed totally cool starting up. But I was no Cinderella, nor was I a fucking idiot. Nothing good could come from this, aside from the sex. The sex was more than good with Gem, and by the look of Ollie's elephant trunk...

"Stop it, Stella," I scolded myself under my breath as I packed up my camera. "You have a vibrator at home. There's no need for this lunacy." Since starting my unexpected career as a paparazzi photographer, I'd spent a whole hell of a lot of time alone. Which had, in turn, seen me develop a habit of talking to myself out loud.

Slipping my camera case into my backpack, I dropped my empty smoothie cup into the trash and walked back down the block to where I'd left my motorcycle. It was the one good thing that'd come out of my relationship before Dillon, and I loved having it as an option for easier parking. On busy weekend days in known celebrity hot spots, it was near impossible to park the Bel Air, but the bike was a breeze.

I slowed as I approached, though, recognizing the height and build of the man lingering nearby with his back turned. He smoked a cigarette with absolutely no regard for the passersby as he exhaled, and when I approached more cautiously, he dropped the butt onto the pavement.

"Stella Charles," the man greeted me with a yellowed smile. "Thought I recognized your bike."

"Donnie," I replied with a nod. He was a colleague of sorts but certainly not a friend. He was the kind of pap that gave the rest of us a bad name and had more harassment charges against him than he probably knew what to do with. He was also Dillon's cousin. "What's up?"

He shrugged. "Nothing much. Just wanted to give you a heads-up, I snapped a couple of pictures the other night and sold them to *The Nightly Mail* for big bucks. Huge bucks. Real sweet payday, that one. Best I've had in ages!" He grinned widely, genuinely pleased with himself.

I arched a brow. "That's great. Good for you." But also at the same time... "Why do you need to give me a heads-up?"

Donnie swept a hand over his hair. "Ah, well, professional courtesy and all. The pics were of you and your hot new boyfriend Seven Harrison. Hell of a bold move, that, crossing the line into their world." He pulled out another cigarette and lit it up while I stood there flabbergasted. "Anyway, they're being published online sometime today or tomorrow, I dunno. Just wanted to do right and tell ya, girl."

He tipped his chin in a little farewell, then swaggered off down the street without waiting or really even caring what my reply might be. What the fuck could I even say to that?

My image of Clara Belle was set to publish tomorrow with *Bright Starz* but if *The Nightly Mail* was hitting publish today... What did it matter? I'd been paid already. And I knew full well there were no images of me and Seven together, but I had driven Gem and Ollie home in my convertible with the top down. We could have been snapped literally anywhere between Malibu and Hollywood.

Stupid.

Oh well, no use crying over spilled milk now. I climbed on my bike and headed across town to the ritzy hotel where a bunch of hugely popular YouTube and Twitch streamers were currently staying while a convention was in town. They were a hot commodity, the streamers, and most paparazzi were too old-school to step away from the A-listers to see the dollar signs elsewhere.

My phone vibrated as I parked across from the hotel entrance, and I paused to check it. I figured it'd be Ollie or Gem, or possibly even my dad. But I was surprised to see an unsaved number calling instead.

Then a sinking sensation hit me, and I reluctantly answered the call.

"We need to talk," Seven growled down the phone line, and I sighed.

"We really don't," I disagreed. "And I'm at work, so I don't have the time, patience, or energy for your pissy attitude, Demon Spawn."

"And invading people's privacy to take their picture is more important than meeting with me, is it? This is urgent, Stray. Do you not get that?" He was *furious*, that much was abundantly clear.

At the same time, though...fuck him. "Is paying my mortgage and ensuring my electricity stays on *more important* than your fragile ego, Seven? Yes. Yes, it really is. Eat a dick and lose my number."

"How much?" He snapped before I could hang up.

I frowned, confused. "How much, what? I didn't sell the images if that's what you're implying. I haven't seen them, don't know what story is being run, and didn't even know they were taken until literally half an hour ago."

He gusted a frustrated huff. "How much is your time

worth, to leave work and come to the house so my manager can work damage control?"

My lips parted in shock, then I scoffed. "You're not serious."

"I am. How much do you stand to earn if you work the remainder of the afternoon?"

Disbelief rattled me and I raked my fingers through my tangled hair. "I don't know, Seven. Maybe nothing, maybe twenty grand. There are no guarantees in my line of work."

He didn't respond immediately, but my phone pinged in my ear.

"I'll tell Jerry you're on your way," he snapped, then hung up, leaving me staring at the Venmo confirmation for a twenty-thousand-dollar transfer into my account.

My hands shook with blind rage as I texted his number with my response.

Stella: Eat. A. Dick. I'm not for fucking sale.

But I didn't send the money back. If he was so rich he could pay me twenty grand without my consent, then he damn well deserved to lose it. I hoped he was holding his breath waiting for me because I would rather eat broken glass than do as he commanded.

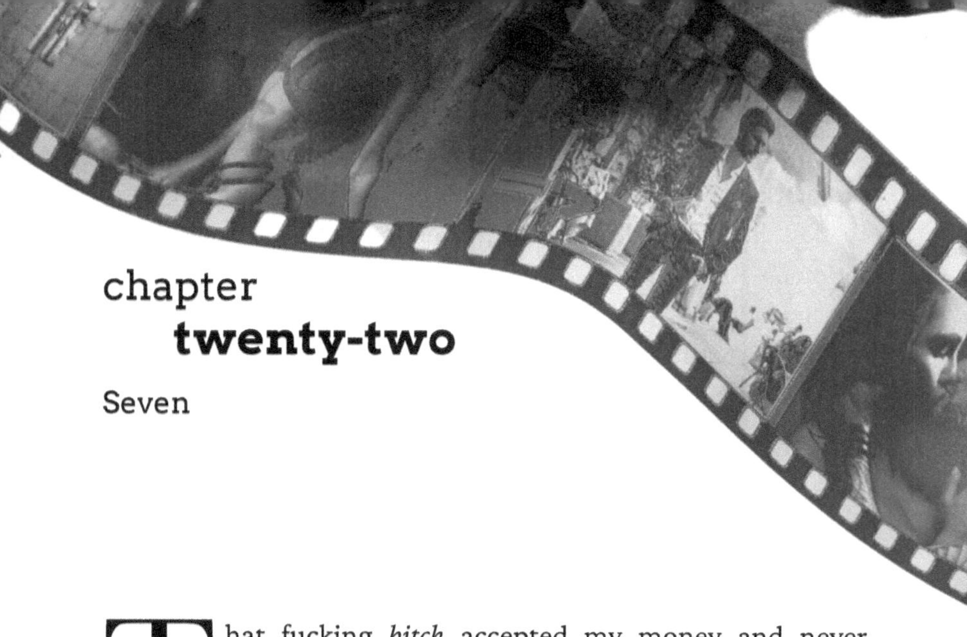

That fucking *bitch* accepted my money and never showed up to discuss damage control on the tabloid trash that was about to be published in *The Nightly Mail*. I paid her twenty grand, for fuck's sake. What more did she seriously want for a couple of hours out of her day?

"Gem! She needs to be here to discuss how we—" I started on my twin again, despite knowing full well that he would not back me up on this.

"Nope!" he cut me off, not even letting me finish my sentence. Dick.

I glowered, fists balled at my sides. "Gemini, you fucking owe me. This infatuation you have with that stray cat is ruining my reputation, and if we don't get ahead of it, then—"

"Technically, Sev, I did you a huge favor the other night when your stunt double held up production *again* so I figure we're about equal. Beside the fact that neither I nor Stella sold those images, we can't be held responsible." Gem was totally unconcerned, scrolling through the images that Jerry had sent on his laptop. Ollie was in them too, of course, but the story was all about *Seven's Mystery Woman* thanks to the lovesick-puppy way Gem was staring at her in them.

The photo of her pulling into our driveway and leaving again *hours* later was damning enough. Especially because the article noted Gemini Harrison was on set for *Keeper's Pursuit* that night.

Fuck my life.

"Jerry?" I pleaded, turning to our shared agent for some kind of backup. Gem was flat refusing to contact Stella and ask her to come over, and Ollie was in the middle of a press event for his upcoming release so was absolutely no help at all.

Jerry had been quiet for a while, letting my twin and I bicker like children while he tried to work out a damage-control plan. In fairness, he'd been our agent since we were fifteen and cut ties with our parents, so he was pretty used to our twin shit by now.

"Jerry, help me out here," I prodded him. "If we are spinning this story, then *she* needs to be in agreement. Legally, if possible."

Gem scoffed, and I extended my middle finger his way. In fairness, though, the NDA was entirely useless when she wasn't the one selling sensationalist shit to the trash rags. That was more wasted money.

"Okay, we have two options here, so far as I can see," Jerry said thoughtfully, his fingers steepled as he pondered it inside his devious mind. He was the best agent in town, and we were fucking lucky to have him on our side. "Either we get ahead and correct the story to the truth, that all those images are of *Gemini* and not *Seven*, effectively taking the air out of the scandal bubble..."

I didn't hate that idea. Then I could play the part of victimized by the media for once.

"Is now a good time to mention there's another Seven Harrison image hitting *Bright Starz* tomorrow?" Gem spoke up, looking the tiniest bit guilty. "Sorry, Bro. Clara Belle was super drunk at the party last weekend and thought I was you, so I took the opportunity to say a few things...”

I groaned, dropping my head into my hands. “I hate you.”

Jerry sighed. “Look, you want my professional opinion on this whole thing?”

Not really... “Yes,” I grumbled, irritated as all fuck. It’d been two weeks since Clara broke up with me and the sudden celibacy was making me all kinds of bad-tempered. I was used to having her *at least* blow me once a day. Her high sex drive was one of the major reasons I’d stayed with her so long. And now all I had was my hand and a bunch of bullshit rumors about a feral stray woman who couldn’t leave my brother alone.

“Your popularity is benefiting from this,” Jerry said, not beating around the bush. “Regardless of what Carriage Pictures is threatening with their morality clauses, you’ve had a massive uptick on casting inquiries in the last week, and there’s been a spike in viewing across all your movies. The viewers *love* a love scandal, Seven. There's a great opportunity here to spin something financially beneficial. Or we could come clean about the images being Gem and *his* new girl, which would undoubtedly see a rise in his personal stardom again.”

“Which Gem doesn’t want,” Gem said with a scowl. “If this drama is paying off in new roles and bigger contracts, let Seven keep it.”

I looked from my brother to my agent and back again. Gem had been really firm for a while now that he wanted to get out of acting entirely, so being suddenly thrust into the tabloids would really not sit comfortably with him. I could already see the idea stressing him out with the way his jaw clenched and his fingertips drummed the counter.

No one spoke for a few moments, then Jerry swept a hand

over his graying hair. "What's the image in *Bright Starz*, Gem? I'm assuming this is one Stella did sell?"

He nodded. "Yeah, I deliberately pissed off Clara and she slapped me in front of Stella's camera."

Jerry nodded. "So the image is her slapping Seven? What's the story?"

Gem shrugged. "Beats me." Then he winced. "Unless they reached out to Clara for comment...in which case I *might* have fucked up."

I groaned again. "What did you say, Gremlin?"

He snapped a glare my way for the use of his old nickname. "I don't remember the exact wording, but I did maybe mention the fact you were planning to propose at the premiere for Mirage and, uh, rubbed her face in the fact that you were taking your gorgeous new girlfriend instead." He winced again. "Okay, I can see how this might have complicated matters. In my defense, I'd had a bit to drink and wanted a good photo for Stella to sell."

I was going to kill him. That was the *only* solution here: I needed to kill my brother.

"Stop it," Jerry scolded before I could launch myself at Gem and choke the life out of him for fucking with my private *and* public life all at once. Why the fuck couldn't he hook up with a nice, normal *fan* like he used to?

"Sorry," Gem mumbled, at least having the decency to look apologetic. "I wasn't thinking."

"All right, but you only said that to Clara Belle, yes?" Jerry asked, his mind clearly going a thousand miles a minute. "But if she repeated it to *Bright Starz*... Hmm. Okay, you two need to decide who is taking credit for these photos and this new relationship with Miss Charles. Which one of you is owning them?"

Gem and I exchanged a long look, and it was the kind of moment where I could read his mind with perfect clarity.

"God damn it," I sighed. "You fucking *owe me*, Gremlin."

The relief on his face was undeniable. Media attention had never sat well with him, and the last thing we needed was another incident like when we were sixteen. The press had been relentless on him and his girlfriend that year, and when they split up, Ollie and I caught him cutting his own arms. We knew something needed to change. Since then, we'd done everything possible to shift him out of the line of camera lenses for his own mental health. And yet here he was, sleeping with the devil herself.

"All right, good choice," Jerry said with a nod. "Here's what we're going to do."

He then spent the next half hour outlining the plan that he'd somewhat concocted to not only spin the story in my favor away from Clara's bullshit, but also to save my Carriage Pictures deal. According to Jerry, I'd split with Clara weeks ago and had been keeping the news private out of respect for her reputation, that the original images of "me" and Stella were taken well after my relationship with Clara had ended and therefore wasn't cheating at all.

In Jerry's version of events, Stella and I were madly in love and trying our best to stay out of the public eye to preserve the purity of our new relationship.

I had to admit, the way he pitched it…I was sold. There was only one problem, but it was a big one.

"How do we get the stray to agree to all of this?" I asked, cutting my gaze to my twin once more. "She hates me."

Gem nodded, not attempting to spare my feelings. "That's true, she does."

"You're very charismatic, Seven. I'm sure you can convince

her," Jerry scoffed, shaking his head in amusement. "Or if need be, I'm sure Gem can talk to her?"

Gem shook his head, the stubborn fuck. "Sorry, Jer. Not that I don't want to help, but right now I'm fighting to even get her to go on a date with me. Asking her to fake-date Seven when he literally tried to hold her hostage and extort her into signing a legal document?" He grimaced dramatically. "I think we'll have better luck asking Hell to freeze over."

Jerry threw up his hands. "Well, this plan only works with her cooperation, so I suggest you two put your heads together and work it out. Fast. Ideally before *Bright Starz* finalizes tomorrow's story so we can get ahead of it all. Oh, and don't forget she will need to attend the premiere as your date, Sev. That will be your public debut as a couple."

Oh. We were already fucked. I may not know a lot about Stella Charles, but one thing I was *positive* about? She was a stubborn, spiteful bitch. If I even hinted that this would benefit me, she'd say no purely on principle.

Jerry's phone rang, and he flapped a hand at us to say he was leaving, answering the call before he even got out of our front door. He paused on the doorstep, picking up a package and placing it on our foyer table before continuing on his way.

Ollie was pulling into the driveway as Jerry left, and I decided I would ask *him* for help, since Gem was being a selfish dickwad. While I waited for him to park, I opened the package and found it was full of panties. Used panties. Gross. Our fan group was fucking intense some days.

It took us the better part of an hour to get Ollie up-to-speed on everything, from the photos to the tabloids, to Jerry's idea of how to spin it all. Then I asked very nicely if he would please speak with Stella to gain her cooperation.

Ollie, fucking asshole, burst out laughing.

"What's so funny?" I growled, glaring at him through narrowed eyes.

He shook his head with a wide grin playing across his lips. "You. Why don't you just *pay her* to come to the premiere?"

I blinked at him in confusion. "What?"

Ollie sighed like I was a dense fuck. "You don't need to appeal to her good graces or beg for a favor. You also don't need Gem or I applying a guilt trip—which neither of us would agree to anyway. You simply have to offer her a business proposition. You already paid her to sign the NDA so she's not talking to reporters about anything, so all you actually need is for her to show up at the premiere. So...*pay her for her time.*"

I was a little taken aback by that suggestion, despite the fact that was literally what I'd tried to do today. "She's not a prostitute, Ollie. That seems a bit insulting doesn't it?" Pretty sure I already knew what her answer would've been. So what the hell could I do to make the offer sweeter?

He snort laughed. "Good, because she's not going to actually fuck you, Sev." Then he smirked Gem's way. "Me, on the other hand..."

Gem threw a piece of his sandwich at Ollie's head and glowered. "Stop hitting on my girl, asswipe."

"She's not your girl, Gem," Ollie snarked back, grinning like a hyena. "She's Seven's now."

Fucking hell, I was already regretting this stupid plan.

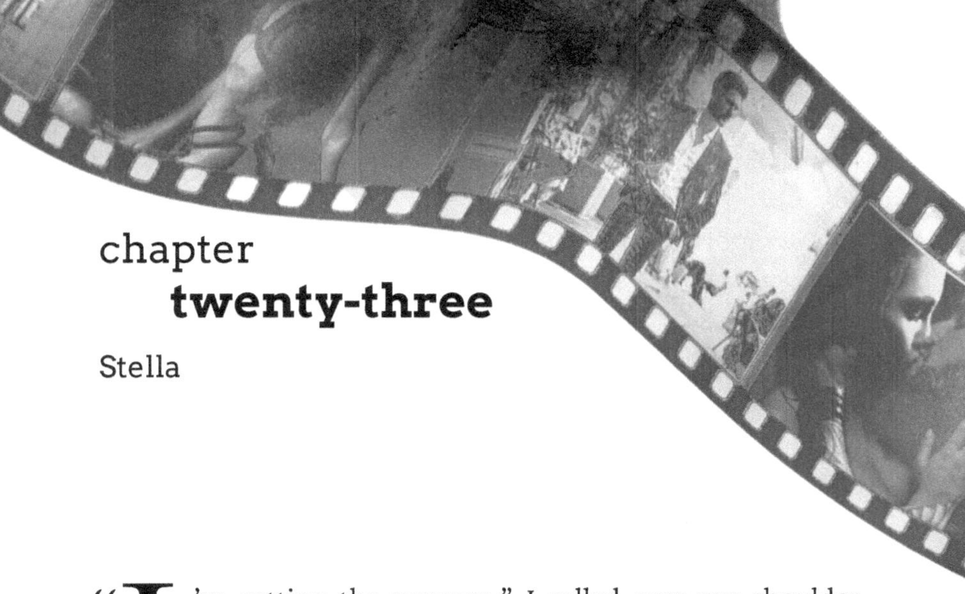

chapter
twenty-three

Stella

"I'm getting the popcorn," I called over my shoulder, laughing as I headed into the kitchen.

"Don't forget the beer!" Dad sounded good today, despite the raspiness in his voice.

"I'll get right on that." As it was, I just snorted. There was no beer. Dad had apparently gotten a friend to drop some off, then Mom found it during her shift, and she made a show of pouring it out. That had to have been fun.

Dad called me after she left to try and get me to replace it. I wasn't really willing to do that, but I did come over and let his afternoon nurse go home early. He'd been grumpy until I pointed out one of his favorite actors had a new movie that just hit streaming and we could watch it.

Smothering a yawn, I pulled out the microwavable popcorn with the extra movie butter and tossed it in for three minutes. As the machine fired up, I opened the fridge to examine our drink options.

The doorbell rang and I tilted my head back with a yawn. Shutting the fridge, I headed for the front door with a half-smothered yawn. I'd spent most of the night on a stakeout at the house being used by the latest *Married with Benefits* season that moved a dozen couples into the same place to see what would happen when they had to play musical beds every other day.

Fuckery was what happened. Fuckery and drama, and the public ate it up if the ratings were to be believed.

"Shutterbug," Dad coughed as he called.

"I got it," I called back. "You stay put." Dad had been pushing it lately, at least that was what all the nurses said, and Mom had complained about. He wanted to do more on his own, but he was a fall risk.

Stubborn man.

Whoever was at the door rang the bell a second time before I got there. The sound of the popcorn going in the kitchen and the scent followed me. Almost immediately, my stomach growled. I'd have to see if we had any Raisinets or Milk Duds hidden in the kitchen.

Opening the door, I blinked stupidly at the last person I expected to see standing on the stoop of the little A-frame in Burbank. Seven Harrison glared at me from behind the dark sunglasses—I didn't have to see his eyes to feel the icy heat.

"Not interested," I told him as I pushed the door closed again.

He landed a palm against it to stop me. "You know *Slick*, you might want to make sure I'm my asshole twin's brother before you shut the door in my face."

I snorted. "Don't call me that," I ordered. "You are no more Gem than I am."

That had his eyebrows raising.

"Are you for fucking real? Is your head so far up your own ass that you think I'd mistake you for him? I *like* him." I let the rest of it dangle there, and if he got the impression I didn't like him, well, served him right. "So you can just fuck right off."

Not that I could close the door, because he was still holding it open. The microwave timer beeped to say it was done, not that I couldn't tell from the rich, buttery scent of popcorn in the air.

Blowing out a breath, Seven kept his hand firm on the door while he pulled off his sunglasses. "Do you mind if I come in?"

"Yes," I said flatly. "I absolutely do mind. Go. A. Way."

Despite the vain hope the rejection would send him away, he offered me no such reward.

"Look, I can stand out here and we can hash this out on your porch, or you can let me in and we can figure this out like adults."

"Ooooorrrr," I said, elongating the word, "we could go for that radical third option of you going the hell away. I dunno, I'm just spitballing."

"You must be radically good at sucking dick for Gem to be so far gone on you."

"Well, don't worry, you'll never find out," I fired back.

"Trust me, I have all my shots and I'm still not interested."

What a dick.

"Now, the paps could be anywhere, you know. They do like to follow me. As you are *well* aware. So, by all means, let's stand here and chat."

"I hate you," I muttered, then pulled the door wider.

"I hate you more, Stray," he muttered as he passed me. Closing my eyes, I shut the door and steeled myself with a deep breath. He and his brother were night and day. Gem was sweet, sexy, and fun.

Seven was an asshole.

"Hey, Shutterbug," Dad said, and I whirled to find him leaning heavily on his cane with one hand on the doorframe to the living room, where we'd moved his hospital bed. He stared at Seven Harrison with narrowed eyes. "We have company?"

"No one you need to worry about, Dad," I said, hurrying

around Seven to intercept Dad before he fell. "And you aren't supposed to get up on your own. We've had this argument."

"Yes, we have," he said in an easy tone as I got an arm around him and he settled his arm on my shoulder. "We know it only frustrates you when I do what I want, so let's just pretend we had the fight already and you can introduce me to the actor standing in our foyer."

"Harrison," Seven said, following me over and offering his hand to my father. "Seven Harrison, Mr. Charles."

Dad studied him for a moment, the sharpness in his gaze and the fixed attention he focused on Seven belied any weakness. With care, he propped his cane against his leg before he accepted Seven's handshake.

"Interesting. What can we do for you, Mr. Harrison?" Dad's tone carried a warning, and Seven spared me a look.

"Actually, it's what I can do for Stella—and I'm guessing you from the looks of things."

Seven shoved his sunglasses into the pocket of his denim jacket. An odd choice for a man who was far more often photographed in suits and slacks or button-downs unless he was filming. The casual look was way more Gem. Then again, that made sense; he was probably trying to avoid notice.

"What can *you* do for my shutterbug?" A continued warning threaded through Dad's question. Yeah, this was not something I needed Dad worrying about.

"Dad, why don't we get you tucked back in and I'll grab the popcorn? Once I get rid of Mr. Harrison, we can watch our movie."

"What movie are we watching?" Seven asked as he stripped off his jacket. "I can get the popcorn for you if you want."

This was rapidly cycling out of hand.

"Grab me a cold beer from the fridge while you're at it, Mr.

Harrison, and I won't even complain if you take a couple of minutes of our time."

"We don't have any beer in the fridge," I said, shooting the demon spawn a warning look. "And Mr. Harrison doesn't need to stay here at all."

"I don't mind—Stella," Seven countered, and I swore I heard the unspoken Stray at the end of the sentence even as he smiled. "I think this is an excellent time for me to get to know your dad. I bet he'll even have some thoughts on our predicament."

Not waiting for me to respond, he headed for the kitchen despite me glaring after him. I could hardly drop Dad and rush after Seven to get rid of him.

Dammit.

"Come on, Dad," I said. "Back in bed."

Dad let me walk him over. He was slow to slide into the bed and didn't hide his grimace too well. I got him tucked in before I grabbed his cane and returned it to by the bed

"Shutterbug." He didn't raise his voice or glare, yet Dad seemed to encapsulate everything he wanted to know in those three syllables.

"I'll get rid of him." The deflection wouldn't work. Dad's dark green eyes were so much like mine, I could read the rejection in them clear as day.

"Are you in trouble?" Now he was worried. I was going to kill Seven Harrison.

"No, sir," Seven said from the doorway as he returned with a red bucket full of popcorn and some sparkling waters as well as two bottles of iced tea. "I didn't see any beer in the fridge, but there were these teas. If that won't work, I can see about getting some delivered."

"No," I snapped before Dad could respond. "Dad doesn't

drink even when he wants to." The last I punctuated with my own glare at Dad.

"Hmm" was Dad's only response. "Fine, I'll settle for tea for now."

"So what movie were we going to watch?" Seven wanted to know.

"Was going to show Shutterbug one of my favorites from back in the day," Dad said, motioning Seven toward the chair I usually sat in next to his bed. That hadn't been the plan, but I was fine with changing it entirely. "Have a seat. You can join us, but no spoilers if you know them."

"My lips are sealed," Seven said with the easiest smile on his face that I'd ever seen him wear. He set the popcorn down and set Dad's drink up before he glanced around the room, then at me. "Need me to grab you another chair, Stel?"

"I'll be fine," I said through gritted teeth. I had a folding chair I could grab and it would put me on the far side from him. "There's really no need for you to stay."

"But I want to." The dick made a great show of taking a seat. The pair both gave me the same look of expectation.

I had no idea how this happened, really. Any of it. But this was how I found myself watching *Ladyhawke* with Dad and Seven. Weirdly, Seven knew the movie—or maybe not so weirdly.

I'd heard of it but never watched it. As much as I tried to enjoy it, I kept finding my gaze tracking to Seven. There had to be an easy way to get him out of here. No doubt existed within me that his appearance here had everything to do with the asinine demand to see me about damage control thanks to Donnie selling those images.

The popcorn turned to ash, and after the one time my hand collided with Seven's in the bowl, I just skipped having any more. I finished an entire bottle of sparkling water and I'd never wished for it to be alcohol so much in my life.

The lightest of snores escaped Dad's mouth as the movie came to the end. The triumph of the star-crossed lovers had left tears in my eyes. After blinking them back, I swiped a hand over my face before glancing at Dad.

He was sound asleep. With care, I eased the popcorn bowl off the side of the bed where he'd braced it. Seven rescued it from me and took Dad's empty drink bottle as I pulled Dad's cover up. Once I changed the station to one that ran marathons of Dad's favorite shows, I nudged the volume down.

It only took me a couple of minutes to get everything set for Dad, so I could leave him to doze while I dealt with Seven. To my surprise, Seven didn't say a word until he followed me into the kitchen.

"What happened?" The quiet question came out far kinder than anything else Seven had ever said.

"He got hurt, took a couple of blows to the head, and it revealed a glioblastoma we didn't know was there."

It was hard to escape the kind of terror that hit that day. Even now, well after Dad survived some of the worst parts…

I cleared my throat. "As it turned out, it was a lucky discovery. They could do something about it, but treatment has been intense and it took a lot out of him."

"Probably expensive too," Seven mused, and I turned from the sink, half-ready to lash back at him but there was no cunning or guile in his eyes. He looked more thoughtful than anything. "Does he have a good prognosis?"

I swallowed around the lump in my throat. "So far," I said, keeping it as vague as the doctors seemed to do. "Options are good."

"Yeah," Seven said slowly. "I would imagine they are."

After rinsing out the popcorn bowl, I shifted it over to the rack to dry. I wiped my hands with the dish towel as I faced him. "Thank you for not bringing up the earlier discussion in front of Dad."

"How did you put it? I'm a hard-ass, not a complete dick."

"I believe I said I was a photographer, not a pervert."

One corner of his mouth kicked a little higher. Uh-oh, was Seven Harrison showing some humanity? Breaking news.

"True." He glanced over his shoulder, but I'd pulled the door to the living room mostly closed. When he looked at me again, he said, "I would like to sit down and work out a deal with you to help with the damage control."

"I have no damage to control," I reminded him. Was it kind of annoying to be *in* the images? Yes. That said, it didn't interfere with my job so much as serve as a reminder to be careful.

"No," Seven said slowly, pushing the word out between his teeth. "I'm sure you don't. At least until word gets to the media with your name and occupation."

Was that a real threat? Or was he bluffing? Folding my arms, I leaned back against the counter. "Oh no, whatever will I do? My reputation will be... Oh, that's right, I don't care what people think of me."

I wasn't sure if it was the statement or my deadpan recitation, but Seven actually huffed a laugh.

"True, but I think you do care about Gem's."

I frowned. "What does Gem have to do with this?" *Besides the obvious that he's in the photos.*

"Except that he is in the images?" Seven echoed my unspoken words. "Well, Jerry only had two ideas for dealing with this fallout *and* salvaging the negotiations with Carriage Pictures. The first is we date—it puts us in front of the story and in charge of the narrative. We let people know that Clara Belle and I broke up weeks ago, and I was just letting her set the tone. Then the photos broke, so as much as I wanted to let her make the decisions, I don't want there to be any mistruths out there about you. I was very single when we met, and it was passion at first sight."

I snorted. "Hate is a passion, I suppose."

"Truly." He gave me a faint smile as he shook his head. "Regardless, now that we're in the open, we're in the open. Then it's a romance and not cheating. I'm a dashing hero who was trying to protect your anonymity, but now I will step in front of it to keep you safe."

"You're really spreading that on a little thick," I said dryly. "Don't you think?"

"It's a story, Stray, and this is Hollywood after all. That's all I'm asking for here. Help me sell the *story*. It'll be a few nights of your life and it'll get your dirty little boots in doors you'd probably never be welcomed through otherwise."

For all the smoothness he'd shown in describing the conditions of our "fake dating," he'd shifted to a far more patronizing note.

"A few nights *is* hours and hours of time that I'd have to spend with you, right?" Because that was already a turnoff. "In addition, I wouldn't be able to work which is lost money."

"I already offered to compensate you," he said, adopting a far more mollifying tone. "I even sent you a deposit to get you to show up to talk to Jerry with me."

"I told you I wasn't for sale."

"You still kept the money," he reminded me.

Arms still folded, I lifted my shoulders. "What you do with your money is none of my business. You dropping it into my bank doesn't win you anything."

"So it would seem," he responded. "While we could continue to argue and debate that, I really am here hat in hand…"

When I glanced at his empty hands and then back up, he gave me an impatient look. Oh, there it was—real irritation in blue eyes even as his nostrils flared. Maybe there was something cracked inside of me because I much preferred this to his attempts to "play nice."

He wasn't nice and I wasn't a fan; he didn't need to play a part.

"With my *metaphorical* hat in hand," he added smoothly. "If you need to be compensated for your time away, then I am more than willing to meet your demands. You negotiated fifty for the NDA and twenty for an appointment you didn't bother to show up for."

I could dispute that point, but I wasn't going to repeat myself.

"Therefore, I would imagine that any evening requiring more than an hour will require commensurate compensation. Let's say twenty-five thousand per instance."

I raised my brows. "More than an hour can mean anything from an hour and five minutes to two days."

"Accepted," he said far too agreeably. "Let's say more than one hour, less than four hours, twenty-five thousand. Additional hours can incur a penalty of one thousand per hour."

"Twenty-five thousand for three hours is eight-thousand three hundred and thirty-three dollars. One thousand per hour is chump change."

Lips pursed, he narrowed his eyes. "Five thousand per additional hour over three, with a proviso to add an additional five thousand if it exceeds three extra hours."

"So if it's an evening that ends up at least six hours, I make thirty thousand atop of the twenty-five thousand?"

A muscle jumped in his cheek. "Additional twenty

thousand. I meant only an extra five thousand, not five thousand extra per hour."

"Oh, damn. That's a deal-breaker. No dice. Have a good evening."

Seven exhaled a hard breath. "Fine, but it will only be three thousand extra per hour. So slightly less than the first three hours, but only a thousand less if it is a *full* extra three hours. If it's two hours and fifty-nine minutes, no deal."

The speed at which he caved to the requests said he really wanted to close this deal.

"You said that the made-up *we're dating* story was only one of two solutions. What's the other one?"

Dipping his chin, Seven studied me for a long moment. The sobriety in his expression stilled any smart-ass remark I'd been considering. Whatever the other choice was, he really *hated* it.

"The other one is Gem steps forward, debunks the stories, and tells everyone it was him and not me. He'll have to do a round of interviews, probably a couple of appearances. One of the late shows, I'd imagine, and maybe a couple of radio shows or podcasts."

I frowned. That seemed overkill to clean up a story about Seven dating me. Then again, killing a blind item or piece of celebrity gossip with the truth was never easy. People preferred the salacious to the sainted.

"It'll put Gem back in the headlines, and it will probably stir up a lot of interest in our previous work, particularly when he was onscreen, and the demands will start to roll in again."

As disinterested in having that attention on Gem as Seven appeared to be, it didn't sound like jealousy or envy. No…

"Gem doesn't want that." It was and wasn't a guess. Gem being aggrieved because people always mistook him for Seven, and being genuinely stunned when I recognized him also spoke volumes.

"No," Seven said. "He doesn't. If I can't convince you, then…I'll eat the damage to my reputation and the deal. I won't like it and I'll probably curse your name, but I'll do it."

I didn't care about him cursing my name so much. The fact he was willing to give up something that seemed to mean a fuck-ton to him for his *brother*?

That mattered.

"So three thousand extra *per* hour in addition to the initial five thousand for each hour after the first three, to be a total of twenty-four thousand. If it's under three hours, then you also prorate by the hour, so it's more for the extra forty-five minutes than twenty minutes."

He frowned but nodded. "However, we will round *down* to the quarters rather than round up unless it's so close it might as well be."

Dickish but acceptable. "If it exceeds six hours?"

"Stray, if it exceeds six hours we are stuck together, trust me, I'll make it worth both of our whiles."

Somehow that didn't comfort me.

"For how long?"

He winced, running a hand over the back of his neck. "Not going to lie, at least through the next premiere and all the press tours coming up." He paused. "Possibly longer."

"It'll keep the attention on the project and your new relationship instead of Clara Belle?" At his nod, I snorted. "Probably earn you some latitude if the film sucks if they like the salacious side better."

His scowl was almost funny. "It doesn't suck."

Too easy to bait. "Uh-huh, so you say. And I have to go to the premiere?"

"Yes," he said, with about as much enthusiasm as I felt. "We don't have to like it. We just have to go."

I snapped my fingers, smirking. "Ah, so it does suck. Got it. This all sounds like I need new clothes."

"I'll take care of all wardrobe costs. I can give you a couple of shops where you can get everything you need, and they'll send me the bill."

Rolling my eyes, I huffed. "They can also leak to the tabloids that you're dressing up your girlfriend." I knew how controlling the story played out.

"Hate the game," he reminded me. "Do we have a deal?"

Did we? It sort of sounded like we did. For Gem if nothing else. "Are you putting all of this in writing?"

Seven grimaced. "I would prefer not to, if it's all the same to you, but if you insist, then we'll make it happen."

"Hmm...I want a deposit. A good faith one. For three dates. So essentially three appearances. I'll put the money in a savings account and not touch it. If everything works out, I'll refund it for whatever the last date is and you only pay me for exactly how many we have. That way if you do something that messes this up, I have the money to help offset some bills."

Dad's electricity was paid and so was his water and garbage. My electric, however, needed a good infusion and I was really not ready to give up that apartment.

"I'll pay you for a full week. We'll call it seven days. You keep it as long as you don't screw this up and throw the story or the narrative. We'll call it a bonus for good behavior."

"Fine. Seven days." I wasn't going to turn down the extra cash. I stuck my hand out and he gripped it. "Deal."

"Good." He pulled out his phone, and a few minutes later mine pinged. I was probably going to end up answering questions about all the money at some point.

My accountant, if no one else, got bitchy about unexplained funds.

He didn't waste any time grabbing his jacket and heading

to the front door. "You'll need to stop seeing Gem and Ollie both. Clean break. No phone calls, no dates. Nothing. This relationship between us needs to be beyond reproach."

"Nope, hard pass," I said, pulling open the door for him. "That's not a part of the deal we just negotiated." His jaw dropped. As much as I wanted to enjoy the expression, I gave him a not-so-gentle nudge and he took a step. "Text me when and where I need to show up, and I'll let you know if I can make it."

I didn't wait for him to agree, just closed the door and leaned back against it. All of my calm fled as my heart raced. I'd just agreed to sell my time for a fuck-load of money to put on a show for the media.

It was official—I'd lost my mind.

chapter
twenty-four

Stella

Despite the intensity of Seven's negotiations, I didn't hear from him for the next four days. Then I woke up to a messenger at the door to my apartment with a fat, white box and two bags as well as a card in a heavy envelope. The card was from Seven and was short and to the point.

Red carpet premiere tonight, party to follow. Will exceed six hours. Deposit will clear your account thirty minutes before I pick you up. Be ready by three.

The neat, clipped strokes of the pen were hard, little slashes. If the way a word was written could convey the emotion beneath it, Seven had definitely mastered the technique. I almost didn't want to see what he sent me to wear, but if he was going to pick me up at three, I would need to start getting ready.

The Portia Levinge Couture gown he sent was legitimately one of the sexiest and most irritating outfits I'd ever worn. First, it fit me like it had been painted on. The body sheath—supported by two thin spaghetti straps—was pure lace and utterly see through.

Lace panels framed the solid strapless black bra and t-backed panties. It literally meant my ass cheeks were going to be on display. As ready as I was to argue against wearing anything like it, I tried it on.

I looked...*really* good. That was without doing my hair or putting on shoes. The unsettling sensation had me vaguely ill. It took me a while to shake off the anxiety, but I was ready to go when Seven showed up.

To my shock, he had a driver with him and he was utterly attentive until we were in the car, then he ignored me all the way to the theater in Hollywood, where the red carpet premiere was going to be.

Press was everywhere, with lights flashing as the stars made the slow walk. "Normally," Seven said as we inched along with the line of other cars dropping off their passengers, "I'd tell you to take one picture with me as we got out and another right at the carpet, then I'd let you go ahead while I paused for the quick questions and photo ops."

Oh, I was going to throw up. There were way more people present than I'd expected even after seeing my share of these from the far side of those velvet ropes. I'd never been a fan of these meat walks. They were there to get attention for the movies and to give the news and stock sites some B-roll.

"That means just stay with me," Seven continued. "I'll keep a hand on you, and if I step away, just stay there, I'll be right back. I don't want you moving into the theater on your own. They'll eat you alive." That last part was muttered under his breath, and I got the feeling he wasn't referring to the press.

I registered every single word while concentrating on even breaths, so I didn't vomit on the spot. I'd rather face Dillon beating the crap out of me again than get out of this car and begin that walk.

This was a terrible idea. The worst. Did I really need the money that much? Fuck. Yes.

There was no more time to think of an escape plan. Seven pushed the door open and climbed out before turning to hold his hand out to me. Keeping a count of my breaths to try and silence the churning wheels of my thoughts, I clasped Seven's hand.

Then we were standing together with his hand on my lower back as he turned us toward the roar of the fans and the paps alike. Cameras flashed, and the only thing that kept them from blinding me was the sun was still up—one nice thing about arriving in daytime. Course, it also meant I was squinting from the sun and trying not to frown as I kept my pace even with Seven's.

"Well, well, look at the pretty little slut!" The voice was all Dillon and full of taunts. As much as I gave a little jerk when I heard it, I didn't turn toward it.

Seven drew me closer when he paused to answer questions. It wasn't until he squeezed my hip that I jerked my attention back to the reporter who looked at me expectantly.

"It's a lot," I admitted aloud. Her smile and nod said that it satisfied whatever question she'd asked. Then we were on to the next and the next. It had only been thirty minutes by the time we stepped into the lobby of the hotel.

"You all right?" he asked in a rough note with a frown, but Seven's manager or agent—whatever—Jerry hurried over to intercept us.

"Stella. Give us a moment," Jerry said to me as he drew Seven away. I hoped I managed to keep a neutral expression in place as people passed. I recognized more than a few of the actors who were here. Before I could get a good look, Seven was back and then we were heading into the theater.

There were little bags on each seat. Swag for those coming to the big premiere. We were seated in the middle with the director on the other side of Seven, along with more actors, family, significant others, and fans. Thankfully, someone bought us drinks and popcorn.

Mine was a sparkling water that Seven opened before he handed it to me. I'd never been so damn grateful to sip the cool, bubbly refreshment. Not that Seven gave me much of a chance to thank him. Then the movie was on and I spent the next two hours and ten minutes being utterly enthralled.

I'd never been a fan of testosterone-overdosed movies with stunts so outlandish it looked like they belonged more solidly in a cartoon than reality. On paper, that's all *Speed Wars* had looked like, but the film was actually...

Not bad.

Humor peppered the script with sharp and witty dialogue. Seven played everything utterly deadpan, not even an ounce of a smile, but it gave him this growly gravitas that was compelling. More than once during the actual high-speed chases and car races, I was holding my breath.

In those scenes, it wasn't Seven behind the wheel—it was Gem. The words from the other night tickled the back of my mind. He'd had to go and crash stuff on set. When there was a particularly brutal accident, I clasped Seven's arm tightly. At some point, he covered my hand with his and then he was holding my hand.

I didn't let up until Seven managed to climb out of the wreckage. Seven and Gem were both fine. When the movie ended with cheers, laughter, and applause, I was pretty blown away.

Then the lights came up, and there were people offering their congratulations. It took a while to weed through all of them, then we were back to the car.

"What did you think?" Seven asked as he loosened his tie. After, he pulled out more water from the cold storage in the back.

"Not really the train wreck I expected," I admitted before taking a long drink of water.

He snorted. "You really don't like my movies, do you, Stray?"

"I—"

His phone rang before I could finish the answer. He held up a hand to me before he answered, then spoke to whomever was on the phone for the rest of the drive. Or it was probably better described as him listening to whomever was on the phone while only giving one- or two-word responses.

Thirty minutes after leaving the theater, we pulled up to a ritzier location in the hills. Security at the gate kept most of the press and fans back. There were a select few photographers getting pictures of arrivals, but it was one or two and then people went right in.

Seven posed with me, one arm around me and a smile on his face. Hopefully my own grin held up and I didn't look like I was being murdered. Then we were at the main doors and inside.

With a glance at his watch, Seven looked at me. "We're leaving at ten fifteen. That's in a little under two hours. Meet me right here."

I blinked. "Are you serious?" He was just going to dump me here while he did...what?

"Yes. What are you going to do?"

I opened my mouth, then closed it. I had no idea what I was supposed to do.

"This is the job, Stray. Don't get confused. We're not on a real date." Then he was striding off to follow the sound of other partygoers.

The last thing I wanted to do was go in there and mingle. The front doors were opening again, and I couldn't really just sit here in the foyer without looking even more suspicious.

A party was in full swing in the huge ballroom, which was visible through the double doors under the main arch made by a pair of dual staircases that circled upward.

Music played. Glasses clinked. There were people dancing. More were laughing. Still more were slipping off to the sides for chats.

Once in the main ballroom, I acquired a glass of wine and downed it like it was a shot. Then I set the empty on another waiter's tray while I stole another. I wound my way slowly through the room. There were canapés and little treats along with the free alcohol.

Seven's costar in the film, Robert Duncan, greeted me easily and motioned me to join him as he took a quick photo with me. Thankfully, someone else wanted to talk to him, so I slipped away without saying a word.

Being on this side of the camera was terrible. I did a sweep of the room. If there was a corner table or something I could go sit at, then I could just drink and eat in peace. There was no solitude or serenity to be found down here. Not with a constant stream of new arrivals.

After finishing another canapé and snagging another drink, I made my way out of the ballroom. The place had appeared to be a large estate when we drove in. Ascending the stairs, I studied the architecture and the art. It gave a faintly French countryside palace or castle vibe. Everything was in cream or gold, and the art seemed even more opulent than the setting.

I wandered away from the music and the crowd. It was truly beautiful. I should have brought my camera. The way the light played in the halls and flickered from the wall sconces just offered so many perfect shadows to study.

There were doors that opened into new sitting rooms and other doors that were closed. The deeper I went, the more interesting the place became. There were large French glass doors that opened to a stone balcony, so I slipped out there.

The cool breeze was welcoming, as was the quiet. A hum from the vehicles arriving and departing drifted over the building, but it wasn't super loud. As it was, I just enjoyed the view and the low stone wall.

This seemed more Venetian than French but I was not complaining. As much as I wanted to linger, I knew I probably shouldn't hang out here. But when I tried to go back inside, the doors were locked.

I backed up to look along the building. The balcony actually stretched along it for several feet. Maybe there was another door.

There were two more sets of double doors. None of them were unlocked. I drained the wineglass, then flattened my hands on the top of the stone wall and looked over the edge. It wasn't that far of a drop to the garden below. I could take the heels off, but I'd probably break an ankle if I landed on the hard stone. I headed for the other end. Maybe there was grass there?

No, but there was scaffolding that had been set against the building. They were replacing some of the siding apparently. Leaving the glass on the railing, I pulled off my shoes. With them stowed in one hand, I swung my legs over and made the short hop to the scaffolding.

It vibrated with my steps more than I liked, and the light was minimal under here. Took me a moment to find a ladder that let me climb down to the next level. There wasn't one to let me go from this midpoint to the ground.

"Fuck," I swore.

"Snow?" The very last voice I expected to hear drifted out of the dark, followed by the man himself stepping under the draping to look up.

"Ollie?" Surprise and delight curved through me. The

alcohol had definitely taken the edge off my nerves. Ollie's presence blunted the irritation at my current predicament.

"At your service," he said with a slow grin. "Have I mentioned how fucking fantastic you look right now?"

I glanced down at myself, then at him. Like Seven, he was also in a suit. "Were you at the premiere?"

"Maybe," he said. "Sometimes I show up, do the perp walk, then head right out the back door."

My mouth fell open. "Seriously?"

"Yep." His grin was all mischievous charm. "Nobody really cares if we watch our own films. So why waste the time?"

"I get that…" Though guilt raked across my belly. "I didn't see you in the movie."

"That's cause I wasn't in it." His grin widened.

"Oh." Relieved, I shook my head. "So you went to the premiere for Seven?"

"Sure," he said with a chuckle. "Let's go with that. Now, you want to tell me what you're doing up there?"

I sighed. "I got stuck on the balcony. I went out to look but the doors were all locked and no one else was up there. So then I saw this…" I waved to the scaffolding. "But apparently there's no ladder down to the ground."

"Probably put away to keep kids from getting into trouble."

Oh. Yeah, that made sense.

"Come on, Snow," he said, moving to be just below me. "Drop. I'll catch you."

It wasn't that far, but still. I frowned.

"Trust me," he practically crooned. "I won't let you get hurt."

I glanced at my shoes and then dropped them. He caught them easier than I expected and then set them aside.

"Good girl. Now come to Daddy."

I made a face. "Ew. Don't call yourself that."

"Fine, I'll let you call me that." The blatant, bold-as-fuck come-on made me laugh.

"I am *not* calling you that, either." Still, I was laughing as I eased out between the bars that served a rail on the scaffolding. I was going to have to dangle and then drop.

"It's always an option if you change your mind," he said from directly below me. "Also, I'm really loving the lingerie choice. That ass is far too nice to cover up."

Shooting a look over my shoulder, I raised my eyebrows. "Stop staring at my ass."

"Come on down and I promise I'll stare at everything else with the same focus."

The man was utterly incorrigible.

Utterly.

Blowing out a breath, I just trusted that I had enough alcohol to not tense up too much when I fell. That would help reduce broken bones, right?

"You can do it, Snow," Ollie said. "Jump."

I pushed away from the railing and let go. The fall seemed forever but also like it was over in a split second.

He caught me easily and I found myself chest to breast and his lips right there.

"Gotcha," he whispered. Then he slanted his mouth over mine. His lips were cool, almost chilly, but they warmed as he teased my mouth open. The strokes of his tongue were firm and sweeping. The demand heating up the contact. He tasted like beer, nuts, and I could have sworn garlic bread.

My stomach growled as he deepened the kiss, and I wrapped my arms around his neck. It was my turn to chase his tongue. I savored every little delicious sample he gave me.

"Hungry?" he asked in between nipping kisses before he laved his tongue over my lower lip.

"Starving," I whispered.

For a lot more than just garlic cheesy bread.

His eyes were hot when he leaned back a little to lock gazes with me. "How starving?" The layers beneath that question unfurled fresh waves of heat in my system. Ollie was so hard against me and his arms so tight that I could feel every inch of him, clothes or not.

I got the double entendre in the question. Got it, embraced it, and answered both parts. "Desperate."

"I know you came with Seven," he said in a rough voice. "But do you want to get out of here?"

It was that or climb Ollie right here and right now.

"Yes," I said. I didn't want to think about all the whys and why nots. "He got his pictures at the premiere and out front."

"Yeah," Ollie said slowly. "Cool. I know a quiet way out of here and I can have a driver scoop us up away from the press, then drop us at my car." That was a lot of moving parts, but it sounded like a plan to me.

"Should we tell Seven?" I mean, he was paying me to be here, but if I left early, well, it would save him some money. That was just good business sense.

He dipped to grab my shoes without ever putting me down. "Fuck Sev," he said, then we were striding through the garden and away from the house.

Okay, there was something sexy as hell about Ollie taking charge like this.

To be fair, I really was hungry for garlic cheesy bread *and* Ollie.

chapter
twenty-five

Gemini

I checked the time on my way to the kitchen. Another hour or so and Seven would be done with that first appearance. Stella had texted earlier to tell me she was going to be with him for the evening.

Guilt assaulted me, particularly when she assured me that it was only a few hours and she would message me the moment she got home. As grateful as I was that Seven was not asking me to take it on the chin with the press, I really hated that it meant Slick was getting dragged into the middle of it all.

This was way more than she'd asked for, selling that one blurred photo of us. But here we were, and the best I could do was make up the time spent with my brother, since he was such a dick where she was concerned.

The alarm panel let me know the gate had opened while I was checking the fridge. The housekeeper often put meals in here we could reheat easily. This was great when one of us was on a specific diet for a role. Tonight it would do in a pinch, but I shut the door to check the cameras.

It was a little too early for Seven to be back, but if he was, then maybe I could head over to Stella's and take her out for real food. The car coming up the drive, however, was not Seven's or his driver.

It was Ollie.

That made sense. He usually skipped out on most premieres, particularly if he didn't have to do press after. That meant we still needed to figure out food. I diverted back to the kitchen, unsurprised when the door to the garage opened up to let Ollie in.

"Hey, I was just thinking," I said, as I turned, only to blink as Stella drifted in dressed in... Wow. I almost swallowed my tongue. Flushed cheeks and lazy smile in place, she prowled through the kitchen, making a beeline toward me.

"Gem," she said with only a bit of slurring. "I didn't know you were going to be here."

"Hey, Slick." The lace dress left nothing to the imagination; her bra and panties were obscured, but they also highlighted her curves. "You look downright edible."

"She does," Ollie said drolly. "Doesn't she?"

When Stella wrapped her arms around me, I looped mine around her waist. Her pupils were definitely dilated and the color was high in her cheeks. "Are you drunk?"

"No," she answered immediately, then paused to hold her thumb and forefinger together. "Okay, maybe a little. But in my defense, there was a lot of wine and champagne—big glasses —and very few canapes. Like micro-crackers."

Her wrinkled nose was adorable. Ollie's indulgent smile was also hard to miss. "So you let Ollie snake you away from Sev?"

She waved her hand in a dismissive gesture. "Seven dumped me as soon as we were inside. He left me instructions for what time to meet him at the door and then he disappeared."

"Sounds like Sev," I admitted.

"I don't really like him," she told me. "You are the much better twin."

Ollie snickered, and when I shot him a dirty look, he didn't even pretend to be contrite.

"I appreciate that, but why don't we get you some water and some food?" I'd deal with my brother later. He wasn't going to use her as a beard if he couldn't look after her.

"Food is probably a good idea," Ollie said. "I was going to stop somewhere on the way home, but she's a lot drunker than I realized."

I could see that.

"Okay, Slick, let's—"

"Gem," she said before I could finish. She cupped a hand around my nape, and I tilted my head to meet her gaze. "I kissed Ollie."

"Wait—"

"Or maybe he kissed me. It could have been that he kissed me. I jumped off the scaffold and he caught me. Then I think I kissed him. Yeah, I'm pretty sure it was me kissing him." Ollie had gone dead still at her pronouncement and I speared him with a stare. "Anyway," Stella continued and blinked up at me. "I kissed him and I liked it."

"I see," I said slowly, not entirely sure where to go with this. Ollie hitting on my girl hadn't escaped me, but she'd pretty much dodged him and now...? "Do you want to kiss him again?"

Yeah, the dick in question perked right up as he leaned against the counter and stared at her.

Stella tilted her head, stroking her fingers up and down my nape, just caressing the skin. It felt damn good and was really distracting too.

"Yes," she said after a beat. "I kind of do. But I want to kiss you again too." Then as if to prove her point, she tugged me and pushed upward at the same time.

Her mouth was hot and fierce under mine. Falling into a kiss with Slick had rapidly become one of my favorite things. Those silky, kittenish licks could drive a man insane, but I'd also felt that tongue on my cock. She'd been made to drive me crazy.

"What do you think?" she whispered against my mouth, her body one slow, sensuous rub against mine. "Could we maybe do a threesome? I've always wondered what that would be like."

A threesome?

My brain short-circuited for a moment as I drowned in her drugging kiss.

"Hold up," Ollie announced loud enough to puncture the moment. "Time-out."

He tugged her right out of my arms and turned her to face him.

"Hey—"

"Wait," he said to me, before he locked his gaze on Slick. "Eyes on me, Snow."

"Oh, why do you keep calling me Snow?" She sounded so put upon. "I am not an ice queen."

"Completely the last place I was going with that," he told her. "You are hotter than hell, Snow. Don't mistake the name for anything other than admiration."

"Really?" I demanded as I stared at him, and he gave me a careless shrug before focusing on her again.

"Oh. Okay, so you want to kiss me, then?" She was all playful and soft and cuddly—it was enough to make me want to punch our best friend and steal my girl away before she tried to kiss him or he kissed her again.

"Yes," he said, but stopped her dead with a finger to her

lips as she strained up to meet him for another burning connection. "But we're not doing any of that until we get you hydrated and food in your stomach."

"Aww." The complaint was almost adorable and a huff of laughter escaped me at the sound.

She twisted to look at me.

"You'll kiss me, right, Gem?"

"Absolutely, Slick," I said, holding out a hand. She pulled away from Ollie and came right to me. There was something infinitely empowering about having her focus all that passion on me. "But Ollie's right. You should probably eat and hydrate. I don't want you hungover or regretting your choices in the morning."

"I'm not really hungry," she said. "And I feel good right now... I mean hot. I should probably take this dress off. It's not like it covers much."

She was going to be the death of me. "We can get you a change of clothes *after* you eat. Come on. Let's get you some water. Ollie will cook."

"Fine, then can we kiss and have a threesome?" The forlorn pout in her voice was equal parts cute and irritating, especially when she looked up at me so hopefully. Apparently she was intent on killing me.

"First we're doing food, and yes, I can absolutely make you something," Ollie said, already rolling up his sleeves. "And so we're perfectly clear, Snow, I am not saying no."

It was my turn to glare as I coaxed her over to the table. "Are you insane?"

"Nope," Ollie told me. "In fact, I'm a damn saint because she is absolutely delectable at the moment, and she ground up against me when I caught her. I could have fucked her in the car and I think we'd have both enjoyed it, but I brought her home, where both of us can be here. Because I'm not an asshole."

While he spoke, he opened the fridge and retrieved one of the large bottles of water before he carried it over to us. Stella had slid off her shoes and tugged the dress up some so she could sit. The lace seemed to be bugging her.

Her legs didn't quit.

"Drink," he ordered her and set the bottle on the table in front of her.

"You're bossy," she retorted, those green eyes of hers filled with a bewitching twinkle.

"I've heard that before." Then he shifted his stare to me. "In fact, I need to steal Gem from you for a minute, Snow."

"Hmm." She hummed a little sound before she propped her chin in her hand and wrapped her free hand around the water bottle. "You can *borrow* him, but I want him back."

There was something altogether possessive in her voice, and I, for one, thrilled to hear it from her. "I'll be right back, Slick. I promise."

"Good." She gave us a wide smile. "I'll be right here where I can see you both. Think you can give me something fun to watch?"

"I'll think about it." I chuckled in spite of myself and then followed Ollie toward the fridge. He was pulling out everything he would need to make breakfast.

That would be fast.

"Pancakes or waffles, Snow?" he called over to her.

"Surprise me," she said, her smile easy and open.

"What are you doing?" I asked Ollie and he paused to stare at me.

"I'm making her food, then we're going to feed her, and after we sober her up, we're going to see if she was at all serious about that threesome request."

Irritation flamed through me and I glanced back at Slick where she gave me a little wave.

"I guess the question, then," Ollie continued, "is what are you going to do?"

"I don't know," I admitted. It wasn't the first time we'd shared a girl. Though the last time it hadn't been simultaneously. "Ollie...she's important to me."

"I know she is," he said, turning to face me with eggs in hand. "I like her too."

Fuck.

What the hell did I say to that?

It took about twenty minutes, but we loaded the table with waffles, fried eggs, bacon, and sausage. He'd fried up a storm. Thankfully, Slick dug right in, and while she was still flushed and relaxed, she didn't seem quite so far gone.

Ollie tracked every bite she took, and I had to admit so was I. When she finished, I got up to make us all some coffee. It was getting late and she'd definitely sobered up somewhat.

"Tell you what, guys, let's have the coffee, and give ourselves a bit of time to digest and then we can go swimming," Ollie suggested.

I shot him a look but he had his gaze firmly on Slick.

"You just want to get me to agree to skinny-dip," she countered. "And we are one and one, game wise, so you're going to have to beat me at one more game if that's what you want."

My dick went hard at the husky note in her voice. "You really like betting don't you?"

She grinned at me. "I really enjoyed our bet."

So had I.

Ollie rose. "Come on, Snow."

"Where are we going?"

"We're going to play that last game, but don't get

comfortable. I plan to win and then we're skinny-dipping." He strolled out of the kitchen, but Slick didn't follow—she glanced at me.

"It's okay," I said and surprisingly, it really was. "If you want to find out...I'm in."

Once I committed, I meant it. The way she licked her lips made me feel damn good about that decision too.

"You sure?" she whispered, and it wasn't distrust in her voice. She wanted to reassure herself and I was important enough that my opinion mattered.

"I'm very sure," I promised. "You aren't losing me, Slick. No matter what."

Her grin was all sunshine. "Guess we need to find out if I'm losing that game of pool."

"Let's go, Snow. Get that gorgeous ass out here."

She bit her lower lip. "Are you in if I cheat?"

"Depends," I said slowly. "How are you planning to cheat?"

She rose to her feet and then she peeled that lace dress up and off, leaving her in the strapless black bra and the black thong. Fuck me, she was beautiful.

"Like this," she said, then sauntered toward the living room.

"Oh, he is so screwed," I said under my breath. Then again, so was I, and I was pretty fucking happy right here.

chapter
twenty-six

Stella

Okay in all fairness, I had to agree I was pretty drunk when Ollie saved me from the scaffolding at the party. Sure, at the time, I thought I was just a little tipsy, but once I had sobered back up to *actually* tipsy, I realized the difference.

Thankfully, neither Ollie nor Gem had been put off by my drunken proposition. Instead they'd taken it in their stride, with Ollie going into full food-Dom mode. That's what I'd started calling his overbearing concern for my meals. Food Dominant. Surely there was a proper name for his fixation somewhere out there, but this worked in my brain.

I totally threw the game of pool. Barely even tried. Why? Because I wanted to go skinny-dipping, damn it! Until, of course, we headed out to their backyard and a breeze made me shiver.

"You said it was heated, right?" I asked Ollie, hesitating as I eyed the water. Then again, the intruder who'd broken in had enjoyed herself swimming laps in the nude, so maybe it was warmer than it looked.

Ollie just grinned, stripping down to his boxer shorts. These didn't have a comical elephant trunk, but they *were* grey, so I'd allow it. Elephant Ollie leaned in close, gripping the back of my neck and crushing his mouth against mine in a kiss that was over far too quickly.

"Jump in and find out, Snow." He kissed me again, then dropped his boxers and executed a perfect backward dive into the pool, splashing me with admittedly not-freezing water.

Gem waggled his brows at me, silently daring me to back out, and I bit my lip. This was about more than just skinny-dipping in their pool; it was a whole metaphor for what I was diving into with the two of them...together...and how it was going to ultimately play out with my business arrangement with Seven. Shit, this was a whole fucking mess.

Swallowing hard, I averted my eyes for fear of losing my nerve, shimmied out of my underwear, and dove straight in the deep end.

The water was not *hot* but it also wasn't cold enough to shock me. Immediately when I resurfaced, my eyes stung and I regretted how dramatic that pool entry had been with how much makeup I was wearing.

"You coming in?" I called to Gem, trying to wipe the streaking mascara from underneath my eyes without looking like an idiot.

"You okay?" he fired back, sitting on the side of the pool with his legs dangling in the water. He dragged his T-shirt over his head and held it out to me. "Here, use this. Your wet hands are only making it worse."

Trying to squint in an attempt to save my eyeballs, I swam over and accepted his dry T-shirt to clean up my face as best I could from inside the pool. It probably left me looking like I was cosplaying Heath Ledger's Joker but...whatever. Take me as I am and all that.

"Damn, Snow, you never heard of waterproof mascara?" Ollie teased, swimming over to me with lazy strokes, his dark hair slicked back. Fuck, he was stunning. It was no wonder he'd made it so big in show biz.

I splashed him as he approached. "Ha-ha, funny guy. I wasn't planning on swimming when I got ready for a fucking movie premiere."

He ducked under the water to dodge my splashes, then grabbed me around the waist and made me yelp with surprise. He pulled me under, my legs automatically wrapping around him as his mouth found mine and we sank lower. Somehow we managed to avoid drowning as our tongues danced together, and I nearly forgot where we were until my lungs started to burn.

Breaking away from his kiss, I pushed away and swam for the surface to grab some oxygen.

"Holy fuck," I gasped, panting as I looked around for Ollie. He took way too long, and when his dark head finally broke the surface, I gusted a heavy sigh of relief.

"Show off," Gem called, still seated on the side of the pool in his underwear as he sipped a beer. Music played from some outdoor speakers and a soft glow of deep green light now illuminated the pool, whereas it'd been dark when I jumped in. Gem must have had the controls on his phone; otherwise, that was really coincidental timing. "Ollie had to learn how to hold his breath for ages while filming *ScubaMan* a few years back."

That made sense. I loved that movie but not for the plot. Mainly for the fact Ollie was half-naked and dripping wet for 80 percent of the scenes, which in turn had me—and plenty of other female viewers—dripping wet as well.

"Are you coming to join us, Gem?" I asked, swimming back over to him and bracing my hands on his knees to pull myself up out of the water. It totally exposed my breasts to him, and his pupils blew wide as he took in the view. Then he obliged my silent request, cupping the back of my neck and kissing me deeply.

I moaned as his teeth tugged my lower lip and his thumb pressed under my jawbone to tilt my head back more. It made me melt into him, letting his legs cage me in against the side of the pool. The water swirled and gently lapped the tiles, then Ollie's hands rested on my hips as he swam up behind me.

"I could definitely get used to using the pool like this," Ollie murmured in my ear as he pressed in close, his hard length brushing my ass. His *huge elephant trunk*, I should say. The water was shallow enough that he could stand—just—but too deep for me, so I had to rely on Gem's grip to hold me above the water. Not that he was letting go anytime soon, with how firm his grip was on my neck.

Gem's other hand found one of my breasts, and I whimpered into his kisses as he tweaked my hard nipple. Fucking hell, this was *not* how I'd thought my night would play out when Seven ditched me at the after-party. I wasn't mad about it, though. Not at all.

Ollie kissed my neck, his hand slipping around from my hip to dip between my legs, and I parted them eagerly for him. We didn't need to play at being coy here—they both knew what I wanted. He groaned as his fingers dipped into me, and I gasped against Gem's mouth.

"Holy shit, Snow," Ollie whispered in a husky voice as he found my clit and started toying with it, aided by the pool water. He crushed in closer, his erection griding against my ass like a fucking tease...or a promise.

Gem swiped his tongue over my lips then, withdrew just far enough to whisper. "If you change your mind..."

"I won't," I replied, already damn near shaking with desire. Ollie's fingers pushed deeper, and I rocked back onto his hand, hungry for more. "Pinky promise." I held up my hand, pinky finger extended, and Gem chuckled, releasing my breast to link pinkies with me.

"All right, in that case…" He unlinked our pinky fingers, then tugged the waistband of his boxer briefs down just enough to free his hard cock. "I want your mouth on me, Slick." His hand on my neck guided my face closer, and I eagerly stuck out my tongue to lick his hot tip.

Gem moaned at the contact, and it was one of the sexiest sounds ever, making me clench around Ollie's fingers inside me.

"What was it you said, Gem? I love meat." Then I closed my lips around him and surged forward to take as much of his dick inside my mouth and throat as possible.

A strangled curse escaped him, and Ollie crushed me in tighter against the wall of the pool as he thrust his fingers harder. Rough, stubble-scratchy kisses decorated my shoulder and neck as he pumped his hand, and I gagged on Gem's cock. Fuck, he was bigger than I remembered—not that it was a bad thing but I did need to grip his base with one hand for stability.

Gem's hips rocked, thrusting ever so slightly into my mouth as his fingers tangled in my wet hair. I did my best to take him deep, my cheeks hollowing as I sucked and my tongue tracing the ridges of his veins as I committed them to memory.

Meanwhile Ollie's thick shaft had slipped between my cheeks and he was griding in the most excruciatingly teasing way. He was doing a fucking good job with his fingers—I could easily come at any moment already—but I wanted more. If we were having a three-way, I didn't want us to cut corners.

I tried to arch my back, pushing back against him with invitation while my mouth was otherwise occupied, but he just fingered me harder as his teeth indented my shoulder.

Shit.

Keeping my fist around Gem's dick, I popped my mouth clear and turned my head to meet Ollie's dark gaze. "I need your dick inside me, Ollie. I don't wanna come unless it's on your cock."

His pupils blew wide and he licked his lips. "I don't have a condom, Snow, and we're in the pool."

Fuck. Those were very logical explanations. But... "Just pull out and come on my back then. Please, Ollie, I need—"

My words cut off as Gem fisted my hair and slammed his cock back into my mouth so hard I gagged again. His musical laughter that followed prevented me from being mad about it —even more so when Ollie swapped out his fingers for the broad tip of his cock a moment later.

I moaned around Gem's girth as Ollie gripped my hips tight and pushed into my tight cunt slowly and carefully, savoring every millimeter.

"Shit, Slick," Gem groaned as he rocked up into my mouth again. "You're a natural."

"So fucking tight," Ollie groaned, his fingers digging deeply into the flesh of my hips. "I haven't been bare in a chick's pussy in...forever. Holy crap, Snow, I could get used to this."

I couldn't reply, but I wholeheartedly agreed with getting used to this. My pussy was *full* thanks to Ollie's incredible size. He really wasn't exaggerating with those elephant-trunk boxer shorts. And Gem's thick cock filled my mouth so much, my lips and jaw already ached. The way his abs flexed as he rocked into me was crazy sexy, though, so I was in no hurry to finish him.

My back arched more as I pushed back on Ollie, making him thrust harder and causing the water to splash around us with the movement. There was no holding back when my orgasm stole through my body, building to almost painful levels before crashing so hard, I needed to gasp for air. Except, of course, all I managed was to open my throat wider for Gem's next thrust and then I choked.

Choking while coming was a new experience…and not a bad one, weirdly.

"*Fuck*," Ollie moaned, kissing the side of my throat as my pussy gripped him like a vise, his breathing heavy. "Fuck, Snow, I can't hold out." He thrust hard a couple of times, pushing me farther into Gem's lap before swiftly pulling out and blowing his load on my butt cheeks and lower back. That part of me was still underwater, though, so all I got was a quick burst of warmth before the pool water washed it off.

Gasping, Ollie shifted his grip to my tits, one in each huge hand as he all but lifted my mouth off Gem's cock. His embrace pulled me back into the water, just in time for Gem's release to shoot all over my face.

Luckily, I closed my eyes right at the last moment and avoided *that* painful experience, taking it on my cheeks, chin, and lips.

"Oh my god," Gem panted, a hint of amusement coloring his voice, and I grinned wide, then licked my lips to catch a thick load of his salty cum on my tongue. "*Shit, Slick…*"

Laughing, I slithered out of Ollie's grip and ducked my head under the water to wash off my face before I ended up with an eye infection. Fucking in the pool definitely had its benefits, that was for sure.

When I resurfaced, swiping my hands over my face and hair, I wondered for a moment whether the intensity of my climax had given me double vision. Gem seemed to be in two places at once.

"Oh crap," I muttered a split second later, when Seven swung his furious glare my way.

His eyes narrowed. "Oh crap is fucking right. We need to

talk, and I would prefer to do it when you're fully clothed, Stray. I'll wait in the library."

I scoffed a slightly unhinged laugh, shaking my head. "No thanks. I'm quite comfy as I am."

His brows hitched and he folded his arms across his chest. He'd ditched the jacket at some point, and his shirtsleeves were rolled up in a stupidly sexy way. It wasn't fair that he looked so much like Gem...because now I was staring at his slacks and wondering just *how* identical they were.

"Okay, then. I'll wait right here. Get out." His glare was heavy and a little bit heated as he planted his feet and watched me, unblinking, as I floated in the pool.

"That's enough, Sev," Gem said, intervening as he grabbed a stack of towels from one of the loungers. "Fuck off. Seeing Slick naked is *not* in your budget."

"Seconded," Ollie agreed, hopping out of the water totally naked and seemingly unbothered by that fact. "This is a private party, bro. Invite only. Snow, did you invite Seven?"

I swiped my tongue over my lips, letting that scenario play out in my head for a moment. "Nope, I sure did not."

Seven's brow dipped in a scowl. "We had an arrangement, and you—"

"Save it," Gem snapped, tossing a towel to Ollie and giving Seven a shove in the direction of the house. "This isn't appropriate."

I thought for sure Seven was going to stand his ground and argue, but after a couple of moments sharing eye contact with his twin, he jerked a short nod and stalked back into the house.

Once he was gone, I let out a long breath and let myself sink back beneath the water. What I would give to grow some gills and never return to the surface...

chapter
twenty-seven

Stella

Much to my disappointment, I did have to eventually resurface for air, but Gem was right there waiting with a dry towel. He wrapped me up like a human burrito, then tossed me over his shoulder while I cracked up laughing at the absurdity of it all.

My wet hair hung down over my face, so I didn't catch sight of Demon Spawn as Gem carried me upstairs to his bedroom where he laid me out on his bed and proceeded to eat my pussy like a starving man while my arms remained trapped in the towel prison.

When I came, I bit my lip to keep from being too loud, but Gem wasn't satisfied.

"Try again, Slick," he growled, then bit my inner thigh hard enough to make me yelp. "This time scream my name."

I was nothing if not obedient—at least as far as Gem was concerned, anyway. And when he was willing to put in the work...

"*Oh, uh! Gem!*" I screamed it this time. "Yes! Gem! Don't fucking stop!"

Apparently, I wasn't the only obedient one.

He let up on me after my second climax tailed off,

chuckling smugly to himself as he licked his lips—and mine—to clean up, then helped me untangle from the towel. The man was a god; he carried me right into the shower with him and rinsed us both off before toweling me down and setting me on the bed again.

"I'll grab you some clothes," he murmured, disappearing into his massive walk-in closet while I lay boneless and more than satisfied on his bed.

He returned with a T-shirt and a pair of boxer shorts, which were both designer label and felt incredible against my skin. Better still, they smelled like him.

"Jealous," Ollie muttered with a pout as we returned back downstairs with flushed faces and easy smiles. "Remind me to hold the towels next time."

"Next time?" Seven barked, already pacing a hole in the floor in front of the bar. "There won't be a next time. Do you have no concept of the agreement we made, Stella? Do you seriously not fucking comprehend the fact that you arriving at a party with me and the leaving with *him*"—he jerked a thumb in Ollie's direction—"could completely fuck the story we only just started to craft?"

"How do you know it was him?" Gem asked, flopping down on the sofa with zero fucks about Seven's rant. "Could have been me. I do love to rescue a damsel myself. And if it was me, then no one would be any the wiser..."

Seven glared daggers. "It wasn't."

"Chill out, Sev," Ollie added. "No one saw us, and what happens in the privacy of our own home is also no one's business. Not even yours, funnily enough."

"It *is* my business because I'm literally paying the stray by the damn hour for her time and you two are out there playing hide the pickle in our pool. Which, by the fucking way, I expect you to sanitize before the morning because I do not need to swim in a pool of your semen."

Ollie and Gem exchanged a long look, while I wrinkled my nose. "Pickle is a bit inaccurate, isn't it?" I muttered, mostly to myself. "Cucumber is closer to reality. Or a zucchini? One of those ones they grow for farmers markets and shit, where they win prizes for their enormous…um…vegetables."

"Technically I believe the Langelang Giant Cucumber is sliced to make pickles so he's not totally wrong," Ollie offered thoughtfully, making me grin. "And those can grow up to twelve inches long." Then he winked, and my pussy throbbed. Crap, I had it *bad* for Olivier Griffiths.

"Would you two shut the fuck up about vegetables?" Seven exploded, throwing his hands in the air, his face red with anger.

I squinted at him, pursing my lips. "You must be a carnivore. This hatred toward vegetables isn't necessary, Spawn. They never did anything to hurt you."

Gem snickered, grinning like he was really enjoying himself as he extended a hand to me. Before I could take it, Ollie grabbed me around the waist and sat the both of us down in an oversized armchair together.

"There was that one time with the carrot—" Gem started to say with a sly look.

"Shut the fuck up, Gemini," Seven hissed.

My lips parted with a question burning the tip of my tongue, but Ollie squeezed my hip, silently telling me not to ask. Well, fuck, now I was extra curious what'd happened with the carrot.

"You," Seven said, redirecting the conversation back to me, "need to explain why the fuck you thought it was okay to just *disappear* from a party where you knew no one and had no mode of transport."

I tilted my head, eyeing him with curiosity. "Were you worried?"

His face darkened and he spluttered. "Absolutely not. Why the fuck would I worry? But our agreement—"

"Was done. I attended the premiere, arrived at the party, posed for pictures. You ditched me, remember? *This isn't a date, Stray*. Ring any bells? The way I figured, we were done for the night. Don't worry. I won't charge past nine."

His jaw tensed, the muscle of his cheek twitching. "That's not the point."

"Spell it out for me, Demon Spawn. What exactly *is* the point you're trying to make? Because I had a whole bucket load to drink as well as several orgasms, so I'm *tired*. Hurry up and say what you wanna say so I can go home."

Ollie's arms tightened around me when I said that, like he didn't want to let me go home. As tempting as it was to propose a sleepover, that was taking things far too quick for my liking. Threesomes? Fine. Sleepovers? Whoa, baby, pump the breaks.

Seven glared at me for the longest time, then folded his arms once more. "We can discuss it when you're of clearer mind. There's no point trying to talk sense when you're so obviously intoxicated."

The way he said it was so incredibly condescending, there was no way he wasn't trying to pick a fight. Like he was deliberately pushing buttons to see what might blow up.

Well, sucks to suck because I was more than fine with that decision.

"Okay, suits me," I said with a yawn. "Can one of you boys drop me home? My date unfortunately lost his manners somewhere along Sunset Boulevard and I seem to be stranded."

Ollie chuckled and Gem grinned, while Seven seemed to have steam coming out his ears.

"I'll drive you," Gem offered, already getting to his feet. "Ollie has to be up for an eight a.m. press junket."

Ollie groaned, hugging me against him as he buried his face in my wet hair. "Not fair," he complained, but reluctantly let me go when Gem offered me his hand.

"This conversation isn't over, Stray," Seven called after us, like it was his one last effort to pick a fight.

I snorted a laugh. "Try harder, loser. I'm way too high on dopamine right now."

The amusement carried me all the way out to the garage, where Gem led me over to a modest little Honda Civic. As he opened the passenger door, he said, "I don't like to get noticed."

An unfamiliar affection rippled through me. "You also don't have dick envy," I murmured, pushing up on my toes to nuzzle a kiss to his jaw. "So I like it."

His snort of laughter was real, and I loved the way he seemed to light up. "What am I going to do with you, Slick?"

I winked as I climbed into the offered passenger seat. "Apparently, pretty much whatever you want. Why? Am I boring you?"

"Not a chance in hell," he promised, then shut the door before he circled to the driver's side. When he held out his hand again, I set mine in his. He didn't move so much as dip his head to kiss my knuckles, then he locked eyes with me.

"Address?"

There was a downbeat and an upbeat before laughter rippled out of me.

"You mean you haven't snuck it into your phone already?" Ollie had. Seven had. But Gem? We'd talked a lot and met elsewhere; he hadn't come to my apartment. Not yet.

"Might need to up my stalking game," Gem said, stroking his thumb along the side of my hand. "Or it could be I am savoring the fact that my girl keeps coming back to me and there's a reward in being the one who is found."

"Synchronicity?"

"They made a movie about it," he reminded me with a wink.

Yes, yes they had.

"Right, well, I like cheating—as you might have noticed earlier."

"I like cheating too," he told me with a grin and then handed me his phone. It was unlocked and the name of my contact was Slick.

Grinning, I typed the address in with my thumbs and then passed it back. "Tag," I told him. "You're it."

It was in this happy, dopamine-infused bubble that we drove to my place. It was just nice to hold hands, listen to the radio, and enjoy the night driving. Not that we got a lot of open driving, as the traffic grew thicker the closer we got to my place.

Instead of dropping me off, which I expected, he parked and climbed out. After opening my door, he reached a hand out to help me up. Wearing only the pair of pool slides Gem had given me in place of my stilettos when we left his place, I was acutely aware of how tall he was.

"I can walk to the door on my own." I was more than used to seeing myself inside. The nice thing about my apartment was we had access to garages that were a separate rental fee. Mine wasn't right next to the apartment, but it did mean that I didn't have to worry about the Bel Air while out. That or my bike.

"I know," he said. "Just like the idea of making sure you get in safe and sound. Indulge me?"

I made a big show of thinking about it as he closed the door and slipped an arm around me before settling his hand on my waist. "I suppose," I said. "But who will walk you back to the car?"

"You could do that," he said, eyes twinkling as we crossed the lot toward the breezeway to my place. "Then I'd have to make sure you got back to your apartment."

"Oh no," I said, exhaling a mighty sigh. "We'll be forever trapped in a loop unless you stay with me!"

"*Or*," he said, stressing the single syllable, "you come back home with me. I have a very big bedroom, and you slept very well the last time you stayed."

It was near impossible to suppress my smile. Before I could respond though, Gem's smile fled and his eyes narrowed as he looked ahead. I turned, frowning.

My front door was open.

"Oh, man..." There'd been break-ins a few months earlier, but I thought they'd caught those guys.

"Wait," Gem said, tightening his arm around me. "Let me go first." Without waiting for agreement, he tucked me behind him and headed for the door. Once there, he nudged it inward with a booted foot.

Inside it was...just destroyed. The sofa was torn up, every cushion shredded. Stuffing hung from everything. Broken glass decorated the floor. The hard shells of books were open, their pages ripped out and scattered. The television had a huge hole in it.

The smell of cat urine and worse seemed to just waft out of there. Splashes of paint were on the walls, the carpet. The little wooden card table I'd saved from a dumpster in college, then sanded to a new color was in literal pieces.

Everywhere I looked, there was destruction. The photo prints Dad had framed for me when I moved in as a housewarming present were broken, the prints sliced and more. My stomach fell away like I'd just taken a tumble off a cliff.

A scuff of shoe against pavement had me twisting, and Gem with me. Dillon strolled around the corner, his dark eyes alight with a kind of malicious glee that his thin, fake smile couldn't mask.

"Oh, that looks terrible," he said, pausing to glance past us into my apartment. His smirk faltered only briefly when he looked at Gem. Dillon definitely wasn't happy to see him, but then he turned that unfriendly gaze back my way. "Must have really pissed off the wrong people this time."

"Why don't you fuck off?" Gem said, his expression tightening.

"Hey, man," Dillon said, raising his hands as if in surrender. "Just saying...looks bad. You know what she does for a living right? Your actor boyfriend does know, doesn't he?"

"I think you misheard," Gem stated, taking a step forward. "I said fuck off before I make you fuck off."

"I'm out." He just kept right on smirking as he backed up and then he turned left.

"You know that asshole?" Gem asked, pulling his phone out as he glanced from me to the door to where Dillon had gone.

"Unfortunately... Oh, the dark room." That reality sank in and I hurried in, avoiding Gem trying to snag my arm. My new camera and equipment was all secured in the new camera safe in the car, in the garage that was also locked. I also used mostly digital for pap shots.

The dark room was just for me...

The door of the second bedroom that I'd converted was off its hinges and the smell of the chemicals was eye-wateringly bad. I'd almost missed it in the other room because of the urine smell, but in the hall, it was impossible to miss.

So much wasted film. Canisters ripped open and exposed. Images torn up and shredded. Everything had been overturned or broken. Glass was everywhere. The chances of recovering anything were slim to none.

"I'm sorry, Slick. Come on," Gem said, tugging me with him. The brief look I got in my bedroom said that room had fared the worst of all of it. My clothes were also part of the mass destruction, along with the bed, the pillows, and everything.

"This is Gemini Harrison. I need to report a break-in, burglary, and destruction of property." He kept talking, and it gradually sank in that he was calling the cops. When the call ended, he pulled me against him, where we stood in the courtyard outside the apartment. "I need to make a couple more calls, then you're going home with me."

"Gem..."

"No," he said, shaking his head. His grim expression and firm tone allowed for no argument. "Someone broke into your place and did that." His phone buzzed and he swore. When he showed me the screen, I wanted to swear too.

Get the Inside Scoop on Seven Harrison's new mystery woman, celebrity photographer Stella Charles...

"Oh my god."

"We're going to take care of this," Gem said. "We're going to take care of everything."

Dillon had something to do with this. He had to have.

Right?

chapter
twenty-eight

Olivier

"You know what's at stake," Seven said, arms folded as he glared at me. "Still you showed up to, what? Bring her home to just get laid? What happened to bro code?"

I'd grabbed a shower and a change of clothes. Now I was attempting to relax before I crashed. I did have a junket the next day, and I wasn't remotely interested in any of it, not when I was waiting for confirmation that Stella was home safe and sound. My glance at the phone went unrewarded.

Knowing my luck, Gem was just going to spend the night there. Lucky bastard. I'd be stuck here with Sev and his bitching.

"Are you even listening to me?" Seven demanded.

"You're going to have a heart attack before forty if you don't find some Zen." I decided to get a drink if I had to listen to him bitch much longer. "No one saw us. She's with Gem, which is the same as being with you right now, as far as the press is concerned, and I'm not a complete moron. I do know how to keep my personal life out of the press."

Seven's expression tightened. Good, that meant he understood the dig. Our careers were important to us. I loved acting. I loved the art of filmmaking. Playing the media game and walking the tightrope between public and private personas was also the job.

I'd controlled that narrative, thank you very much, and cultivated the playboy image. It meant no long-term commitments on display even when I'd had them. Seven couldn't take a shit without it making Page Six. That was never going to be me.

The alarm let out a warning beep to let us know Gem was back. Good. I swapped the unopened beer out for water and turned to the door from the garage.

"Hey," I said as she came through the door. "Snow, baby, I wasn't expecting you back so soon! I am, however, not all sad to see Gem persuaded you to stay here tonight."

"I'm not sad," Seven added as he joined us. "I'm pissed. So much for not being on the clock."

"Sev," Gem snapped. The warning in his tone suggested Seven had pushed his twin about as far as Gem was willing to let him. Better he figured it out now before he ended up with a broken nose. "I insisted she come back after what we found at her apartment."

"What did you find?" I crossed to where Stella stood, arms wrapped loosely around herself. For the first time since I'd met her—and that included when that prick had been strangling her—she seemed fragile and lost. "Hey," I murmured, rubbing my hands against her biceps. "You're freezing."

Her hair was also still damp. They couldn't have been gone more than ninety minutes.

"Someone broke into her place," Gem said as he started some coffee. "Trashed it. Tore everything up. Someone dumped all the chemicals and it smelled like cat piss everywhere."

"What the fuck?" I glanced at Snow. "Does this have anything to do with that prick...?"

"Maybe, but Gem doesn't think so." She shuddered. "Even though he was lurking nearby to gloat about it."

I wrapped her up, sharing body heat, and she didn't pull away.

"One of the dirtier tabloid sites got your name and address somehow and published it online." Seven actually sounded disturbed as he scrolled angrily through his phone. "Fuck."

He locked gazes with his twin, but it wasn't one of their usual silent battles. If anything, it only lasted a beat of time before he shifted his attention to Stella.

"You need to stay here," he said, shocking the shit out of me, and if Gem's little jerk was any indication, him too. "We'll get you set up and I'll replace anything destroyed."

"You don't have to do that," she said, sounding so weary, it made my bones ache. "Really, I can go stay with my dad. It's not ideal, but I need to check on him too."

"As much as I'd like to say that would be fine, if they found your apartment, how long will it take them to track you to your father's place? Someone probably *gave* them your info, and who's to say they won't hand over your dad's address too?"

Instead of answering, Stella banged her head lightly against my chest. I only knew a little about her dad, but what I knew was he was sick and took a lot of care. "We have security here," I said. "You even heard it, remember? You staying here is totally reasonable, especially for selling the dating story."

"Though we may want to get you two broken up sooner," Gem said, "rather than later. Might take the target off her."

Could be. It would also clear the way for me to officially date her. I could keep her shielded, then we'd have all the time we wanted.

"You can definitely stay with me," I said. "It'd be a fun sleepover, and I have plenty of room for you."

"She's sleeping with me, dickhead," Gem informed me. The coffee was ready and he poured her some. I nudged her over to the counter, so she could drink it. "Already decided that before we came back."

"Fine, you can swap back and forth." I was willing to make that concession. "It'll be no trouble at all."

"Excuse me," Seven interjected into the silence. "Is Stella staying here as a guest to be protected or just a bedwarmer and fuck buddy for you two assholes?"

I frowned and I wasn't alone.

"Hey," Gem said. "I would never treat Slick like some one-night stand or easy lay."

"Good, then we'll set her up in her own room and suite. It's not like we don't have the space. Then if she doesn't want to fuck one of you two losers, she can say no and not have to worry about where she sleeps."

Yeah, it might not be Gem who punched Seven at this rate.

Stella cleared her throat, pulling all our gazes like a magnet. "Look, I don't want to be any trouble or cause for strife…"

"Stray, shut it. You're here now. Gem was right to make you come back. We should probably make arrangements to get your car and anything else salvageable."

"She's already here," Gem said. "I brought her bike, and she drove her car. They're both in the garage. I'll get a ride back for my car later."

"Fine, then let's get the green room ready."

"Green room?" She was still way paler than I cared for, but she seemed to be rallying.

"It's the color palette for the room. Our decorator decided to do the rooms in color themes because, and I quote, 'we are impossible to work for and don't seem to know what we want.'" The woman had been very talented but not remotely patient.

Seven shrugged. "It works. Anyway, come on. Bring the coffee with you if you want."

I don't know who was more surprised by the active role Seven took in leading Stella upstairs to the guest room with us trailing after. Having her own room was nice, but that didn't mean she couldn't sleep in one of ours or I couldn't go sleep with her. Right?

Gem had gotten a night with her sleeping in his bed already. That meant I had dibs on next.

The green room was not on the same side where my room or Gem's was. Seven's room was closer, but at least it wasn't in the same hall.

She put her coffee cup down as she turned in a slow circle. "This seems like a little too much and..."

"It's not enough," Gem said, and I was inclined to agree. "But for now it will have to be. Just...promise you'll stay here until we figure all of this out?"

You could practically feel the exhaustion rolling off of her. "Fine," she said, raising her hands in surrender. "I'll stay. But the moment it becomes too much, I go. Agreed?"

"As long as it's safe for you," Seven said, "I have no problems kicking you to the curb."

"Thank you." She sounded so dry.

Seven shrugged. "Don't mention it. Seriously. For now, we'll let you get some sleep."

"Does this mean I get hazard pay?" The question was so wry and deadpan, I damn near laughed aloud.

Looking *less* amused, Seven just said, "Don't push it."

Gem and I both looked at Stella for the invitation to stay.

When she pressed a kiss to the corner of Gem's mouth, I took the hint. Not tonight.

"Go on," I said to Gem. "I just want a couple of minutes, then I'll head for my own bed. Promise. Scout's honor." I held my fingers up in the Vulcan blessing of *live long and prosper* and smiled wide.

Rolling his eyes, Seven dragged his twin out and the door closed behind them. I faced Stella who looked at me with those hypnotic emerald eyes. Dressed in borrowed clothing, she looked damn good even if the sweatshirt was too big and the shorts hit below her knees.

"Disheveled kind of suits you, Snow."

A flash of amusement softened her darker mood. "That's what you wanted to stay to talk about?"

"No," I said, closing the distance and cupping her face in my hands. "I wanted to say I'm sorry. I know how slimy it feels when someone invades your privacy, how vulnerable that can make you. I'm even more sorry that helping us landed you in that position."

Was she dating Seven for me? No. She was doing it for Gem more than his twin. Yet her actions helped them both out, and they were my family. Helping them meant helping me.

"That makes you one of us," I said. "Make a list so we can replace anything you need. We'll take care of getting that place cleaned. Maybe get you moved into a building with better security?"

She tilted her head back with a groan, and I made some kind of soothing sound.

"I know, it all costs money. We'll figure it out. *Bright Starz* paid real well, didn't they?" We'd put a call in and I'd personally volunteered to write a check for anything she brought them, if they didn't want it. Stella was proud as hell and would never just take the money directly, no matter how much she needed it.

"Yeah…most of the stuff in the apartment was just stuff…"

"But?" The past few weeks had given me some insight into the stubborn, gorgeous woman who wouldn't let us spoil her the way I wanted to, so I just made sure she never had to worry about food.

"There were personal things that were in there."

"They can't be replaced." I rubbed her biceps again. "Give me a little time to chew on this. I bet I can find a way to make it up to you."

Another laugh escaped her, and when she wrapped her arms around my neck, I lifted her for a real hug.

"It's going to be all right," I promised. Then, because I was saintly, I asked, "Do you want company or would you rather sleep alone? I know what I would prefer, but I think in this case Seven is right: you get to decide."

She squeezed me once and then eased back, and I let her go. "I'm just…wrecked. I need to sleep. Honestly, I think I need to go into a coma for a few hours. Then I need to check on my dad. Can I have a rain check?"

"Anytime," I promised. A knock on the door interrupted anything else I would have said, so I answered it.

Seven stood there with a stack of T-shirts and leggings in hand. The look he gave me was bored. "I have these. They're not going to be much but they will be closer to you in size."

Stella eyed him, then the stack and finally crossed to us and took it. "Thank you."

"Not going to ask me who owned them?"

"Nope. Clara Belle wouldn't be caught dead in these and there's no other woman's underwear to ick me out. Beggars are definitely not choosers. Good night, Ollie…Demon Spawn."

The fact she shut him up so efficiently amused the hell out

of me, but I nudged him into the hallway and let her close the door behind us.

Studying Seven, I tilted my head to keep an eye on him as we headed away from her bedroom.

"What?" he demanded.

"Nothing, just trying to figure out where you found that unexpected scrap of humanity."

"Fuck off, Ollie," he said without heat. "I'll take care of arming the security system. Get some sleep."

"Yep," I said, then headed to my room.

Alone.

While the very beautiful, curvaceous, and hot-tongued Stella slept a few doors away.

Life could be cruel and kind.

chapter
twenty-nine

Stella

I was scrolling through the blind items and updates on social media that loved to post celebrity spotting. I'd missed a couple of breaking scandals this week living with the boys. The sex was incredible—so no complaints there—but I swore Seven had something new every damn evening.

While I could try my luck at day shots, the best scores were during parties, which, by and large, happened at night. People drank, they got tired, their judgment grew questionable, and if I was in the right place at the right time, then I would have it made.

When my passenger door opened, I jumped. Then Ollie slid into the seat next to me. "Hey Snow."

"Ollie." I tilted my head to give him a once-over. "What are you doing?"

I flicked a look out of the car. I was parked not far from Mann's Chinese Theater. There were some rumors about filming permits for right at the theater, which could lead to some fun shots. Although today wasn't looking promising.

"I'm helping," he said, grinning. "I came disguised, see? I even brought my own secret spy camera." He palmed something from his pocket and held up what could be a laser pointer from the size of it. "Takes pictures in bursts. So you can get a lot all at once. It's not noticeable, so we can get up close if we need to."

If *we*… "Ollie, you do remember which side of the line you actually live on when it comes to the paps, right?" Though I had to admit, his enthusiasm was *adorable*. Probably wise to keep that particular compliment to myself. His disguise consisted of jeans, a button-down shirt that was open over a dark T-shirt, a dark baseball cap, and sunglasses.

"Hence the disguise." He shook his head. "I'm starting to worry you don't listen to me, Snow. But it's fine. I'll forgive you."

Tongue against my teeth, I fought the urge to laugh. "Gracious."

"I can be," he said firmly. "So what are we doing? Who is the target? Need me to flush the big game out of a store?"

Since we were nowhere near a store, it was a safe bet the answer to that one was no. Before I could answer though, my phone rang.

Dad's contact information popped up. "Hey, Dad," I greeted him, holding up a finger to Ollie's lips to silence him. "Everything good?"

I'd made it to the house once to make sure he was stocked up and to check in with Mom while she was on shift. When they divorced, I doubted she ever planned on being his at-home care nurse, but she hadn't hesitated when asked.

We might not be as close as some mothers and daughters —yeah, I'd always been a daddy's girl—but I could rely on her. She'd always come through. She was getting frustrated with Dad pushing it constantly, and I was going to arrange some downtime for her, but that meant getting more money in, which meant more photos.

I wasn't paying rent right now—my apartment was totally

uninhabitable—so that might be enough to bring in an additional nurse to cover her shifts for a week. It was something to think about.

"Everything is fine, Shutterbug. But I need a favor."

"As long as it's not asking me for contraband of any kind to sneak past Mom or the other nurses, I'm in."

He coughed through a laugh. "Sometimes, I wonder where you got your sense of humor."

"Me too, then I remember who raised me." His chuckle deepened at the verbal poke. "What's the favor, Dad?"

"Shutterbug, you know I love you and your mother more than life itself."

Uh-oh.

"But I need a break from her and I'm pretty sure she needs one from me."

That fell right in with my line of thought, but I still had to bite back a smile. I hadn't told either parent about the break-in and vandalism. Frankly, the police seemed to have almost no leads. Their bottom line had been that I'd been fully doxed online. It could have been literally anyone, since my photo, name, and address were out there for any psycho Seven Harrison groupie to find.

Their less-than-helpful responses had frustrated Gem so much, he'd said something about hiring his own detective. I thought I'd talked him out of it, since the police had a really valid point. Maybe.

"Done," I said without needing him to convince me more. "I'm already trying to work out a plan to give Mom a few days off. That means we'll probably have to use one of the nurses you don't like as much."

"I don't care if I like them," he admitted. "I don't generally feel bad when they tick me off and I scold them. Your mother has been letting me get away with it, and I just...I can't be a bastard to her, Shutterbug. She doesn't deserve that from me."

She'd probably been letting him do it for the same reason he didn't want to do it to her: they still loved each other. Living together and sharing a life together just wasn't in the cards. They disagreed on too many things, but their divorce had never been about a death of feelings.

"That's 'cause you're the best," I reminded him. "But if you can hold out another couple of days, I just have to get everything squared with the home-care staff."

"Have I told you that you're my favorite child?"

Funny guy, since I was an only child. "Yes, many times, and I'm glad, but I'm still not bringing you beer."

His laughter this time wasn't populated by a phlegmy cough, so I'd take that as an improvement. Then we were getting off the phone and I met Ollie's curious gaze.

"I want to meet your father."

Six words I never imagined coming out of Ollie's mouth. "How about—"

"It can wait, obviously. We need to get you settled and he's healing, but I want to meet him. He's only met Seven, and I don't think that's the impression I want him to have." He rubbed his jaw, looking thoughtful.

"I'll think about it," I said. "You like to cause trouble."

"I do," he admitted without shame. "I suppose I could curry favor with your dad if I brought him beer, but that would definitely cost me points with you. So what if I bring him some fake beer that tastes like it and has no alcohol content? He gets to enjoy the flavor and you don't have to worry about him."

That was...ingenuous. "I don't know if he'd go for it."

"No harm in trying," he said. "Right?"

"Right," I admitted. Then my phone vibrated with an update. Oh, good. Celebs spotted at the Grapevine. It was a fun, little wine bar, very popular with younger actresses. "I need to go."

"I'm in," Ollie said, grinning. "Really, put me in, Coach. Make me work for it."

This was never going to work, but I headed for the Grapevine anyway. There were a couple of B-list actresses having lunch with an agent. I checked them out through the telephoto lens.

Nothing about the meeting looked squirrelly or even particularly interesting except...

"Do we know if he's the agent for both of them?"

"No idea," Ollie said. "Let me check their website. It usually lists all the clients."

The blonde was definitely working the agent; she was leaning forward and the dress she was wearing was cut low, so the man seemed to be in an intense conversation with her breasts. While I wasn't there, I could practically hear her talking...

"Yes, please focus on my breasts some more. I see that you completely respect me. You're really listening to my issues, and I feel like I can rely on you to represent me in my attempts to make it onto the A-list somewhere. On it, not under it."

Next to me Ollie chuckled and I cut a glance at him.

"Am I wrong?" I motioned to the man who hadn't lifted his gaze from the actress's boobs the entire time we'd been sitting here.

"No," Ollie admitted. "She's also *not* his client yet. I'd imagine this is her vetting a possible stepping stone, because he has a higher caliber of actor in his stable and she's looking to trade up."

"So a better agent can do that?"

"A good agent is better than a good script. Everyone thinks

that a good script is the unicorn. It isn't—there are a lot of good scripts out there. But those scripts don't always have four quadrant appeal, nor do they promise to make back the investors' money and turn a profit. You want to make a good script into a movie, you get to be your own executive producer and find the financing. Then you can make art, and there are people who appreciate it."

"But money is in the spectacle."

"Exactly. I don't really see her talking to this guy as anything more than testing the waters." He shrugged. "Then again I don't know her, so I don't know what her chances are to make a break somewhere. A good agent, though, they will fight for that script for you. They will fight for you to get the roles you want and need. They make your success vital to their own."

"Is that Jerry for you guys?"

He shrugged, then leaned back in the seat. "So far. He's repped us since we were kids—well, teenagers. He came in and listened to us, not our parents, then worked with us to get what we wanted. So far so good."

I smiled. "I'm glad." I snapped a few pics, but I doubted they would be good for anything. Still, it didn't hurt to have a backup for another story down the road. "It's nice that you have someone keeping your best interests at heart. I can imagine it's a lonely life."

My phone rang again, and I frowned at the number. I didn't know it so I sent it to voicemail. I'd been getting a lot of those unknown caller or blocked caller numbers. Some were spam. Others were gossips. A couple of the really odd ones had been my college roommate from freshman year and a woman who'd lived next door to me up until last year, asking if we could "meet for drinks," as if that were something we did.

The phone buzzed again. Blocked number.

"You should turn off the ringer for unknown numbers."

"Not always helpful to me. Some of these could be about work or tips—occasionally it's about Dad."

A third blocked call came through and then three messages popped up in rapid succession.

Blocked Number: *Hey, it's Flip. You should put me in your contacts. I wanted to reach out and see if maybe you could help me set up an audition with Seven? You guys seem like a cute couple.*

I stared at the message, and Ollie leaned over to look at my phone. "Who's Flip?"

"I—" I shook my head. The name was familiar. "I don't know."

"Maybe some random, just block him."

Sounded like a plan when "Flip" sent through another message.

Oh you should watch Dirt-TV tonight. They're covering your first date with Seven and I'll be in it. Hope you don't mind, but it's such an adorable story.

Groaning, I leaned my head back against the seat. "Flip the bartender. From Cactus."

"I'm sorry, Snow," Ollie murmured. "Celebrity gets a weird reaction out of people."

"I know—it's how I pay bills but this..." I stared at the message, then just cleared it off the screen. "I think I need a drink."

"Well, it just so happens that I know a great place."

Someone jogged up to the passenger side of the car and knocked on the window. Two someones. They backed up a little and looked in the car. They were practically bubbling over with excitement.

"You're busted," I warned Ollie.

He rolled the window down. "Hello, girls, what can I do for you? We're in a bit of a hurry."

"Can we get your autograph Mr. Griffiths?"

"Please," the other girl said. "We love you so much."

"Well, since you love me so much," he said, before signing the one girl's book and the other girl's backpack. He declined to sign a boob though. "Sorry, ladies. Even if you had an ID declaring your age, I'm afraid I have to draw a line somewhere."

Then he conceded to taking a selfie with them, but he didn't get out of the car. "Now, I'm afraid we need to go."

"Of course," the first girl said, then she stole a look at me and let out squeal. "Oh my god, you're Seven Harrison's girlfriend."

Kill me.

"Yes," Ollie said. "She is. But shh." He pressed a finger to his lips. "The fame gets to her and I was trying to show her that we can have normal dates too."

"So you're on a date?" girl number one said, eyes wide.

"A fake date?" the second girl said. "'Cause you can't date your best friend's girl. Right? Doesn't that break the code?"

"Girls," I said, before Ollie dug us in any deeper. "Ollie's doing a little stint pretending to be a photographer—" I patted my camera. "I'm just here as his beard. But you're drawing attention, so could you..." I made a shooing motion.

"Oh, yes, sure, sure! Bye! Thank you!"

"I can't believe they recognized me," Ollie mused.

"I hate to be the one to break this to you, stud, but you still look like you even in the hat and sunglasses. You aren't Clark Kent."

His grin didn't diminish.

"What?"

"You called me stud."

I rolled my eyes and then focused on the traffic.

"I like it," Ollie continued. "Stud. I accept that as my nickname."

chapter
thirty

Stella

It felt like cheating, it really did. It felt *wrong*...but at the same time, I was having too much fun to let something silly like morals get in my way. Not when I was reaping the benefits in such a spectacular way.

"Okay, so Jerry found out that Candice Irons and Jeremy Rogers have been hooking up at the Mon Claire Hotel every Wednesday at two," Gem told me with a wide grin after hanging up his call. "It's only a half-hour drive from here. We've got time to grab lunch on the way if we leave now."

I got to my feet and grabbed my boots to pull them on. "Let's do it!" Because worst-case scenario, Jerry's tip didn't pay off and I still had a nice lunch out with Gem. Unlike my covert dates with Ollie, I didn't need to hide my affection for Gem.

A few days ago *The Nightly Mail* had splashed photos of us across a four-page spread after someone papped us making out on the beach. I wasn't even mad about it because the photos were *scorching* hot. Seven was initially pissed, but as Gem pointed out, it was a freebie. We were selling the Seven-and-Stella story and he hadn't needed to pay me for it.

Gem and Ollie were going out of their way to get me the inside tips on where to photograph other celebs. Particularly elusive, big-ticket ones, that tabloids paid big money for. To my surprise, Jerry was on board with our gaming the system and had been slipping us tips himself.

Seven *hated* it, but none of us gave two fucks what Seven liked.

"Where do you want to do lunch?" Gem asked as we headed out to their enormous garage. We took one of Seven's cars—a sleek black McLaren—and Gem had raided his twin's closet for a Hugo Boss sport coat and collared shirt. If not for how intimately I knew Gemini Harrison, I'd have easily been fooled that he was Seven. No wonder Seven had done so well in the action-movie industry, with such a perfect stunt double.

I shrugged, settling into the low seat of the sports car. "I'm easy."

Gem's lips curled in a sly grin. "Well...in that case..."

Laughing, I shook my head. "This morning in the shower with Ollie wasn't enough? Damn, Gem, here I was thinking I was the sex addict in this ménage à trois." It'd been a lovely shower. Gem had washed my hair for me while Ollie had held me aloft, impaled on his cock. Then they'd swapped so Ollie could comb the conditioner through my lengths. The sweet, floral scent every time my hair moved turned me on now.

"Let's hit up the new Yakiniku restaurant. I've heard great things about it," Gem suggested, driving us out of their very secure property with all the casual confidence of...well...of Seven.

"Hai Dozo? I heard they have like a six-month waiting list for a table," I commented, shaking my head. "Also, their seating is all outdoors and super visible to paps."

Gem grinned, all teeth. "Good. I'll make sure to look extra infatuated with you as we eat, as if that'd be a hard ask."

"Seven ought to be paying you for all this work you're putting in as him," I grumbled, but really...I much preferred to be out with Gem than faking it with Seven. "What's he doing with all his free time now that you're doing the heavy lifting for his reputation?"

"He's studying for the role Carriage Pictures is offering," Gem told me with a sigh. "It's a big deal to him and would majorly elevate his career to the next level since it's slated to be a huge franchise. Spin-offs, small screen, merch—literally all the things. And if he signs on at this stage of the project, he stands to take a cut of *every* facet of the franchise, rather than just take a wage for his role."

Okay, I guessed I could understand that. It seemed like a lot of pressure, though, with the morality clause he'd mentioned so many times. His private life had to be squeaky clean and his reputation gold-plated. The fake cheating scandal really could have fucked things up.

Weirdly, in the two weeks I'd lived in the guys house, I'd softened toward Seven a little bit. Not a lot. He still made me want to smother him with a pillow full of snakes. But I no longer actively tried to sabotage his career—because he meant a lot to Gem and Ollie and they meant a lot to me.

Crap. I was developing *big* feelings. This was going to hurt when it ended.

If it ended.

It didn't have to...did it?

Who was I kidding? This wasn't my happily ever after.

"I can get us in," Gem said, circling back to the question of our lunch spot. "Or rather, Seven can." He winked, and I couldn't fight my grin. For a guy who hated being in the spotlight, he sure was having fun pretending to be his brother.

Sure enough, the restaurant practically fell all over themselves rearranging tables to accommodate us, and Gem took every opportunity for PDA while we waited. He was so fucking sexy, it was easy to forget we were on full display as he kissed me in front of dozens of other diners.

"I guess my invitation was lost in the mail," Ollie drawled, pulling up a chair to join us a few minutes after we were seated. "Snow, baby, you look fucking delicious today. Your hair, in particular, seems very clean." He kept his voice low enough to not be overheard, but my cheeks flamed nonetheless.

Gem kicked him under the table and Ollie pouted. The inability for *him* to show public affection toward me was starting to wear thin.

"Aren't you supposed to be doing a sit-down interview with *Men in Film* today?" Gem asked, handing over a menu anyway. "Slick and I were on our way to Mon Claire to snap some pics of naughty, cheating celebs."

"I was, but it finished early. Then I spotted *Seven's* McLaren in the valet here and figured I'd come join you. I do so love to eat out." He licked his lips, holding eye contact, and I shifted in my seat. He really did enjoy *eating out*, that much was true.

I groaned, shaking my head. "Stop it. You're going to give some other random photographer the shot of their life in a minute, when I drag the both of you into the bathroom." Because much like the entire dining area, the doors to the restrooms were far too visible to literally any hack job with a telephoto lens.

Normally, there wouldn't be much worth photographing when it was just rich and famous eating their lunch. But I had no doubt the story would go wild if I got caught getting double dicked down in the bathrooms.

"So Seven was whining about the whole paparazzi thing this morning over coffee," Ollie said, shifting the subject smoothly, then paused strategically as the waitress came by to take our orders.

We all waited until she was gone again before continuing. "He's permanently whining about everything involving me," I muttered, letting my leg rest against Ollie's under the table. From my other side, Gem's hand had found my knee and stroked little circles on my thigh. "I should *probably* find somewhere new to live." Since we'd all agreed that the security in my previous apartment was basically nonexistent.

Ollie hummed thoughtfully, slouching in his seat. "It wouldn't send the best message though, would it? You've been living with Seven for two weeks now. If you suddenly moved out, it'd seem like things were on the rocks between you."

I smiled, shaking my head. "You just don't want to lose the easy access to my bed, Olivier."

"True," he agreed. "But also, optics, Snowy my sweet." His wink was far too sexy for this time of day.

I sighed, shaking my head and trying to ignore how *insanely* attracted I was to the both of them. I'd thought maybe the appeal would wear off once I'd let them fuck me stupid for a couple of days, but it was only getting worse. I liked them both so much it actually made my chest hurt.

"Well, I can't stay forever. We will have to brainstorm something. When is Sev supposed to sign this deal anyway?"

Gem shrugged. "No idea. They're dicking around with contracts at the moment."

Our drinks arrived then, and the conversation shifted between the boys to discuss the press tour that Ollie was currently in the middle of. It was for a movie set to release in a couple of months, and he seemed genuinely excited about it. The amount of promotional work the studio had him and the whole cast doing said they had high hopes for some accolades too.

"...are those ones all with Violetta?" Gem was asking when I tuned back into their conversation, having just briefly being lost staring at the line of Gem's jaw and thinking about whether I could discreetly palm his dick under the table.

I frowned. "Violetta Dulce? She's in the movie with you?"

Ollie quirked a brow at me, tilting his head to the side. "Yes. She's the leading lady."

I blinked a couple of times, storing that information in my brain. "Oh. I didn't know that, I don't think."

Gem's fingers squeezed my knee lightly. "Do you not like Violetta, Slick? She's pretty new. I've never worked with her."

I bit my lip, asking myself silently whether I was seriously jealous of a woman simply doing her job. Violetta Dulce was a goddamn knockout though. *Stunning* didn't begin to touch on her beauty. She was a former Miss Universe contestant turned actress after a social media boom, but from what I'd seen, she was actually a good actress.

And Ollie had already mentioned it was a "high-heat" movie, and that meant the gorgeous woman had been kissing my man.

"I haven't crossed paths with her," I admitted, swallowing back my childish jealousy. "She doesn't even live in LA, I don't think?"

Ollie shook his head. "Nah, she has a place up in northern Cali somewhere. She's just here for this series of interviews, since we have to do them together. Chemistry and all that, you know?"

I pursed my lips, nodding. Logically, yes that all made sense. But the feral cavewoman part of my brain was freaking right the fuck out. I didn't know enough about Violetta to know whether I should be so worried or not. If it were Clara Belle or any of the other countless vapid actresses I was familiar with, I wouldn't give it a second thought.

"Do you enjoy acting, Ollie?" I asked thoughtfully, taking a sip of my Chardonnay. "Does it make you happy?"

His gaze was confident and open as he replied. "One hundred percent, yes. It's what I was born to do, and I couldn't imagine doing anything else with my life. I hope I'm still playing the dashing villain and tragic hero when I'm old and gray." He practically sparkled when he spoke about his acting. It was beautiful. "What about you, Snow? Do you enjoy what you do?"

I used to. But now? I wasn't so sure…

Being on the other side of the camera had given me a fresh perspective on the lives of the celebrities whose scandals paid my bills. I had nothing else, though, so I gave a tight smile and nodded.

"Sure. Love it. Oh, look, here's our food…"

chapter
thirty-one

Seven

Gem got roped back onto my set full-time, and he didn't even bitch at me about it which said a *lot* about his mood at the moment. Something about Stella had changed my twin…and not in a bad way. As much as she irritated me and made me want to push her into a crocodile-infested swimming pool, I couldn't deny how happy Gem was. Or Ollie for that matter, and if that wasn't a shock, I didn't know what was.

Ollie was a perpetual bachelor. A player of the highest degree. He didn't date—not seriously. He fucked around and flicked them away the second they started developing feelings. That'd been his MO ever since we hit puberty and he started being asked to sign chicks' tits.

Until now.

Until her.

Stella fucking Charles.

"What are you doing?" I asked when I found her sprawled on the sofa in her underwear and one of Ollie's favorite T-shirts. The fabric was all hitched up from her awkward position and the underside of one boob was exposed. Why the *fuck* was I so turned on, staring at that curve? Probably because my fake relationship with her had totally killed my sex life. I couldn't exactly go hooking up with anyone else with all eyes on *Seven and Stella.*

She glanced up at me, totally unconcerned by her lack of clothing. The infuriating woman had *no modesty* at all. The other day I'd walked in on her sucking Gem's dick in the gym bathroom and she hadn't even flinched. Just winked and continued with what she was doing, while Gem threw a towel and told me to fuck off.

I'd thought about that way too many times since then.

"Watching TV," she replied. "What does it look like I'm doing?"

I scowled, eyeing her weird pose hanging half off the couch with a leg slung up over the backrest and her hair on the floor. "Yoga? I don't know. Stop it, though. You're irritating me."

She scoffed and made no move to get up. "Me *breathing* irritates you, Demon Spawn. Go brood in the library if you have an issue with me."

Footsteps in the hallway reminded me why I'd vacated my library in the first place. Our cleaner wanted to vacuum in there and I couldn't deal with the noise.

"Oh, I'm sorry," the woman said, pausing in the doorway. "I didn't realize you still had company, Mr. Harrison."

"You're fine," I replied, moving closer to where Stella sprawled on the couch and nudging her leg aside to make space for me to sit down. She obliged, but then placed her leg across my lap once I was sitting. I guess it was a good thing she was willing to sell the story.

The woman glanced curiously from me to Stella and her very obvious lack of clothing, her eyes widening. "I just wanted to apologize, Mr. Harrison. I knocked over a glass in your library and it'll take a little longer to clean up the breakage. I didn't want you accidentally getting cut."

That was annoying, but I bit back my sigh of frustration. "That's fine, Martha, wasn't it?"

The woman frowned, her lips pursing. "Flora."

"Right," I replied. "Sorry."

"Seven's in no hurry to get back to his library," Stella drawled from her weird position, using the remote to select the next episode of whatever trash she was watching. "He was just telling me how much he *desperately* wanted to suck my toes while I watch *Is It Cake?*"

The cleaner—Flora—gasped in embarrassment, shock, or horror, or a mixture of the three, before disappearing back down the hall to continue her work.

"I'd rather suck on a poisonous snake than your toes, Stray," I growled, smacking her foot off my lap. The motion unbalanced her position and she slid off the sofa onto the floor headfirst. Which, to my disgust, ended up with Ollie's T-shirt over her head and totally exposing those lush tits in all their upside-down glory.

"Dickhead," she snapped back, rolling and rearranging herself to sit on the floor with her back to the sofa. Her T-shirt was back in place. "Snakes are venomous, not poisonous, you moron."

I puffed out a long breath, folding my legs to hide my thickening cock. It wasn't *her* that I was attracted to—it was just tits in general that turned me on. They could have been Flora's and I'd still be rocking a semi right now.

"Whatever. I was going to offer you something nice, since you generously waived our agreed fee for your public appearances with Gem, but now I changed my mind."

Her head whipped around, suspicion etched over every inch of her pretty face. "You don't do *nice*, Demon Spawn."

Okay, she had a point. That wasn't to say I didn't ever do nice things, but as far as our interactions went? Yeah, her point was valid. "Well, I don't *now*. Are you seriously sitting here watching a reality TV show about cake making?"

Her eye roll was infuriating. "It's about cake *decorating*, dumbass. The whole point is that they're so realistic you don't know which item is real and which is cake. See this one?" She gestured to the TV where on the podiums there were five different sneakers. The camera zoomed in on one. "Is it cake?"

I wrinkled my nose, confused. "No. That's a shoe." Then watched in fascination as the host took a huge knife and cut straight through the toe of the shoe. "Holy crap, it was cake."

"See, it's genius," she muttered, utterly enthralled once more by her show.

Somehow, don't fucking ask me how, I sat there watching the rest of the episode with her—plus two more—and got genuinely fired up when I guessed the wrong bag of cash at the end. Then cursed when I saw what time it was.

"Get dressed, Stray," I ordered. "We were supposed to leave twenty minutes ago."

"Leave? For what?" She did get up off the couch, where she'd made herself comfy a while ago, so that was a step in the right direction.

I blew out a sigh, raking my fingers through my hair. "Does it matter? You didn't have any plans today anyway. Come on, I'll pull the car around."

I started for the door when she called after me. "Is this a paid date, Spawn?"

Sassy bitch.

"Sure. Whatever. Just put some pants on, for the love of fuck. And a bra." Although, I couldn't say I'd be too disappointed if she forgot that part.

Damn it. I needed to get laid so freaking bad.

I pulled out one of my lesser-used cars—a Mercedes—and

waited impatiently for Stella to slide into the passenger seat, sadly fully clothed.

"So are you telling me where we're going?" she asked, weaving her inky hair into a loose braid over her shoulder.

I could tell her, but why make things easy? "Nope. You're getting paid for your time, Stray, just go with the flow. Better this than lurking around behind bushes taking photos of my colleagues anyway."

"I don't lurk," she grumbled, folding her arms and staring out her window.

We were quiet most of the drive, our only conversation happening when I tried to put on the radio and she insulted my choice of station, then I obviously had to make fun of her for her shitty taste in music.

"Okay, why have you brought me here?" she finally asked when I pulled into the warehouse parking lot.

I smirked, then climbed out and went around to open her door for her. "You have no idea where we are, do you?"

"Absolutely no idea," she replied, agreeing. Just then, the door to the closest warehouse opened and a gray-haired woman in overly large chunky-framed glasses stepped out with a severe scowl.

I suppressed a shudder.

"Seven, you're late. And you brought a friend."

"Sorry, Janice, my girlfriend and I just lost track of time this morning. You know how new relationships are, all hot and heavy." I kept my hand on Stella's elbow, keeping her right by my side as I approached the scowling woman. "This is Stella, the light of my life."

Stray snorted under her breath and I squeezed her elbow in warning.

"Stella, baby, this is Janice Greenbriar, senior photographer for *Notoriety Magazine*."

I'd somewhat expected some fawning or awe for meeting such a well-established and highly regarded photographer. Surely that was the position all paparazzi aspired to? Photographing celebrities *with* their consent and gaining accolades for their artistic merit, rather than just the salacious content? But Stella just looked Janice up and down and gave a tight-lipped smile.

"Hi," she offered, folding her arms under her breasts to make it clear she wasn't going to shake hands or anything.

I wondered briefly, as Janice ushered us inside, whether Stella could sense how little I cared for Janice and was emulating my vibe or if she was just always rude to people she'd never met.

Little explanation was necessary when we entered the studio space, and I was quickly ushered into wardrobe and makeup, leaving Stella to her own devices for a little while. It irritated me that I found myself anxious to know what she was thinking. She remained quiet, sitting on a stack of pallets and watching Janice set up the lighting.

I didn't like shooting with Janice, but *Notoriety* was one of the biggest magazines right now. It wasn't an offer I could turn down easily, so I gritted my teeth and reminded myself I was an adult and a professional as Janice posed me how she wanted.

Janice, unfortunately, liked to be *hands on* with her posing. I used to think it was just her artistic style, but after speaking with some colleagues, that was not the case.

"Whoa, what the fuck?" Stella exclaimed after twenty minutes into the photoshoot, pulling *everyone's* focus. I was wearing nothing but a white button-down—unbuttoned— and a pair of white briefs, and trying to keep my head in the zone. Professional. "Did you seriously just adjust the position of Seven's dick with your hand, Janice?"

The photographer's spine stiffened and her lips tightened before spinning to face Stray's accusation. "I posed my model to get a better shot, yes," she snapped. "Do you have a problem with that?"

Stella's wide eyes swung to mine, then back to Janice. "Is that a joke? Yes, I have a problem with that. You can't just grab a man's *penis* without consent, regardless of your profession. What the actual fuck?"

Janice must have been fuming, her shoulders were shaking but she had her back to me. All I could do was shake my head at Stray and silently ask her to let it go. The shoot would be over soon, and we could leave.

I had thought that bringing my *girlfriend* would mean Janice kept her hands to herself. I'd also hoped that the *Notoriety* editor was going to be here, so I could introduce Stella and maybe help her get her foot in the door at the magazine. Apparently, I was wrong on both counts.

"I didn't—" Janice spluttered. "Seven consented to this shoot and as such—"

"Sev, *babe*, did you tell Janice it was okay to touch your special place? Are you comfortable with her groping your meat stick in the name of photography?" Stella fluttered her lashes at me, the sarcasm loaded on heavily.

I almost laughed. Almost. It would have been funny if we weren't literally talking about *my dick* here.

"I'd prefer she didn't," I admitted out loud, since Stella had already burst this can of worms right open.

Janice whirled back to stare at me in horror, like I'd just accused her of sexual assault. "Well, I never. If that's how you feel, Seven, then I think we're done here."

"Great idea," Stella agreed, not letting me say otherwise. "And before you go feeling like the victim here, Janice, consider how this all might have played out if the genders were reversed. If an older *male* photographer was caught adjusting a younger actress's vagina flaps *for the photos*, I seriously doubt that'd be acceptable, do you?"

Janice seemed shocked speechless, as was I.

Stella needed no response, though, striding over to wardrobe and grabbing an armful of my clothes and shoes. "Come on, Seven, we're leaving. And, Janice? Don't be shocked when you see Sev's written complaint to your boss about this inappropriate conduct. Bye!"

Stunned, confused, and bewildered...I followed.

"Stray, what the fuck?" I whispered as we reached my car. I was still in nothing but my underpants and shirt, barefoot, but she wasn't waiting around for me to dress. The moment I unlocked the car, she was tossing my stuff inside and strapping into her seat.

Shaking my head with disbelief, I just got in and started up the engine, driving us out of the lot.

Neither of us spoke for a good portion of the drive, then I said the only thing that could fully form in my head. "You're not like other girls, Stella."

She snort-laughed so hard, I thought she was going to hurt herself, tears leaking from her eyes as she shook with mirth.

"Oh my god, Spawn, do you ever hear yourself speak? I'm just like every other girl. Literally a dime a dozen. If I'm *not like other girls*, then you've been spending way too much time around vapid airheads like Clara Belle. You've lost touch with real women. Don't worry, precious. I'm here now to bring you back to earth."

Great. My own personal reality check. Just what I always wanted.

Then, an even more disturbing thought crossed my mind.

Had Stella just saved me from sexual assault? Was I the helpless princess in this fairy tale? *Fuck.*

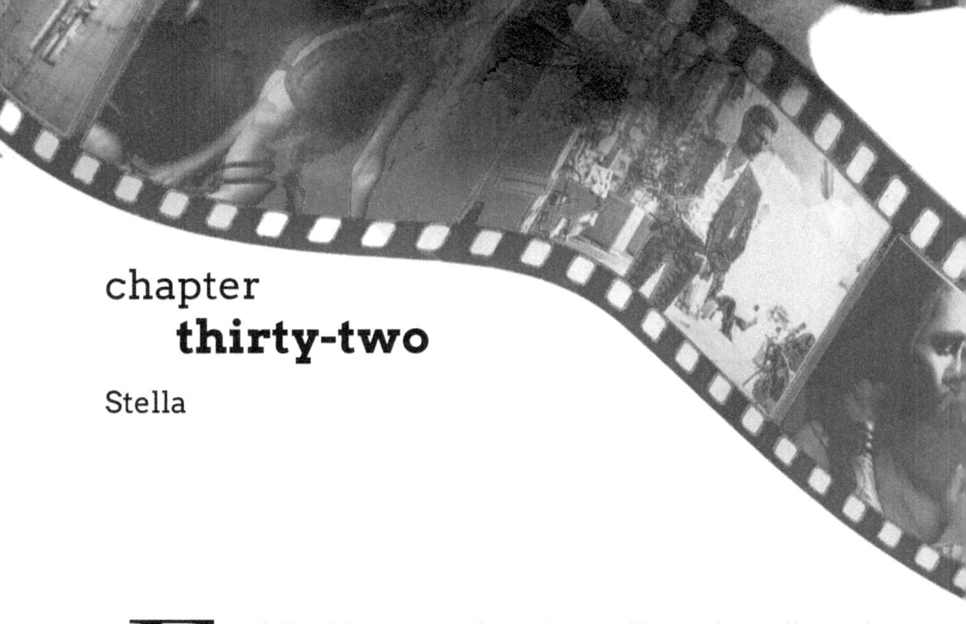

chapter
thirty-two

Stella

"**F**uck." I blew out a breath as Ollie and I collapsed together on the bed. My heart still raced and my body hummed.

"Pretty sure we just did," Ollie murmured into my ear. "But give me a few minutes and I will absolutely go for round two."

"Three," I said, holding up three fingers over my shoulder. "Pretty sure it will be three."

He scraped his teeth over my shoulder in a playful bite. "Three is definitely a lucky number, Snow." The drag of his cock leaving me had me groaning. "Stay here." He added a slap to my ass before he rolled off the bed.

I pushed my head up, the bedhead I had going on was probably impressive because Ollie loved to put his hands in my hair, fist it, and then fuck. I licked my lips and made sure no drool had escaped. There was just something downright fierce about the way he fucked.

To say I was more than a little drunk on him would be a bit of an understatement. Add Gem to this and I was living in some hedonistic dream. That was a sobering thought. Dreams ended. Sometimes it was better to wake up before they became nightmares.

Ollie wandered back out from the bathroom with a damp cloth and a glass of water. "Drink," he said as he handed it to me. I opened my mouth to say something, but he stole a kiss. "Hmm, I could get used to this."

He left me to drink before he went to wipe me down. Another unexpected facet of this fantasy life I was existing in: Ollie and Gem seemed to both thrive on looking after me. It was as unsettling as it was unfamiliar. I'd had boyfriends before. I'd even had lovers.

I couldn't say any of them had been like Ollie or Gem. Hell, most were more like Seven—if Seven and I were fucking and he was still a surly bastard. It would probably take an epic amount of fucking to get the stick out of Seven's ass and make him relax.

Making a face at that thought, I downed the water like it was a shot of vodka. Once I set the glass down, Ollie flipped me over and looked down at me with a gleeful smile. Then he was burying his face in my pussy like he had challenged Gem to a duel at dawn for who was the best at it.

Oh, fuck, that idea just fired up my libido and I didn't even try to fight my screams. Boneless as hell when he finally took a break, I grinned at his very stiff cock.

"Round four?" He grinned and at my laugh, he added, "That's not a no." It most certainly wasn't.

He pulled me up and over his shoulder giving me a gorgeous view of his very tight ass. "Ollie? Is this how you plan to do calisthenics every morning?" I had to know as he carried me into the bathroom.

'Cause that was how he'd bribed his way into spending the night in my bed. We were going to get up early and work out together. Or I could have coffee and watch him work out—he just wanted the time. I think I liked this plan better.

Apparently, so did he because his wicked laugh was also not a no.

Thirty minutes and another orgasm later, I practically floated out of my room with Ollie strolling beside me. He still needed to swing by his own room for clean clothes. Not that I minded the *long* walk to get there. Those extra dozen steps or so were a killer.

I leaned on the doorframe and pointed a finger at him. "Uh-uh. Not coming in. You get your clothes on and then we're going downstairs. I cannot live on sex alone. I require coffee." At his smirk, I grinned. "And according to you, I also require food."

"Hmm, I'll just lure you back up here after breakfast." He rubbed his hands together like some kind of evil villain and this had been his dastardly plan.

"I thought you had more interviews today." I was pretty sure he had some streaming services doing "on the set" and "behind the scenes" specials. At least I thought that was what he meant.

"Ugh." Ollie groaned. "I don't think I want you so aware of my schedule anymore."

"No?" I grinned as he pulled out a cheerful if a bit subdued Hawaiian-print business shirt. He held it up in front of him and then looked at me. "I like it. It makes you look even more dark and mysterious."

His snort just made me grin. He slid the shirt on and buttoned it up on his way to the door. Once he squeezed in with me, he dipped his head for a kiss that I'd been expecting and welcomed.

Yes, we had places to go and things to do. I had a lot to do, including getting my own place again. Before I got too comfortable.

At the same time, I didn't want to go anywhere. I enjoyed

this playful side to Ollie, particularly when he was all relaxed. When I nipped his lower lip, he chuckled.

"Disciplining me now, Snow?" His eyes danced with all the possibilities.

The man was terrible. Absolutely terrible.

"Someone has to. You're a menace." I wouldn't have it any other way.

Laughing, Ollie wrapped an arm around my shoulders as I slid mine around his waist. We headed for the stairs, sidestepping one of the cleaners who was coming up the stairs.

She froze in place, her eyes wide and her expression uncertain. I offered her another smile. "Good morning."

The woman nodded briefly, then stepped hastily out of the way.

"Come on," Ollie said, tugging me along. "Let's go feed you. You definitely need to keep up your strength."

I didn't mind if I did.

Sadly for me, Ollie apparently miscalculated the time for his interview and a scorching call from Jerry had him giving me a quick kiss before he headed out. Ollie had been planning to make breakfast, but with his absence, I went for cereal.

Someone—Gem I was pretty sure—had seen me sneaking the bowls of Cocoa Puffties. I loved the cereal a stupid amount. They'd had an unopened box in there, so I hadn't felt any guilt for the first bowl. Not really for the second or third bowls either.

But then a new box showed up. I hadn't eaten the cereal in front of them. A girl's gotta keep some of her dirty little secrets. The indulgence of the too-sweet and absolutely, deliciously chocolatey goodness was something I wanted to continue to enjoy.

Bowl in hand, I drifted into the dining room. There were places to eat at the breakfast bar in the kitchen. We'd had exactly no meals in here since I arrived, which was fine—the kitchen was more comfortable.

A stack of mail and a large flat package waited there. Munching on the cereal, I drifted over to look at the address label on the package. I recognized the *Notoriety* address and the warnings to *do not bend*.

It had to be photos.

I wrestled with my conscience for a solid thirty seconds before I set the bowl down and pulled the tab on the seal for the package. Hard cardboard kept the photos flat, and folders protected the photos themselves. Setting the pieces aside, I flipped open the first one.

With a frown, I studied it. Then moved to the next. Then the next. One after another, I paged through the images. There had to have been fifteen or twenty sent over in total. Likely culled as the best from the three thousand she took on the day.

If these were the best, I had to grimace. "Shit. Shit. Oh my god, what was that woman thinking? Clearly she wasn't, 'cause she has no idea what she's doing." She'd been more interested in sexual assault than focusing on the task at hand. What a creep.

With a sigh, I set the last one down.

"My thoughts exactly," Seven said from the doorway. I only startled a little because I hadn't even realized he was home. "It seems that opening my mail and rifling through it has distressed you. I don't know if you're aware, but it's actually a federal offense to open someone else's mail."

"I'm your girlfriend, Seven, basically de facto at this stage. But that's beside the point because *these?* They're shit. Total steaming dung piles. Every single one." I was sorry I had opened the package up too, but I couldn't unsee the travesty of what she'd sent over.

His eyebrows skyrocketed. "Excuse me?"

I strode over to him, took his arm, and walked him back to the table. Parking him in front of the images, I started flipping through them one at a time to show him.

"Shit." I slapped it down.

"Shit." I slapped down the second image.

"Only slightly up from shit, but I can't even tell if you're supposed to be human." Down went images three through five.

Six through fourteen were next. "These are hardly an improvement. You look like the wax display of you at Madame Tussauds…"

"There isn't a wax of me there."

"Could have fooled me," I said with a scoff. "Because we have evidence right here."

"What about this one?" It was the last one in this stack. The first one I'd opened. "What's wrong with it, Stray?"

"It's soulless. You look like a two-dimensional replica of yourself, flat and lifeless. I don't even know how bad you have to fuck up a shot to do that. I was there. The light wasn't the worst. You can do a lot with a little, and you were in white and on full display but all she manages to capture is a sexless, unappealing facsimile."

His mouth fell open through my diatribe. Yes, it was a damn diatribe. I took photos for a living, but I also understood the art. The woman had the easiest subject in the world—personality excluded—and she failed utterly.

"You think you can do better?" The words landed on the table like a proverbial gauntlet.

"I could do better pictures than this with a store-bought instant camera and the photos developed in a nineties-era Kodak machine." That wasn't arrogance; it was a straight-up fact. "I sure as fuck couldn't do any worse."

He shifted his position to meet my gaze with his unreadable expression. "Then prove it, Stray."

It was my turn to stare at him. "Excuse me?"

The corner of his mouth kicked upward. "You heard me." Then he picked up my bowl of cereal and handed it over. "You shouldn't let those get too soggy."

"I won't. I don't use too much milk anyway." Then as if to prove the point, I took a crunchy bite of the cereal. It bought me a little time to consider my next words. I glanced at the photos again, then Seven.

His eyebrows raised in silent challenge. "Are you up for the task or not?"

I scoffed, nearly choking on my delicious cereal. "I'm more than up for it. But I need to get a studio. If we're doing it, we're going to do it the right way."

"You can't just take the photos here? We have light. You have a camera, a shiny brand-new one thanks to the bullet holes you're putting in my bank account." There was just a touch of mocking to his tone.

I shrugged, not rising to the bait. "Sure I could. But it wouldn't be my best work. If you want me to play, then we do it my way or we don't do it at all. Honestly, Seven, I have nothing I need to prove to you so if you're happy to let *Notoriety* publish that crap...have at it."

Folding his arms, Seven tucked his chin for a moment. He seemed to be calming himself, smoothing over his irritation. When he raised his head, he seemed far more patient.

The desire I had to pop that mood and make him lose his temper was *right* there. It actually caused me some physical pain to bite back the urge.

His expression was back to carefully neutral again, making me remember how very different he was to Gem. His twin was an open book, all the time. "Tell me what you need and I'll make it happen."

Well, shit, he must see how bad those images are after all. I wasn't about to deal with him booking some random studio. He knew all about film and the conditions it took to get the right lighting. If he didn't, he should.

No, he just wanted control back and to probably make me prove myself in some shitty environment with fluorescent lights or some crap. Absolutely not.

"How about I just tell you when *and* where to be, what to wear, and what to do? Will that work for you, Spawn? Because if not"—I pushed the shitty photos across the table to him again—"Janice has you sorted."

"Fine," he said with gritted teeth. "Dazzle me with your brilliance."

"As if that will be hard." I pulled out my phone, scrolled through my contacts, then called in a favor. The whole time I spoke to the studio owner, I could practically *feel* Seven trying to figure out what the rub was, what game I was playing.

"Sunday afternoon?" I flicked a look at Seven. He nodded his head slowly. Good to know. "I get the whole place, no one else?" The affirmatives were the answers I was waiting for. "I'll cash app the money to you. Thanks, Patton!"

Off the call, I pocketed the phone and reclaimed my cereal. "Sunday afternoon."

"So I heard," he said. "What time?"

"Noon until seven. But I can extend it to nine if I give them ninety minutes' notice."

"Think I'm going to need that much time?"

"Honestly? The thought had occurred. You seem to be as good of a model as you are an actor from what I saw." Then I took a bite of the cereal before it really did lose the crunch.

He huffed, but it held an edge of amusement. "Am I going to need a safe word?"

I glared at him. "Don't push it, Spawn."

chapter
thirty-three

Stella

I worked miracles this week, including sitting through the weirdest "publicity" date with Seven so far. Instead of an event, private home, or restaurant, we'd gone to a regular movie theater where they were airing a Seven Harrison marathon. We were seated near the back—the last row had clearly been set aside for us. Unfortunately, with Gem tied up on set once more as Seven's stunt double, I actually had to attend these dates with Seven himself, rather than Shadow Seven—as Gem jokingly called himself.

The first movie to air was the schlockiest, most insane fantasy movie I'd ever seen. I barely recognized any of them from their parts. Gem and Seven shared the role of the prince, until the prince was cursed. Then Seven and Gem battled outsiders and each other as the competing parts of the prince's personality. As for Ollie? I may never let him live down the pageboy haircut they made him wear.

Overall it was ridiculously cheesy and kind of adorable.

"Hopefully that didn't suck for you," Seven whispered against my ear before he stood. The audience was applauding as Seven was introduced. He stood in front of the packed auditorium and told stories about his time on that set.

Then he took questions. At the end of that, he rejoined me and they put on his next movie. Leaning toward him, I had to know: "How long is this marathon?"

"Five more movies, Stray. Don't worry. I'll cover the overtime."

Rolling my eyes, I leaned back in the chair. This was one of their first truly teen movies. A pair of brothers and their best friend pitted against vampires in a beach town. It was absolutely terrible.

I loved every minute but only because of Gem being in it.

By the time we left, Seven had taken pictures with lots of the fans, answered questions, and played the good sport about everything. It was—enlightening. It also gave me some ideas.

Sunday afternoon found Seven driving, despite my objections, in a fancy hybrid SUV. I had to take my camera equipment out of the safe, but I had a bag to bring it all with me.

Everything else I'd need would be at the studio. Seven had asked me what to wear—now there was a question I didn't get every day. I'd told him to dress like he had for the *Notoriety* shoot and to bring a couple of other outfits with him, something more casual and relaxed, along with something we could make dressier.

I really didn't see me dressing him up more. He was too uptight as it was; we needed to loosen him up. Excitement threaded through me. This wasn't about catching some scandal or documenting bad decisions to be sold later.

After entering the code for the lock, I opened the door to get us inside. "Make yourself comfortable," I told him as I began my sweep. I'd used this studio before. I just wanted to see what my best options were going to be.

"What time are you expecting the makeup artist?" Seven asked, hanging his garment bags on the clothing rack at the side of the room, where some Chinese screens were set up for changing.

I grinned to myself, shaking my head as I turned on the lights and set down my equipment. "You like wearing makeup for photo shoots, Spawn?"

"What?" he replied, looking confused. "No, but it's... That's just normal for all editorial shoots."

I raised my brows, meeting his eyes across the small studio. "Do you think you *need* makeup, Spawn? I've got some concealer and blush in my purse if you wanna borrow it."

His eyes narrowed in a glare, and I tried really hard not to laugh at him. He was making it impossible to remain straight-faced though.

"I'm teasing, Spawn. Chill the fuck out. You're handsome enough just as you are. You don't need makeup. In fact, I daresay that was contributing to the whole wax-mannequin vibes you were giving under Janice's lens."

Seven grunted, like my statement shocked him. "You think I'm handsome?"

Okay, now I had to laugh. "Oh, that's news to you? I'm literally fucking your identical twin on a daily basis, Seven, Of course I think *you're both* handsome. You're not on good terms with logic are you, hot stuff?" I snickered, rolling my eyes. "Let's start with jeans and a T-shirt, no shoes. Give me a few minutes to test lighting."

Not waiting for his response, I turned back to my task of ensuring the studio was set exactly as I wanted it and then set about tweaking my camera settings to align with the light. This was very different from my usual long-range telephoto snaps, and if I was being honest, I was terrified of fucking it up.

I'd talked a big game about Janice's photos and had no actual confidence that my images would be better, but I had to try. I couldn't let Seven approve those lifeless, stiffly posed images in a magazine as big as *Notoriety*. After seeing her touch him inappropriately, I wanted even more to rob her of that payday too.

"Is this good for you?" Seven asked from right behind me, making me jump a little as he shocked me out of my internal musings. I spun around to find him right there in my personal space, making me retreat a step.

He'd dressed as I asked, but the T-shirt hugged him in all the right ways to highlight the muscles he worked so hard to maintain. If not for the permanent scowl set on his face, I could have been fooled that he was Gem, dressed so casually.

I nodded, my head whirling with ideas for posing. "Yep. Stand over there on the tape mark, so I can check lighting against you."

He did as he was told, not making things difficult at all, which was...unexpected. I slid into professional mode, acting like I carried out studio shoots with major celebrities every damn day, while internally I was sweating buckets that I couldn't make it work.

Five frames in, I relaxed. I *already* had gold. Why the hell had I been so worried?

Letting the anxiousness slip away, I confidently guided Seven through the poses I had been researching all week from my favorite editorial shoots over the years. He nailed them all. Every damn one. It blew me away, considering how stiff and awkward he'd been in front of Janice's lens, which made me think that likely wasn't the first inappropriate interaction they'd had.

Gross.

We stopped after a couple of hours, and Seven ordered us food and drinks delivered so we could refuel. As we ate, he told me more about the current project that Gem was working with him on. It sounded downright dangerous, and when I sent

Seven to change into the next outfit, I popped off a quick text to Gem. Just checking on him.

"Okay, how do you want me?" Seven asked, reappearing out from behind the changing screen, and I nearly dropped my phone. His hair had become messed up while he changed, and he was back in the same outfit he'd worn for Janice: white button-down unbuttoned and a pair of Calvin Kleins that left absolutely nothing to the imagination. Fucking hell. This identical-twin thing was starting to mess with my head because my pulse was racing just from looking at Seven.

I needed to swallow hard before finding my voice. "Um, just give me a sex. I mean a sec." *Fuck!* "Give me a *second* while I drag that couch over." Hiding my flaming face with my hair, I hurried across to the side of the studio where an assortment of props and furniture was stored. I wanted Seven on the brown leather Chesterfield, but it took more effort than anticipated to make it move.

Thankfully, I had a big, strong man there to help, and between the two of us, we got it into position under my lights.

"Sit," I murmured, waving a hand at the leather seat as I adjusted the height of the diffusers and dialed through the warmth of the lights.

He once again did as he was told, and I tried really freaking hard to keep my mind out of the gutter when I caught him rearranging his dick in those tight, white underpants.

Once I was happy with the light, I stepped back to where I'd left my camera, then glanced over at Seven. He'd slouched back on the couch while waiting and had an elbow propped up on the arm with his legs spread wide.

"Fuck," I muttered. "That's perfect. Don't move."

His brow dipped ever so slightly as I quickly fixed my camera settings and took a few test shots. Then I sighed and shook my head when I looked at the previews.

"Can you..." I pursed my lips, analyzing the little image on my camera screen. "Can you stay exactly as you are but this time try putting a little more *sex* in your eyes? Look at me like I'm Clara Belle."

I raised the camera back to my face, clicking a few shots before grimacing. "Okay, scratch that, you look fucking constipated. Can you just pretend you're looking at someone you *actually like*? Give the camera your best panty-dropper smolder, Seven. I know you've got one in there somewhere."

He shifted slightly, then *wham.*

Fuck. I think my own panties just drowned with the instant flush of heat as his gaze hit me through the camera lens. *Holy crap.* I was unprepared.

"Like that?" he murmured, seeking validation.

"Uh-huh," I replied in a somewhat strangled voice. "Perfect. Move around a bit, try some different positions."

He did as I asked, such an obedient man, and my throat tightened with desire. I tried to mentally remind myself it was just the identical-twin effect. I was so intimately familiar with Gem and they *were* identical, so my body just thought he was Gem.

Right?

Right.

"Hold that," I ordered when he struck a pose with one leg hitched up on the sofa and his head tipped back into the light. "Don't move for a sec." I just needed to fix the way the shadows were falling over the side of his face, which I did with a minor tweak. Then when I tried another shot, I realized his shirt wasn't quite right.

"Stay there," I murmured. "I need to fix this." I put my camera down, then moved over to where he posed on the couch and tugged the edges of his shirt farther apart, revealing his golden, toned abs in full flex.

"Stray," Seven said in a rough voice, pulling my gaze away from his abs, where I had just zoned out. Fuck, had he just caught me checking him out? "Is that drool on your chin?"

Panicked, I wiped my face of all expression. Then instantly groaned when Seven's lips curved in a smug-as-fuck grin. Totally busted. "You're an asshole," I muttered. "It just so happens you're a sexy asshole. Don't let it go to your head, Demon Spawn."

Forcing myself to take a step back, I turned away to retrieve my camera once more as I took a few calming breaths. This was *Seven*...not Gem. Except, that was part of the problem.

Swallowing hard, I brought the camera back to my eye and tried to focus on the art. Except he took that moment to run a hand through his hair and flex his body, and an embarrassing sound escaped my throat. Fuckity fuck, had he heard me? Surely not. It had been quiet. Just in case, I fake coughed a couple of times.

Nice. That covered it up.

"Okay, try a different pose," I suggested but as he shifted his position, I spotted a big problem through the lens of my camera. A big...hard...problem.

"Seven!" I gasped, lowering the camera and putting it down on a stool so I could gesture wildly at the issue. "This isn't a shoot for *Playgirl*. No one needs to see that."

He shrugged, unconcerned with the way his briefs were stretched out of shape. "I don't know what you want me to do about it, Stray. I can't control the fact that my dick thinks you're looking at *me* like that."

My mouth went dry. "Like what?" My question was so high-pitched, it was comical.

Seven smoldered at me, fisting his dick through the fabric as he shifted on the seat. "Like your head is blurring the line on which Harrison twin is here, maybe thinking about having

Gem bend you over the arm of this sofa and fuck your pussy until you screamed."

"I'm not!" I protested, my cheeks heated. "That's...insane. Trust me, Seven, I could tell you two apart in the dark."

His brows rose with curiosity. "Ah, so that look in your eye is just for me? Good to know."

Panic. Utter panic. "What? No, that's not what I said. You're twisting my words, Seven."

His lips pursed, and his hand shifted on his cock. "Am I? I don't think I am."

I forced a humorless laugh. "Well, trust me, Seven, you could literally kiss me right now and I'd feel absolutely nothing for you. My panties are bone dry, in case you're wondering. All of this is doing *nothing* for me."

Somehow I'd drifted closer while we spoke, and quick as a whip, he sat forward and grabbed my wrist in his strong grip. A sharp tug pulled me off balance and I tumbled into his lap with a startled gasp, which he smothered with a bruising kiss.

My brain totally short-circuited. I hadn't been lying about knowing him and Gem apart well enough that I wasn't picturing Gem in his place—that was the fucking problem. I was attracted to *Seven*, and now that he was kissing me, I lost all grip on my protests. My lips parted and his tongue delved inside with determination while his fingers flicked open the button of my jeans.

Shock rippled through me as I realized he was taking me at my word, and I tried to squirm away but his grip on my wrist was impossible. Within seconds, his hand was inside my jeans, and inside my utterly saturated panties with his fingers slipping between the folds of my heated, swollen pussy.

"Liar," he growled against my mouth, and it was the kind of feral sound that made me whimper with need. Almost against my will, my hips rocked against his hand, encouraging his fingers to slide deeper and I moaned. Fuck. I was totally busted now, but at the same time, so was he.

A deep rumble vibrated his chest as I stroked my hand down his body, then stroked my thumb over the slick tip of his erection, already poking out of his underwear like the garment simply couldn't contain all that meat anymore.

Seven groaned, then released my wrist to roughly yank my jeans and panties down in a frantic motion. I helped by kicking them off my legs, not breaking our kisses for more than a few breaths, then his hand returned to my pussy and he thrust two fingers inside.

When I tugged his underwear down to fully fist his cock, he made another of those growling noises and swiftly manhandled me to kneel on the couch. I whipped my shirt over my head and unclipped my bra in record time, then gripped the backrest as he stood behind me.

His fingers swiped through my aching lower lips a couple of times, but right when I thought he'd insert Tab A into Slot B, his palm cracked down on my ass cheek and I yelped.

"What the fuck, Seven?" I gasped in shock as he massaged the already-heated flesh.

"That's for lying to me, Stella. Do it again and you won't like the result," he explained. Then smacked me again, harder, and my pussy clenched. "And that was just for fun." Then he slammed his cock into my tight cunt with one brutal thrust that saw me scream out loud.

My whole body tensed and quivered, but the heat swirling through my core promised such a good time, I couldn't even be *that* mad about it. Still, considering he'd just proven he and Gem truly were identical in all departments, he could have taken that entry a little slower. That'd ache later for sure.

"You're such an asshole, Seven," I moaned, even as I rocked

back on his thick cock like a greedy whore. "You didn't have to be so rough."

In answer, he smacked my other ass cheek with an open palm, then hissed a breath as my pussy clenched around him. "Yes, I did." He replied. "So you'll be too sore for another of your marathon fuckfests with my brother and best friend later."

A low chuckle rolled out of me then, my breath coming in short, sharp pants as I rocked on his cock, increasing the depth of his thrust. "You'll have to try harder than that, Sev. I have plenty of stamina."

"So I've heard," he grumbled, then smacked me again, and I yelped loudly. "I'll settle for making sure you can't sit without thinking of me. Especially when your sweet pussy grips me like that, holy *fuck*...Stella." Another smack, and this time I cried out.

My backside was flame hot and so freaking sensitive, I could hardly form complete thoughts. I needed to come. That was all I could focus on. I needed to come so freaking badly, and those smacks with his cock buried deep inside were building the pressure to something terrifying.

"Holy *shit*," I moaned when he delivered another few smacks in quick succession, swapping sides. "I'm so close, Seven. I'm going to come..."

"Good," he grunted, planting a foot up on the sofa to fuck me deeper. "Come on my cock, Stella. Say my fucking name while you do."

Instead of smacking me again, he reached around and found my clit with a brutal pinch.

"Fuck!" I exclaimed. "Shit...*Seven!*"

He didn't slow to wait out my climax; instead, he grabbed a fistful of my hair and jerked my head back as his hips pumped. He fucked me with all the pent-up frustration of *weeks* of living together. He hadn't been joking when he said he wanted to make it hurt—I'd bet anything I couldn't walk straight later—but that ferocity only intensified my orgasm further.

When he came, it was buried deep inside me with absolutely no effort to pull out—like he wanted to fill my pussy with his cum regardless of potential consequences. Both Gem and Ollie had been fucking me without protection, but they'd been crazy careful about pulling out at the last moment.

Thank fuck for my IUD, that's all I had on that subject.

He grunted as those hot jets filled me up, his fist tightening in my hair as he dipped a kiss to the top of my spine, groaning my name. "*Stella…*"

"I still hate you, Seven," I whispered between gasps for air.

He laughed then, and his cock jerked inside my throbbing pussy in the most incredible way. "The feeling is mutual, Stella."

Fucking hell, we needed to stop using each other's real names. This was feeling way too intimate for my liking. Then as he slid his thick cock out of my slick core, he slapped my ass and I jerked like he'd electrocuted me. He laughed harder then, and it was an infuriatingly smug laugh.

"Gem's going to skin you alive," I grumbled, pulling my clothes on over my *exceptionally* sensitive butt. Then dread curled through me. Would he also skin *me* alive for this?

chapter
thirty-four

Gemini

Seven fucked Stella. It was painfully obvious from the moment they arrived home from their photoshoot. Her lips were puffy and pink, her cheeks colored, and her eyes glassy. I knew that look *extremely* well because I took great joy in causing it. But the smug-fuck smirk on Seven's face and the stiff way she was moving got my blood pressure rising.

"Gem, you're back early," Stella gasped when she locked eyes with me. I was in the kitchen, halfway through reheating a meal that our chef had delivered earlier, and the moment our gazes met, she flushed with guilt. "We need to talk."

My jaw tightened as Seven slapped her backside and she visibly flinched.

She. Flinched.

"What...*the fuck*...did you do?" I snarled, fists balled as I considered actually murdering my brother.

Panic etched across Stella's gorgeous features, and she physically stepped between my twin and me like she could stop me from killing him for whatever he did to hurt her.

"Stop! Gem, he didn't hurt me!" she exclaimed, holding her hands up like she was trying to break my stare down with

Seven. "Or, rather, he didn't do anything I didn't enjoy," she amended with gritted teeth.

Seven's grin curved his lips again, and he gave me a pointed look. Our twin link said everything I really needed to know—he liked her a whole fuck-load more than he was ever willing to admit out loud. This had been brewing since the minute the two of them met—it had just been a matter of time. I knew it; Ollie knew it; *Seven knew it*. The only one who seemed surprised was Stella herself.

I narrowed my eyes, my jaw tight, but I calmed down somewhat. She'd enjoyed whatever Seven did...and I found it extremely hard to maintain a grudge when I could feel the calm satisfaction radiating from my twin. He wasn't using her for a quick fix to toss her to the curb later—he was giving in to his undeniable desire.

And she was reciprocating, it seemed.

Jealousy was a totally new emotion to feel between Seven and me, and yet there it was, bitter and acidic as he bent to brush a kiss over her cheek.

"Now I know why Gem calls you *Slick*," he murmured, then chuckled as Stella threw a hard elbow into his abdomen. She wasn't messing around—she actually wanted it to hurt—but Seven just patted her backside again and walked away laughing.

Once he was gone, I eyed Stella more carefully. "Are you okay?" I asked with dread. What if she said she wasn't? I trusted Seven as much as I trusted myself. More. But if Stella felt—

"I'm fine," she grumbled, her cheeks pink again. "Seven's just a dick, that's all. Nothing new...except, uh..."

"You had sex." I wasn't going to make her flail around searching for the words to tell me what I already knew.

Her eyes widened, but she nodded.

I sighed, running my hand through my hair. "Do you... Does this change us? You and me? Ollie?"

She shook her head violently. "No. God no. Unless this changes things for you? Seven was... That was a one-time thing. Never to be repeated. We still hate each other, if that's any reassurance."

I couldn't help but smile at that because I knew perfectly fucking well once wouldn't be enough for Seven—not now that he'd had her for himself. He would already be hooked, just like me and Ollie.

"This changes nothing for me, Slick. I'm perfectly happy to share you with my best friend—hell, I *enjoy* sharing you with him. Why would my twin be any different?"

The relief that washed through her was visible, her shoulders sagging, and I reached out to pull her into my embrace. Her arms wound around me, and I held her tight— right where she belonged, except that her hair smelled of Seven. I needed to get her in the shower and fix that.

I said as much, and she groaned. "As much as I want to take you up on that...I think I need to put some ice on my backside before I can engage in any more fun."

Motherfucker. Acting on impulse, I flicked open her button, spun her around and yanked her jeans down to see what he'd done with my own two eyes. All over her perfect ass were raised red welts in the shape of Seven's hand, some already turning purple with bruising.

"Seven's a *fucking asshole*," I growled as she giggled and tugged her pants back up.

"I know," she agreed. "That's what I keep saying!"

Scooping her up into my arms, I let the uncertainty slip away. So long as she still wanted *me* even after having Seven, that was all that mattered. "Come on, Slick baby, I'll take care of you. Wanna watch some Netflix in bed with me? I'll be on my best behavior and provide ice packs for your backside."

She snuggled her face into my chest, her fingers linked behind my neck as I carried her up the stairs to my room, my dinner totally forgotten. I set her up in my bed—lying on her belly and propped up with pillows so she could watch TV—then ducked back downstairs for supplies: popcorn, drinks, and frozen gel packs.

"Oh my god, Gem," Stella laughed when I returned. "You're too much."

"Or just enough," I countered, getting cozy beside her and placing the ice packs on her backside. Seven had really left a mark—no doubt exactly as he intended.

She sighed as I settled in beside her to watch the movie she'd picked. It was one of Ollie's newer ones, and he'd love to know she was watching it. After a while, her eyelids started drooping, so I dimmed the lights and lowered the TV volume so she could drift off if she wanted.

"See?" she murmured, sounding half-asleep. "This is why I love you, Gem. You're so thoughtful."

I froze. "Say that again?" But she was already asleep.

I'd heard her, though. Her soft voice echoed through my head over and over, getting louder and clearer in my brain. *I love you, Gem.*

She'd said it, and there were no take backs. Nope, not now that I'd heard it with my own ears.

Grinning like an idiot, I turned off the TV and rearranged us under the blankets so she snuggled into my arms, just how I liked. "I love you too, Slick," I whispered, despite the fact she was fast asleep.

The next morning, she woke me up in my favorite way. With her lips wrapped around my cock and her hand cradling my balls like precious jewels.

"Do you have plans today?" I asked her sometime later, as she lay boneless and sweaty, draped over my chest. My dick was still parked firmly inside her and I'd happily just leave it there until it hardened again, if I hadn't made other plans already.

"Mmm," she replied, lazily tracing the ridges of my traps with her fingertip. "I did, but it's not important. Why?"

"Remember how you offered to take me on a date?" I kissed her hair, teasing my fingers down her spine. She fit so well in my arms. "Before this arrangement with Seven, remember? You wanted to take me for a drive into the hills away from all the prying eyes?"

She lifted slightly off my chest to squint at me with those sooty lashes of hers framing her gorgeous green eyes. She took my breath away all the time. "I remember. You offered a hike and a picnic. I countered with a drive."

I dropped a kiss on her nose. "Exactly. So do you want to? I'll drive."

Her smile was like a ray of goddamn sunlight. "I'd love to." Then her pussy tensed around my cock and I started to get hard again. Her smile turned sly, so there was no point even trying to hide it. She just had that effect on me...

To save on time, we took our party into the shower, where Ollie found us, strolling into the bathroom right as I came all over Stella's perfectly lush tits. He started to question the redness and distinct handprints on her backside, but she was *very good* at distraction and he quickly forgot what he was asking as she deep-throated his monster cock.

"Holy *fuck*," he moaned, gripping two fistfuls of Stella's wet, black hair. "You've been working on that. Shit, Snow, you're such a good girl taking my cock that deep."

"Fuck," I chuckled, grasping myself. "I can't come again so fast. I need to rehydrate or something. Don't take too long in here. Stella and I have a date." Then I left them to it because I loved Ollie...and I loved Stella too. They made me happy.

Would Seven fit into this with us? It was already perfect, but maybe it could be better with him.

It was midmorning by the time Stella and I finally left the house, but that meant I had tons of time to pack a full picnic spread in the trunk of my car. Our plan was to drive up into the hills and walk to the waterfalls about half an hour from the parking lot. Then we could swim, picnic, fuck, whatever we wanted, and all without the constant scrutiny of media.

Except we barely made it ten minutes up the winding road of Angeles Crest highway when I realized we were being tailed.

"What is it?" Slick asked after I glanced in the mirror for the fifth time in a short span of time. "Is someone following us?"

I sighed. "Yeah. Probably, uh, paps."

She scowled, shaking her head. "We don't claim anyone who engages in risky business to get shots. Risking vehicle accidents just to get a photo? So not okay."

Yeah. I agreed. And yet, the car behind us sped up to tailgate-level closeness and another glance showed they weren't alone, another car seemed to be right behind them.

I needed to keep my focus on the road and driving safely, but every fiber of my being wanted to get Stella away from these leeches so even without meaning to, I sped up.

The road was winding up the side of the hill, and it was impossible to take the corners too wide or too fast, but the car following us seemed to have no regard for their safety as a man literally started to climb out the passenger window with his camera in hand. He stopped only when his entire upper body hung out in the wind, raising his camera to his face.

"Is he fucking serious?" Stella exclaimed, then stuck her hand out her own window to show the photographer her middle finger. As funny as it was, she'd probably just given him a major payday.

"How the hell did they know this was my car?" I asked aloud, shaking my head. I drove the most mundane, nondescript Honda Civic for several reasons, one of which being that it wasn't a *celebrity* car and could go totally unnoticed.

Stella growled an angry sound, looking over her shoulder. "I'd bet my life savings it's Dillon. You left your car outside my place the night it was ransacked. He probably took notice and sold the info."

I grimaced. "He's a real peach."

Just then, the second car's driver put their foot on the gas and sped up, overtaking the paparazzi guys and coming up level with us in the wrong lane. A frantic glance across showed me the car wasn't carrying more professional stalkers with cameras but instead a bunch of girls. All with their shirts lifted and tits wobbled around as their driver kept them level with us.

"What the fuck?" Stella exclaimed with a mixture of laughter and panic. "Is this a regular occurrence for you?"

"It's really not," I admitted. "This seems to be your influence, Slick. The fangirls are losing their minds with jealousy like Clara *never* experienced."

Stella started to say something, then gasped sharply. "Gem! Look out!" She screamed her warning right as a semi-truck came around the next corner, headed straight for the fangirls. I steered as far over as possible, dropping my foot hard onto the gas to give them space in our lane to pull in, but the paps remained hot on our tail.

There was no other option for their driver but to swerve the other way, and a split second later, the most almighty crash rang out on the side of the hill.

"Holy fuck," I exclaimed, braking as fast as I could without endangering ourselves. A glance in the mirror showed a thick plume of smoke already rising from the trees where the car had disappeared over the ledge and a sick feeling of dread curled in my gut.

The paparazzi car had stopped too, and both men were already out with cameras in hand. One ran toward the crash scene, camera raised and, presumably, shutter clicking like mad while the other approached my car. Fucking hell. That was the last thing Stella *or* Seven needed—so I made a choice I knew would haunt me forever.

I stepped on the gas and reversed back the way we'd come, passing close enough to the pap that he actually flung his camera as he threw himself to the side. I'd never have hit him. The camera though? I experienced a bit of glee as I ran right over it.

Once we were at the side of the road closest to where the girls went off, I was getting out of the car. "Call rescue services."

"What are you going to do?"

"Get down there and see if I can help." I circled to the back of the car and flipped open the trunk. Thank fuck I'd left my climbing gear packed in there.

Stella was getting out of the car, phone to her ear as she described where we were. The truck had stopped some way down the hill and the driver was hurrying up to us.

Three things happened at once: the pap whose camera got broken—so sad, moving on—charged toward us; the other photographer was yelling, "They're alive"; and the stroke of helicopter blades echoed in the distance. Hopefully that meant rescue efforts were already on the way.

"You bastard," the pap said as he reached us. Then Stella literally put herself bodily between us. The pap shoved her, and before I could punch him, she slammed her knee into his junk and he went down howling.

"Yes, I'm fine," Stella continued. "The man tried to assault me, but he's going to be too busy getting his dick out of his throat to do it again."

That was my girl.

"You got more of that?" the truck driver asked when he saw what I was doing. He also had a fire extinguisher in hand. I slung the first-aid kit over my shoulder and then handed him some rope.

"Be careful," I told Stella, and gave her a kiss. I pressed my keys into her hand and then eyed the guy on the ground who was still groaning. "You think about touching her again and you won't have a dick to hold on to."

Turned out the truck driver—Dale—was a decent enough climber himself. The route down was steep, but we made it swiftly.

The girls were somehow still alive.

The other photographer had also taken a tumble trying to get down there and had broken his leg. What a shame. We had most of them stabilized as the ambulances and cops rolled in.

One girl had to be airlifted. I was pretty sure she'd broken her pelvis. Another girl had a lot of lacerations; some were pretty deep. I gave one of the paramedics a number for a plastic surgeon we knew. I'd call him too. She might need some help with the scarring.

The fact no one died was a fucking miracle. We had to answer questions. The pap Stella had kneed was in handcuffs and in the back of a cop car when I got back up there.

"Don't worry, Mr. Harrison," a fresh-faced cop that looked like he still used pimple cream and was going to be late to his third period in high school said. "He got verbally abusive with Miss Charles. We put him in the car to cool off. Once my partner gets everyone's statements, we'll make the call on what to do with him."

Fine by me. I slid an arm around Stella, and she hugged me tight. "That's fine. We'll be right here to make the statements when you're ready."

We never got to the waterfalls or to the picnic, and I found myself filing another police report. The whole time, there was a helicopter circling overhead. This story was going to go viral.

Dipping my head, I kissed Stella and soaked in the connection. She dug her fingers into my nape, and when I lifted my head, I studied her fierce expression.

"You okay?" In all the excitement, had I missed something? "You weren't hurt with the sudden deceleration were you?"

"You're a damn hero," she said, and I blinked. "I'm more than fine. Just wish..." Then she glanced to where there was tape keeping people back. The full rescue effort had closed off this section of road, and we'd gained more than a few lookie-loos.

Pressing my lips to her ear, I whispered, "Seven and you are going to get all the credit. I'm more than okay with that, Stella. I might make him look good, but I don't want that attention. I never have. But those girls were foolish and who I am or want to be isn't their fault."

"I know," she said, then smoothed her hands down my shirt. "You're amazing."

"Right back atcha, Slick."

It took another two hours before we were able to give our statements. At least I could feed Stella from the packed picnic we had. That said, when we were free to go, I was more than happy to get her back in the car and away from all of this.

"You might have a hard time topping this date," she warned me with a sly grin. "Unless I can convince you to do the lifeguard routine and save me when I get a cramp."

I snort laughed. "So you have fantasies about men in red board shorts?"

"And out of them," she hummed. "I'm not fussy."

My dick stiffened obediently. "It's a good thing we have a pool."

"Oh," she said with a little smile. "Feel like rehearsing until we get it just right? Might take a while."

The rest of our lives if I played my cards right.

chapter
thirty-five

Stella

As proud as I was of Gem, I couldn't stop thinking about the accident. Reckless driving on the part of the paps trying to get a picture of us aside, the fangirls had taken needless risks to flash their tits at Gem. Yes, I understood that they thought he was Seven and apparently his fans were just that obsessed, but it was a phenomenally stupid idea on their part. They'd nearly died, for fuck's sake.

One of the two paps who'd been there was under arrest. He'd gotten mouthy with the cops and since they'd had enough to book him, that's what they had done. Good. Maybe he'd develop a brain cell while he was in jail. Honestly, who was going to buy some boring shot of us in a nothing-special Civic on the way to a date? It was an idiotic idea put into action by some idiotic people. My gut told me Dillon was probably involved and that just made it even worse.

Curled up in a chair in the library, I scrolled through social media on my phone. I'd checked in with Dad but he had a doctor's appointment today. Mom was back from her break and they both seemed a lot happier for having had the time apart.

Dad had also seen the news reports about the accident and

the images of me and "Seven." I'd messaged him from the crash site once I spotted the press helicopter. So then, I'd gotten a running commentary from him in text messages about the angles from the story.

The next-to-last message from him had left a mark: *Just promise me that you know what you're doing, Shutterbug.*

Did I know what I was doing?

What started out as a one-night stand—a very *good* one-night stand and some lucky shots—had morphed into so much more. I didn't want to go over the mental list of how much *more* because it would just leave me fighting anxiety all over again. I wasn't used to this level of emotional attachment.

By some small mercy, when I *had* slipped into a panic attack after the whole crash mess, it'd hit me when I was alone and I was able to get through it privately.

If it'd been an hour earlier, I'd have been wrapped around Ollie—who'd been *livid* when he got back and found out everything that had happened. If it had been a couple of hours later, Seven would have had a front row seat to my meltdown. He'd silently plucked me out of my bed and carried me to his, but I'd been too exhausted to ask what the hell he was doing.

Drained, shaking, and defeated, every muscle in my body ached. I mentally made an executive decision to discuss it with him later since taking me to sleep in his room was wildly out of character for us.

He was gone when I woke up, the only evidence that I hadn't imagined it all being that I was still tangled up in his charcoal sheets with the distinctive smell of him clinging to my skin—almost like he'd bear-hugged me all night long.

Weirdly, they were all gone today. Gem had more stunt work to do.

"I thought this film was finished," I said when he told me

before leaving the house. Seven had finished his scenes weeks ago, and I'd thought he said filming was complete.

"Pick-up shots, Slick," Gem said with an indulgent smile. "Seven's finished all of his principal photography, but with me there, they wanted to polish some of the set pieces. We have maybe another week and we should have everything."

"Be careful." I'd worried about the work before. After the accident, I couldn't escape thoughts of just how risky his job was.

"Don't worry, Slick," he murmured before he kissed me. "I have the best reason in the world to come home."

There was a preview screening for the press for Ollie's new movie today—two of them, actually, a private one on the studio lot and another larger one tonight with the red-carpet treatment. Ollie had been poking Seven and Gem to make sure I got to go or he'd threatened that he'd take me as *his* date.

Even that didn't really help me shake the unsettled feeling in my gut. In my opinion, celebrities courted the press and the public. They needed us more than we needed them. But...those girls could have killed themselves with their actions. The paps could have caused more than one accident. If Gem hadn't been such a good driver or if the trucker hadn't been aware of what he was doing, it could have all ended so much worse.

The hashtags about the Harrisons and the accident were everywhere. So were pictures, including swoony comments on them about how heroic Seven was. *The perfect man on-screen* and in real life.

Too bad he was with such a shrew.

Shrew?

I rolled my eyes at the wildly outdated term, but there was a hashtag that caught my attention: #stellamustgo. That didn't bode well. Nor did the one next to it: #freeSevenHarrison.

Oh goody, that one was trending. Like I was somehow holding him captive? That was new.

I clicked that one first. The sheer volume of posts, links to other social media sites, reels, clock app videos, and more had me sitting up slowly with bile rising in my throat.

There was intense, and then there was *this*. All of the messages had a clear theme. They didn't want Seven back with Clara Belle—not all of them anyway. She had some fans, but most were happy they were apart. They didn't think it had been a real relationship anyway.

But me? Oh, they wanted me gone yesterday. They'd have happily seen me die in that crash.

He's a ten, except he has an ugly bitch noose named Stella around his neck.

#Steven is a terrible fate for our man Harrison. He deserves better. She's ruining him.

Those were mild. The more I doomscrolled, the bat-crap crazier they became.

Stella's a dirty pap. I bet she has the goods on him.

OMG #stellathedevil is she blackmailing him?

We have 2 #freesevenharrison, have u seen this?

The photo accompanying it was blurred, so I had to click to clear it up. It was a photo of Gem, me, and Ollie at the restaurant when Ollie slid in to join us for our lunch date. We were all laughing, but Ollie was holding my hand.

The replies to that particular image began as angry and descended into vile. Oh and look, a new hashtag. #stellatheslut

If you didn't want everyone to know what you were doing, don't do it in public. Celebs *wanted* to be photographed and they *wanted* the reputation. That was my firm belief for the entirety of my paparazzi career, and I was unapologetic in the images I sold with that belief.

Except...I didn't want any of this.

I wanted *them.*

This was—fuck, this was a mess.

As much as I told myself to stop doomscrolling, I couldn't seem to come back up from this particular rabbit hole. I ended up on some Reddit board where Seven's fan group seemed to live. The Stella hatred there was next level.

They had pictures of my car. My motorcycle. Someone had found my driver's license picture. Were they fucking serious? There was a picture of me in high school in my goth phase that had lasted a solid minute. Every single image included something else about me they didn't like.

I was too tall. Too skinny. Too fat. My ass was round. My ass was flat. I had big boobs. I had no boobs.

"Make up your fucking minds," I snapped at the screen. My absolute favorite was that I was a clout chaser followed by a gold digger.

Then they brought Dad and wild conspiracy theories into it, and I wanted to throw my phone across the room. Or vomit. Or scream. Or...run.

Everyone knows that once upon a time, Seven; his twin brother, Gemini; and their best friend, Olivier Griffiths, were the hottest tickets. They got the Snatch Squad nickname because they had their pick of girls. They still could, but Stella is going to drag Seven down. I heard that after her father's accident, Stella Charles started down the celebrity pap road to make the celebrities like our beloved Seven pay for her father's mistakes. She's probably blackmailing him with sex pics and videos now.

Assholes. They were all fucking assholes.

This chick just went on and on. She had so many posts. Oh and look, a special set of links to all her platforms. It was more of the same; the vitriol grew more and more heated the closer we got to today. Apparently, she'd been on a crusade about me from the day the first story broke.

Oh, wait, that was on me. After all, I'd sold that picture myself. *Fucked yourself, didn't you, Stella?*

When a video popped up on her feed, I hit play. The woman who popped up lip-synched to some disparaging song with text prompts describing me. Worse, she looked like me. Well, the hair was mine and the clothes looked like...

I frowned and hit pause to look at it a little closer. They were exactly like mine. Had she gone out and bought clothes to mirror me? That was...

Fuck my life. Those were my clothes. Stolen out of my ransacked apartment, no doubt.

"Miss?" The snap of a voice jerked me out of the hellscape I had gotten lost in, and I looked up to find one of the cleaning ladies in the door. I swear, these women had stealth powers. They appeared and disappeared without warning. "I need to clean in here."

"Oh, sorry. Let me get out of your way." Probably a good idea to take a break. Empty coffee cup in one hand and the phone in the other, I headed for the kitchen. I had to scoot around her because, unlike other times, the cleaner did not shift to let me pass. Maybe I'd been holding her up enough that she finally had to say something. Ugh.

In the kitchen, I stared at the immaculate state of the space. The coffee from earlier was gone and the pot cleaned out. Apparently, she'd already finished this area.

I needed more coffee, though, so I started a fresh pot. While I waited for it to brew, I opened up the notifications on my phone to stare at the updates to the hashtags that had populated in the last few minutes.

The doorbell rang, and I glanced at the wall monitor. No one had buzzed up to the gate. But the cleaners didn't either, so maybe it was more staff. I found Jerry at the front door, his phone at his ear, and he gave me a harried look when I opened it for him.

"No, Marcus, I'm not sending them to New York for that opening. Seven already said he would do the Los Angeles, London, and Sydney red-carpet premieres. He's going to be on planes for four days. So New York will have to be a pass…"

"Come on in," I murmured softly as Jerry strode right past me. I closed the door, relocking it, and then waited for him to look at me.

"Sorry," he said, covering the mic on his phone with a finger. "Almost done. Just resume whatever and I'll follow you."

"Seven isn't here. Nor is Ollie or Gem."

"I know," Jerry said with a nod. "I'm here to see you."

That didn't bode well. Cycling through all the reasons he could be here to see me, I headed back to the kitchen. Thankfully the coffee was done brewing.

"Fantastic," Jerry said. "That's what I like to hear. Yes, he'll absolutely be bringing Stella with him. So they can get lots of pictures. The press is just *loving* the two of them right now and I have no doubt they'll be stronger than ever by the red-carpet date."

I shot him a look. He almost sounded genuine, despite the fake dating being his idea in the first place.

"Sounds good. Just remember what I said: vet the paps we let in. No more daredevils." Then he was off the phone.

"Where am I going?" I asked. "And do you want coffee?"

"I'd love a cup. I'm supposed to be cutting back." One of those statements wasn't like the other. "I've only had three so far, so I can't hear colors yet."

A snort of laughter escaped me and I poured him a cup.

"You should stay off the fan sites," Jerry said with a wave toward my phone. It was still open to one of the ugly Stellahating hashtags. "In fact, I'd avoid anything that involves your name in a hashtag. You'll never see anything you like."

"So I've discovered. You didn't say where I was going..." I took a sip of my own coffee. It wasn't really helping with the jangling of my nerves.

"To the red-carpet premieres. Seven's star is rising, and we're really close on that contract. Carriage Pictures is far more amenable to a couple of conditions now, particularly after the accident. They want to lock Seven in."

"It was good publicity, I suppose." That made sense. After the car crash, he was being hailed as a hero and the news was gushing over how kindhearted "Seven" was to stay and help. He'd also gotten some calls from a couple of directors that were hot right now, including one that preferred to only work with the same set of actors on every movie. The man also eschewed the studio system and did things his way.

Two years earlier, Nolan Kristoffsen left the studio he'd had a business partnership with for two decades and took his film business elsewhere. Then the first film released with that studio swept all the awards, the accolades, and made nearly a billion dollars.

His call had been one Seven had taken personally, and he'd positively glowed afterward.

"Exactly," Jerry said. "It's rising and rising fast. We don't want it to flame out. A lot of people are going to claim he's an overnight sensation, but you and I both know this is years of hard work in the making."

"No argument there." Seven was insanely dedicated to his craft.

He gave a small nod with a slight smile. "Good, because I need your help."

"My help?" I blinked. "To do what?"

"To convince Seven that you have to attend all these premieres."

I frowned. Suddenly that smile on his face was somewhat more sheepish. "It sounded like that was already the plan."

"It's *my* plan," Jerry said firmly. "Not Seven's. He's already vetoed having you attend because he doesn't want you to have to face that media gauntlet. Red carpets for a movie of this size will be wild, but I think you can handle it, Stella. You're tough."

Seven said no? That was insulting. Wasn't me showing up at these things fairly crucial to the whole fake-dating bit? Of course, we weren't so fake now...now that he'd been inside me.

chapter
thirty-six

Stella

"This is a terrible idea," I said as Seven backed me right up onto the hood of his car. The engine was still warm, and it let out little pops and crackles as it cooled. A lot like me and Seven. He'd barely parked and closed the garage door before he was dragging me out of the car and onto it.

"The worst," he agreed, mouthing kisses along my jaw to my throat as I undid the buttons on his shirt. The tie and jacket were already gone. He gripped my hips and lifted me up onto the hood itself. When he slid his hands down to my legs, I gave a little jolt at the heat of his palm on my inner thigh. "Fuck, I love that this dress has a slit. You need slits added to every single outfit."

"Excuse me?" I tilted my head back but he wasn't listening. He was kissing a path to my breasts, and he'd already dropped the spaghetti strings to bare them. The outfit had little cups in the top and you couldn't really wear a bra with it comfortably.

He palmed each breast and then sucked one of my nipples against his teeth so hard, I groaned. *Holy shit, that hurt and felt so goddamn good at the same time.* I yanked his shirttails out of his pants as he thrust three fingers into me.

Where the fuck had my panties gone? Seven fucked hard and furious. He didn't give me time to think about anything. Probably wise, because I was already swollen from fucking Ollie before I had to get ready and then Gem in the shower afterward.

The dopamine infusion made the evening so much more pleasant and almost took my mind off all the crazy stalker fans. Yes, I was starting to see them everywhere.

"Fuck," I swore as Seven bit one of my nipples hard enough that it stung.

"Focus, Stray," Seven ordered as he spread my thighs wider. "I'm working here."

A laugh bubbled out of me. "Apparently not well," I lied. "Or your dick would already be in me, Spawn."

That got his head up, and I had about three seconds to reconsider the challenge. Then he had his pants down, his dick out, and holy shit, he slammed it in so hard, I swore I felt my uterus quiver at the idea of him trying to reach it.

"Paying attention now?" The dark, delicious note in his voice had me arching.

"Oh, fuck yes," I moaned, not that he waited for the endorsement to start rocking into me. No, he shifted my hips higher, and I locked my ankles behind his ass. It had me sprawled out on the hood of his car while he set an unrelenting rhythm.

"That's it, Stella," he growled. "Take every fucking inch and then beg me for more."

No, I was absolutely not begging for shit. Except... I locked eyes with him. "Make me."

His lips pursed and his eyes went practically incandescent with that challenge. "If you insist."

I was so damn close to orgasming, I wasn't ready for him to retreat so abruptly. From long, hard thrusts, he shifted to shallow, barely there dips. When I tried to pull him in with my thighs, he let out a dark laugh.

"Not until you beg for me, Stray."

Ass. Hole.

I glared up at him as he grinned at me. He stroked one thigh, then between us, to where he was inside me. But the contact was so barely there and gone again.

"Fuck, I hate you," I groaned, already regretting my infatuation with his moody ass.

His responding chuckle only made it worse. Dick.

"Just one little *please*," he whispered, leaning over me. I could feel him everywhere and I just wanted him to—

"Goddammit," I growled.

"Mm-hmm," he said with an almost mournful shake of his head.

"*Seven.*"

Then he slid his hands under my ass and there was a finger probing right at my asshole. I snapped a look at him.

"You can do it, Stella," he coaxed, the agony of those half thrusts leaving me vibrating on the edge of frustration. "I know you can."

I seized his open shirt and hauled myself up until we were nose to nose. "Fuck me like you mean it, Seven," I ordered him.

"That's not begging," he murmured, then nibbled a little kiss along my lower lip. "I could just leave you like this, I suppose."

I glared. "Fine." I'd just get Gem…

"Gem is wrapping up the last of the night stunts tonight."

I groaned and almost slumped backward. Damn his mind-reading abilities.

He clicked his tongue thoughtfully. "And come to think of it, Ollie's doing that interview with late night and isn't even in the city. It will be *hours* before either of them get back."

"I hate you," I promised him again.

His grin was pure triumph. Sadly, the dick was right.

"Please, Seven," I simpered at him, batting my eyelashes. "Please give me your dick and fuck me like an animal."

Laughing, he dragged me into a kiss that devoured me before deepening his thrusts again. He didn't make me wait or beg for it as he fucked harder and deeper until I was pretty sure there would be an imprint of him on my bones.

The last thing I expected was the thrust of his finger into my ass. The burn and the pressure shoved me right over, and I was screaming his name.

"Fuck! Fuck! Fuck! Spawn!"

Well, close enough.

I was pretty sure I blacked out when he finally let go and came. His broken breathing matched my own as I surfaced. That was something. I had no idea how long we lay there, but eventually Seven eased out of me.

Didn't matter. I could still feel him.

"You know," I said, "I must like you a little bit."

"Yeah?" He was stripping off his shirt and then dabbing it between my legs. Oh, fuck, that was way too much contact. I squirmed but he didn't back off. "Just blotting some of this up, though I don't mind if you walk through the house with my cum on your thighs."

Leaning up on my elbows, I planted my barefoot against his chest. Where the hell had my heels gone? Problem for another day. "You like the idea of your cum running down my legs."

"I do," he admitted, and when I blinked, he grinned. "Surprised?"

"That you said you like anything about me?" I raised my eyebrows. "You could say that."

"Come on, Stray." He peeled me off the car hood, and it was

definitely peeling me off—my sweaty ass had gotten a little connected. We both paused to look at the very clear ass print on the hood. "Hmm, I might keep that. Could start a whole new trend."

The house was quiet as he guided me inside, collecting some of our discarded clothing as we went. The code he entered was familiar now. They'd given all of the codes to me. There was even one to send an alert to the cops, and another that would send alerts to them.

Seven paused in the kitchen, where he collected drinks and snacks. Oh, food sounded good. Then he took my hand, and upstairs we went. I could have just gone to my own room, but he had the food and he went into his.

I let him bully me into the shower—*after* I put my hair up. I didn't want to wash it again right now. His cock was all up and straining when we got out, and I decided to do him a solid and sank to my knees right there on the tiled floor.

Edging him might have also played into my plans because it was my name he chanted before I let him come. His release had me choking because, just like with my cunt, he didn't back off.

Finished, he dragged me up and then carried me to his bed, where he proved that Gem and Ollie were not alone in their pussy-eating skills.

I lost track of orgasms. When he flipped me onto my stomach and thrust into me even as he smacked my ass, my endorphins lost their damn minds. Pretty sure I mewled like a kitten when we were done. Or maybe I was just purring.

This time when he got a cool rag, he was careful with cleaning up his mess and then setting something chilly against the fresh welts he'd left on my ass.

"This isn't too much, is it?" The soft question roused me from my stupor, and I glanced up to find him studying me.

"No," I said "Not really. Unexpected? Sure. But I like it in the heat of the moment. The next day or two of feeling it every time I sit down? Debatable."

His smile was so wide and beautiful, I forgot how to breathe. "I never want you to forget what it feels like to have me."

"I had gotten that impression," I teased him, and he shocked the hell out of me by nuzzling a soft, almost-sweet kiss to my lips. Then he straightened and reached for one of the apple slices he'd grabbed in the kitchen along with some cheese.

The first bite was pure crisp fruitiness with the edginess of the sharp cheddar. "Hmm." I pushed up on my elbows and he took his time feeding me and himself. Then we split some water.

"I've been meaning to ask you something," Seven said, and I flicked a glance up at him. The emotion in his eyes stymied my next smart-ass response.

He offered up more fruit and cheese, and I accepted them and sucked on one of his fingers. His pupils seemed to dilate farther as he watched me. Then he slid his free hand up to loosen my hair and stroke his fingers through it.

"Will you stay in here with me tonight?" It was an invitation. The last time, after the car crash and my subsequent panic attack, he'd just brought me in here and that was that. We hadn't discussed or acknowledged that it'd even happened, and I hadn't slept in his bed since.

My heart did an uncomfortable twist.

The weight in the question threatened to suffocate me. Ropes of tension looped around me...but ultimately I wanted to stay.

"Unless you were planning on carrying me to my room, I guess I have to. Not sure I can walk after all of that." I was aiming for casual and nonchalant and wasn't totally sure I nailed it.

The smile kicking up one corner of his mouth made my stomach bottom out. The ease in his expression, the openness in his eyes, and the warmth in his smile were absolutely devastating to my equilibrium.

He just did *not* need to know that—his already enormous ego did not need the boost.

"If I wore you out that much, I better keep you close, so I can look after you." He fed me another slice, and this time he added a thin wafer of dark chocolate. Oh, having expected the cheese, the chocolate had my eyes drifting shut and another moan escaping me.

Instead of turning on a movie or music, we just lay there, with him feeding me and absolutely seducing my senses with his apples and chocolate and drugging kisses.

When we were done, he wrapped me up, tucking my head to his chest. I stayed there 'cause I was too damn spent to move —that was my story and I was sticking with it.

Lights out, he stroked his fingers up and down my back, the light massage sending me deeper. I was so ready to sleep. "You really are something special, Stella." The soft words threatened to leash me to him forever. "More than you know."

Yeah, I couldn't do this. It was too much and I was going to end up making a fool out of myself with words like *love* and *want* and *need*. So I walked my fingers up to press against his lips. "Shh. Sleep now."

He nibbled one of my fingers, then captured my hand in his. "Mine now."

"Shut up," I growled. "Or I will go sleep somewhere else."

My eyes snapped open as a shock rippled through me. Seven Harrison made me feel safe. Like Gem and Ollie. That thought was going to leave a mark. Fuck. What was I supposed to do with that? With all of them? I couldn't decide this now, so I closed my eyes again. Despite the surprise, I was also exhausted and warm. The asshole was still chuckling when I finally fell asleep, wrapped up securely against him.

A wild shriek woke me with a jolt.

The room was mostly dark and the bed next to me empty. But I could still smell Seven—and feel him. Blinking with sleepy confusion, I jerked my head at the movement of a woman right next to the bed.

Woman? What the shit?

Three things hit me at once.

One, she was dressed like one of the cleaners, and she looked just like the woman from the reel who'd been cosplaying as me.

Two, she looked really pissed off.

And three, she had what looked like a weapon in her hand.

I tried to roll away as she swung it, and it slammed into the pillow where my head had been.

Then she shrieked again. "You slutty whore! You're fucking *dead*!"

Being one of the featured guests on Laurent West's *Late Night on the Right Coast* meant a twenty-four-hour turnaround. Still, there were perks to flying first-class and nonstop. If only Stella wasn't still tied firmly to Seven's contract negotiations, then I could have lured her to come with me and we could have made it a long weekend in the city.

Next time, I promised myself. Maybe she'd like Broadway or sightseeing. Either way, I'd stayed long enough to sign autographs for the audience and the fans waiting outside the studio, then headed out to dinner and drinks with Laurent and a couple of the other guests.

It was good networking, but as much as I enjoyed the opportunity, I would rather have left earlier. As it was, I crashed for about three hours in a hotel room by the airport, then boarded a flight first thing in the morning. Time difference was a wonderful thing.

A driver waited for me at the airport, and I only had my carry-on, so I didn't have to wait for luggage. If only the drive from LAX wasn't quite so dense with traffic. Still it would barely be seven by the time I got to the house.

Perfect.

Hopefully I could kiss Snow awake. If she was up, I'd see about luring her back to bed. Twenty-four hours was far too long to be away from her. The closer we got, the more I felt like humming.

I used my code to let us in, and the driver took me up to the house. I made sure to add a generous tip and waved the man off as he left. Once I was inside, I disarmed the alarm, then reset it.

After I verified the driver was out, I headed for the stairs. The downstairs was quiet, which was perfect. Seven was always an early riser but could be doing laps in the pool or blowing off some pent-up tension in the gym. Totally fine by me.

I was halfway up the stairs when the first shriek ripped through the air. While I couldn't identify who was actually shrieking, there was no way *that* sound heralded anything good.

Racing up the stairs, I hesitated where the halls split. Snow's room was to the right, Seven's straight ahead, and mine and Gem's were to the left. The wild sound repeated, far angrier this time, and it came from straight ahead.

A part of me really hoped this was just Seven pissing Stella off. The man had a gift for pushing her buttons, and it was so obvious he got thrills out of having her bite back. I would happily sweep in and steal her away. At the same time, that scream didn't sound like her.

"Get the fuck away from me!" That voice, however, did. All playfulness vanished. Whatever was going on was bad...

Not letting myself think much past that, I shoved the door to Seven's room open. Thankfully, it wasn't locked. Light from the hall spilled inside. It didn't really give me much time to track what was happening.

Stella was on the far side of the bed, stark naked and wild-eyed. Another woman, armed with a knife, was lunging at her.

"Stop!" I yelled the word, hoping it would shock the woman or surprise her enough to make her stumble.

"Ollie!" Stella waved an arm at me, like she wanted me to get out. So not happening. Her assailant lunged forward, slashing the knife in the air.

The world slowed—I was never going to get there in time. Light from the hall glinted on the blade as she sliced toward Stella's outstretched arm. A hiss escaped Stella as a line of crimson decorated her flesh.

I wrapped an arm around the woman's middle and locked a hand around the wrist of her knife-wielding arm. "Stop," I ordered her again as I hauled her backwards. I had no fucking idea who this woman was, but I didn't care.

She was in *our* house and attacking the woman I loved. No way in hell was I going to let this continue. Despite the size difference, I found holding on to her incredibly difficult, considering how wildly she started fighting.

Legs kicking back at me, she tried to stomp on my feet. She kept trying to jerk her hand out of mine as I increased the pressure. I just wanted her to let go of the damn knife.

I narrowly avoided her head slamming back into my face. Then she twisted and bit down on my arm so hard, I was pretty sure she ripped skin through the shirt.

"Fuck." I gritted my teeth through the pain, but even my nerves spasmed and my fingers unlocked briefly. She sliced with her weapon, but I flung her away with all my might. She hit the side of the dresser with a sickening crash, knocking something off that thudded to the floor.

"Ollie." Stella sounded exhausted and *pissed right off*. Not that I could blame her. She stopped at my back, which was good. I had no intention of letting her get past me.

"It's okay, babe." I tilted my head toward Stella, but I didn't take my gaze off the woman crumpled in front of the dresser, panting wildly as she glared at us. "Just stay behind me. I'll deal with her."

The woman's lip curled in an ugly sneer. "Of course you want to protect the slutty whore cheating on Seven. What kind of shitty friend are you?"

Oh good. One of Seven's rabid fangirls. "Tell you what, Looney Toons, you get some help for your defects and I'll get back to you on that. Now put the goddamn knife down." This was insane. Somehow she'd managed to hold on to it through everything, like it was glued to her hand. Crazier shit had happened in Hollywood, I guessed.

Every bedroom had a security panel near the bed. All we had to do was hit the panic button. But that panel was on the *other* side of the bed from where we were.

I really should have triggered the security before I got up here. *Idiot.*

Stella's attacker was dressed like one of our cleaners, but I couldn't place her face to save my life. Her hair was done like Snow's, like if she were the Dollar Store version of Snow or something. Black box-dye could never replicate my girl's inky tresses.

Now would be a great time for Seven to stroll in—or Gem. Fuck, I'd even take Jerry if he moved his ass. The wild-eyed look on the woman's face kept me on my toes. Twice more, she tried to get past me, both times with a feint, and both times, I blocked her.

Yeah, we were not getting anywhere this way.

"Snow, babe," I said, holding the rabid chick's gaze. Granted, she wasn't foaming at the mouth or anything but she might as well have been. She also wasn't firing on all cylinders. "I need you to get out of here and head to your room or mine or even Gem's. Just get there and close the damn door, lock yourself in, and hit the alarm."

"She's not going anywhere!" Oh look, Looney Toons found her voice again. "Neither are you. Seven needs to be *free*. You two can be a lovers' murder-suicide pact. He might be upset for a little while but then he'll be free, and I'll be here to take care of him."

"Houston," I intoned, "we have a problem. Actually, we have several." I wanted her to focus on me, despite how ridiculous it was to try and reason with a wannabe murderer. I kept one hand outstretched to her and moved it whenever her gaze started to wander to Stella.

With my other hand, I motioned Stella to the door. She'd have to go over the bed and that was fine. I'd tackle Lady Straightjacket here before she could get to Stella. And once Stella was out of the line of fire, so to speak, I could hopefully talk the crazy lady down—or at very least disarm her so she couldn't do any more damage.

We just needed an opening.

"Problem number one," I continued in a conversational tone, like she wasn't threatening my naked girlfriend with a bloody knife. "Seven and I have been friends for years. I hate to break this to you, but we've never let a woman come between us unless we were the ones making her come."

Confusion creased the knife-wielding bitch's face. She really thought Stella was *cheating* with me, and it'd never crossed her mind that it was all fully consensual.

"Problem number two," I said, "one of the first things we're taught is to never stick our dicks in crazy. So you'd be shit out of luck, even if you succeeded in killing us."

I swore I could see the loading sign playing out over her head. Stella moved, hurtling herself over the bed as the psychotic lady snapped her gaze forward. She let out another of those banshee shrieks. It was enough to make my ears bleed but I launched forward to block her from reaching Stella nonetheless.

She managed to slice down my left forearm, but I caught her and her knife arm again. This time, I didn't let go. She was *not* getting near Snow.

Twisting, I held her hand away from me and bashed it against the footboard of Seven's bed. The knife finally clattered away from her loosened grip. Now I just needed to secure her. Somewhere else in the house, the alarm went off, likely triggered by Stella.

I didn't get long to enjoy the victory as the woman raked her fingers down my face. It didn't quite draw blood, but fuck, it hurt to get nailed in the eyes. I jerked my head back, and she tried to take advantage of my distraction to surge past me.

Stella was out of sight, but I couldn't risk this woman getting anywhere near her. Lashing out an arm, I caught her around her waist and shoved, sending her flying backward.

There was a heavy thump as she hit the wall, and she crumpled to the floor in a heap once again. I shook my head to try to clear the stars and scrubbed at my watery eyes thanks to her claws.

"Oh my god," Stella exclaimed, and I snapped my head over to look at her. She was in the doorway, wearing a T-shirt and wielding a baseball bat with violence and determination etched over her gorgeous face.

What a picture.

I looked back at our assailant—she wasn't moving. If anything, she lay awkwardly against the side of the dresser and there was blood leaking from a crease along her scalp.

"Fuck," I swore and double checked where the knife landed before I approached the woman.

"Ollie, be careful…" Stella was ready to back me up and she came right in after me, but I waved her off.

Mad Maxine wasn't moving. I crouched down and gingerly checked for a pulse. She had to have one; she'd been screaming a minute ago. The blood kept trickling downward steadily.

The sinking feeling of dread hit me a few seconds later. A shout echoed up from downstairs and the alarm cut off a moment before the sound of feet pounding on the stairs reached us.

The men who burst in had black suits and guns drawn—private security. "Mr. Griffiths? Miss Charles? Are you both okay?"

We'd made sure that security knew Stella belonged here. "She attacked us," Stella blurted out, and all at once, she was explaining, spilling the whole story without even pausing for a breath as she recounted the whole saga from the moment she woke up.

Her hand found mine, and I dragged her close for a hug. I didn't give a damn if security saw it—or got a good look at Snow's gorgeous legs.

She also didn't pull away until she found I was bleeding. Leaving the knife where it was and the room untouched, we retreated downstairs while our security called the incident in to the police.

I called Peter, my lawyer, while Snow pressed a cloth to my arm. Then I groaned when I called Jerry to fill him in.

Seven chose that moment to show up with fucking *pastries* of all things. When the fuck had he gone out for pastries? Gem was also heading home. Paramedics showed up and so did the coroner.

The house was a total circus, but Stella stayed with me. I made the paramedics treat her cut first, then let them look at mine. When the cops wanted to separate us, I shot a look at

Seven. He nodded and went with her. He also called another attorney to represent her.

Holy shit. I'd killed someone.

There were going to be consequences, but as much as I wanted to find some guilt for it, I couldn't. That bitch would have murdered Stella if I'd been even a minute later.

So no, I didn't feel an ounce of guilt. Not even for the publicity fallout we were going to face.

Stella was alive. I was alive. Seven and Gem were safe. We were all together.

It was a good fucking day.

chapter
thirty-eight

Stella

The story wasn't going away anytime soon. It was at the top of the gossip sites, the news stations, and even the papers in a lot of major cities: "Fan-club president dies in attempt to murder Seven Harrison's fiancée. Olivier Griffiths is real-life action hero." Somehow I'd been upgraded from "girlfriend" to make the drama more dramatic.

Meanwhile, we had to deal with the arduous fallout of the whole incident on our end. Police interviews. Crime scene investigators. Doctors appointments with documentation of my injuries and Ollie's. Then came the litany of questions: How had she gotten in? Why was she there? Why was that morning the day she snapped?

Ollie and I were separated during the questioning. Seven refused to be removed even when the attorney he hired for me showed up. Peter couldn't represent Ollie and I both. Even if he was willing, he couldn't physically be in two places at once.

The questioning seemed to go on forever, or so it seemed. I still wasn't sure who told them I was Seven's fiancée. At the time, it hadn't really seemed that important. Then Page Six announced it.

The hardest pill to swallow in all of this was the fact that the woman who attacked us and died was the president of one of Seven's online fan clubs, a woman named Karen Tyler. She'd also been employed by the company that provided our house cleaners.

She'd had access to the house and the guys for months. The invasiveness wasn't lost on me. Seven was furious because what else had she been doing in the house? The police were going to search her place and continue their investigation, but all three guys reluctantly admitted they'd "lost" a lot of underwear in recent months.

Since Ollie and I had basically told them the same story, they weren't charging him. They did, however, ask him to restrict any travel for a while. It was so late when we left the station, the sun had already set. Gem, however, waited for us in the lot with coffee, food, and a warm hug that I desperately needed.

Gem had gone to see my dad at some point when we were at the police station. With the breaking news, he wanted to be the one to let him know I was okay. He also wanted to relocate him. Since the house was the epicenter of the investigation, he arranged to move Dad into a place nearby with increased security and in-home care.

As for the four of us? We were staying in another mansion that Jerry had secured for us. Increased security included a manned security gate and a patrol. I'd never imagined that would be a life I wanted to live.

The media was everywhere—the press, the paps, all of them. The only time we left was for Ollie's red-carpet premiere, and we went together, all of us. The questions and the press of the crowd were insane.

One other piece of crazy that came out about Karen Tyler and her attack: she'd been egged on by Dillon. Apparently, he'd been feeding her all the info. While the police were still investigating him, he'd been blacklisted. Peter also got a restraining order filed against Dillon to keep him far away from us.

Two weeks after Karen Tyler died, the house was released by the cops and the death labeled self-defense. She'd died trying to attack us, and all Ollie had done was shove her back when she'd tried to charge me. Her death was an accident.

When Peter called us with the news, I did something I wouldn't have expected in a million years: I burst into tears. Something hot and fierce broke inside of me, and everything came out in a torrent.

Ollie wrapped me up tight and held me while I cried, then he released me to Gem while Ollie went to get us drinks. Eventually, Gem surrendered me to Seven. None of them teased me about the waterworks or the fact that I was the worst crier. My eyes got all puffy and my nose ran. It was pretty damn awful.

"Hey," Seven said when the crying slowed to hiccups. "You get that all out of your system, Stray?"

I lifted my sore and swollen eyes to glare at him. "Don't start."

"I never finished," he murmured, rubbing a slow circle against my back.

"Pfft." When I stuck my tongue out at him, he laughed.

"Slick," Gem said, "we have a proposition for you."

"A deal as it were." Ollie picked up the thread.

"A negotiation," Seven added. "But we're not discussing terms until you're up for it."

"I'm up for it," I said, sniffing, then accepting the tissue to wipe at my eyes before I blew my nose.

For some reason, the fact it actually made a honking sound had Seven flinching but then struggling to control his laughter, which made me feel better.

"Thank you," I said to Ollie as he passed me a drink. It was a cold glass of wine, and I was more than ready for it. "Should I be drinking before we talk terms for this proposition slash deal slash negotiation?"

"It's going to take a while," Gem said. "Last time I checked, you enjoyed a good wager."

I did, but what did that have to do with anything? Ollie and Gem grinned as they looked past me. Seven was curiously silent on this part.

"Okay, spill it, boys." I had most of my equilibrium back. They were all safe and here, and we were together. My dad was fine and doing well, thanks to the guys. Then because I shouldn't be sitting in a lap to negotiate, I got up and paced over to a second sofa, where I took a seat and eyed all three of them. "Anyone? Bueller?"

Seven snorted, a faint smile on his lips. "Excellent reference."

I saluted him with my wine. At least I still had my sense of humor. The three looked at each other and then as if by silent consensus, they stuck their hands out.

"Oh my god, are you seriously going to rock, paper, scissors this?"

"Yep." Ollie grinned at me. "Very democratic of us."

The part that made me laugh was the twins. They took Ollie out in the first round. He slid past them to come sit next to me. He even stretched and dropped his arm over my shoulders. The boys kept choosing the exact same thing.

"We're going to be here all night, and they're both going to do scissors this time." They stopped on scissors at the same moment I said it. Their glares amused me. After setting my wine down, I flicked open my bag and pulled out my change purse. I fished out a quarter and tossed it to Gem. "Flip the coin because now I want to know what you three are up to."

Gem flipped the coin and let Seven call it.

"Heads," he said.

With a smirk, Gem revealed the tails-up coin.

"You palmed it," Seven said. "Don't think I don't know that trick."

"Whatever, boys, deal with generational trauma later. What's up?" Admittedly, the more hell they gave each other, the better I was feeling. I also liked Ollie being right here, where I could lean against his shoulder.

"You remember how we met?" Gem said, eyeing me.

"Pretty hard to forget. You were in my spot."

He blinked. "What?"

"That corner stool. It's my favorite, and you were sitting in it. So when I had the chance to get it, I had to take it." Had I not mentioned this before? I could have sworn I did.

"I thought that was a joke." The shocked look on Gem's face was priceless. "So if I hadn't been sitting in your spot…"

I shrugged. "I might not have talked to you." Then, because he looked so genuinely troubled by that, I continued, "Which would have been a terrible shame. Though I still think you hitting on Flip as Seven would have been hilarious."

Seven whipped his head up to stare at me. "Excuse me? Also, who the fuck is Flip?"

"No one," Gem said, his grin growing. "Just a guy, and you owe me, Sev. I had to clean up at pool to make sure she didn't win that bet."

"Eh," I said. "I still feel like I won." Gem held my gaze and all the warmth unfolded in my chest. I adored that man.

"Me too," Gem said with a sigh. "You surprised me that night. You keep surprising me. I love how you do it. I love you."

Oh, my heart lodged in my throat.

"While our first meeting wasn't as prosaic," Ollie said, "I'm really fucking glad I got there in time to deal with the asshole. Just wish I'd broken his legs now."

"Me too," Gem and Seven said in one voice. No, that wasn't creepy at all.

"Still, Snow—you know why I call you that, don't you?" Ollie studied me.

"No?"

"Snow White's hair was black as ebony." He slid his fingers through my hair, combing it. "I'm pretty sure I fell for you that night when you stubbornly refused to go to the hospital or see a doctor, and I had to drag you back to the house."

I bit my lip. That was so damn sappy, and it made the tears burn in my eyes all over again.

"You stole my heart, Stella Charles. You aren't allowed to give it back. But I'm with Gem—I don't want this to end."

This...all of us?

I shifted my gaze to Seven. All three went quiet until Gem smacked Seven. "Not funny. Play nice."

For his part, Seven smirked. "Stray is never going to buy me being nice."

"Nope," I said. "I much prefer you being you. Even when you're an asshole."

"Then let's say you've been a thorn in my side from the beginning. Mouthy. Irreverent. *Stubborn*."

I shrugged on the last.

"You're also brutally honest with me when few people are willing to be. Even if I don't like hearing it, I like that you'll say it. I could wish you had better taste in movies, but then...you like me *despite* the fact that I'm an actor. I like that—"

Gem elbowed him.

"Fine, I love that about you." He shot a look at his twin. "Fuck off, Gem. I didn't interrupt your pitch."

"That's because his pitch was good," Ollie volunteered helpfully.

A laugh escaped me, and I smacked Ollie's thigh. "Seven is doing just fine, even without a script."

"Thank you," he murmured.

"Don't mention it," I retorted. "Seriously just...continue."

"All of us want you to stay," Seven said. "You may have noticed that we've been talking. We don't always agree on everything, but on this we agree: we *want* you."

"We *love* you," Gem stressed.

"We can't get enough of you," Ollie added.

"Guys..." I paused to gather it all together before I downed the glass of wine. Courage was courage, and if they could be this open with me, well, time to suck it up, buttercup. "I love all of you, but...can we really make it work? I mean three of you and one of me? What will the columns say? What about your careers?"

"Come on, where's your sense of adventure?" Seven started. "We can make anything work if we want it badly enough. The three of us are living proof of that. You, Stella Charles? So are you. You wanted to take care of your dad, and you did whatever was necessary, even dealing with an ass like me."

"As for the three of us and the one of you," Gem said, stepping up to answer my other questions, "not sure if you've noticed, Slick, but it's *been* working for us. Yeah, we butt heads, and some of us are greedy fucks. I don't care that Seven is your public boyfriend. I wouldn't care if Ollie was. Or both. Whatever. I don't give a *fuck* what the columns say."

"As for our careers," Ollie said, "financially? We're solid at the moment. I've been thinking about doing more producing, so if the parts dry up, I'll find that perfect script and make sure it gets made. If the choice is my career or you? I choose you."

"Carriage Pictures?" I looked at Seven.

"I had Jerry lay it out for them. He wasn't a fan of playing hardball, but I'm not letting a deal derail our lives. I'll still make movies whether it's for Carriage Pictures or B64 Studios."

I swiped at the tear that escaped and shifted my gaze to Gem. "But you hate the attention." They'd all made that clear, even if I couldn't see it for myself. Gem liked occasionally playing Shadow Seven, but he hated being in the spotlight as Gemini.

"True. We'll figure that part out. Maybe I'll shave my head and get a tattoo. I can still double for Sev when he needs it. They have CGI; they can airbrush out what they don't like." He blew out a breath. "The only thing that makes this all work though is if you say yes."

I wanted to say yes.

"But," Seven interjected, "we know exactly how stubborn you are, so here's the deal, Stray. You and me, one-on-one, pool. I win, you give us six months to prove this works."

"And if I win?"

"You get whatever you want," he said. "But I'm not planning to let you win."

Let me win?

I pursed my lips. "Whatever I want?"

"Whatever you want."

I could always stay anyway—*after* I kicked his ass.

"Deal."

Three months, two weeks, and four days later…

"Rack them up, boys," I said, polishing the tip of my brand-new cue stick. It was a gift from Gem for our *almost five-month anniversary*. I wasn't entirely sure that was a thing, but I kind of liked it.

The look on Ollie's and Seven's faces would have been worth the gift even if I hadn't already loved the deep blue marble pattern on the handle offset by the silver bands. It was perfectly balanced and felt just right in my hand.

The amused smile on Gem's face when I pulled out the stick-polishing cloth had sent me into a fit of giggles. Laughter that only grew when Seven *glared* so hard at his brother he looked like he was going to have an aneurysm. Gem never missed an opportunity to remind them that it was *our* pool game that brought me into their crazy lives in the first place. It was also thoughtful as hell.

Ollie had his phone in his hand, and I had a feeling from the intensity of his thumbs flying over the screen that he was looking for a way to one-up Gem. The competition between the three of them was something they took *very* seriously.

Almost too serious, sometimes, but they had so much fun and were far too entertaining for me to truly mind.

"Ahem," I said, bumping Seven with my hip. "Are you having a stroke, Demon Spawn?" That effectively yanked his attention off Gem and put a stop to the silent but amusing contortions they were using to argue with each other versus their words.

Their "twin shit" as Ollie liked to call it.

"No, Stray," Seven practically growled, wrapping his hand around my nape to drag me to him as he dipped his head and gave me a long and *very* thorough kiss. Shivers raced over my skin and my nipples beaded to hard points. Seven had been gone for the past three weeks for reshoots on a film in the UK, and I'd missed him like crazy. He'd tried to take me along but lost a pool game to Ollie and then to Gem so two-to-one, I stayed here.

Against my lips, he said, "Don't tempt me into tossing the rules out. I could just as easily tie you to my bed and deny you orgasms until you agree to join me when I head back to set."

Holy fuck. That threat went straight to my cunt and I was clenching around emptiness even as I fisted his shirt.

"Don't threaten me with a good time, Harrison," I warned him, and he grinned. Then he bit my lip sharp enough to sting. "Don't think you get to duck out of this game either."

"Not going to happen. I plan to win today." We were three-and-three. "It's the tie-breaking game, after all."

With that, he let me go and headed over to the table. The room suddenly felt chillier as he racked the balls. Gem threaded his arms around my middle and pulled me back against him.

"Are you going to put us out of our misery?" he asked against my ear.

"Hey, I wasn't the one who said best two out of three, then

best three out of five, then best four out of seven." I'd won that first game fair and square. "And I wasn't the one who then had to leave for a few weeks." Which officially put our bet on hold.

Ollie glanced up from his phone and grinned. "We didn't mind the last three weeks of sleepovers."

I rolled my eyes. Technically, I should have already moved out. While I had been looking and even gone to see a few places, Gem or Ollie, and once Seven, all kept finding something wrong with the prospective place: It was too far away. It was too small. It didn't have the best security. It was too close to Hollywood. Too close to Burbank. It didn't have a doorman. It had security, but it was half-assed.

A week earlier, I'd dared the boys to come up with a place they would accept, so Ollie had a few places sent over for us to go look at. Seven and Gem both decided those weren't good enough either, for one reason or another. Thank fuck 'cause the last place was a co-op and it had required a six-figure down payment.

"Rub it in," Seven muttered as he got the balls racked up. "Speaking of which, Stray, you and me tonight. My bed. No excuses."

"Win the game first, Demon Spawn, and we can talk terms. Until then...this is anyone's game." At his smirk, I couldn't resist tweaking him. "That's polite for *it's my game.*"

His nostrils flared and he gave me a sidelong look. "You keep thinking that, Stray."

Ollie sighed and tilted his head back. "Maybe you should've used Gem as your Shadow Seven, so he could win this game for you."

"Damn," Gem said before he nuzzled a kiss to my temple. "You're right, he should have."

I laughed, tilting my head back to look up at him. His

whole new look was really working for him. He'd shaved his head, and over the past few weeks, while Seven was gone, he'd begun to grow in a short beard. I could definitely get used to it, especially with how soft his facial hair was becoming.

"I'm not taking that bet," I said. "You two were the ones who insisted Seven had to win it."

"Our mistake," Ollie said, then grunted when Seven elbowed him out of the way. "All future bets will be handled by Gem or me."

Gem and I snorted at the same time. Seven shifted his dirty look to Ollie.

"You do know that you're *not* helpful right?"

"Wasn't even trying to be, mate," Ollie told him, affecting the Australian accent he'd been working on for an upcoming role. I wrinkled my nose when he glanced to me. He winked as he shrugged. "Still a work in progress."

"Demon Spawn," I said before he could do the break and suddenly found myself the focus of all that intensity in his eyes. He ran so damn hot, the man was a volcano of simmering emotions and wild passion.

It was seriously wild how attractive I found that side of his nature.

"This is our final game," I told him. "Win or lose, we're not extending it past today." As entertaining as it had been, I really wanted *my* prize.

Lips pursed, Seven finally blew out a breath and nodded. "Fine. Win or lose. Last game." He settled into position at the end of the table and readied for the break.

"Don't fuck this up," Ollie muttered.

"Really feeling the support there," Seven deadpanned. "Mate."

Gem huffed out a laugh and I leaned into him as Seven

made the shot and the break. He was stripes and I was solids. Seven really hated stripes—he called them bad luck. To be fair, he'd lost every single game to me when he wasn't shooting solids.

It was a tight, tense game. He sank one of my balls by mistake, and it left me with just the eight to sink. Yeah. I could make that shot.

The question was, did I really want to win?

"Eight in the corner pocket." I sank it in one smooth strike. *Hell yes!*

"Dammit," Seven swore and the tension in the room skyrocketed. It was almost electric how their tempestuous emotions raked over me.

"Fuck," Ollie swore, and Gem actively glared down into his drink.

"I'm sure you all meant to say congratulations," I said, not remotely repentant for having kicked Seven's ass. "So...are you boys ready to pay up?"

Three gazes fixed on me.

"Excuse me?" Seven asked.

"If I win, I get whatever I want...right?" I raised my brows, daring any of them to dispute it. Seven white-knuckled the cue stick in his hand, and I was really proud of him for not throwing it. My Demon Spawn had temper control issues.

"That *was* the bet," he said slowly. "So...I take it you're planning to collect right now?"

They all looked so profoundly disappointed. What did they think I was going to ask for? Public humiliation? Maybe they thought I'd ask to move out permanently, no questions asked. It was enough to give me a tiny, itty bitty smidgeon of guilt.

But not enough to prevent me from collecting.

"Absolutely. I've waited *weeks* to get my prize. So no excuses."

"We're not making them, Slick," Gem promised. "What do you want?"

I drank in the sight of them, one at a time, letting the tension knotting in my belly unfold. The past few weeks had given me plenty of time to imagine exactly what I wanted and in great detail.

"I want you." I put my cue stick up, right on the rack where it belonged. Gem had rearranged it to make a spot for my stick.

"Me?" Seven eyed me with more than a little suspicion.

"Yes," I said, grinning wider. "I want all three of you..."

"All three of us," Ollie repeated. I swore, I could practically see the light bulb that went off over his head as what I was saying registered. "At the same time?"

We hadn't done that. Not yet, anyway.

"Mm-hmm. So let's go, boys. Time to pay up."

My beautiful twins stared at me with identical dumbfounded looks. I wished I had my camera just to snap that picture. The fact that all three were somewhat frozen delighted me. *Always good to know your limits, I suppose*. But I knew damn well what I wanted...and had been wanting for a while.

Experience had proven that Seven didn't care for sharing as much as his brother or Ollie. Today, however, that was going to change. They wanted six months to prove we could work.

Well, that proof needed to start with my four-way. Or was it a three-way? A three-on-one way? I headed for the stairs—since I planned to be incapable of moving when this was done, we should at least be close enough to one of our beds to use it.

Halfway up, I tugged my T-shirt off and tossed it aside. No cleaning crews in the house, the doors all locked, and the security system armed—no one to interrupt...

Just to be sure, I paused near the top and pulled out my

phone. No messages I needed to address, so I stuck it into do not disturb.

"Are you coming, boys?" I asked over my shoulder. The split second between inactivity and the three of them moving all at once was almost cartoon levels of amusing. From my position at the top of the stairs, I had a front row seat to their actual race.

Seven elbowed Ollie and then shoved Gem at him before he hit the steps. He was halfway to me when Gem damn near knocked him over the railing to pass him and I winced.

Maybe I should have added a caveat about injuries. Seven hit the top step a split second ahead of Gem and swooped me up and over his shoulder. Laughter bubbled through me as I met Ollie's amused gaze. He wasn't racing up the stairs so much as stalking up them. The shiver that went through me at the heat in his gaze...

Seven headed straight for his room. Fine by me. He had a huge bed. All of them did, really. It really was one of my favorite parts about this house.

Oh, fuck, who was I kidding. *They* were my favorite part of this house. I landed on the bed with a bounce. Seven stripped off my shoes and tossed them even as Gem unbuttoned my jeans. They each grabbed a pant leg and tugged them right off.

When I would have pushed up on my elbows, Ollie dropped onto the bed and fused his mouth to mine. No room for talking, debating, wagering, or even groaning. His tongue tangled with mine as he fisted my hair and someone stripped my lace panties away.

Cool air against my cunt didn't last long, not when Gem pressed a kiss against my clit that had me bucking almost immediately. Holy fuck. I couldn't catch my breath or deal with the sudden surge of electricity rioting through my system.

Or the orgasm that had me writhing. Gem was relentless,

his tongue vibrating my clit as he thrust his fingers. Fuck, that man knew exactly how to get me going. I was screaming right into Ollie's mouth. My bra vanished in a whisper of fabric.

"Move." Seven snapped out the command, and my hips bucked as if they were desperate to obey him.

Ollie dragged his head up and I got my first look at his swollen mouth and sexed-up eyes. "Chill the fuck out, Seven. I'm kissing our girl."

"And she said all of us, and so far the only one actually getting her off is Gem."

"So glad you noticed," Gem retorted in a husky voice. My breath came in swift, shallow pants. At least I thought it was. Honestly, I couldn't really feel my legs at the moment. Then Ollie was teasing a finger around one of my nipples. "So why do we have to move?" Gem asked.

Oh right. Seven said something about moving. I lifted my head to see where he was, and for a moment, I was struck by the sight of the twins. They were both naked.

Funnily enough, the only one still in clothes was Ollie, but I was drinking in the sight of Seven and Gem in all their glory. Seven had just one tattoo, freshly inked before he left for the UK. It was a small one he'd had done on his right bicep that matched the one Gem got on his left bicep. It was literally just the astrological sign for Gemini with a numerical seven incorporated into the center.

I was debating getting one to match it, since Gem and I had gone for an eight ball. There was just something poetic about both of us having a matching eight ball both for the game and the answers. It was fucking stupid how much I loved the matching tats. Ollie was working on what he wanted for us…

"Hey," I said, now that I had two brain cells to rub together. "Weren't we doing something?"

"Yes," Seven said. "Flipping you over." When I opened my

mouth, he held up one finger to silence me in an almost imperious fashion. My eyes narrowed. "Ollie, give Stella something to do with her mouth."

Fuck. My heart did a little ping-pong like it always did when Seven used my name. The intimacy was almost too much.

"With pleasure," Ollie murmured as Gem winked at me before he gripped my hips, and then I was flipping onto my side. It put me eye to eye with Ollie's beautiful dick, and I opened my lips for a taste.

Gem propped one of my legs up and then resumed his carnal exploration of my clit, but wait...

Warmth spread across my ass as lube trickled against me. Oh—oh we'd been discussing this, but the guys hadn't—

"Hey," Ollie protested as he thrust all the way to my throat, and I swallowed around him. "We have wagers on who gets her ass first."

"Well, Stella won her wager and you're fucking her mouth and Gem already went for her pussy. So this ass—" He landed a hand against one ass cheek in a stinging crack of his palm struck, and my whole body lit up. "This ass is mine."

"Fuck," Gem exclaimed in between teasing licks and thrusts from his fingers. "Slick is very much on board for all of the above."

The soft laugh that left Seven would probably serve a supervillain. "Somehow, I thought as much." Then he landed another slap. While the heat of that pulsed through me, he had two fingers in my ass. That added a whole new burn.

Seven approached my ass with the same intensity and focus as he did all projects he was emotionally invested in: thoroughly, laser-focused, methodical... He wasn't taking any chances in just slamming his dick in and hoping for the best.

Instead, he took his time with lube and fingers while I desperately tried to focus on sucking Ollie's dick.

I used to think I was good at multitasking. Apparently, I was wrong. More than once, Ollie thrust into my throat with my hair firmly gripped in his fist, growling a reminder to give his dick the attention it wanted.

Not wanting to let anyone down, I redoubled my efforts so much that Ollie lost control and blew his load with no warning whatsoever, making me choke and splutter on his salty cum.

"Fuck, Snow, I'm sorry," he groaned with an edge of laughter. "I don't even know what happened. Did you just use *teeth?* Shit, maybe I'm into a bit of pain too."

Seven took that as a hint and smacked my ass with a crack of his open palm. I yelped and tensed around his fingers, then Gem sucked my clit and I exploded. Literally screamed as I came so hard I saw stars, Seven's slick fingers buried to the knuckles in my ass and Gem's face in my pussy.

"That's it, Stella," Seven purred, stroking my heated ass cheek with his free hand. "Good girl. That'll be the first of *many* tonight."

I gasped, a panicked sort of whimper escaping in lieu of real words, since my whole body was still trembling and buzzing with my climax.

"Careful what you ask for, Snow," Ollie laughed, shifting aside and stroking his spent cock lazily as he reclined against the headboard. I knew from experience how quickly he could get hard again, but it looked like he was trying to beat a personal record...and I was excited to see if it worked.

"Take her mouth, Gem," Seven ordered in a gruff voice. "I don't wanna risk you licking my balls while I push in."

Gem laughed but did as his twin suggested as he slipped into Ollie's vacant position at my head. "You ready for this, Slick? You're unleashing a beast."

"Three," Ollie murmured in agreement.

"Never been more ready in my life," I groaned, then turned my head to stare at his twin behind me. "Are you going to fuck my ass, Seven, or just play with it?"

His brows rose, and a thread of anticipation tightened around my lungs. What was that saying about waving red flags around bulls?

Seven withdrew his fingers, gripped my cheeks in two firm handfuls, then thrust the tip of his cock into my ass with a smooth motion, making me yelp.

Gem laughed, then swept my hair up in his fist and smacked my lips with the tip of his cock. "Open up, baby girl. Let's give you something else to focus on."

I eagerly parted my lips and flattened my tongue for him to push in, but my mind was 100 percent focused on the unfamiliar sensation of Seven's dick slowly pushing deeper into my ass. It was...not painful—not after all the prep and lube he'd dedicated to the task—but it was *different.*

"Relax," Seven growled, his fingers biting harder into my flesh as he pushed in farther. "Don't fight it, Stella, because I have the patience of a saint. If this takes all damn night, so be it, but I *will* be blowing my load inside this tight hole."

Oh shit, dirty-talking Seven Harrison should be illegal.

"That's it, beautiful," Ollie murmured, shifting closer to stroke my spine encouragingly. "Relax into it. Let Gem into that well-trained throat too. I know you can take them, Snow baby. You're so good at this. So perfect for us."

His praise was blowing my fucking mind, and I forced my body to comply. I'd sucked enough dick in the last few months that he was spot-on in calling my throat well-trained. I could deep-throat all three of them without a second thought most days, but the whole *anal* situation had me a little distracted.

Shit. This was only two of them too. I still wanted Ollie in my pussy as well? Yes. Unquestionably yes. But I needed to get used to the anal thing first.

I wasn't a quitter. I could take it—just like Ollie said. I'm *good* at this…and this poly-relationship could work long-term if I could take them all at once. I was utterly convinced.

"*Yessss*," Seven hissed as I focused on letting my ass open, and he thrust in so far his hips slapped my ass. "Perfection. Do you want Ollie now, Stella? Or not yet?"

He withdrew a little as he spoke, rocking his hips rather than full-on fucking me. Letting me adjust and get used to the sensation which…I was really starting to enjoy.

My mouth was far too full to respond, though, and Gem pushed deeper into my throat like he wanted to keep me gagged and force Ollie to make his own decisions.

"So fucking pretty," Gem murmured, tugging on my hair to force my eyes up to his. "This mouth was made to be fucked, Slick."

"And this ass," Seven groaned, sinking in once more and making me moan.

"But only by the three of us," Ollie whispered firmly, snaking a hand beneath me to rub my clit. I tensed at the added touch, and both twins made an identical hissing gasp as my muscles tightened. "Just us…but so fucking perfect for us, Snow." Then he pushed two fingers into my pussy, and I let out a long moan around Gem's thick cock.

Fuck that felt good.

Seven took the cue to increase his intensity, fucking me more deliberately as Ollie thrust his fingers in my soaking cunt.

"You like that, don't you?" Ollie commented thoughtfully, then added a third finger. It was a lot, filling me to almost an uncomfortable tightness, but I knew from experience that his cock was bigger.

Seven grunted, slamming in harder still. "She fucking *loves* it." And smacked my ass *hard*. "Shit, that's amazing. Again, Stella. Clench up like that again for me." Another smack, and I couldn't have disobeyed if I'd tried.

"I need to get in on this," Ollie groaned, kissing my spine. "Boys, rearrange."

Seven huffed a heavy sigh, then withdrew from my ass and Gem reluctantly released my mouth just long enough for Ollie to slip in beneath me. Gem politely shifted to the side so his friend wouldn't be treated to a close-up view of his balls and asshole, then roughly grabbed my chin to reclaim his position in my mouth.

"Nice," Ollie murmured, reaching down to line up, then thrust up into my slick cunt. "Fuck yes, like coming home. Your pussy is incredible. I can't wait to take a turn in that perfect little ass…"

"Mine," Seven growled, then reclaimed his spot and pushed deep.

I cried out at the *intense* stretch and feeling of absolute fullness, but Gem's hard length muffled any more noises as they all buried balls deep within my body. It was, in a word, *perfect*.

Ollie was right. I definitely could take it, and better than that, I loved it.

The three of them worked with the kind of intuition and teamwork that only years of friendship and brother bond could produce, making me come *over and over* to the point I worried I would dehydrate or maybe lose function in my limbs.

When Seven finally came, it was with a roar and buried *deep* inside my ass. Then Ollie and Gem immediately switched positions to take their turns, while Seven lay back and watched, occasionally kissing me with his hand wrapped around my throat until he was hard again.

I totally lost track of time.

The guys were *very* careful to duck into the bathroom and clean up after fucking my asshole, which was appreciated for how many different rotations we hit...until eventually we all just *collapsed*.

Utterly spent in all the best ways.

"Six months...?" I murmured into the sleepy darkness sometime later, simply sensing they were all still somewhat awake.

Seven tensed beneath me. "That *was* the agreement," he confirmed. Six months for them to convince me this relationship could work out long-term.

We really hadn't dealt much with paps and media, but that was largely due to our sneaky ways in avoiding the public eye. It helped that I no longer worked in the celebrity-stalking space.

"We still have time left," Gem pointed out, his hand finding my spine and stroking a gentle path.

I sighed, utterly content. "We don't need it. I'm convinced already. I love the three of you so much it physically hurts some days, and the idea of ever leaving...it's my worst nightmare. I'm in it for six months, six years, six decades. However long you want me, I'm yours."

The collective sound of relief gusted through our shared bed, and I brushed a kiss on Seven's chest.

"And we're yours, Stella," Seven replied in a husky voice, kissing my hair.

"Forever," Ollie agreed, his hand on my butt squeezing reassuringly.

In the quiet darkness, Gem's lips found mine, and he kissed me softly, letting his mouth say everything he didn't have the words to express. He's been mine since that first night over margaritas and nachos, and there had never been any doubt about it.

These three sexy-as-fuck men, with all their crazy fans and soaring careers...as insane as it still seemed...they were perfect for me and undoubtedly my happily ever after.

THE END

afterword

This is what can happen when you lock two writers up in a cave, and put one in charge of the other in order to hit a deadline. Squirreling happens. Procrastitation happens. A lot of saying the word "no" happens. To be perfectly fair, if you're thinking this sounds an awful lot like what happened with *I'll Be Home...* you wouldn't be wrong.

Except this wasn't a holiday tale and there's fewer puns, and instead of Dasher we have Doordash. That said, thanks for reading. We hope you had as much fun with the story as we did writing it.

Also, if you're wondering, have we already talked about the next time?

We're going to have to go with NO SPOILERS!

xoxo
   Heather & Tate

Reader groups:
<u>facebook.com/groups/heatherspack</u>
facebook.com/groups/TateJames.TheFoxHole

347

about the author

Tate James is a USA Today Bestselling Author of Contemporary Romance and Suspense Romance, with occasional forays into Fantasy, Paranormal Romance, and Urban Fantasy. She was born and raised in Aotearoa (New Zealand) but now lives in Australia with her husband and their adorable crotchfruit.

She is a lover of books, booze, cats and coffee and is most definitely not a morning person. Tate is a bit too sarcastic, swears far too much for polite society, and definitely tells too many dirty jokes.

A few places you can find her

facebook.com/tatejamesauthor

instagram.com/tatejamesauthor

tiktok.com/@tatejamesauthor

bookbub.com/authors/tate-james

bsky.app/profile/tatejamesauthor.bsky.social

pinterest.com/tatejamesauthor

also by tate james

Madison Kate

#1 HATE

#2 LIAR

#3 FAKE

#4 KATE

#4.5 VAULT (to be read after Hades series)

Hades

#1 7th Circle

#2 Anarchy

#3 Club 22

#4 Timber

The Guild

#1 Honey Trap

#2 Dead Drop

#3 Kill Order

Valenshek Legacy

#1 Heist

#2 Forgery

#3 Restoration

Bluebell House Duet

#1 Forced Proximity

#2 Trauma Bonded (TBD)

Boys of Bellerose

#1 Poison Roses

#2 Dirty Truths

#3 Shattered Dreams

#4 Beautiful Thorns

The Royal Trials

#1 Imposter

#2 Seeker

#3 Heir

Kit Davenport

#1 The Vixen's Lead

#2 The Dragon's Wing

#3 The Tiger's Ambush

#4 The Viper's Nest

#5 The Crow's Murder

#6 The Alpha's Pack

Novella: The Hellhound's Legion

Box Set: Kit Davenport: The Complete Series

Dark Legacy

#1 Broken Wings

#2 Broken Trust

#3 Broken Legacy

#4 Dylan (standalone)

Royals of Arbon Academy

#1 Princess Ballot

#2 Playboy Princes

#3 Poison Throne

Hijinx Harem

#1 Elements of Mischief

#2 Elements of Ruin

#3 Elements of Desire

The Wild Hunt Motorcycle Club

#1 Dark Glitter

#2 Cruel Glamour (TBC)

#3 Torn Gossamer (TBC)

Foxfire Burning

#1 The Nine

#2 The Tail Game (TBC)

#3 TBC (TBC)

Undercover Sinners

#1 Altered By Fire

#2 Altered by Lead

#3 Altered by Pain (TBC)

about heather long

I love books. Not just a little bit, but a lot. Books were my best friends when I was growing up. Books didn't care if I was new to a town or to a class. They were always there, my trustiest of companions. Until they turned on me and said I had to write them.

I can tell you that my own personal happily ever after included writing books. I've always said that an HEA is a work in progress. It's true in my marriage, my friendships, and in my career. I am constantly nurturing my muse as we dive into new tales, new tropes, new characters and more.

After seventeen years in Texas, we relocated to the Pacific Northwest in search of seasons, new experiences, and new geography. I can't wait to discover what life (and my muse) have in store for me.

Maybe writing was always my destiny and romance my fate. After all, my grandmother wasn't a fan of picture books and used to read me her Harlequin Romance novels.

Links:

Facebook: facebook.com/groups/HeathersPack

instagram.com/HeatherVLong

bookbub.com/authors/heather-long

amazon.com/~/e/B002BMBCUC

also by heather long

82nd Street Vandals

Savage Vandal

Vicious Rebel

Ruthless Traitor

Dirty Devil

Shamelessly Loyal (Novella)

Brutal Fighter

Dangerous Renegade

Merciless Spy

Reckless Thief

Fierce Dancer

Dirty Dancer

Bay Ridge Royals

Shamelessly Loyal (Novella)

Battle Lines

Deceptive Truce

Wicked Surrender

Violent Chaos

Desperate Victory

BLOOD Brothers

Burn

Lure

Blue Ivy Prep

Problem Child

Mad Boys

Party Crashers

Money Shot

Bravo Team Wolf

When Danger Bites

Bitten Under Fire

Cardinal Sins

Kill Song

First Chorus

High Note

Last Word

Chance Monroe

Earth Witches Aren't Easy

Plan Witch from Out of Town

Bad Witch Rising

Fevered Hearts

Marshal of Hel Dorado

Brave are the Lonely

Micah & Mrs. Miller

A Fistful of Dreams

Raising Kane

Wanted: Fevered or Alive

Wild and Fevered

The Quick & The Fevered

A Man Called Wyatt

Heart of the Nebula

Queenmaker

Deal Breaker

Throne Taker

Lone Star Leathernecks

Semper Fi Cowboy

As You Were, Cowboy

Shackled Souls

Succubus Chained

Succubus Unchained

Succubus Blessed

Shackled Souls (Omnibus)

Standalones

Kiss of Fate (w/Blake Blessing)

Taste of Karma (w/Blake Blessing)

I'll Be Home… (w/Tate James)

Overexposed (w/Tate James)

Switchboard Duet

Talk to Me

Don't Let Go

Untouchable

Rules and Roses

Changes and Chocolates

Keys and Kisses

Whispers and Wishes

Hangovers and Holidays

Brazen and Breathless

Trials and Tiaras

Graduation and Gifts

Defiance and Dedication

Songs and Sweethearts

Legacy and Lovers

Farewells and Forever

Hellos and Happily Ever Afters

Wolves of Willow Bend

Wolf at Law

Wolf Bite

Caged Wolf

Wolf Claim

Wolf Next Door

Rogue Wolf

Bayou Wolf

Untamed Wolf

Wolf with Benefits

River Wolf

Single Wicked Wolf

Desert Wolf

Snow Wolf

Wolf on Board

Holly Jolly Wolf

Shadow Wolf

His Moonstruck Wolf

Thunder Wolf

Ghost Wolf

Outlaw Wolves

Wolf Unleashed